# AMERICA the Beautiful

## A Ku Klux Klan thriller based on American history

by

# Oswald Mould

Published by
Filament Publishing Ltd
16 Croydon Road, Waddon, Croydon,
Surrey, CR0 4PA, United Kingdom.
Telephone +44 (0)20 8688 2598
Fax +44 (0)20 7183 7186
info@filamentpublishing.com
www.filamentpublishing.com



ISBN 978-1-912256-31-0

Printed by IngramSpark

# About the Author

Oswald Mould is a retired Registered Nurse and has worked in the mental health field as a Psychiatric Nurse in the New York City Health and Hospital Corporation for three years. Before this, he worked for 11 years for the State University of New York at the Downstate Medical Centre, including six years as an Emergency Room Nurse in the Resuscitation Unit and for five years as a Radiology Nurse. He also worked for five years as a Trauma One Emergency Nurse at Harlem Hospital of the New York Health and Hospital Corporation; at the Interfaith Jewish Medical Centre as a Medical and Surgical Nurse; and as a Visiting Nurse.

Before working as a nurse, Oswald worked in the computer industry, in the corporate world of Wall Street and as a civil servant. He witnessed the September 11 attack on the original twin towers of the World Trade Centre, which he describes as "a horrendous incident that pushed me into nursing, because I had already qualified as a nurse." After the crisis, his company moved the IBM facility in upstate New York, where Oswald had to commute approximately 100 miles daily.

Oswald has completed four manuscripts and plans to release one a year as he settles into retirement, commuting now between New York, London and the Caribbean.

The author says he was influenced by the many racial incidents of young black men being killed by the police in New York and other parts of the USA. He felt the need to do something about it and decided to write his first book. He states that "enduring the pain of racism is common among black men, for we have to live with it daily in some form or another." He channelled his feelings into his fictitious characters and wrote this, his debut novel, as a gripping, emotional and relevant demonstration of the racial problems inhibiting America's growth and development in its embrace of diversity.

His comprehensive research, included the history of the lynching and hanging of African Americans, the dark, disturbing history of the Ku Klux Klan (KKK) and how for decades its members terrorized African Americans in the South through harassment, shootings, hangings and burning the homes of innocent people while they slept. The author carefully researched the United States Air Force Academy and the Vietnam War, which is based around three main characters whose lives are strongly emotional and relevant in today's world.

The reader is taken inside a psychiatric unit and experiences the lives of the inmates through the eyes of a psychiatric nurse, caring for a patient who tells his life story. The story begins when the main character is ten years old and he is forced to watch the hanging of his father and uncles by the KKK and how it affected him thereafter. The book draws from the author's experiences, knowledge, emotions, perceptions and his imagination. This story is a historical thriller. It is a gripping action-packed, brutal, purposeful, emotional and revealing fictional story based on American history.

The author says that "after reading this story...readers will see the United States of America in a way you may have never seen it before."

# Contents List

# Acknowledgments

I would like to thank my wife Cheryl, my daughters Rhea, Reisha, Tanisha, Tanisha's husband Arron and his father.

I would like to thank Chris, my publisher, Wendy, my editor, and Emma, my website creator.

I would like to thank my sister Angela and my cousin Victoria. I would like to thank my friends Mrs. Jerrilyn Wiggan and her daughter Charlene. I would like to thank my former ER coworkers for taking the time to read my novel: Tamara Drummond, Jackie Reid, Shelly Blackmon and Yonette Parks. I thank Kwasi for informing me of the King Alfred Plan which I added to give another dimension to my book.

# Preface

There are deep flaws in the American justice system. Have you seen the brutal beating of Rodney King? Too far back in history for you? Did you see the strangulation of Eric Garner? Did you see the execution of Philando Castile? What about the murder of Tamir Rice? All of the officers who took part in these brutal beatings and deadly shootings were acquitted. Sean Bell, Amadou Diallo, Timothy Stansbury, John Crawford... and the list goes on. Thousands of men, women and children we know not of have been murdered and their killers were never brought to justice. Simply because they were Black.

It was common practice in America over the centuries to hang black men, women and children. It was treated as a festive occasion. Many families would pack their picnic basket and go to the plan site of the execution to watch while they ate their meal as the lynching procession unfolded. The young children watched in awe as they were being taught by their elders that this was the appropriate treatment for the coloreds. They too would train their children to do the same. It bore similarities to the audience watching the gladiators at the Roman Coliseum. But these victims were not gladiators – they were black men, women and children who were at the wrong place at the wrong time, who were falsely accused of crimes because they were black. Most were hanged without a trial. From one generation to the next, racism became entrenched in the psyche of white America. From the Ku Klux Klan to mob injustice, it was the white way, the American way. Thousands of black men, women and children unjustly met their fate through a hangman's noose.

As an author, I am committed to revealing the past and changing the present to make America's future an enlightened one.

For as technically advanced as we have become as a nation,  we have not really evolved beyond our stone age mentality. We as a nation remains divided, segregated, and in disharmony because of our practice of white supremacy. We see it in our government and in our racial divide. We easily think of killing those we do not know instead of thinking of getting to know, understand and accepting them. We threaten weaker nations with sanctions and war if they do not accept our ideology of democracy while at home our Congress fights to prevent its citizens from receiving health care because it was created by the first Black president. We overthrow governments of brown skinned people if it's in our best interest, disregarding the interest of the people and government who we overthrow, while at home we find reasons and means to mass incarcerate the minority Black and Hispanic population. Many of the things we do were learned from what we practiced during the times of slavery and Jim Crow. We learned them as we headed west to achieve our manifested destiny during the plains wars, as we killed all that was not white. We learned from the upheavals and riots of the segregated inner cities of America during the Civil Rights wars and many more incidents like those at home and abroad in which we were involved. They were America's labs. They were America's research and developmental centers as we became the great beast we are today, all because of acceptance of white supremacy.

America projects itself as the freest, most prosperous, most beautiful nation on planet Earth and its brainwash is successful as we hear the chant "USA, USA!" over and over again. Truthfully America's republic was built on noble principles. We see that as we read her Declaration of Independence. However, most of its black disenfranchised citizens will never get to experience the nobility of America's beauty. For in their schools, the board of education has placed police officers who will quickly arrest and incarcerate its students, hence the term 'the school to prison pipeline'. We have seen those videos also. Based on zero tolerance policies, we find vast numbers of black and Hispanic students being suspended and expelled from schools all over this nation. It is noted that many Black and Hispanic students end up in jail for minor infractions and while being suspended stand a higher chance of being incarcerated. Most students that are suspended or expelled end up dropping out of school, never completing their education, and end up in a life of crime. The vast majority of students disproportionately subjected to these suspension and expulsion for minor infractions are Black.

So, the horror of America continues to be heaped on its Black population. They are denied entry to America's prosperity. Their unpaid labor as slaves was the catalyst to America's early prosperity and wealth. Their unpaid labor as slaves laid the foundation for prosperity as we evolved to become an industrialized nation. Yet they are constantly denied, barred from accessing the prosperity they created while being forced to slave for over four hundred years. The vast white privileged population continues to benefit from centuries of our forefathers slaving. It benefits them to keep the racial conversation there, never wanting to examine how they have benefitted from slavery. In denial, they make statements that excuse them from being accountable for their forefathers' actions which have left them vast wealth.

From slavery to segregation, from Jim Crow to mass incarceration, from Ku Klux Klan to sanctioned police murders. When does it end? When does the horror cease? When will America allow all her citizens to experience her true noble beauty? Or is her beauty only superficial, skin deep, and horror her real character? African Americans come to live in fear of their police force, knowing they stand a greater chance of being killed by the police rather than the criminals that prey on them. We now make choices when we are victims of crimes, as we daily see videos of police killing our people when we call them to report crimes against us. Their use of deadly force has us questioning our options. Should we arm ourselves and whenever approached by a police officer be prepared to live or die knowing their intent is to kill us? Or should we continue down the same path we have been travelling and whenever we are approached by a police officer accept that among the options here is that we will be killed even if we are unarmed victims? So far to date, the justice system has not held any officer accountable for murdering unarmed black citizens.

As Black men, we know racism and prejudice exist. We experience it daily from white women who tightly grip their purses when they appear in our presence or white owned businesses giving us attitudes when we seek their services. And those are the vanilla cases. We were the ones victimized, yet still through the white media we have been libelled, slandered and dehumanized as the white population is taught to hate and fear us because we are criminals. We were the ones who were enslaved. We were the ones who were brought here shackled in the pit of some ungodly slave ship and sold into slavery. We are the ones whose continent was divided up and colonized, raped of its natural resources. We have reasons to hate. We have been the victims, yet the media, the greatest divisive factor of all, is the hate factory for white supremacy and its the main propaganda machine. Its members see themselves as a free press as their bias destroys the integrity, credibility and reputation of poor people as they see fit. They should have some form of regulation and accountability, for fake news can be more destructive than real news.

Our justice system is corrupt and racist. It is an intolerable affront to us Black people as we see murderers dressed in blue with badges constantly use deadly force on people of color, and they are not held accountable by being acquitted by their peers. How does it feel to know we cannot count on our justice system to find a man guilty when he openly – on video – kills an innocent unarmed Black individual? This is a system that should never be corrupted or tainted by racism. It should not have any dealings with for profit business or harbor greed incentives. It's a system that should not have laws that target any ethnic or racial group. We should never be afraid of the police, but they have given us several reasons to be afraid of them. Our enemies no longer come dressed in white cone hats and sheets. They come dressed in blue, carry a badge, and a gun. They use deadly force to resolve any problems with Black people. No doubt about it - they are the modern day Klan sanctioned killers of the state.

Read this book, and read of one man's horrifying journey through Beautiful America. It's a thriller.

# CHAPTER 1: Mr Stuart

"It was a hot summer's eve in 1958. The five of us set off on our return trip home. Early that morning we had left with a list of things to purchase, such as groceries, clothes and household items. We could not afford a car, so we walked. We cherished these walks to the various towns close to our home; it was like travelling to a foreign country. We found it invigorating and did it almost every weekend. It firmly bonded us and cemented our relationships so even eternity could not erode them. The group consisted of my father, David, and my uncles Joe, Steve and Robert. Dad said the walk would make me strong but we jogged most of the way to the town. Uncle Steve said, 'When they were in the military, ten miles were nothing in comparison to what they had to do in their drills.' They often said they wanted me to follow in their footsteps and become a soldier. They fought for their country in Europe and the Pacific in WW2."

The person telling this story is one of my patients. For confidentiality reasons, I cannot reveal his name, so I will refer to him as Mr Stuart. He has a long history of mental illness with multiple admissions to many of the mental health institutions in Brooklyn, New York. He hallucinates, believing that he sees and hears things that are not there. Mr Stuart is a black man in his early sixties. He was diagnosed as a schizophrenic and a psychopath. Mr Stuart decided to tell me his life story, a dubious honor I somehow earned. As his mental health nurse, I did not ask his reasons for telling me his life story. It appears he is attempting to develop a relationship by opening up to me. When I feel secure that he will not go back into hiding, I will grill him as to why he needed to tell his story. But first, the foundation of his trust must become solid or he will slip back into his cocoon. Most patients are paranoid and don't like the stress of being questioned and so I will temporarily refrain.

"Which branch of the military were your father and uncles' members of?" I finally asked, once he had been talking for some time.

"The army," he replied. "My father and all his brothers were army men. They fought against Hitler and the Nazis in Europe and against the Japanese in the Pacific," he said, repeating the information, which he was apparently proud of and thought would impress me. Without getting the response he wanted, he returned to his story. "However, this night was very different. I remember it as if it was yesterday. It was a few months after my tenth birthday."

"Mr Stuart, in your chart it says you hear voices?"

"I do," he stoically replied.

"What do the voices tell you to do?"

"To kill people," he replied unemotionally. I wondered if he could be telling me the truth, for his face betrayed no qualms about what he has said.

"Have you ever acted on those commands?"

"Many times," he said without hesitation.

"How many people have you killed, Mr Stuart?" I found myself asking, needing to know facts.

"In total close to a thousand people," he replied in a matter of fact manner as I sat there stunned by his answer. The number sounded so unimaginable I could not fathom or believe it.

"I am a grim reaper," he said without a smile.

"For sure," I replied, dismissing his statements as the grandiosity of a crazy old man. No one could have killed that many people and be out walking the streets, I thought.

"Mr. Stuart," I said, "grandiosity is a symptom of mental illness. I don't believe our law enforcement is so inept as to have allowed a man with a resume of so many killings to fall through the cracks. Were you a member of the military and involved in a war when you killed these people?" I was trying to discern if there was any truth to his statement.

"A lot of them were enemy soldiers in a time of war and the rest were enemies with bad intents," he replied.

"What do you mean by bad intents?" I asked.

"I mean they would have killed me if I did not kill them," he replied with a look of disdain. He fell silent, and studied me, as if he was reading my thoughts.

"It's your prerogative to think what you want. I want to reveal my life story and I really don't want any unnecessary interruptions as I do," he gruffly stated. He looked at me darkly, warning me not to push him again for a while. For a fraction of a second it was not Mr Stuart's face I saw; it was the face of the evil that lurked within him. It sent a chill down my spine as fear took hold of me. I wondered what dark, barbarous deeds would be revealed in his life story. Yet there was something about him that made him different from the other patients. He was well groomed, neat and clean. Outwardly, he was not anyone's perception of a psychiatric patient; I never heard him screaming or acting up. He was well disciplined and always had self-control. There was structure to his life and everything he did seemed to be well thought out. However, he said he was hearing voices telling him to harm others and that's why he was here. No one knows what lurks in the minds of men until they choose to reveal the thoughts that dwell there. In this, his judicious moment, he was choosing to expose the depth of sanity he possessed and the depth of insanity that possessed him. I was not an eager listener to his story, for it hinted of being a troubling one. Yet, I wanted to know when his insanity started, where it took him and what he did on account of it.

Mr Stuart's behavior at best was described as guarded. He was sometimes characterised as a loner. I had never heard of him being verbally abusive or agitated but he did show signs of antisocial behavior. Agitations leading to threats of violence are common behaviors of clients in their most acute psychotic state. This usually happens after they become non-compliant in taking their medications for significant periods of time. They begin to see things, feel unusual sensations and hear voices commanding them. We have to reality orientate them after bringing them under control with medications. Without their prescribed medications, they frequently lose control in their battles with their psychosis, and become agitated, verbally abusive and sometimes violent after losing their rationality. Mr Stuart did not present any of these signs. He was aware of his psychopathy and sought to control it with medications. He never allowed his medication to run out. If he saw his prescription was coming to an end and he had no refill, he sought out his psychiatrist or voluntarily committed himself to a mental health facility as per this hospitalization.

"Mr Stuart when did you discover and accept that you were mentally ill?"

"It was during the early years of my marriage. My wife Jackie noticed the symptoms and insisted that I see a doctor. I was diagnosed and placed on medications."

"Mr Stuart, were you a soldier and did you fight in the Vietnam War?"

"Yes, I was," he replied.

"You went through the Vietnam War without anyone noticing your illness."

"Yes, I thought I was normal. It's easy to kill when I am not on medications and later in life when I need to, I stop taking them."

"What!" I said in amazement. "You are saying when you wanted to kill you stop taking your medications?"

"Yes, I told you - I am a grim reaper. It made planning to kill and killing easier."

With that statement, I realized I was unearthing a deadly monster. It had taken a long time working on developing a trusting relationship with him, as I did with all my clients. Now here we were, him wanting to tell me the story of his life and me fearfully being drawn into it. There are 24 other patients on the unit with their own stories and complaints, all seeking my attention, wanting me to be their audience, making it difficult to narrow my focus to one individual patient. It is foolhardy to do that in a psychiatric unit because it is important to know what is going on with all the patients. Some harbor thoughts of suicide while homicidal thoughts dwell in the minds of others. I must always be aware of my immediate and ever-changing environment. There are those who are diagnosed with depression, those who are bipolar, as well as those who are symptomatically hallucinating. I must be aware of their presence to maintain my safety as well as theirs.

"Where are you from?" I asked.

"Alabama," he countered. "It was a dangerous place for a black man then."

"Tell me a place that is not a danger for us today," I said, stopping and looking in his eyes where I was confronted by the pain and hate he had endured. The experiences he had to cope with as a black individual in such a hostile and demeaning society had taken their toll. In that moment, I chose to listen with my heart and soul as well as my brain to make the necessary connections before he chose to put his barrier up and close me out for being judgmental. I pulled up a chair and looked in his eyes and with sincerity I said: "Mr Stuart, I will listen to your story but if any emergency or something that requires my attention comes up, I must go, do you understand? But feel free to approach me anytime to continue with your life story."

"Yes," he replied and he went directly to where he had left off.

"As day turned into night the full moon reflected the sun's light over the landscape, making it easy for us to see and be seen. We walked across the open grassy fields. There was a large swath of land covering several hundred acres. Recently it was used in bearing and harvesting wheat, but at the time it was in recovery stage and was overwhelmed by short grass and weeds. We were walking, talking, laughing enjoying the journey home, but this night was destined to be different. In the distance, I saw a lone tall, vibrant, muscular, healthy oak tree, standing like a sentry guarding the grassy fields on a hill on this otherwise flat landscape.

"It towered over everything, looking magnificent. I was told by my father that generations ago this countryside was covered by these magnificent trees but only this one survived the saws of the determined loggers as they harvested the forest while clearing the land for farming. Its thick sturdy trunk was held in place by its strong muscular protruding roots that anchored it deep within the ground. Its burly branches reached to the sky to greet the sun each day. Its healthy luxurious plumage of green crowned this grand survivor, but this night it seemed ominous, like a shrouded dark figure waiting to do something harmful to us. As we walked in the direction of the tree and I listened to my father's and uncles' tales of fighting Hitler's armies in Europe. That's when I began hearing a dull muffled beating sound. It was hardly audible at first so I did not give it much attention. Eventually it got louder, so I asked my father what was making that sound. At first he did not hear it, so my Uncle Joe put his ear to the ground and listened.

"It sounds like several horses coming in this direction," he said as he got up.

"Run! Run!" shouted my Uncle Steve. He dropped the bag of groceries he was carrying on his back and we took off in the direction of the lone oak tree. "The tree is our only chance! We must get up the tree," he shouted.

"Why are we running, father?" I asked after we had gone a distance at full speed, not aware of the deep dark reason behind this fearful flight.

"For our lives, son," he said glancing back. "If we are lucky we will make it", he gasped between breaths as we sprinted in the direction of the old oak tree. I still did not understand. He continued to explain between each breath he took. "The only people that ride in large groups at this time of the night are the night riders, the Klan," said my father. "We must make it up that tree before they get us; it's our only means of surviving this night."

"My heart skipped a beat, triggered by the fear that took hold of me when I heard my father's reply. I looked around as I ran, hoping to see somewhere else to hide. There was nothing but the flat open fields lit by the glow of the full moon. I felt the tremors of the ground below my feet getting stronger by the seconds from the distant beat of the galloping horses as they quickly closed the distance between us. I looked behind; they were still not in sight. I dreaded the thought of them catching us, but heard the sound made by the hooves of the galloping horses getting louder and louder by the second as they made angry, thunderous contact with the ground. The earth below my running feet began to shake, as the fear in me grew stronger. They were gaining on us and the thought made me run faster. I looked back and I saw the hooded riders in their white robes, which were billowing in the wind as they urged more speed out of their galloping steeds to accomplish their deviant deeds.

"Ahhhhh!" I screamed in pain as I went down. I had stepped in a gopher hole and my right leg popped as I fell forward screaming in agony and fear. I knew right away my leg was broken but I was more concerned about the immediate peril. Terrified, I looked again to see where the Klansmen were as I struggled to get my broken leg out of the hole. My father and uncles who were slightly ahead of me came to my rescue. My father lifted me up onto his back and began running but that delay and my added weight slowed him down. His brothers were not about to leave him behind - they were military men and would fight to the death rather than abandon each other. That was the deciding factor. The Klansmen had seen us as they appeared above the horizon for they headed in our direction. They quickly gained on us as I clung to my father's back. I urged him forward by shouting, "Run father run! Run - they are gaining on us." I was overcome by fear, knowing our death was imminent if we were caught by these men, dressed in white sheets. My injury had slowed us down – they were rapidly gaining on us and it was becoming apparent we would not make it to the tree. I was gripped by fear, knowing what they represent and what would be the outcome if we were caught. We continued running for our lives but the oak tree was just out of reach. In a matter of minutes, we were surrounded by them and the battle for our lives began.

"My father placed me on the ground near him to protect me but even with a broken leg I stood and took my place with them as he and his brothers, my uncles, stood tall and prepared for their final battle. The enemy this time was neither Hitler's armies nor the Japanese in the Pacific. No, this time the enemy was our white neighbors dressed in white sheets who had a long history of terrorizing us, intimidating us, assaulting us, burning down our houses while we slept, shooting us down and lynching us black folks.

"We were severely outnumbered, there were at least 50 of them and we knew this was a fight to the death for I knew their only intent was to hang us.  As we were locked in battle one of them rode his horse into me, which sent me reeling to the ground. Quickly several of them swarmed me and attempted to tie me up. I kicked, punched and bit them as I tried to get to my feet. Then one big one punched me in the face. My head snapped back, hitting the ground. I blacked out and when I regained consciousness I was tied up by all four limbs with my hands behind me.  I looked around and my uncles and dad were still fighting them. They swarmed my father grabbing him as he struggled and fought them off, but they were relentless and again they swarmed him, getting hold of his arms. He kicked one in the guts and as he went down kicked him again in the head. Then one took a baseball bat, swung it like a club with all his might, and brought it down on the side of my father's head. I screamed as I saw my father's body go limp. They continued to punch, kick and beat him with the bat. I screamed and then shouted, "No! No!  Leave him alone!" and I cried for my words fell on deaf ears as they mercilessly continued to beat the defenceless body of my father.

"They bound and gagged us, then dragged our beaten, broken, bloody bodies across the field to that big old oak tree. All the time, they were celebrating their victory by calling us niggers and taking a whack at our now defeated defenceless bodies. I screamed as the anger welled up but the gag muted my sounds. I cried as I realized the inevitable was at hand and I was partially to blame. If I did not break my leg, we would be up that tree instead of being dragged to its hangman's noose. I looked around and saw my father, his back to me, clothes were partially ripped from his body, tattered and coated in a mixture of blood and dirt from his wounds from the preceding battle. He was not moving; his bound, bloody body lay motionless on the ground a distance away. I did not know if he was dead or alive and then he turned towards me and I saw his face swollen and covered in blood. His eyes were swollen shut but as I peered I saw he was looking directly at me saying something. I strained to listen. He could hardly speak above a whisper.

"'I love you, son. but my journey here on earth is coming to an end. If you live, you must carry on, you must be strong and make your mark on this earth. Find your purpose and live for it but you must also be ready to kill and die for it. This should not be happening; it is inhumane and should be stopped."

"I will stop it one day, father. I will put an end to this even if I have to kill or die." A group of them came over and started beating him with a whip and I cried as I was made to watch my defenceless father scream and beg as they whipped and kicked him repetitively. To them we were less than the animals in the fields. I saw others had grabbed my Uncle Joe whose condition looked worse than my father's. They lifted him onto a horse and they led it to the tree where a hangman's noose was already hanging from one of its many sturdy branches. They placed it around his neck, and then slapped the horse, which galloped off. I screamed behind the gag as I heard his neck snap and saw his swinging body suspended in the air.

"Why had God deserted us? What evil had we done to be treated like this? What hate lingers in the heart of men to treat his fellow man like this?

"Then it was Uncle Steve. I closed my eyes, I could not watch. I heard the one in charge shouting to take the gag from his mouth. I heard Uncle Steve cursing at them as they whipped him, kicked him and punched him while they dragged him defiantly struggling to the waiting obliging horse. They were shouting, 'You stinking filthy nigger! This is what you get for coming into our town and trying to mix with us white folks.' They placed him on the horse to meet the same fate as Uncle Joe and soon he was hanging from a noose beside his dear brother, dead to the world. I cried as I was made to watch these heartless callous acts.

"Uncle Robert had managed to free himself while he lay on the ground, still not in any better condition than his brothers. He waited until they approached him and as one of them picked him off the ground, he struck like a rattle snake, quickly disarming him of his pistol and unleashing a barrage of lead on them. Briefly it inspired me as I saw some of them meeting the same fate as my uncles. His aim was true and deadly and five of them went down. But the rest responded with more than a hundred shots fired in his direction and he too was dead. I felt some joy to see he had inflicted pain and suffering on them as I saw them trying to revive their dead after the skirmish. They too were feeling the pain and anguish I was feeling. However, that brief deadly encounter only stirred them in to greater anger as they approached my father. He was bleeding profusely from the trauma inflicted to the side of his head. Through the blood I saw his brain where his scalp and skull had been peeled away from the baseball bat. They grabbed him and lifted him to his feet and I rose to mine even with a broken leg. He was limping and they hit him in the face but he was already unconscious and offered no resistance. He was still breathing and they lifted him onto a horse, placed him in the saddle, put the noose around his neck. I had managed to free myself and charged at them, but I was no match and they quickly overpowered me and tied me up again. When I was finally subdued I saw my father swinging from the end of the hangman's rope twitching away the last remnants of his life. I was now overcome by grief.

"There was a boy of no more than sixteen years of age among them. He had briefly lost his hood in the battle. I looked at him and knew I would never forget his face. He had an ugly scar that ran from his left forehead interrupted by the deep orbit of his left eye, then continued down his left cheek and ended just above his left upper lip.  Another rider handed him a hood, which he quickly put over his head. What I saw in that boy's face let me know then that the difference between men would continue to stimulate hate for generations to come. I looked around, overcome by fear.  I saw evil in their eyes and heard the hate in their voices. I did not realize that I was next.

"It was mental torture as I saw the limp lifeless bodies of my father and my uncles hanging from the thick branches of that oak tree. Minutes ago, we were talking and laughing. I shouted at their lynched, hanging bodies but they did not respond. I could not believe it. I did not want to accept it. They were dead. Why? Because they were black. In that moment, I lost my innocence and hate took its place in my heart. From that moment on, I lived with hate for white people for what they had done to me and my family. The Klan members laughed and called me a worthless nigger. They desecrated the bodies of my father and uncles. I screamed and shouted for them to stop as they cut off my uncle's privates and I cried and cried for I felt so helpless to protect them. I moaned as I watched them prepare to depart as they gathered themselves and their dead. I laid there bound by my legs and arms, not accepting, hoping that my father and uncles would come back to life. So suddenly their lives were violently extinguished.

"As they prepared to leave the boy turned to me. 'Nigger - one day soon it will be you who will be hanging from a tree, just like your pa. I hate you niggers. You are the reason why the South is like this. If it was up to me, none of you would be allowed in this country. I would wipe you all from the face of the earth," he said and then rode off.

"In that moment, I stopped crying to hear what my white counterpart had to say. When his delivery was finished, I stored every word in my memory just like this violent, brutal incident. This moment of infamy would lead to my salvation. I would be fuelled by the hate of this crime and those spoken words would inspire me to do unnatural things. Then one of the cowardly Klansmen hit me from behind with a blunt heavy object and I passed in and out of consciousness.

"The full moon cast an eerie light on the battle field as if in disgust at what had taken place there. It seemed as though Mother Nature, distraught by the event she had witnessed, wept in earnest as dark clouds appeared. Her tears fell to the ground in the form of torrential rain drops. Lightning lit up the sky above as thunder roared. Then it was silent again. The rain stopped and the thunder and lightning ceased as suddenly as it had begun. My body lay there on the ground below the oak tree by the hanging bodies of the departed as their spirits were welcomed into heaven while in the distance the fading sound of hoofs were heard no more and the ground ceased to tremor. In the heart of men, hate would continue to exist and this evil would continue to repeat itself in the United States of America in some form many times over before it would be acknowledged as a crime.

"I don't know how long I was there.  But I made myself a promise. If I lived no matter, how long it took, I would avenge the death of my father and uncles.  I knew who they were, the Ku Klux Klan, and that was all I needed to know. I would hunt them down and kill every single one of them for what they did to me was inhumane.

"Incredible as it may seem I was found there on the ground by a white family who cut me free and buried my father and uncles under that old oak tree. They tried to comfort me. They even took me to a doctor to have my broken leg placed in a cast. But there was nothing in the world that could comfort me. I did not feel the pain from my broken leg for the pain of my broken heart was far greater. I remember rocking back and forth in a catatonic state in their car repeating over and over, 'I hate the Klan.' I must have said it a million times, even as the doctor, who was white, attended to me. I don't remember what he said; I don't remember what he did for nothing penetrated through the grief I felt that day.

# CHAPTER 2: 24 Hour Letter

"One set of whites violently, traumatically took your world apart and another tried to repair it," I thought out loud as he paused.

"I see it now, but how can you heal a broken heart after a trauma of that magnitude? I used to wonder how many more of us black folks were buried there under that old oak tree. I sometimes wondered if that was the purpose for its existence and one day after the cast was removed I returned with an axe and started to cut it down. It took me weeks but finally it fell to the ground and that brought me some satisfaction knowing it would not be used for that purpose again.

"For years after I could not speak I was so angry. I would try but words did not come out of my mouth. I dreaded the nights the most for they were the worst. Each night I relived that horrible event through my nightmares. In those dreams, I was there again reliving those moments, being chased by them in the fields, being captured and it was me they were about to hang beside the bodies of my father and uncles until I was dead. I can still hear them saying things like, "Hang that nigger. The only good nigger is a dead nigger." I would wake up screaming, my clothes soaked in perspiration. I always hoped my nightmare was only a bad dream but when I went to my father's room, my auntie who had moved in to take care of me was in tears and she would hug me to comfort me and say things to warm my heart. Then one night my father and my uncles came to me in a dream. They told me not to worry and to let Ed teach me how to hunt. They said to let him teach me how to use a rifle and a bow and arrow. They said he would help develop my skills in hunting, tracking and the use of weapons as I formulated my purpose in life. They said he would present me with reasons to live and I should commit myself to learning and understanding them.

"Yes father," I replied, with tears rolling down my cheeks.

"Who was Ed?" I asked.

"Ed was my auntie's husband. His father was an Apache Indian and he had taught Ed to be an Apache warrior. "Never forget who you are," Ed said to me as he began to teach me. "Never forget the reason why you are learning these skills.""

"Where was your mother?" I asked.

"She died about two years before that incident," he replied.

"What was the cause you committed yourself to?" I asked.

"At first, I did not understand but as the years passed, I finally understood I was committing to avenging my father's and my uncle's lynching."

I found myself staring at him. knowing full well what he meant but needing to hear him say it. Even then, it was not credible to me because so many patients have claimed to be born killers but have never harmed a fly in their entire lives.

Suddenly the conversation was shattered by the crisis alarm system. I was still looking at him when he said, "Somebody needs your help, doc, you better hurry, go."

"Yeah," I said. "We will continue later," I got up from the chair and headed to the nurses' station. The alarm went off again, indicating that help was needed on unit eight. There are ten psychiatric units each with 25 beds for patients in the hospital. It was common practice for some units to sound the alarm when a patient lost self-control and became agitated, which quickly progressed to violent behavior. When the alarm sounded, which was a cry for help, the ancillary staff would leave their units and go to the unit in crisis. The hospital police would also respond to the alarm, to observe and if needed, assist in keeping order. We converged on unit eight and were informed by the charge nurse that a young black male was becoming progressively psychotic and agitated. I saw him at the end of the unit. He was approximately six feet, weighing about two hundred pounds. He was swearing and threatening violence if his personal space was invaded. The charge nurse tried to talk him down but that only seemed to infuriate him. He began threatening to kill anyone who came close to him. I ushered forward a little and began speaking with him from a distance, addressing him by his name.

"Mr Franks, I have some PRN medications for you."

"I don't want any fucking medication," he replied to me, in a raised voice.

"This medication will help you to feel better, allowing you to regain control over your psychosis, calming you down so your behavior will be appropriate again."

"I am telling you all, the first one of you who comes over here, I am going to bust them up," he said, showing his fist. "I am going to fuck you up."

"Are you hearing voices, Mr Frank? Is that the reason you are acting the way you are?"

"Yes, I am hearing your voice, motherfucker, and I don't like it at all. Get the fuck away from me and take your medication with you," he said as he grabbed a plate with food and threw it at us. There was no doubt in my mind he meant what he said earlier but now he was a danger to others. This behavior could not be allowed to continue.

"Mr Franks, there is no need to be afraid. We are here to help you and the first step is for you to calm down. We will not hurt you."

"You calm the fuck down and get the fuck out of my room, nigger."

"I want to give you some medication to help you overcome your psychosis and assist you in regaining your control over it. Will you take it?" I asked.

"What kind of medication is it?" he countered.

"Ativan, Haldol and Benadryl, IM," I said.

"That shit is going to knock me out," he spat. He grabbed a chair and threw it at us.

With that, the male techs and hospital police swarmed and subdued him, and held him by each limb as he struggled against them. They lifted him and carried him screaming and kicking. He was injected with his PRN medication for agitation and left locked in the quiet room. A staff member was assigned to stay and observe him through the glass of the locked door. He was no longer a danger to himself or others so I returned to my unit, to find everything as I had left it. Soon a patient was asking for a towel and soap to take a shower and another was asking for additional clothing from his belongings. We responded to their needs and none of them displayed any dreaded behavior. The stress remained at a low level on the unit as the staff kept a vigilant look out. Any patients seen pacing back and forth were approached and gently probed for their reasons displaying these early signs of agitation. They were cared for before they reached a crisis level. Through our diligence, we were having what had become to us as a normal day on our psychiatric unit.

I was sitting at a desk in the nursing station when Mr Stuart approached me and requested a sheet of writing paper and a pen.

"What are you writing?" I asked.

"This will be my 24-hour letter," he replied. "I believe I am well enough to go home."

"Is your legal status voluntary?" I asked.

"Why don't you check my chart and see," he shot back.

I did and he was, which gave him the right to submit a letter instructing the institution to release him in 24-hours. He had voluntarily hospitalised himself since he had run out of his medications to prevent the psychosis from taking control of his mind. He had an appointment with his psychiatrist booked but the date was one month away and he had feared he would lose control to his demons. But now he was feeling better. There were no reasons to keep him. He had already met all the criteria needed for discharge. He was never considered a threat to others or himself and he now denied having any visual, tactile or any other type of hallucinations. He also denied any suicidal or homicidal ideation.

"Mr Stuart, will I ever hear the end of your story?" I asked, but hoping to get something that I could use to deny his discharge and extend his stay.

"You are a busy man with a lot of people demanding your time. In addition, I really don't believe you are sincerely interested in my story, although I want you to hear and understand it," he replied looking me in the eyes.

"Time is a commodity in my job, to meet the needs of my clients. Until you are discharged, you are still my client and I will have time for you," I said earnestly.

"A well-rehearsed response," he said.

"Mr Stuart, you reached out and I responded half-heartedly, you sensed my lack of interest and it affected you, causing you to withdraw. Now I am reaching back to you because you thought it necessary to reveal something that is important and maybe a key to your treatment. Maybe it is so important that you will not be psychologically healthy until you have divulged what is on your mind. It may take more than your voluntary stay, but it has to be said for you to be free of all your sufferings, and I will listen."

"When?"

"Finish your story, Mr Stuart," I said.

"Son," he said smiling, "my story will take more than a few minutes or even a few hours. As a matter of fact, it is the story of my life and I have been on this earth for almost 60 years. I cannot summarize my life into hours."

"That's what I love to hear, Mr Stuart - a story of life. It means as a patient you are analysing your past to see where you have been and where you are going."

"Just listen to my story and don't give me any fucking philosophy," he said.

"That was a joke," I said.

"And not a good one either," he shot back.

"Story time," I replied, sensing that this was not one of my more therapeutic moments. We walked together back to his bed in the unit. It was quiet in the nursing station as he sat down and gathered his thoughts.

"Ed taught me how to hunt. He taught me how to track animals and how to use a bow and arrow. Later he taught me how to use a hunting rifle. From the time, I was 12 until I was 18 we hunted in the forested area of Alabama and her bordering states at least once a week. One thing he kept drumming into me was that I should always make the first shot be the kill shot. He showed me the areas of the body that would bring about instant death when penetrated by a bullet. He had me practice by shooting at those areas on wooden cut outs of the animals we hunted. For target practice, he placed tin cans at the top of the fence post of the hog pen. I shot them off to develop my marksmanship. When we went hunting he only allowed one bullet in my gun at a time. We went hunting for fast moving wild game such as wild hogs, rabbits and birds. I learned to make every bullet count. However, one day I developed a clearer understanding of his thinking. We were out hunting and were confronted by a black bear. The bear stood up on its hind legs and growled at us. He looked so ferocious, standing over ten feet tall. His paws were huge and terrifying. I was instantly gripped by fear. I brought my rifle up without taking time to aim and fired my single shot hitting him somewhere in the shoulders. This angered him even more and he began to chase us. We had become prey to this beast who was intent on tearing us apart for hurting him. For miles, he chased us. At times, we could not see him but we heard his loud growl behind us as he crashed through the dense undergrowth.

After a time, we entered a bushy, narrow isthmus between two lakes. I did not hear anything and I thought the bear was dead. However, Ed knew differently and was prepared for the bear to ambush us. As the injured bear charged, I screamed in fear. Ed took time to aim and fired his hunting rifle hitting the bear in the head. It crashed to the ground with a thunderous thud within a few feet of where I stood. On that day, I learned the need for patience and came to understand what he meant by making that first shot be the kill shot. Again, he showed me the areas to aim for to bring down a prey with that single shot. Those lessons became a part of me as I grew and matured into a young man and again when I became a sniper in Vietnam. Those were among the best days of my life.

"From the time I was 12 until I was 18, I seldom heard voices. However, after my 18th birthday, the voices started again. It was the voices of my father and uncles telling me to join the army. It was during the earlier part of the escalation of the Vietnam War. I knew if I joined I would go there but I did not mind, in fact the thought was thrilling because I was used to killing although I had never killed a man before."

That statement sent chills down my spine. I knew then I was dealing with a man that was a cold blooded, heartless killer even if his killing was sanctioned by the Government under the terms of war. He enjoyed killing. I sensed it in his demeanour even as he excused his killings as an act of war. I sensed he was born to kill for he was so comfortable talking about it, and to make matters worse, his military training made him more proficient at it. So far during his stay as a patient he made no gestures or showed any signs of wanting to do me or any staff or patient harm. I knew the reason behind this calmness he portrayed. It was his way of coping and never losing control. "How many men have you killed so far in your life Mr Stuart?" I asked again wanting to hear if he would repeat the number he had stated earlier.

"I am telling a story, nurse Gordon. When I am finished, you do the maths. I will not be hiding anything," he replied.

I looked at the clock and saw it was almost 3:00 pm. I still had three charts to write and I had to find out detailed information about the other patient I was assigned to chart on.

"Mr Stuart," I said "we have to cut this now. I must complete my preparations for the oncoming tour. We can continue this tomorrow."

"What time tomorrow?" he asked.

"I am not at liberty to give you a specific time Mr Stuart," I said. "You see how things can be unpredictable on the unit. When I have some time, I will come and we will talk then."

"Sounds like a plan to me," he said.

"Mr Stuart," I continued. "You have been here two days, tomorrow is your third, as a voluntary patient. With a 24-hour submitted letter, you will be discharged and what about your story, will you be able to finish it by then?"

"Nurse Gordon, will you promise to listen, understand and take the appropriate actions when necessary?"

"I do," I said, not grasping the depth of this commitment.

"Give me the letter," he said and I handed him his 24-hour letter. He took it, read it and said, "Understand this commitment you have made. I am giving up my freedom," and he tore up the letter. "What I will reveal to you in my story will lead to my demise either by you acting or not. I want to die with honor in God's eyes and that may not be so in the eyes of man." I looked at him not knowing what to say, not fully grasping the depths his story was taking. Those simple words "I do" had committed me to a happy marriage but now it was committing me to a dark troubling future. I wondered what craziness I had allowed myself to be manipulated into.

I went to the nursing station where I immediately got his chart and started a detailed study of his psychiatric history. There was no prior documentation of the story about his father and uncles. I attained a listing of all his prior hospitalizations on the computer. His first hospitalization was in 1979 but there was nothing documented in any of his charts about what he had told me. I wanted to know why something as important as that was never documented. It was the tragic event in his life that changed everything, including his perception of people. His whole life was shaped and defined by that incident. I approached the psychiatrist to whom he was assigned.

"Dr Charles, you have been treating Mr Stuart for various psychoses for several years now. Has he ever said anything to you about his parents?"

"Mr Gordon, Mr Stuart selects the topics he speaks of and one of those he does not speak to me about are his parents. When we approach that subject, he becomes selectively mute or moves onto a different topic. He once told me they were dead."

"Did he tell you how his father died?"

"No," replied Dr Charles.

I summarised to the doctor the story Mr Stuart had told me.

"Do you believe him?"

"I see no reason why he would create a story like that."

"Did Mr Stuart avenge his father and uncles' deaths?" asked the doctor.

"At this point he has not reached that part of the story but I do believe he will eventually reveal that."

"You must find out. Apparently, Mr Stuart trusts you. The story he is telling may also be confessions of things he has done in the past. You must listen, understand and respond therapeutically to his revelations."

"Then what?" I demanded.

"We are bound by the laws of confidentiality. Whatever he reveals stays here, between the staff and in his chart."

"Even if he admits to being a serial killer."

"Those are the laws of confidentiality."

# CHAPTER 3: Thy Son Will Learn from Thee

It was a summer's night in 1958 when Christopher Carson came face to face with his destiny. Carson had been taught by his father to be a Klansman from the time he was eight years old. He had taken it to heart and put into practice all its racist rhetoric. He was the 20th generation of the Carson family. The Carsons were originally from Scotland and were among the first white settlers of Virginia. They then moved south to Alabama. They were active in the war of Independence and in the Civil War, fighting for the Confederacy. With the defeat of the Confederacy and the period of black growth during the Reconstruction era, they took to wearing the Klansman's garb and adopted the philosophy of white supremacy, terrorizing black folks in the South to regain what they had lost in the war. Young Christopher Carson was the fourth generation to have worn the Klansman's robe. The Carsons were wealthy, influential, prominent and well respected, though many nights they joined Klan members to go 'nigger hunting' as they called it. They dressed in their Klan attire, saddle their horses like the old days and headed out to end the miserable, pathetic life, as they saw it, of some unfortunate 'black man'. Carson participated in this ritual many times and never thought of it as illegal or wrong. It was the white way of life, the right way of life in their view and no one disputed it but the Negroes.

Early that hot mid-July summer's day of 1958, a Klan member saw a group of young black men in town and got information about them. Later he got word to the rest of the Klan and after they left town, the Klan was prepared to do what they had been doing since the emancipation, to keep Americas' hate alive as they dehumanised, terrorized and hanged black men. Carson as usual went with his father on the hunt and as they chased the group and captured them his father shouted, "Don't harm the boy, but hang the rest of them. Let him watch and see what awaits him when he steps out of place and become an uppity nigger." So they did, but Carson now at the tender age of 16 had adsorbed, experienced and witnessed so many lynchings that it no longer affected him. He had come to enjoy seeing black men and women twitching and kicking as the last remnants of life were squeezed out of their broken, mutilated bodies while they were hung. This was their murderous method of choice, besides burning down the homes of blacks while they slept.

Carson observed with disdain the black boy his father had decided to spare. He observed as the boy made courageous but futile attempts to save his father's life only to be pummelled and beaten down by the Klan members who wanted to hang him. On seeing his family members meet their demise the boy broke down and Carson watched him as he began to scream. Carson detested any such show of emotions. His father commanded his men to tie up the boy as he lay there in the field crying, shrieking, and grieving. Carson then rode over to the bound and grieving lad and said, "Nigger, one day soon it will be you who will be hanging from a tree, just like your pa. I hate you niggers. You are the reason why the South is like this. If it was up to me, none of you would be allowed in this country. I would wipe you all from the face of the earth."

Carson rode off into the night with his mentor and the rest of the Klansmen who had accompanied them. As they rode away through the open quiet fields, their burning torches flickered and burned no more. Soon this night would only be an insignificant memory to him, just like the people they had hanged. They did not matter to him, as in his mind they were not humans, due solely to their skin colour. As far as he was concerned, these sub-humans were not a creation of God and were meant to be the white man's slaves. If they were not his slaves, they could not and would not be allowed to live where the white man lived.

As Carson arrived home, he caught up to his dad who was making his way into the study of their large plantation house.

"Dad, did you see how those niggers tried to fight us off like they believe they had a chance against our superior numbers? When we were about to hang them, they began crying and begging for their lives. They are nothing but a bunch of cowards. Those fucking niggers don't deserve to live."

"I am proud of you, son, within you are the vestiges for the future of the white race. Our ultimate mission as Klansmen is to see that America remains a white man's country. The only way we can accomplish this mission is by punishing any nigger who steps out of line and creating laws that make the others fear the thought of venturing out of their place. Son, to keep them in place will take a few hangings to remind them who are the bosses, who makes the rules and what is their role here. They must know and accept that this is a white man's country," said his father as he removed his Klan sacrificial robe.

"Father, I will always remind them. I will always let them know who are the bosses and the purpose of them being here. Did you see how that nigger shit and pissed himself up when we were about to hang him? No white man would lose his dignity and allow that to happen to them. Bubba Ray stuck a hot cattle's prod up his ass. Did you hear him scream?" He said as he laughed. "The other nigger was as big as a horse. Charlie cut off his penis while he was still alive, Charlie says he is going to cook it up and eat it, which will make his bigger, like those niggers. You know Charlie, he hasn't got shit down there, nor does he have a lick of sense."

"They aren't human, son, not like you and me. They are like the beasts of the fields and God gave us white men the right over all animals, to do what we please and he has not shown us any disfavour in our treatment of them so we must be doing the right thing. Son, my father always told me never allow any Northerner to come down here and tell me how to run things, for they sometimes want to dictate civil laws to us. This is the South and we do things our way and these niggers like the way we treat them. I wish your mother was still alive to see you today - she would be so proud. You know we once hanged a nigger for looking at her. She was certainly a pretty woman," he said as he picked up a framed picture of his deceased wife. "Wish she could have had more of you before she passed on. You are the future, son. You know we are descendants of Vikings. Our forefathers were once raiders. They conquered villages all over Europe and took what they wanted and needed. We are the descendants of great warriors whose ships and swords paved their way into history. We must not forget our past. We must not forget who we are. You, my son, will one day carry on this tradition and pass it onto your sons."

"My father taught me everything," said a jubilant but reflective Ian Carson as he spoke to his son. "He taught me the importance of being a white man and the need to protect our womenfolk, especially from those niggers. He taught me the need for education. I went to school and became an attorney then after several successful years of practice I followed in his footsteps and ran for Congress. I remained in congress for four terms before I became a senator. Like my father, I aspired to be president. I campaigned but dropped out of the running because of insufficient funds. A change is coming to the South, my son. I can feel it. I can see it especially since the military went and started treating those niggers like they are equal to white men and they got rid of segregation. Now, whenever those boys get out of the military, they just don't want to act like they used to before they went in. Now you see them trying to disrespect the white Southern way of doing things. They want to eat at the same restaurants as us, use the same bathroom as us, and drink from the same water fountain as us. Soon they will want our women too. There is a change coming, son, but we Klan's men must stand firm and prevent it from ever happening. We are the gatekeepers of the white race and it is our duty to prevent any of those people from intermingling with us and destroying the purity of our race."

Without question, Carson accepted the words of his father. Like his father and the many generations of Carsons preceding him, they all had allowed themselves to become a vessel of this hate. Brainwashed, in time they became the leading catalysts for this type of thinking and were among those that directed and defined American hate over the centuries.

Followed by millions, the Carsons and their friends had conducted genocide during the Plains war against the American Indians. They branded indigenous people as savages who blocked their path as whites headed west after the civil war. While a Carson stood in Congress lighting the fire for war against the Indians, another sold guns and whisky to the Indians. The slaughter of these proud nomadic people was inevitable. The Indians looked different and lived on lands that were wealthy with minerals. Their food supply, such as bison, became target practice for many wealthy whites as they rode along the railroads through what was once Indian country. These beautiful animals were almost wiped from the face of the earth so the Indians could not eat and use their skins for clothing. Many more battles were fought where this brand of treachery exemplified the thinking of white America to the rest of the world before the Indian tribes succumbed to defeat and were forced to live on reservations.

"When will we be able to get rid of those niggers, father?" inquired the young Carson.

"Son," return a thoughtful Ian Carson, "there are laws preventing us from wiping them out."

"Well, Hitler almost wiped out all the Jews in Europe so why can't we do the same to the niggers here?" asked the young Klan boy.

"Did you note the price he paid for his atrocity? Son, you have to be wise. This nation's laws will not allow it."

"What if there was a race war father?"

"There would be no excuse to wiping them out."

"There will be a race war, father. I will see to it. Us whites must protect and defend ourselves from those niggers," answered the young Carson before he allowed his father to complete his thought.

"We cannot go about slaughtering them like that, son - people will not allow it. What we must do is use the laws to do it for us. Create laws to stop the growth of their population."

"How is that father?"

"A friend in the senate recently revealed a plan to me that would inhibit, stymie and cause a continuous decrease in the black population."

As his interest peaked, the dedicated Klan boy listened intently.

"What is the plan, father?" He craved this insight and his father, a connoisseur of words as well as alcohol, poured himself a shot of bourbon before he continued.

"The first step is to prevent them from getting jobs. We plan to get to most corporations through word of mouth that most companies should not hire those people. We will bring in drugs such as cocaine, heroin, marijuana and we will hire their young people, the future of their community, to sell these drugs to their own. In the meantime, we will create laws. We will make laws that will incarcerate them for decades if they are found with any drugs in their possession."

Years later, many political officials including the young Carson, were elected to get tough on crime and laws were passed that lead to the incarceration of millions of young black men and women. Many received life sentences for non-violent crimes, such as possessing or selling drugs. Those found guilty were punished as severely as someone committing a crime of first-degree murder. This legislation, intended to disproportionately incarcerate the black population, made its way through the House, then the Senate and was signed as law. Such was the American justice system at the time.

"I do not understand, father," acknowledged the young Carson. "These laws will take so long to work. If there was a war, we could wipe them from the face of the earth in weeks, not in scores of years."

"Such are the ways of laws. But with laws the population will not cry foul, for they will have committed crimes that will justify their sentences, whereas an outright genocide would not be tolerated by most Americans."

"As we speak father, in Birmingham niggers are sitting at the counters of the Woolworth' s store, demanding to be served like us. They do not want to go in their areas anymore. They are refusing to sit in the back of the bus. They are refusing to give us their seats when all the seats in the front of the bus are taken."

"As I said, son, there is a change coming. We must start to create laws that will prevent their growth even when we allow them to sit at the counter with us. With more black men and women in jail, there will be fewer and fewer black babies born each year. We are going to build prisons all over this nation to put them in. What will be left outside will be an ageing black population that's passive and controllable. In time, they all will be dead and we won't even have fired a shot. That is the beauty of the law. Give you an example – in 1896, Plessy versus Ferguson, the court ruled that separate but equal was constitutional and that ruling became the backbone of segregation. From that, we created laws that separated and disenfranchised niggers throughout the South until they had no rights at all".

"You think that will work again father?' demanded an impatient young Carson.

"Yes, son, the Jim Crow laws returned supremacy back to the white man in the South after the Civil War. Those laws have been active from the end of the reconstruction period, for almost 100 years and they have succeeded in keeping the niggers in place during that time. Those laws made their way from the South to the Midwest and then all over America. White power became the American way instead of just the Southern way. The North won the Civil War and emancipated the slaves, but we won battle for supremacy."

"Father, are you blind? The niggers have revolted. They are winning the Civil Rights war! If this keeps up they will soon have the right to vote and elect other niggers into office. They are gaining power, father."

"Son, times are changing and the laws to prevent the growth of the nigger must change and adapt to these new happenings otherwise they will become obsolete. These new laws are meant to keep them powerless, penniless, uneducated, and most of all, decimate their population. These new laws will be more effective than the Jim Crow laws were. They will start the inadvertent genocide of the nigger population. We will first steer their men into a life of crime by not offering them any other opportunities. They will end up where we want them, in prisons all over this nation where they will become a non-paying workforce for our companies. Those that the laws do not get, the drugs will get. You will live long enough to see what I mean. Watch and see what I am talking about. The niggers are powerless. They have no source of income, they don't own any business, they have no political representation that will not sell them out in a minute and their schools are not teaching them anything worthwhile."

"Father, things do not remain the same. There are always constant changes going on. Your laws and your drugs will account for a good portion of the nigger population but what about the rest? That is why I want a war. I want to account for the total nigger population. I want them all dead."

"That is an ambitious goal son, but may not be an achievable one. You must be realistic. Do you want all niggers in this nation dead or do you want all niggers on the planet dead?"

"We will start with all the niggers in this nation and then work on the rest of the planet after," replied the young Carson. "We are Americans, the most powerful nation on the planet, no nation will dare question, intercede or try to stop us out of fear of our retributions."

"Hitler thought the same way son..." But without allowing his father to finish his statement the young, brash Carson interrupted. "Hitler was a fool. He started too many wars, he should never have attacked Russia, he should have kept them as an ally and they would have won the war. But my objective is the niggers. They are all over the world and they are not wanted wherever they are located. Most countries would be happy to rid their borders of them; we will offer them our assistance. Before you know it, father, we will be raising the Confederate flag in Tim Buk Tu."

"Son, most Klansmen would welcome your thinking but I think it's a little too ambitious. Even my plan will one day be exposed for what it is. We must come up with something new. Whatever it may be, it must be sanctioned as the law of the land and that will make it legal for generations to come before they realize the damage it has done." The young Carson listened impatiently, while he formulated his own plan for an outright war of the races.

"Soon you will be graduating from high school. You will start attending either the US Air Force Academy or West Point Academy."

"I want to go to the Citadel, father."

"No son. I want you to be exposed to more than the Southern ways. I want you to become worldly and wise. You are an intelligent boy. I want to prepare you for leadership. I also want you to look your best. That scar on your face must go. I will make an appointment with one of the best plastic surgeons in the country to remove it."

"Thank you, father. I want to look as good as I think, one day I want to be president of this great nation, the United States of America."

"You will be son, that you will be."

# CHAPTER 4: The Psychiatric Unit

At 7:30 a.m. the medication nurse starts each day by counting the narcotics medication while the charge nurse and head nurse are briefed on the patients in the unit. This particular morning was moving at its usual pace with each staff member attending to their individual patients. The head nurse was preparing for the unit rounds, a meeting that included the unit chief, who was a psychiatrist, his assistant, the psychologist, social workers, the art and activity therapist and case workers. The charge nurse had the charts of the newly admitted patients and the census reports. The census reports were integral to this meeting. It consisted of the patient's name, age, gender, legal status, psychiatric diagnosis, medical diagnosis, patient assigned psychiatrist, social worker and clinician's notes of the patient's response to care. After the nurse's report was presented, the census report became the focal point of discussion, with the psychiatrist leading the discussion on the individual patient and the treatment team members interjecting with information based on their individual discipline. All of this was leading to the patient's progression and readiness for discharge or the need to have the patient relocated to a long-term facility because of his worsening condition. Every morning, this group would meet and discuss the patient mental condition and progress.

I was informed by the head nurse to accompany her to a morning report. I had represented nurses in the unit rounds many times before, so was familiar with all its nuances. When I asked why I was accompanying her, she explained that I had made a breakthrough with Mr Stuart and she wanted me to share my information with the group, as the information could prove valuable.

When it was Mr Stuart's turn, I informed the staff of his 24-hour letter, that his status was voluntary and his behavior appropriate in all occasions. The therapists agreed regarding his behavior and the art therapist displayed some of his work. The feedback was unanimously positive. I mentioned that Mr Stuart was telling me his life story and had said that as a young pre-teen, he had witnessed the brutal lynching of his father and uncles by the Klan.

"This," I stated, "pushed him over the edge and still today he occasionally hears his father and uncles voice giving him instructions."

"What kind of instructions?" Inquired the psychologist.

"He said the voices command him to kill others and that he lives to avenge the death of his father and uncles. He has mentioned he has killed at least 1,000 people, all of them enemies. He has just started his story so I look forward to hearing and discerning the truth from what is plain falsehood. I need more time to listen and determine if Mr Stuart's hallucinations would make him a danger to others or himself," I replied. "At this time, Mr Stuart has denied having any hallucinations. His story is about his past— it's both informative and revealing. I will continue to engage him in conversation to get him to reveal his inner thoughts. But I cannot advise discharge now, until I am able to ascertain without doubt what the voices are telling him to do and if he has ever acted on what they have commanded him."

"Keep me informed," said the unit chief. "I do not want someone who could be a danger to others allowed to be free on the streets. In fact, do not engage Mr Stuart. Allow him to come to you and do not appear to be too eager to listen."

"Won't that let him walk away?" I queried.

"He wants to talk. When you can, you listen, and engage him, but don't go looking for him. Let him come looking for you — you will get his unguarded story then."

I realized what he was saying and accepted that as my strategic mode of operations. We quickly evaluated the rest of the clients on the census and moved to meet the three new patients who were admitted on the unit during the previous night tour.

The first was Mr John Curtis. A 23-year old male, he had a history of being schizophrenic. He also had a long history of drug usage and multiple mental health hospitalizations. At the tender age of eight, he had killed his stepfather who had beaten his mother into a coma. He stabbed his stepfather in the back of the neck several times and then called 911 and reported his crime. His mother never recovered from the coma, her brain was bashed in, causing massive brain haemorrhage. He lived in one foster home after another up to his 19th birthday. Currently he considers himself to be a big-time drug dealer but in reality, he is a violent street thug, a mugger and a thief when he is not incarcerated. When Mr Curtis was led into the room, I noticed his tremendous intimidating presence. He stood a good six feet three inches and weighed close to 300 pounds of muscle. There was an undeniable meanness to his disposition that seemed easily ready to render itself to violence. He was seated at the end of the table and the members of the care team introduced themselves after the chief gave a short speech on the purpose of the meeting. He said nothing when it was his time to speak. He stared and got out of his chair and was taken back to the unit. I was happy to see him go, and in my heart and mind knew of the danger that accompanied him to the unit.

The next patient was Ms Morales, a 45-year old female with a diagnosis of depression. Her hair was matted and uncombed, partially hiding the patchy scaly skin growth invading her face. She was not concerned with her general appearance. She took the seat at the end of the table without making eye contact with the care team as she began speaking, "I have been hearing voices telling me that I am a worthless, a good-for-nothing bitch forever, and that I must kill myself." She had made several attempts over the years, but never anything fatal. Her attempts included several overdoses of her medications or pills, only to call 911 and end up in the emergency room where she was saved time and again. She had several scars on both wrists from her various attempts, which she wore as a badge of honor. She was willing and ready to tell her peers or staff of their history. Here she was, still surviving after 30 years of attempting suicide, looking wretched, tormented and at least 20 years older than her chronological age of 45. Her cry for help appeared to have been permanently unanswered leaving her in a state of flux. She was undefeated, trying to find the answers to make it all stop so she could lead what she perceived a normal life, but the voices would not leave and no psychiatrist had found a way to extricate them from her head. The only thing left was for her to summon the courage to do as they commanded. I knew one day she would summon that courage and not call 911. I wondered if she ever had a moment of peace and happiness in her adult life. She appeared a victim and would always be a victim of the voices and her inner anguish. We had seen her many times before and knew of her history. This place was her home and when she left to go, she was only visiting her family, later to return.

The next was an unusual case: Ms Me Yoa Matoma, a 21-year old Japanese female whose diagnosis was suicidal ideation, with a recent attempt by drug overdose. She had neither previous mental health nor any medical history. Currently she was a philosophy student at New York University. She had recently married her Anglo-American boyfriend. From his perspective, the marriage was so she could attain her residency or green card. However, she had mistakenly interpreted their marriage as the real thing and so she had sex with him, consummating their marriage. She was really in love with this young man. On seeing her husband in the constant company of another young women, she confronted him. He verbally abused her, and told her to accept the circumstances. She became distraught, concluding that she had disgraced her family's name and so sought to end her life. As a Westerner, this would be a painful situation but something one would eventually accept and adapt to achieve their intended goal. Ms Yoa however, was from a different culture whose views of this event did not bode well. Suicide was seen as the only acceptable solution when one has lost face, been publicly humiliated and disgraced.

She stated in the meeting she was disappointed that she was not successful in ending her life, and would again attempt suicide until she succeeded. I knew she meant every word of what she said and I made a note to change her thinking. She had decided to bide her time so that she would be successful in her next attempt. I remembered watching footage of Japanese soldiers in the Pacific as WW2 was ending. Rather than being captured and surrendering to the American soldiers, many Japanese soldiers found ways of committing suicide. I also remembered the Japanese Kamikaze pilots of WW2 who used their planes as suicide bombers by crashing them into US battleships. She was placed on one to one observation, which meant staff were assigned to be with her always.

Soon morning rounds were completed and I returned to the unit where Mr Stuart was patiently waiting. He had positioned himself where he could observe the on-going activities at the nursing station. I looked at him and he smiled. I went to inform the secretary of required updates to the census, when I noticed Mr Williams ambulating toward the table tennis board. I observed as he picked up a paddle and requested to play a game. I thought this was a little odd, especially for Mr Williams who had been self-isolated for a long time. He had been selectively mute, depressed and reclusive, normally found in his room, asleep or awake in his bed or speaking to himself while gesticulating. Seldom did he venture outside of that environment or interact with his peers. He admitted to hearing voices but never said what the voices were telling him. His involuntary legal status had allowed him to be kept in this facility for months awaiting a bed in a long-term care facility as his condition had not improved. Now I wondered why he had suddenly broken out of his shell.

With no one responding to his request to play, he approached Mr Stuart and asked, "Hey brother, want to play a game?"

Mr Stuart studied him. I watched them curiously from a distance.

"Get away from me," snarled Mr Stuart in a cold, contemptuous voice, hardly audible from where I stood.

"Fuck you, nigger," Mr Williams spat back, as he made his way to find someone else to play with. I wondered why he was so determined to play table tennis this early in the morning. I watched as he made his way from one rejection to the next and called him over to find out.

"Mr Williams," I said as he approached the desk, "why the need to play a game of table tennis now?" With him close by, I sensed he was on drugs and I asked, "Did you have a visitor yesterday?" He looked at me and I saw a change come over him. He went silent and walked away. I checked the records, and he did have a visitor. I called security and soon the five security members arrived and went to search his room. They instructed the clients that shared the room to wait in the day room while they searched. As they did so, another patient came to the nursing station and informed me that Mr Williams had come to their room and asked a friend to hide his drugs until the search was over.

"Did his friend do that for him?" I asked.

"Yes, he did," replied the informer.

"Where?"

"It was a plastic bag with coke in it," he started to say.

"Where did he hide it?" I firmly demanded.

"He swallowed it," he replied.

"What?" I said in disbelief.

"He swallowed it," he repeated.

"You saw this?"

"With my own two eyes," he shot back.

"Who is the individual?"

He gave the name of the accomplice who was also sitting in the day room. I was not sure whether I was being manipulated or not, but I aimed to find out. The search proved fruitless. The patient who was said to have swallowed the bag with the drugs was placed in the quiet room under constant observation while I explained things to management. He was then quickly admitted to a medical floor and an abdominal radiological exam confirmed that he had swallowed the plastic bag with the drugs. He remained under constant observation while the medical team waited for the plastic bag to pass through his gastrointestinal system.

Suddenly, above all the patient fracas of the unit, intruded the angry voice of the most feared patient on the unit.

"What is your fucking problem bitch? What the fuck are you looking at?" This outburst made its way from across the large room, grabbing my attention just as it was meant to, like a hostile vice. It was Big Louie's voice. He was a paranoid schizophrenic and now it sounded like he was getting angry, which was a danger to everyone ,including the staff. He was shouting at the top of his voice. Louie was a young Hispanic male in his early twenties and prone to violence. He was six feet four inches and weighed 360 pounds. He always had a mean and angry scowl on his face. He actively hallucinated but trusted the voices in his head, which made it difficult to treat him. It also prevented him from developing any trusting relationship with his family, staff or peers. From his day of arrival, I had a bad feeling about him. With determination to hide my fear, I always approached him with certainty and kept a good distance from his personal space. He was sitting in the dining area. The staff began converging in that room when they heard the outburst.

"Bitch, I am going to kick your ass," he said, with the determination to execute this task.

"Louie," I heard a staff member shout, "Calm down."

He attempted to pick up one of the steel table-benches. It weighed about half a ton. He lifted it off the floor and attempted to throw it at the other patient who was the object of his wrath. The table turned over in the process and this frightened everyone who was there. I went quickly to the medication room and by the time I came back he was in his room, angrily pacing back and forth and swearing to himself. I could see he had no control of his behavior. Our eyes met as I entered the room and I could see the volcanic anger spewing out, ready to destroy others.

There was a dark evil emitting from him like none I have ever seen before, and it was frightening. There was a dark glow issuing from the lower orbit of his eyes. I felt an invisible dark force that enveloped him and I feared the danger he carried to the unit. In my mind, I thought of what I should say to him that would be therapeutic and also make him aware of his inappropriate, dangerous behavior. He was mildly mentally challenged, very paranoid, and considered everything a threat. Violence was his main solution to most of his problems.

"You see these clients here? They are your peers and I am responsible for their safety just as I am for yours. You lifting heavy objects and throwing them around is endangering them as well as yourself. I cannot allow that behavior, Louie."

"What are you going to do about it, nigger?" he snarled.

"I am going to medicate you, Louie. Don't let this happen again because if you do I will put you in isolation and restrain you. Tie you up like an animal, Louie. And Louie – you address me as Nurse Gordon, not as 'nigger.'"

The nurse prepared the medication and within moments the hospital police officers were there. Louie did not put up any further resistance and willingly took the medication. Soon after, he was sleeping like a baby.

# CHAPTER 5: Self-Discovery

He was sitting on one of the couches in the patient lounge with an ugly scowl creasing his face.

"Good morning, Mr Stuart," I said. "Are you ready to continue from where you left off yesterday?" His evil scowl transformed into a sneer. "We could do this later," I suggested, which brought him to his feet.

Standing he said, "Let's go by one of the tables in the back."

I followed him and we found an unoccupied table in the back and sat facing each other.

"Is there a reason for you telling me this story, Mr Stuart?"

"Don't you want to hear it?"

"It is interesting."

"Then listen. It will become apparent as time goes by."

"I prefer having the rationale for you telling me your personal detail history upfront. It will prevent miscommunication – too much ambiguity and misinterpretation."

"Nurse," he said pausing as if searching for the words to express his thoughts while he looked me in the eyes. "In life, we pray we do the right things. I have done many things and not all were good, not all were bad.  However, I feel the end is coming and I need to relieve myself of my many burdens." he said. "Many things I have done will be open to interpretations down the line, but it won't matter for I have judged myself and found myself guilty. Others in the court of law will eventually do so. But the only judgment that concerns me is that of the almighty."

"Do you want to speak with a pastor?" I asked. "He can pray for your forgiveness."

"If I wanted a pastor, I'll request one. I want to speak with you and with my revelations I will attain solace in my heart.  It will be an atonement of my sins," he said.

"Mr Stuart, whatever you say I have to share it with the rest of your care team. I want you to understand that before you continue speaking with me."

"I am aware that my dark turbulent history will be studied, deciphered, psychoanalyzed by all psychiatrists, psychologists and others to see how they could prevent this monster from committing the deeds he did throughout his life. But the real answer behind my troubled past they will never admit to, as they are in denial of its existence. They have whitewashed their history so as not to bear any responsibilities of their forefather's atrocities and are in denial of their racism and hate. In this country, racism destroys the mind and damages the spirit of black men and women. It stands in the way of their personal growth and most of all, it arrests the mental growth and development of the individuals who perpetuate that type of behavior. Hate has a way of consuming you, not allowing you to see anything else and serve anyone else but it, until it is finished using you. Then it leaves you, its discarded tool, guilty of something heinous to serve the consequences of its directives," he said.

"You hope to bring about positive changes by revealing your secrets," I said. "Through my experience, such revelations will be negatively received and given the worse spin by the media and you will be demonized. They will never arrive at the thought you visualize, not if violence was your chosen method of change. I suggest you keep your secrets, take them with you and be buried with them intact."

"The world has to know what hideous deeds this monster has done through being the victim of hate and racism."

"You are scaring me. Why do you keep referring to yourself as a monster? What hideous deeds have you done to brand yourself a monster?"

"Nurse Gordon," he said, "I don't believe I scare you one bit. I see how you handle these other monsters here and they don't scare you. You are an honorable man; you have a good heart and that is why I wish to tell you my story."

I felt he was manipulating me.

"Are you an American citizen?" he asked. Instantly my guard went up.

"Why would you want to know such personal information about me?"

He smiled again. "We are getting away from the reason we are here, but it would be helpful if you knew some American history. It will help you to understand my life," he said retreating from his question as he met my inquiring, cool stare.

Not waiting, he continued. "Anyway, during my senior year in school, we went on a field trip to our nation's capital; Washington DC. We visited all the monuments to our founding fathers and all the great presidents of our great nation but the thing I will never forget was my visit to the National Archives. There for the first time I read The United States Declaration of Independence. One sentence stood out to me as it has stood out to the world, it says "We hold these truths to be self-evident, that all men are created equal, that they are endowed by their Creator with certain unalienable rights that among these are Life, Liberty and the pursuit of Happiness."

"What was it about that statement that made it so outstanding to you?"

"It is the noblest thoughts of this great nation in one sentence. Although it was not the constitution it also enforced the God given rights of all the members of the human species no matter where they derive. They all have the same rights as any white American," he said without any doubt in his voice.

"Do you believe that?" I inquired.

"I do even if I have to fight for them. In 1965, as a boy I marched with Martin Luther King in the third march from Selma to Montgomery, Alabama. I am so regretful I was not there on Bloody Sunday and a few days later when they were not allowed to cross the Edmund Pettus Bridge," he said.

"What was that all about?"

"That is why I want you to know more about your adopted country's history, Mr Gordon, so that when I reference these things you won't have a need to question me about them." I looked at him a little embarrassed, though more disgusted at his patronising reply. "It was about the right to vote. The constitution grants all American citizens that right. Our democracy is built around it, yet still Jim Crow laws in the south denied us black folks that right so we marched for it, we fought for it and we died to achieve it. In Dallas, Alabama, blacks were the majority population. They made up 57 per cent of the eligible voting population yet still only 130 were registered voters, less than one per cent. So, we decided to change that and were met with great resistance. Many black folks were beaten to a bloody pulp and many would lose their lives, but it was the death of a white supporter that garnered the support needed to bring attention to the social order of the South and the state of Alabama. People understood the South as a place where state endorsed terrorism against its non-white citizens was practiced as the law. In 1965, President Lyndon Johnson introduced a bill that passed into law, the Voters Right Act, which made it possible for all eligible black men and women to vote and made illegal all the requirements the Jim Crow laws had passed to prevent blacks from voting."

"Even after accomplishing that do you believe that white America think all men are created equal?" I pried into his thoughts.

"They don't even want to see us much less think we are their equal in any way, shape or form. Haven't you heard of white supremacy Mr Gordon? Don't they have that in your country? They build penitentiaries to store us and make laws to incarcerate us in large numbers. What do you call that if it isn't racism, Mr Gordon?"

"I have heard of it but I have no time to acknowledge it. It's not practiced in the country I am from."

"Why are you here? The thought of equality is repulsive to them, which is why segregation came about and is still in existence today. Go back to where you came from and make sure American ideals do not influence your country. Surely if the dollar becomes an influence there, racism will follow. It's American as apple pie. Reading the Deceleration of Independence shaped my life as much as that night when the Ku Klux Klan lynched my father and uncles. You should read it, even if you are not an American citizen. The thought is truly divine, so much so that even the corrupt founding fathers could not bring themselves to alter it to read all white men are created equal."

"Words to heal a divided nation, words to give hope to a disenfranchised population."

"Indeed, Mr Gordon, indeed. I graduated from high school on my 18th birthday. It was a milestone but it was also the time I knowingly took my first step into the darkness and into manhood. That night was the first time in more than four years I heard the voices."

"What did the voices say to you?" I asked.

"It was the unmistakable voice of my father and uncles. They were telling me the day was soon approaching when I would get my papers to join the military."

"Did they object to you being drafted?"

"No," he replied.

"Did you object to being drafted?" I interrogated.

"No," he replied again. "The fact is they encouraged me to accept my duties and perform them well. They said to make them proud."

"I never heard anyone say voices could be so pleasant," I retorted.

"My father and uncles loved me," he said, "and I loved them in return." The faint smile disappeared from my face, leaving me sombre and curious.

"What year was that?" I asked.

"The year was 1968," he replied.

The Vietnam War, I thought.

"Yes," he acknowledged, as if reading my mind. "It was the era of the Vietnam war. Within weeks, I received my classification and instructions to report to Fort Dix for basic training."

"Why did you go?" I inquired. He stared at me with an incredulous expression, as if he could not believe what I asked. "Many people fled to Canada to avoid their duties to the country, why didn't you?" I asked. In his face, I saw the grossness of my suggestion.

"I would not have made my forefathers proud," he replied.

"I see you do not know what is to be an American" he retaliated.

"I am still an honorable man," I retorted.

"Just not an honorable American," he shot back. "Having thoughts like that you cannot be a real American."

"Who or what is a real American? This is a nation of immigrants. The only people who can make that claim to be a real American are the Indians."

"They died fighting for their land and their way of life, didn't they? That is what it means to be an American. It is the will to live by their terms or die trying. Look at those immigrants who migrated here. Many have fled tyranny and persecution in their countries. Landing on our shores, they have used the opportunities to live and prosper, like you, Mr Gordon."

"No, Mr Stuart, that was genocide being done by white America on the indigenous population of this country so white Americans could take their land. More than ten million people were killed, massacred, butchered. However, I live here and if this country was attacked," I said, "I would not think twice of picking up arms to repel any invading or attacking force."

"An American does not wait until he has but one choice. He always tries to resolve the problem before then, for his best interest," he said with a scowl on his face. "What about dying?" he interjected, "would you have any fear of doing that for your adopted country?"

"Yes, I would, but the death of my spirit through oppression would be worse than actually dying."

"No," he replied. "If you have life, you have hope. You may be able to bring forth changes against the unseen forces that govern us. Being the minority, I think we are subjugated to the wills and whims of the majority in this country, but there is also that unseen evil that controls us and no matter how we try to change it for the better, the more it become entrenched in its racist ways."

"Without a doubt," I said, "but there are laws which govern us all, so we can fight prejudice in the courts."

"You do believe that?" he rhetorically asked with a smile.

"You still do not know the system. It's called the law and when you look at it, you will see a white man with a gun ready to subjugate and exploit us black folks even in the country you are from. It's no different, although it may not be as obvious as it is here. We are an exploited race, trying to find our way in a society that has no desire for our presence. However, we are Americans and we will overcome, that I know. We the black population of the United States of America, are the soul of this nation. We are the righteous spirit of this nation. If we reach the point of finding ourselves and not destroying ourselves in the process, our contributions to this nation will be astounding. While our white counterparts make weapons of war and force other nations to do as they say or else, we contribute civil ways of doing things. We as a people have made great strides in this nation and for this nation as it evolves. We have shown that money and profit is not our only goal and one day when we are accepted we will transform this nation to live up to its credo that all men are created equal no matter where they live on this planet or their culture. We will make sure that all people are treated equally and not exploited by greed and corruption. Capitalism is a dangerous thing, it has legalised slavery and institutionalised racism wherever it has taken root."

"Can that be changed, Mr Stuart?"

"Yes. And you, Nurse Gordon, are an example of that change. We need more like you, not more like those who hang out at the street corner, wasting their lives away."

We had moved away from his life story to his politics and I wanted to get back to that, so I interrupted.

"What did you do while serving in the military?"

"While serving in the military, I honed my skills as a marksman. I became so good that I represented my platoon in many inter-company shooting competitions. I soon became the best shot in my company and went on to defeat the reigning division champion, a representative of the Rangers' Company within our division. That victory made me the best marksman in our division."

In my ignorance, I continued to question him, "Were you a sniper?"

"No," he said. "I was an infantry man, but I had the natural skills of a sniper. I developed those skills while hunting and tracking prey back in the wilderness of Georgia and Alabama. I loved hunting."

"You seem to relish the defeat of the Rangers' representative more so than any other of your competitors. Why is that?" I probed.

"You are so right," he replied with a smile on his face. "The Ranger core is the sniper unit of the military. They consist of the best marksmen in the infantry and when it comes to shooting long range no other military unit surpasses them. By defeating their best, it vaunted me into military stardom."

"What does that mean?" I asked.

"It meant that I represented my division in all long-range shooting competitions."

"What is a division?" I had never served in the military and needed clarification.

"It's the largest single unit in the military, they are usually two types," he continued. "They are the armoured division and the infantry division."

"I take it you were of the infantry division?"

"Yes," he replied.

"Tell me about the competition that vaulted you into military stardom?"

"Every year the military has these types of competitions," he said. "It starts from the smallest unit of the military, the squadron, where everyone competes. The winner of each squadron competes against each other to represent the platoon. The representative goes on to compete to represent the company and so on up the ladder, until there is a winner representing the division to the single individual remaining, representing the army. In my case the competition was stiff all the way. There were excellent marksmen at every level. At the level to represent my division, I was against a member of our division's Ranger Company. The individual was the current divisional champion and had been the army's reigning champion for two years. The rules were simple; we had targets every 250 yards. We were given five shots at each target.  For the first four targets, we tied. All our shots hit the bulls' eye. At the mile was where we separated. I shot first in the competition. Three of my shots hit centre bull's eye, one went right but still hit the target and my last shot completely missed the target. His first and second shot missed the target, his last three found the target but none were in the bull's eye. That was the first time he had shot at the distance of a mile in the competition. I, on the other hand had won twice before at that distance."

"How did you feel winning that competition?"

"I never felt so good in my life. I was the best at something. I was a champion. I had won. Eventually I competed against other divisions' representatives. I was on my way to win the divisional title for being the best marksman in the military, but my company was shipped out to Vietnam."

"Were you disappointed?"

"A bit," he said, "but once I got to Vietnam I quickly realized you had to be alert to survive. War and death were always in front of you, around you, above and below you. Death and war was a constant there. If you weren't alert, you were destined to return in a body bag. Have you ever fought in war, Mr Gordon?"

"No," I replied, wondering what was next to come.

"You are a fortunate man, Mr Gordon. You never had to experience that savagery of seeing men killed and be killed in large numbers, many by your hands. The Vietnam War –it was hell. Be glad you weren't there." He said this with his familiar ugly scowl and with that got up out of his seat. He had a sombre look on his face as he walked away, as if his memory had banished him into the grip of some horrible experiences he had had there. I wished I could help but he was now hiding behind the wall he had erected. There he was secure, protected, safe from my prying questions, but not from his demons.

# CHAPTER 6: The Ongoing Education Of Young Carson

In July of 1960, Christopher Carson, now 18, graduated from high school. He travelled to Colorado Springs near the Rocky Mountains and not far from Denver to start his higher education at the United States Air Force Academy. The young Carson had met all the requirements to attend this special institution of higher learning but, even if he had not, it was difficult for them to refuse the son of a United States senator. Carson was born with a desire to fly and he spent hours researching and preparing for his destiny and often was in the library reading books about planes. He was drawn to the new jet fighter planes developed by the leading countries around the globe, especially those of the US and the Soviet Union. He bought and made model planes and imagined himself one day piloting them. He was even more fascinated by the research and development done by the US as they went about making planes that ultimately flew faster than the speed of sound. Carson dreamt of one-day mastering one of these supersonic iron maidens. To make that dream a reality, he researched the requirements to be a student of the United States Air Force Academy. He took his SAT several times, gaining one of the highest scores among applicants in the class of 1960. The Air Force was the only thing that rivalled his obsession with being a Klansman.

Carson was amazed at the diversity at the Air Force Academy. Although the clear majority of the students were white males, he found a significant number of African Americans in each class. One day during class break, he was walking with his peers when he spotted a staff officer to whom he felt some kinship. He decided to question him on the presence of so many black cadets.

"Officer, I see many black cadets here. Will they be getting the same training as I?"

"All cadets regardless of their color get the same rigorous training and graduate with the same degree. I must assure you that a percentage of you who start this program will fail either by some character flaw or through the lack of ability to tolerate the rigors of this program," said the staff officer.

"Sir," continued young Carson, "in the South, most niggers do not have the aptitude to complete grade school or get a general diploma much less go to a school of higher education. It is a waste of time allowing them to enter the academy as students. They will ultimately fail. I would not trust one of them to fly a propeller driven plane, much less to be my wing-man flying a supersonic jet fighter," he retorted brashly, which brought a round of laughter from many of the white cadets and resentment from the black cadets' present. Carson did not care if they were offended. His life to date had been an offense to the black race and being in a new environment was not about to abruptly change his racist thinking.

Feeling the need to know more of this young Southerner, the staff officer proceeded to question him.

"Cadet, what state are you from?"

"The wonderful state of Alabama," Carson replied proudly.

"What you uttered regarding blacks – is that a belief you share with the people of your state or is that your own personal belief?" the staff officer asked coolly.

"Both," he replied. "It's strongly believed that blacks are inferior to whites and it is a waste of money trying to educate them because of their limited intelligence."

"I want a show of hands from all of you who share Cadet Carson's point of view," demanded the staff officer. Without hesitation, most of the white cadets raised their hands. He surveyed the group, making a mental note of whose hands were raised.

"Cadets," he barked authoritatively, "you all have an assignment tonight in addition to your other assignments and this new assignment is due tomorrow. The assignment is for all of you who have your hands raised to research and write a paper on the Tuskegee Air Men – on the finding of this group of officers who courageously served this nation during WW2 to their personal battles to improve race relations in our nation."

"Who are the Tuskegee Air Men?" asked a befuddled Carson.

"That is your assignment," replied the officer, "to find out who they are, what they did and when, where, and why the military found that there was a need for them and their courageous contributions in winning the war in Europe against the Nazis."

He turned his attention to the group.

"Some of you men will one day be officers of the United States Air Force. That means that your identity will be rooted in qualities of character. That character will be moulded through four years of intense military training. That character will require you not to be using words like 'niggers' nor 'spic' to address your black or Hispanic fellow officers. That is not the way of an officer of character or an officer of the United States Air Force. Cadets, let this be the last time I hear this racist dialog coming from any one of you. You are now informed that the use of any such words will lead to your unconditional dismissal from this institution. Is that understood, gentlemen?" demanded the officer.

"Yes, sir," they all replied as they came to attention.

"Before I leave, I must inform you that this teaching will be documented in your character files and you will be monitored on how you all cope with racial and cultural issues. Quite a bit of your training will be overseas in foreign countries with foreign cultures. It's required of our officers to understand and respect people of other nations and their cultures. If we do not have respect for our fellow officers who are black or Hispanic, we will not have any for our allies of different color and culture. Lack of respect for others will show itself through our attitudes, intolerance and disrespect in the tone used when we speak with others. Those behaviors will always lead to failure and they will not be tolerated by your fellow black or Hispanic officers or by our allies."

However, what had taken a young Carson a lifetime to learn would not be unlearned in minutes. The prejudice that had become a way of life for him was ingrained into every one of his brain cells. This air of arrogance and superiority emitted from every pore of his body and, like a foul odour, its stench alienated all except those of similar thinking.

Cadet life for Carson was a rigorous test of his fortitude. In this period of his life he had to suppress his racial hatred and focus on the strict honor code of a cadet's life. He wanted more than anything to graduate as an officer. But the hallmark of an officer's character is being able to make morally sound decisions and carry them through. Carson, while he excelled in many character based issues, lacked in the ability to treat men of color with the dignity and respect demanded of him. At the end of his freshman year, with the assurance of being an A student, he allowed himself the freedom of again releasing his suppressed racist convictions. He had discovered that a few black cadets in the academy had formed a coalition. For survival, they had banded together in groups of five with a mentoring senior as their leader. The higher-class members took the lower-class members under their wings to guide them through the difficult times. Their success was evident, for no matter how degrading their assignments, they always came out shining. One day Carson pretended to befriend one of these cadets who revealed to him some of the secrets of his group's survival. Hearing this, Carson decided to form a counter group. He had already befriended a few similar thinking white cadets who believed blacks were not worthy of being Air Force officers. They began a pattern of hazing the black cadets with the intention of stressing them and making their lives so intolerable they would give up and go home. Carson secretly went about recruiting members for his counter group. One day he approached a cadet who he believed would be a great addition. The young man was known for his rational and analytic thinking.

"You said your group is a secret society. What is its aim?" he inquired.

"Cadet Graham, I have formed a secret fraternity whose short-term goal is to discredit as many of these niggers attending this sacred warrior institution so they will leave of their own accord or be dismissed," replied the unrepentant Carson.

"How are you going to do that?" inquired the cadet.

"The question is, are you with us?" he demanded.

"We have an ethical and moral issue here," replied the cadet. "What you are proposing is against the constitutional rights of a group of people and against the teaching of the academy. Why would you want to do that, knowing that your fate will be eventually intertwined with theirs?"

"Does that mean you will not join us?" inquired Carson, now worried he had revealed the goal of his group too early and needing assurance that his secret society would not be exposed.

"Affirmative," replied the cadet. "It sounds too much like the Klan that I know you are a member of. I am a fan of Dr King. His teaching reflects my thinking."

"You are a nigger lover," said Carson, realising that Graham had not been among those students disciplined by the staff officer for raising their hands in agreement to his earlier racist statements.

"I love all people of this nation. I believe they all deserve a fair chance. Given the opportunity, they will succeed. I see you failed to understand the lesson our outcome officer attempted to teach by having you read about the Tuskegee Air Men?"

"In the south I once knew a man," he replied sternly, "who knew too much. He was a nigger lover too. Like you he expostulated niggers' rights. One day he disappeared. He was not part of the group and he was not a nigger."

"Are you threatening me, Cadet Carson?" inquired a calm and unnerved Cadet Graham, but Carson got up and left with a smile on his face.

"As a man of honor," continued Cadet Graham, "I have already made the decision to give my life in service for my country. I do not fear you or your kind. Eventually, you will be exposed for who and what you are. The success you attain will be the evidence to your defeat and your demise. You are truly not a man of honor. Your decision to undo what many men of honor have laboured to do will lead to your downfall. I have vowed to protect my nation and its entire population without discrimination. That is why I am here."

"They are not people. They are niggers."

"They are people and the sooner you realize and accept that, the better it will be. They are Americans like you and I. They have been laying down their lives to protect this nation and its interests for centuries. They have been men of honor long before you and I existed and will continue to be long after we are gone. They are Americans who have fought and died with distinction for this nation. They have served in honor and all they ask is to be treated and respected with honor. They are Americans like you and I and we must respect that," said a strong-willed Cadet Graham.

By the end of his sophomore year Carson and his secret organisation sought to find bolder means of discrediting the black cadets at the Academy. One of his members came up with the idea of catching them in the act of cheating, which was among the Academy's most repugnant unethical act, resulting in dismissal from the academy.

"We will all be taking major exams at the end of the semester. I want each of you to memorise a group of the questions in each exam. We will reformulate the exams, make a few copies and place them among the property of the niggers. We will alert the staff to the nigger who is in possession of the exams. When this becomes public knowledge, we will demand an investigation, which will lead to the expulsion of all of the niggers on campus."

"It's devious," said one cadet in glee.

"It's brilliant," chimed in another. "We will finally get rid of all of the niggers."

"Today the academy, tomorrow the Americas and finally the world," said one of the cadets.

"All niggers must go," said another as they hailed in agreement.

About a week later a well-known black cadet of the senior class was found to have copies of past and present exams among his belongings. He was dishonorably dismissed from the Academy without being granted a chance to explain. It was said he could not prove his case in front of a committee. Not being able to explain why or how these exams were among his possessions he was treated as a liar. With that one incident, all black students now came under the scrutiny of the Academy because it was a known fact they assisted each other to the point of graduation.

Carson had struck his first blow and he made sure the leaders of the black group would meet the same fate. Within days, other members were found to have exam papers hidden among their properties and they too were dismissed. The witch-hunt continued as many of the young black students were dismissed from the academy and their futures were severely damaged. The media got hold of the story and blew it up without further investigation.

As the Academy continued to reel from the increasing numbers of black students involved in this scandal, it looked for solace. How could so many have perpetuated this crime of dishonor in an institution of honor? It was contrary to its teaching and its standard. The administration and faculty wondered where they went wrong, without realising that their response was part of Carson's secret plans. Many of the black cadets were the children of affluent black families, were referred from well-known churches and had excellent academic backgrounds. It was from these groups the Academy sought their candidates. These young black men were among the bright shining stars of America's future.

The Dean was suspicious. He met with his faculty and said, "I think we need to do a deeper investigation into this problem. It seems too convenient that all these young black men were caught cheating and they have all denied this allegation. I have taught many of them and found them to be men of sound moral and ethical character. Not for a moment did they appear to be disingenuous in their denial of cheating. We are here not only to question their character but also the Academy's inability to see what is front of us, as well as these young men's vulnerability in participating in a world that may not be ready and willing to accept them."

"This is also a question of respect," said the outcome officer, who represented respect for human dignity at the Academy. "Did these young men conduct themselves in a manner respectful of themselves, to others, to the institution and ultimately to their country? I would say yes to all of those. I do not in my wildest dream believe they were cheating. They faced each obstacle we presented with courage, vigor and an intensity to defeat and be victorious; be it in athletics, academia, basic training, weaponry or the understanding and belief in humankind. Each of those young men demonstrated that they respected themselves and others. Our military is a microcosm of society, attracting diverse people who we must develop into cohesive units, who collectively must be able to carry out lethal missions. These men had moved beyond their personal biases and saw that everyone was deserving of respect."

"Those men adopted the major four aspects required for service to this nation without a question. Therefore, I find it difficult to see them as cheaters," said another officer.

"Gentlemen," said the Dean, "maybe it was not in your realm that these men found themselves weak and having a need to cheat but maybe in their academic pursuit they found themselves lacking and sought a remedy in cheating."

"There was no lack of confidence in these men, no second guessing to them. They were among our elites and you do not get there by cheating. To sit at that table, you must be considered a major authority by your peers. You must be knowledgeable and act on your knowledge. These men were considered as such," rebutted the outcome officer.

"What they are accused of is out of their character and deserves further investigation."

Another outcome staff officer stood to speak. "Gentlemen," he said, "I received a troubling letter today implying that we made a rush to judgment, but we will be the judge of that."

"We are waiting," said another impatiently.

"Do not rush to judgment, for not everything seems to be what it is. There are powerful influential forces that have roots outside of the academy who want to influence what takes place here. They are well organised, well financed and secretive. However, their goals are quite different from those of the Academy. They wanted to go back to a time when everything was white. The presence of black cadets in this academy is an intolerable affront to them and they will use any means to remove these young black men from this institution. A southern son of the Klan exists in your midst. He recruits likeminded brothers and he preaches white power. He has formed a secret society whose mission is to see an all-white student body and staff at the Academy."

"Is this something to believe?"

"From the result of our discussion, I say yes and I call for an investigation into this matter. I think we owe it to the integrity of this institution to get the truth so we can either vindicate or discredit these men based on a qualitative investigation."

"How do we do that?" inquired one of the outcome officers.

"We could hire a non-biassed outside source to do the investigation."

The Academy decided this was the best course of action. The investigating group consisted of three white males and one black. Two were assigned to be white cadets, one to infiltrate the secret society and the other to investigate the rest of the white student body for their contribution to the scandal. The third was assigned to be an outcome officer and the black investigator was assigned to penetrate the inner core of the black group and find out anything he could on their preparations for exams.

It took a semester for the investigators to find the truth about the cheating scandal. The investigator's documented report spelled out each step of the secret society plan to have the black cadets dismissed. It detailed how they planted the exams among the black student body and alerted the staff. The Academy sent out letters of apology to the black students who were dismissed for cheating and made overtures for them to return. Some of them returned but most went onto other universities after their names had been cleared. However, the Academy was not ready to severely punish its white male students for attempting to destroy the integrity of its black student body. None of the white students who were involved in the act were dismissed. All were reprimanded, except for Carson. The Academy was wary of Carson because his father was a senator. From that day on Carson realized the changes that were occurring outside of the south and he knew he had to put an end to it. Things had to return to the way they were. As he struggled with the reality of the social changes and the opportunities now being granted to blacks, it gave him ammunition to cement his beliefs in racial segregation. He soared up the ranks to pilot of the United States Air Force but in contrast plunged deeper into the abyss of hate as a human. Separation from his southern roots did not reprieve his mind of his southern thinking. At nights in the dark and quiet of his dorm, he lay awake longing for the days of nigger hunting. He longed to see a black man hanging from a tree, twitching, kicking, as the last remnants of life were squeezed out of his body while his broken neck awkwardly supported his head. That was his calling, his true destiny. "Long live the Klan," he prayed to himself each night as he fell to sleep.

His four years at the Academy come to an end and they threw their caps in the air as they were declared graduates. They went in as boys and were leaving as men of honor with a Bachelor of Science degree, as well as being a commissioned officer of the most glorious Air Force in the world. They stood together as one believing in maintaining the freedom of their great nation. This was their immediate goal no matter the colour of their skin. They would work as a unit to accomplish that feat.

All but one revelled in the joyous occasion. As Christopher Carson looked across the crowd of graduating cadets, he felt remorse for his white comrades who had fallen by the wayside on the journey. But there was no room anymore for remorse. He looked to his right and saw many of the black cadets who were once dismissed from the institution now graduating. Their bliss was evident by the smiles and laughter they shared among themselves and their families. They too would be making a journey to achieve the American dream while in service to their country. It was no longer an exclusive white man's journey and this tormented Carson.

# CHAPTER 7: Arrival to Battle

"The day came when we left for Vietnam and we were transported by C130 transport planes. We stayed in Japan for a few days and continued onto Khe-San, a hilly province in Vietnam not easily traversed. From our base there, we could monitor the Ho Chi Minh trail, the major artery used by the North Vietnamese to transport supplies and men to the enemy garrisons in South Vietnam. As an infantry man, I always kept my weapon with me. My chosen weapon was an Enfield rifle. While in transit from Japan I sat beside another soldier who was a young white boy from Kentucky. I noticed that he was eyeing my weapon.

'What type of rifle is that?' He eventually asked.

'It's an Enfield rifle, a British military weapon.'

'Why that?' he questioned, implying that 'made-in-America' is the world standard.

'It's a great weapon. The British used it to rule their empire for decades.' I felt a comfort with the rifle more than I had with any other weapon. It was like an extension of me.

'What cartridges does it use?' He persisted.

'The same as ours,' I replied, holding up the weapon so he could get a better look at it. 'This was one of the best infantry and sniper rifles of the 20th century. It served the British soldiers with distinction and without failure in many wars,' I explained. Our conversation continued until the pilot's voice was heard above the noise ordering us to buckle up.

'Where is your weapon?' I asked him.

'It's in the cargo bay with the rest of my gear, 'he candidly replied.

'I hope you have no immediate need for it.'

'Then my life will be in your hands,' he said. I smiled.

"We touched down as a hot battle was in progress on the edges of the camp.

The pilot reassured us that it was more than five miles away from the landing strip and wouldn't prevent us from landing safely. He explained that Viet Cong forces were attacking the other end of the base. The base camp was over ten square miles with over a quarter million fighting men dwelling there. On landing, we got a true grasp of what was happening. The North Vietnamese and Viet Cong forces had breached our defensive perimeters where the transport planes had landed. The plane I was in was the second of three. It was filled with men, supplies, munitions and other equipment. They opened fire at us and we realized we were sitting ducks on the tarmac. The Viet Cong attacked the planes with small firearms and the North Vietnamese with mortars. Hundreds of them were swarming to the interior of the base far from the previous battle scene. The plane came to a halt and the doors opened. Those who attempted to alight met a quick demise as they were unarmed.

I threw my backpack off and took up position by the open door, opening fire. I couldn't miss as there were so many of them. I kept reloading my weapon and firing. Each bullet counted. I heard a tremendous explosion followed by another, which seemed like it started a chain reaction. I looked in the direction  of the sound to see a tremendous fireball. It was the first plane and had still been occupied by troops and cargo on explosion. I instantly felt no one could survive that incident. The tremendous explosion of the plane made me more determined to make every bullet count. I knew the same fate awaited us if I did not prevent it. I could hear the screams of the men who had survived the explosion as the plane was now engulfed in flames. I saw burning, screaming men jumping from the blazing fuselage of the plane only to meet their demise at the hands of a Viet Cong bullet. I saw a group of the Viet Cong huddled together at the far end of the field with a shoulder held missile launcher. They were now focusing their attention on the plane I was in. I took aim and fired, killing the one holding the missile launcher with one shot. I watched the loaded weapon fall to the ground. Others were scrambling to get hold of it and complete the task; I picked them off one by one knowing that if they retrieved it and had the opportunity to aim, we would meet the same fate as the previous plane. I continued as they made attempts to retrieve the weapon, until they finally gave up. I couldn't disembark from the plane as the other soldiers were unarmed and trying to retrieve their weapons from the cargo bay. I was the only one who had an available weapon and ammunition. But I made them pay dearly. Each shot I fired was a kill shot."

"You did not miss a single shot?" I inquired.

"No, every shot found its mark. I made every shot a kill shot," he repeated.

"Soon their dead bodies were scattered all over the airfield. They began retreating and continued firing from the cover of the jungle. I waited and looked for the flash from the muzzle of their gun and as soon as I saw that I returned fire to that exact spot. I noticed I never got return fire from those areas."

"Why was that?" I asked. "Do you think they moved?"

"No," he replied, "I killed them. It did not take them long to melt back deeper into the jungle for safety, leaving behind their dead and wounded, fearing the lethalness of my weapon. Finally, we could disembark. That was when we really saw the carnage they had done. The first plane that they blew up was still burning. There were no survivors. The plane that landed after us was badly damaged and many of its passengers were killed while trying to disembark."

"Who won the battle?" I asked.

"They did," he replied, "although we killed many more of them than they killed of us. They had made a statement. They were not afraid to bring the battle to us. After the battle, the general was informed of my feat. He came to my barracks to meet me and asked me several questions about who taught me to shoot. I told him I was a hunter from when I was ten years old; I knew the area of the body where I had to hit. He informed me that I had killed 221 men in this battle. I knew that I had fired 250 shots and I knew each shot was a kill shot. I asked him if he had counted those who were killed while shooting from the cover of the jungle foliage. He hadn't, but was not going to risk lives to find out how many of those hiding in the bushes I had killed."

"How did he know that you had killed all these men?"

"First because the weapon was different from all others there. It had a unique signature. Secondly, they were predominantly head shots which became my customary way of killing, and thirdly I was the only one with a weapon," was his reply. "I was decorated with the Congressional Medal of Honor, the first of many medals I would receive while killing in Vietnam."

"Who were the Viet Cong?"

"The Viet Cong was a communist guerrilla conscript army from South Vietnam who were allies of the Communist North Vietnamese. They were among the forces we were battling alongside the South Vietnamese for a democratic Vietnam. During the first week, soldiers who heard of my feat came to see who I was. Many were informative, instructing me to always be alert and aware of my surroundings. That was the key to survive the war. They told me there were several hidden traps and mines that the Viet Cong used to inflict heavy casualties on our forces.

"I was assigned to a squad and instantly disliked by my commanding officer. I didn't know why but I had bad vibes about him. I survived the first week, without killing any more Viet Cong. Still, the buzz continued. Anywhere I went on the base; I was known as the man who used a Viet Cong platoon for target practice. For weeks, everyone talked about it. They said I had singlehandedly saved the lives of the men on my plane and the battalion on the base that day. I continued to build my reputation as a cold-blooded killer and a heartless sniper. I had become a celebrity," he said with pride.

"How is that?" I asked.

"My squadron was ordered to overtake an enemy base. Our own base was highly strategic as we used it to stop the flow of enemy supplies into South Vietnam. But the enemy had countered this by building a base atop the hill overlooking ours. We were at their mercy as they launched waves of artillery at us. We were flown in by helicopter and once there I saw the strategic importance of the hill. From there, the enemy had a bird's eye view of us. From there, they launched their attacks. They had not cleared their base of the trees and thick jungle foliage so it was difficult for our recon planes to see what was happening on the hill. It took several days and hundreds of lives before we captured that hill from the enemy. But it was not long after that they counter-attacked. From the dense jungle in the valley below, close to the base of the mountain, they opened on us with heavy artillery, attempting to bombard us into submission. Our commanding officer called in for air strikes against their artillery positions. Soon thereafter three F4 Phantoms came streaking across the sky dropping incendiary bombs and firing missiles at the enemies' positions. We watched as the explosions mushroomed into huge orange and black fireballs. But that was dwarfed by the horrendous screams of the enemies who were caught in this catastrophic attack. We could now see them because many were on fire, running around screaming as they attempted to put out the flames that were consuming their bodies. But it was almost impossible because it was Napalm fire."

"What is Napalm fire?"

"It's a fire that was a product of the incendiary bombs we were dropping. Unlike regular fire it sticks to you like an adhesive and burns at temperatures close to 3,000 degrees Fahrenheit," he explained. I was aghast at this horrifying information. "Usually there are no survivors. Many people were vaporized by the intense heat of the incendiary bombs, which turned the area into an inferno. We were miles away yet the intense heat was affecting many of our troops. It was a horrendous way to die and I felt pity for them. Their piercing screams were heard above the deafening explosions of the bombs. We watched transfixed by the horror that was playing out in the valley in front of us.

I felt then that I knew the hell and inhumanity of war. A group of F4 Phantoms came flying across the sky dropping more incendiary bombs. Suddenly from out of the jungle, streaking toward the group of F4 Phantoms came a surface-to-air missile. It quickly closed the distance across the sky coming up from behind the jet. The pilots who were flying a close formation did not see it. The missile blasted the middle jet out of the sky, blowing it up into a huge fireball. The explosion must have done something to the wing man's plane. He ejected as he lost control of his jet fighter and his plane plummeted out of the sky and crashed through the jungle, hitting the ground with a huge explosion. The other plane came down with its dead pilot in flaming fragments."

Interrupting him, I asked, "Aren't those planes equipped with radar, to prevent such happenings?"

"Yes," he responded, "bur radar is a double edged sword. It tells you where the enemies are and it also reveals your location to the enemy. In so doing, the enemy can lock onto your radar signals and shoot you down. To avoid that, sometimes the pilots flew with their radar off, especially after they had a lock onto the enemies' position and dropped their load of bombs or fired their missiles."

"You still have not told me how your reputation as a shooter was enhanced during this battle?" I probed.

"Allow me to tell my story in the order it took place," he replied. "Many of us were green recruits and not thinking. We stood atop of the hill, transfixed by what was playing out in the skies above and the valley below. The hill had not been cleared of its vegetation or been flattened by the enemy as we had done on our base, which made it difficult for them to pinpoint us or advance up to attack us. The hill descended at a steep angle of 70 degrees for approximately 2,000 feet before meeting the valley. The country was covered with lush jungle vegetation. We hadn't realized that the enemy, hiding in the lush vegetation, had started to surround us at the base of the hill.

After the F4s had gone back to base, they continued their merciless bombardment on our position using grenades launchers and mortars, unaffected by the aerial assault on them. All around us were constant explosions from their mortar attack and our men were now at the receiving end of the bombardment. We returned fire with all we had. Not more than five feet to my right, I heard a thud and a grunt. I looked over to see a young man on his back, with lifeless eyes open, aimlessly staring toward the heavens. He was still clutching his weapon, a Thompson submachine gun. I reached over and closed his eyes, took the weapon from his lifeless grip, loaded it and placed it over my back. It became a major part of my arsenal, like my Enfield rifle. I never went into battle without it.

"I heard firing behind us and suddenly shouting and screaming. I turned to see what was happening and to my surprise there were Viet Cong guerrillas among us with their AK47s blasting away at our troops."

"How did they get there?"

"We discovered that the enemy had well-concealed egress leading to underground passages, bunkers and camps there in that hill. While we were above, they were massing in tunnels and bunkers below our feet. Almost 100 of them came pouring out of these underground bunkers to engage us in battle. They were coming at us with guns blazing. I grabbed the Tommy gun and responded with short bursts. Preoccupied with the fight for our lives in close hand-to-hand combat, we were not aware that those who had amassed at the base of the mountain began a fast advance up the incline. They were on the verge of overrunning our position. I heard the commanding officer calling for reinforcements before he was shot dead by the enemy. We had no place to retreat to, nor could we surrender. This was a fight to the death. Out of the corner of my eye, I saw a Viet Cong decapitate one of our soldiers with a Samurai sword. The soldier's body was still moving when his head hit the ground and he was still trying to talk. We were caught up in that moment before I opened fire on him. He was dead before he hit the ground. I tore the sword from his grasp.

"For hours, we fought at close quarters, killing, maiming, and trying to annihilate each other. The ground was soaked with blood from the dead and the dying. I became a savage that day, something clicked in me and I began to enjoy every thrilling moment of this deadly contest for life. I no longer wanted to kill with just a gun. I wanted my killings to be up close and personal. I had the perfect weapon for that, the Samurai sword. That sword became my weapon of choice. Moving quickly to avoid being a target, I hacked my way through the ranks of the enemies, decapitating them. In my frenzy I savoured each scream I heard from them, relishing their last gasp of air before I presented them with their inevitable demise. I became fearless, and in the heat of battle I became a killing machine. I was spurred on by every kill I made, energised by the battle. I loved the gore of it as I separated so many of my enemies' heads from their bodies with a savage swing of that sword.

"With one powerful club-like swing. I split the head of a Viet Cong soldier down the middle through his skull and neck down to his chest. I watched as he looked at me in death, before his split brain gave way and I became awash in his blood. I finally experienced the intimate gore of battle before the invention of the gun, when men fought with sword, axes and spears. I found myself enjoying every moment of it. After we beat the enemy into a bloody merciless submission, it was noted that several of their bodies were without heads. When reinforcements arrived, they could not believe this eerie, gruesome battlefield. I was called in and questioned by the officer in charge. I explained to him what had happened. He looked at me, still washed in blood, and accompanied me out to the battlefield. 500 of us against an overwhelming enemy force, at the end of the battle 49 of us had survived. We had killed 1,620 of the enemy. Those of our men who had survived came together to comfort each other. We milled together briefly for a prayer then went out among the bodies, separating our fallen comrades from the enemies. We talked briefly that night and I overheard one of my brothers in arms saying that I was a beast, a merciless warrior, but he was happy to have me on his side than to have me against him.

"We destroyed the underground bunkers and passages and held the hill for another three weeks before the enemy reorganised and made another assault on the hill. That time I was not there. They massacred every one of our soldiers on the hill that day."

# CHAPTER 8: War Hero, American Warrior

In Vietnam, Major Carson and his squadron were greeted and briefed by their commanding officer, General Leech. He showed great interest in the planes flown by Carson's squadron, the F4 Phantoms.

"These are the new F4s," said General Leech as he walked around the plane, examining every inch. "Do you know anything about this supersonic jet you have been entrusted with, Major Carson?"

"I know it's one of the fastest military planes we have in our arsenal, and probably the most technologically advanced," he replied.

"For you and everyone else that is flying this bus, we hope so." General Leech stood in front of the huge jet fighter plane, with his contempt for it visible on his face.

"Why don't you like the plane, General?" inquired Carson.

"It has been the coffin for too many of my young pilots. This plane came with great expectations and many promises from its manufacturers. They said it would end the era of the dogfights. They forgot to tell that to the enemy. This plane came armed only with air-to-air missiles to destroy the enemy and to defend its pilot; great when you catch the enemy by surprise and he is not aware or your presence. But what the manufacturers failed to understand was the enemy would not be a cooperative partner. Many of our pilots went up there believing in their weapon system but when they ran out of missiles they were left defenceless. Like us, the enemy has no mercy. Our planes were falling from the skies like rain drops in a monsoon. Some of our boys took to attaching a pod with a machine gun to their planes so that they would stand a chance when they had fired their last missile. It worked, and the Pentagon finally ordered the manufacturer to build the plane with a gun. You are the first squadron to have the manufacturer's plane with the gun," said General Leech.

"That's quite a bit of history, General," said Carson.

"Yes, and I want you to make the rest a successful one for those who sacrificed their lives to make the Pentagon aware of the deficiencies of this iron maiden. I want you and the rest of your men to fly this bucket of bolts up there and blast those commie bastards out of the sky – send them to their graves in great numbers. I want you to put fear in their hearts so whenever they see these planes coming they will run and hide instead of engaging us in battle. I want your boys to rule the sky over Vietnam to give us air supremacy." He said this with an intense scowl, beating his fist in the palm of his hand to emphasize the seriousness of his demand.

"Yes sir, General. I will make them pay. This plane is a great plane and I believe in it. I have no doubt of its abilities or of mine. I have trained with this plane and I feel one with it. I intend to wipe out the North Vietnamese and their MIGs from the skies so that we will reign supreme over Vietnam."

"That is what I want to hear, Major Carson – a commitment to the strategy of winning this war."

"That is the reason I am here, General, to win this war by any means necessary."

"Don't you get cocky and underestimate the enemy now Major Carson. Those North Vietnamese pilots are as good as any of you boys coming from the Air Force Academy. That is why we have not been able to wrestle the skies from them."

"We will wrestle the skies from them and we will reign supreme over Vietnam, General. That I promise you," he retorted.

The General looked in the Major's eyes, impressed by what he heard. Those words comforted him and he sensed they were prophetic. He had finally found the pilot whom he believed would change the course of the war.

"I want you to walk the walk that will back that talk. You hear me, Major?"

"Yes sir, General, yes sir."

In the following days, Carson and his squadron flew several escort missions over North Vietnam. They were assigned to be protective cover for the giant B52 bombers. It was on the fifth day of this assignment he encountered his first major incident. One of the huge B52 bombers was hit by a surface to air missile, which caused a great explosion in the sky. The shock waves from its blast knocked one of the planes out of control. As it spiralled through the air at over 40,000 feet, Carson radioed the pilot, Captain Willis. But he had lost consciousness and did not hear his radio, disoriented by the unexpected shock waves from the explosion. The tremendous force that gravity exacted on him rendered him comatose as his plane continued to spiral down to the earth.

"Come in Captain Willis, come in Captain Willis, are you with me?" Carson was frantic, knowing what awaited Captain Willis if he did not regain control of his plane. As the Squadron Leader, Carson repeated on his radio "Captain Willis, Captain Willis, eject from your plane," he followed the plane closely. He could see the unconscious captain in the cockpit, slumped over the controls of his inoperable jet fighter. The plane engines were off and it was less than 10,000 feet to the ground. If Captain Willis were to survive he had to regain consciousness quickly. Suddenly Carson saw another surface to air missile clearing the canopy of the jungle. It gathered speed and was streaking up the sky towards the bomber fleet. His attention was now drawn to the missile as it streaked through the sky at five times the speed of sound. Through his radar, he locked onto the site but it was too late as he saw the missile gather speed, on its way to take down another B52 bomber. He looked up in the sky and saw the fireball from a B52 hit by the previous missile. Now locked onto the missile site, he flew his killing machine at tremendous speed with all the ferocity and hate he could muster. He let his missiles fly at targets on the ground as his machine gun blazed with the anger that possessed him. Soon everything in that camp was burning out of control and exploding with such tremendous force that the fleeing enemies became victims of their deadly weaponry. Caught in an explosive chain reaction you could hear their last piercing screams from miles away as they gave their lives for their cause. Satisfied with his handiwork, he headed back up the dangerous blue sky, instinctively alert and prepared to engage any enemy jet fighter hiding in the clouds. He hadn't had time to think of his fallen comrade. He hadn't seen when Captain Willis's jet smashed into the ground nor did he see the fireball that erupted from its blast. A stupefied Captain Willis had entered death's door and was instantly incinerated; his death was so quick he did not have the time to experience the pain. He truly gave his life, his soul and spirit in service for his country.

Days would go by before Major Carson would have another direct contact with the enemy. His squadron were patrolling the skies, this time as interceptors to maintain their sliver of air supremacy over the enemy. It had been a costly war to the US air force. They had underestimated the North Vietnamese's capabilities. Their jet fighters were not very manoeuvrable in comparison to the enemies' MIGs. The F4s, now armed with guns, evened up the playing field; in fact, the Air Force believed technologically they had jumped ahead of the enemy's ageing fighter fleets. They needed a chance to prove themselves right.

As Carson and his squadron of five F4 phantoms flew at 50,000 feet with the sun behind them, they saw a group of eight enemy planes about 5,000 feet below. Quickly they pounced from behind and, before the enemy knew what hit them, three of their planes were blown out of the skies without their pilots having a chance to eject from the planes. The remnants of their planes fell from the sky like meteors, leaving a flaming trail behind as they crashed to the ground. The sky was alive with men intermittently flying their planes well beyond the speed of sound with the intent of shooting down the opposition's aircraft.

Carson got behind another enemy jet plane. As the pilot started to take evasive manoeuvres by breaking to his left; Carson manoeuvred his jet at an angle and fired his gun. The fleeing enemy pilot flew his plane into the fusillade that Carson had fired. Carson and his squadron had vanquished the sky of the eight enemy planes without a loss and now had achieved air supremacy over Vietnam for the US Air Force. Carson himself was attributed three of those kills. That battle had decisively turned the war in the US's favour.

Time went on and the war continued with men from both sides killing and dying for their beliefs as they tried to subjugate each other to those beliefs. Carson was to obtain acehood three times for shooting down over 15 enemy jet fighters. He survived being shot down three times and each time he was plucked out of the Vietnam jungle and given a replacement jet fighter to continue his role in the war.

It was the second time he was shot down that reignited his dark side, which to that moment had been suppressed. It was another bright sunny day when he and his squadron flew at tree top level to avoid radar detection. They flew in a loose formation at subsonic speed to destroy a mobile surface to air missile site before it could relocate. This site had cost the air force ten B52 bombers in two days and the navy had also lost six jet fighters to the missile launching unit. There was a strong need to put this unit out of operation. The unit was located near the North Vietnamese and Cambodian borders. The US was restricted from using Cambodian air space but that didn't prevent them from doing so when they found it necessary. Carrying an assortment of bombs and missiles, they came in from the Cambodian side to attack the site, catching the enemy by surprise. An assortment of missiles, cluster and incendiary bombs quickly destroyed the mobile platforms of the missile site. The enemy did not have time to respond and it was a successful mission. Carson had been promoted to Colonel weeks before he led the mission. He was already a feared fighter pilot, but his ambition was directing him to find other ways to contribute to the war effort.

Still flying at low levels after they had accomplished their mission, they were spotted from above by a squadron of enemy fighters. The North Vietnamese pilots in their MIGs pounced. Instantly one of Carson's squad was blown from the sky. Soon Carson himself was in the crosshairs. He attempted a variety of evasive manoeuvres but his adversary was experienced, fearless and smart. He couldn't shake the enemy fighter who started riddling his plane with bullets before he blew it from the sky with an air-to-air missile. Carson's F4 Phantom was shot out from under him. As it began to burn, he fought to maintain its control but it was hopeless. He ejected before one of its engines exploded. The ejection seat blasted him clear of the explosion and he watched as the plane broke apart and exploded again with a tremendous boom. He felt the shock waves emitting from the final blast of what was left of his fighter plane as it headed to the ground in fragments. His parachute brought him safely down and he landed in the dense manmade forest called the Black Forest.

On landing, he quickly cut himself free of his parachute. He recognised the type of trees and the uniformity in which they grew, concluding that he had landed in a rubber plantation. He checked for signs of the enemy but only heard the sound of birds and other wildlife. He listened and waited for the quiet that would precede an ambush. There was none. Nature has its ways of alerting one to danger he thought – one just has to listen and be aware. He radioed his base with his location and was told where to go for pickup. They were about to dispatch a Huey gun ship to rescue him. He followed the directions and arriving at the site, saw many abandoned warehouses of an old factory complex. Before he proceeded, he took time to check there weren't any enemy fighters waiting for him. The buildings were in different stages of deterioration, some with signs on them in French. He had become familiar with the language at school and, as part of his academy's international cultural training studies, had gone to France for six months where he learnt to speak French fluently.

He continued searching the buildings for enemy activity. It appeared that the war had not touched this place, since it had been abandoned by the French. He wondered why, as he went about his search. The building's infrastructure had remained intact. Then he noticed the tarmac of an airfield that could support large cargo planes. Due to lack of maintenance, it was invaded by weeds in the cracks of its pavement. Its long, wide pavement dissected the plantation into east and west zones with neat rows of trees on either side stretching as far as the eye could see.

There were no indications of the making of tires or other products here from the sap of the rubber tree. It seemed the French were harvesting and purifying the sap here before they transported it to factories in Europe. Suddenly he heard the unmistakable sound of the Huey in the distance coming to rescue him. The warehouse would have to wait, as the Huey arrived in the courtyard to retrieve him.

When Carson's rescue mission was safely completed, he met with his commanding officer General Leech at the barracks outside of Saigon and gave a debriefing report. His report included what he had stumbled on in the Black Forest. He was amazed that such a readymade military site existed and was not being used. "General, I landed in what appeared to be a former French rubber plantation and I want to further explore it for possible military usage."

"Colonel," acknowledged General Leech, "although it appears that it can be converted to military usage, it's not recommended. The buildings are booby-trapped and the periphery of the plantation was mined by the French before they were forced out. When we win this war, they plan to return and continue their rubber plantation. They never gave us permission to use their facility."

"Neither did they deny us the use, General, and we do not need their permission to use the facility as we see fit. I would like to explore the place," he retorted.

"It's a dangerous, isolated place Colonel. Why so much interest in some deserted old factory buildings?" inquired General Leech.

"I feel drawn to it, General. Right now, it could be considered a safe base for covert operations. I ventured into many of the buildings and there were no signs of enemy usage. They have stayed away from it just like the French had intended. Who knows – maybe we can find use for it in the future."

"If the enemy knows we are using it, they will make it one of their targets. They'll reach over the minefields surrounding that forest and blast you to smithereens, Colonel. The only reason they didn't do it already is because they didn't know you were there. But if you were to let your presence be known there, that untouched environment would soon be like the rest of 'Nam, under siege from Viet Cong guerrillas and North Vietnamese soldiers. They would find a way through that minefield in less than a day."

"It does not matter, General. I would like to take some men to accompany me as I explore this place," replied Carson determinedly.

"I have no men to spare for such a foolhardy mission," replied General Leech.

"The danger lies on foot but if we flew over and into the compound we can avert the danger of the minefields."

"Why do you want to explore this abandoned factory Colonel?" General Leech was unconvinced.

"I feel that it could be useful if we know more about it."

"Useful for what, Colonel?" General Leech was suspicious. He stood up and headed to a cabinet where he pulled out a folder and dropped it in front of Carson. "You have not answered my question, Colonel," he said.

"General, I don't know what need it would fulfil at this juncture. But it has potential to one day fulfil our needs."

"Read those documents," said General Leech as he pushed the thick folder across the desk. It contained the history of the rubber factory.

"Nothing here indicates that the plantation was mined and would be a danger. I was exploring before the helicopter came and covered lots of ground. There was no indication of the buildings being mined or booby trapped."

"Colonel, you are a great pilot – but are you able to identify a mine if you saw one? "

"General, you are forgetting that I was trained in identifying and disarming mines while I was at the Academy."

"Aaaaah," grunted General Leech, sensing his defeat. "Submit to the Joint Chiefs a requisition based on what you are planning to use the plantation for, Colonel, and if they are ok with it, they will grant you permission to use it."

Shortly after, Carson contacted a high-powered friend in the CIA who was a member of his secret society. They shared an interest in empowering the group and advancing their ideology in South East Asia. Between them, they planned on using the Black Forest plantation as the base of their operations. Days later, they arrived in a Huey on the grassy overgrown courtyard of the plantation compound and set out to claim the abandoned factory for their own.

# CHAPTER 9: Red Dong

"Tell me about your perception of the Viet Cong," I asked Mr Stuart.

"Why?"

"From television reports of the war, we kicked their diminutive asses all over Vietnam, yet still we lost. How is that? I am perplexed."

"Total misconception. Television only brings to you, the viewers, the battles we won, not the ones we lost. And we lost some very badly."

"Did the enemy put fear in your heart?"

"Fear in itself is a good mental edge to have. It guides and keeps you aware of your surroundings, it makes you cautious in the things you do, but you should never allow it to gain possession of you. Once the battle starts, you have no time to focus on fear; your death will be the result of that. You must focus on fighting and killing the enemy before he kills you. That was our objective."

"How come you survived?" I asked. "The description of how you fought made you a prime target. From your description, you threw caution to the wind."

"I was a warrior and part of being a warrior is to accept death in battle. A glorious violent end was quite acceptable to me; it would have been valiant to meet my death that way. It's the way I sent many men to their graves. The Viet Cong and the North Vietnamese soldiers," he continued, "were resourceful, well-organised and unintimidated enemies. They were clever people who were underestimated, a major mistake on our part. Their resolve was strong and although they were an ambush force, their fight was far greater than their size. Our size proved to be greater than our fight."

"I have never heard of any outstanding military officers from the North Vietnamese regiments or The Viet Cong guerrilla forces. Were there any?"

"The Viet Cong forces were made up of mostly South Vietnamese who were fighting for independence from the colonial powers and for unification of their country. North Vietnam was an independent communist nation who didn't want to be governed by an outside force. They wanted their destiny to be in their hands. But as far as military officers are concerned, there were many great ones on both sides. Among them was one who put much fear in our fighting men. His name was Red Dong. He was a skilful infantry commander and an expert in ambush tactics. He knew how to use the terrain to his advantage. Commander Red Dong fought in two crucial battles, which gave him insight into fighting us. The first battle was at Death Valley. At the time, he was like a first lieutenant, young and inexperienced but a smart officer. We had shuttled troops by helicopter into Pleiku in the Central Highland of Vietnam. There the Special Forces were under constant attack by the NVA/VC forces. We deployed our seventh cavalry there to Landing Zone X. Inadvertently, we landed in the middle of the NVA 66th regiment base camp.

"The war raged on. We called in support from artillery fire and close air support. The battle should have ended when the enemy fled deep into the jungle. But wanting total annihilation, we pursued them; this was a mistake by our military and the beginning of Red Dong's reputation as a warrior and commander. He and his men were waiting for us within the cover of the dense vegetation of the hot and steamy jungle. They were patient – they waited for the moment they could inflict the greatest casualties on us, when they could actually read our dog tags, to open fire on us. We didn't have a chance to recover. They hit us from all sides with everything they had. As we retreated, they cut off our escape route. We were trapped, surrounded and forced into hand-to-hand combat, in which we prevailed after we were reinforced. We suffered great losses in men and equipment. It was one of our worst defeats.

"We weren't able to have artillery or close air support to aid us in that battle. There was no differentiating between our lines and theirs. I remember that battle clearly," he said. "I fought with my sword in one hand and my Colt 45 automatic in the other. If it were not for reinforcements, we would have been wiped out.

"That type of warfare became his signature type of battle. He found means of neutralising our artillery and air support. When we fought him, the battles were up close and personal. His next big battle was during the Tet Uprising. He had taken control of the city of Hue and kept our troops at bay for almost a month. We suffered heavy losses and weren't able to fully take control of the city until we were granted the okay to bomb it, which was first denied us to preserve the historic site. When the battle was over, the city was wasted. Most of it had been burned to the ground during the early stages of the battle and the rest was bombed to smithereens during the latter stages. It was a ghost town with only parts of the old fortified city walls still standing. That battle we won decisively. We inflicted such heavy losses on the Viet Cong forces that we could not envision them recovering from that defeat. Nevertheless, they did. Retreating like ghosts, their survivors vanished from the city. Commander Dong regrouped his forces, gathered new recruits and prepared to battle us again. We could not deliver that knockout punch to him and his forces. They had survived many battles against us, while taking heavy losses but always inflicting heavy damages to our forces. We expected him to battle us again at a place of his choosing. His battle plan was a well-executed ambush of our forces, cutting off our ability to retreat. Nevertheless, our troops were better trained and could usually repel these attacks. But still they took their toll. It was around this time we discovered that Red Dong was from South Vietnam. Our agents found the village he was from and soon we got our search and destroy orders for it. Troop carriers armed with at least three M60 machine guns lead the way. This battle had an ominous feeling, I knew it was wrong but the sentiment of vengeance prevailed.

"We prepared as if we intended for none of the enemy to survive. It was deliberate. When I arrived, the village was already burning. The old men, hysterical women and children were being rounded up. I went into a hut and found a group of our men holding down three young girls, raping them. I watched in disgust as they beckoned me to join them. We questioned the old men but they wouldn't give up any information so the captain ordered them to be killed one by one. I watched as our men opened fire on them. A sickening feeling consumed me as I observed the mayhem that day. Our commanding officers did nothing to stop it. Innocent women and children were slaughtered. I watched the carnage. I remember my commanding officer shouting orders at me but I couldn't focus on what he was saying. All I could hear were the screams of the panic-stricken villagers. What were we doing? I asked myself. I was a soldier – it was not my duty to question why, but to do as ordered. I discovered I still had some remnants of humanity in me, the army did not take it all. I found it difficult shooting down unarmed civilians. I remember telling myself there was no glory in committing atrocities; it was the handy-work of cowards. The bodies of women and children were strewn all over the burning village. There were so many dead that I could not avoid walking on them. I tried to rationalise this as an act of war. Still, this really traumatized me. I was not faint hearted as I had done some horrifying deeds myself, but this was beyond abomination.

"Many died at my hands, but I never conceived of such horror on innocent civilians. I observed a group of men keeping the corpse of an old man from hitting the ground by intermittently opening fire on him. Before he hit the ground one soldier opened fire again, which straightened up his limp corpse as it ripped the remnants of it apart. These sadistic men tried to see how long they could keep the corpse from hitting the ground. I felt then that I hated every moment of this sickening war. It brought out the ugliness in man. Why were we doing these vile deeds to these people? We were killing them by the thousands but they would not surrender.

"I knew as long as I was there it was my duty to kill or be killed. That night as I lay in my bunk trying to forget what had happened, I knew that the next day I would do it again. I cried as a new perspective began to take hold of me. It was bad enough that I was tormented by it in my nightmares, but to concede that there was no escaping the carnage for 365 days was mentally devastating. I tried not to wonder what hell would be heaped on us by the enemy come daybreak. We had levelled Red Dong's village and killed everyone. We burnt their huts and food supplies. We made it personal. We sent a loud message to him. We knew the enemy would try to respond in kind. It was a matter of time.

"They did respond, but not possessing our penchant for unnecessary brutality they did what they knew best. They waited in the jungle for our patrols, search and destroy units and attacked relentlessly. In the span of a week they wiped out five of our units. We sprayed the jungle with Agent Orange, a defoliating chemical, which rendered the trees leafless. It was an eerie sight but it did not stop the Viet Cong from ambushing our patrols. They were so good at camouflaging themselves. It became their main tactic.

"Red Dong's next major battle was at Kham Duc. This time, with a huge force, he managed to surround a US military base. He cut off any reinforcement to the base by any means except by air and portions of the base were overrun by Viet Cong and North Vietnamese soldiers. As the cargo planes began bringing in reinforcements, they became targets for the enemy's surface -to-air missiles. The helicopter gunships did not fare much better. We decided to evacuate the base at night so as to confuse the enemy. Thousands of mines were set up at the outer edges of the perimeter of the base, preventing them from storming it. They began bombarding our base with artillery and mortar fire until the evacuation was complete. As our Huey lifted us temporarily out of harm's way, we conceded the mined base to the enemy. It took about a week, with heavy losses on both sides, for them to accomplish this.

"The reputation of Red Dong grew and the military placed a bounty on his head. They distributed posters with his picture all over North and South Vietnam, which read "Wanted: dead or alive, 50,000 US dollars leading to the capture or killing of Commander Red Dong of the NVA, for the killing of US soldiers." When I first saw the poster, I became fascinated by it. My tour of duty in Vietnam was coming to an end in only a matter of days.  But I could not get the wanted poster of Commander Dong out of my mind. Going back home was becoming less important to me. Motivated by the 50,000-dollar bounty, I decided to hunt for Red Dong after my tour was up. When I was issued my walking papers, I set out on my mission to assassinate him or bring him back alive. I knew I would receive more if he was alive because they could question him. I had become accustomed to the jungles of Vietnam. Without fear, and accepting that my death could occur at any time, I focused on my objective".

# CHAPTER 10: American Warrior, War Criminal

The cries of pain from torture pierced through the darkness of the jungle night. It was an unsettling, eerie sound that captivated the minds of those who heard it. The helpless wail travelled for miles through the canopy of the Vietnamese jungle to the ears of its North Vietnamese and Viet Cong warriors. Like an alarm, it awoke them and brought them to their feet to listen to the blood curdling screams. It made the hair on their backs stand up. They knew they were the cries of their captive brothers. It became a motivational factor, another reason to win the war, to defeat the occupying Americans and get them out of their country. Nothing less would be satisfying to them.

The Americans who listened knew those screams were not emitting from their comrades and accepted it as a fact on their path to victory. The North Vietnamese knew the cry was emitted from a son of their own who by daybreak would no longer be alive. Soon a new screamer would be heard, their agony again carrying through the jungle to the ears of their comrades like a message saying, 'Do not surrender, fight until death, the enemy is merciless and will use any means to get you to talk'. The North Vietnamese listened to the sound and like a radar, they followed it to its source, the Black Forest. The word spread and they planned to rescue their captured comrades. Whenever they heard the nightly screams, it spurred them deeper into vengeance.

In times of war, men are their worst and their best. It is a time when courage and bravery are defined by how many enemies you kill. It is a time of taking sides against each other, dehumanizing each other, branding each other and in so doing, making it easier to kill each other. In times of war, diplomacy has failed and men refuse to communicate and use good judgment. Instead they accept, embrace, and become one with the darkness within their hearts.

When night fell on the land and the sound of battle ceased, a caravan of helicopters could be heard as they flew to the Black Forest. The sole regularity of their appearance was that they flew only at night. Sometimes months would go by without them visiting the Black Forest. Then sometimes they appeared every night of the week. The North Vietnamese and the Viet Cong waited with rockets and other arms hoping to bring down some of these helicopters but they never succeeded. Their irregularity made it impossible. It was said that the Americans never took the same flight path twice to the Black Forest.

After Carson's thorough examination of the French rubber factory, a two star CIA General known as Amadeus Walker got hold of the report and concluded that this was the ideal place to conduct his CIA activities.

General Walker oversaw the prisoners of war and saw the Black Forest as an ideal place to keep his prisoners and make it a high security penitentiary. General Walker never for a moment thought the US would be defeated. As a CIA man, he and his team practiced the dark side of war. It was their duty to do the unmentionable to the enemy and the French rubber factory gave them a place where they could practice these unmentionable things. Torture was the centrepiece. The more ruthless the method, the better it made him feel. He was a cold hearted, bloodthirsty, hateful tyrant. His prejudice became his guide, as his intelligence took a back seat during the war. He wanted as many captives as he could get his hands on, to torture them for information to defeat them. Many times, through torture, the enemy revealed vital information to him, especially about their underground tunnels. But because of the way the tunnels were constructed, the US military could not make an assault on them. Unknown to the US, the enemy was digging a tunnel under the minefields that took them to a remote part of the Black Forest. It was about this time Carson was released from the Air Force and became a member of the CIA.

"General Walker, Colonel Carson is here to see you," said an aide to the general.

"It was a great job you did, Colonel, and I commend you for your brilliant work. You have given us a place to conduct our operations in secrecy. The CIA will always be appreciative of your foresight. Why are you here, Colonel?"

"General, I heard you oversee the prisoners of war," said Carson.

"Yes, Colonel, the POWs are my concern."

"General, I have documents here for you to release several of your most dangerous prisoners so that my men and I can fight them in a controlled environment."

"I do not understand, Colonel."

"You know that the Black Forest is surrounded by mine fields making it isolated and impenetrable. Under those circumstances, we have been granted permission by the Pentagon to use the place as a laboratory for our research."

"What are you studying, Colonel?"

"We are studying the enemy's fighting tactics so we can teach our troops in training what to expect when they arrive here in the jungles of Vietnam. In our studies, we have found that the majority of our fatalities are our new recruits. They are not prepared to fight this war. We must find ways to cut our losses. If we can teach our soldiers the Vietnamese style of fighting, they will know what to expect before they enter battle. We will document everything so that training can be developed at home to prepare our recruits for this type of warfare. As per the Pentagon, when needed, you will supply us with some of your toughest prisoners. We will allow them to escape out into the forest and me and my boys will hunt them down and kill them."

"Colonel, this sound like an error in judgment and it could lead to something that could consume us. How much thinking have you given to this project?"

"This is a Pentagon approved assignment and they have given me the green light to use the Black Forest to conduct my research. I will use it as a laboratory to study the enemy's fighting skills, tactics and strategy. I will be using your prisoners of war in these war games. General, here is the Pentagon's consent authorising my plan." General Walker studied it and saw its merits.

"Colonel, there exists the possibility that the prisoners will overpower you, wipe you out, take your weapons and return here to continue waging the war."

"General, I have some of the most disciplined, war hardened veterans you will ever meet. These men are killing machines. If I felt that any of them would compromise this assignment by losing his weapon to the enemy, I would not have chosen him to be among us."

"Colonel, you are asking me to turn over prisoners to you so you can murder them?"

"This is a war, General, and the idea of it is to kill and destroy your enemy before he does it to you. We must beat him into submission and that occurs by killing, maiming, mutilating as many of them as possible until they are physically and mentally broken, when they see surrender as their only option. We must beat the fight out of them before they beat it out of us. Right now those stubborn gremlin sons of bitches are beating the fight out of us."

"We are Americans, Colonel; no one beats the fight out of us. No one, do you hear me, Colonel?"

"I hear you loud and clear, General. However, look at what is occurring at home and you will see there is more than one way of beating the fight out of us. Our military men are ready to continue the fight, but is it the same with the American people? That's what a democracy is about General, the will of the people, not the will of the military. The fight is being beaten out of the people and they are telling the military to stop this war. Because we are a democracy, we will adhere to the will of the people."

"I am hearing you loud and clear, Colonel, you can have the prisoners and I have one order for you. Do not return until all the prisoners are dead. I do not want any stories circulating that these prisoners' 'Geneva rights' were denied. Dead men tell no tales, Colonel."

"You can rest assured, what goes on here stays here, General."

"Colonel, whatever you are doing was never sanctioned by me, but of course your documents will stand up in the international court of law."

"General, why the need for my documents to stand the test of international laws? There will be no revelation after this research has been completed. It is classified."

"I see, Colonel, that your inexperience in these matters has not taught you to cover your ass. This will come back to haunt you one day. Since you have the documents, I will turn over the prisoners to you, but you will regret this research you are about to conduct. I sense you will use the opportunity to do other deeds from the war games you say you will be conducting. I know you will face an inquest one day. Based on the nature of this assignment, an inquest is inevitable. Yes, the Pentagon did prepare me for your arrival and your plans."

"Will you report what took place here, General?"

"No, Colonel, but I have lived long enough to know when wrong is about to occur and I know that the spirit of those who are wronged will not rest until things are right. Arming POWs with guns carrying dummy bullets is deceitful and murderous. If you are going to kill them, just take them outside and kill them."

"You fail to understand the goal of my research, General."

"No I don't, Colonel. I have a sense you will never understand."

Carson ignored the General's warning, and soon he and 24 men arrived in three Huey gunships at the Black Forest facility. These men were heavily armed and ready to kill. A small force of Viet Cong prisoners were armed and released into the Black Forest. They were given time to establish their resistance and, as predicted, they devised an ingenious ambush before they discovered their weapons were loaded with dummy bullets.

Carson's men were all members of the Sons of the Klan, the secret fraternal society Carson had created during his early years at the Academy. Since then, the fraternal society had taken roots in all branches of the military.

Carson found a new function for the Black Forest rubber plantation. After capturing the Viet Cong prisoners of war, he and his men hanged each one of the prisoners on separate trees. For months, this practice continued under the guise of a sanctioned government study. Carson continued his study to expose Viet Cong war strategy and reported back to the Pentagon. But the hideous side of his work remained a secret.

When the rubber factory went under the CIA control, the screams of prisoners started at night, which was when General Walker's men did their torturing. Even during the cease fire agreements and the peace talks, this continued.

The North Vietnamese commanders planned to attack the Black Forest through the newly constructed tunnels, but because of their losses, such plans could not be implemented. One day a high-ranking North Vietnamese intelligence officer was captured. Getting information from him could decisively turn the war in the Americans' favour. He was instantly taken to the Black Forest for questioning. The North Vietnamese were determined to rescue him and for five days after his arrival, they bombarded the facility into the ground.

Carson and his men were away on a special assignment when the North Vietnamese bombardment occurred in the Black Forest. On their return, they were ordered to go in and search for survivors. General Walker and his staff were killed in the bombardment. More than 50 per cent of the prisoners of war were killed, including the high-ranking North Vietnamese intelligence officer. Others escaped, but many died trying to traverse the minefields. Carson and his men hunted down the remaining prisoners, close to 1,000 men. Most were severely injured or died fighting and those who surrendered were hanged by Carson.

Carson's study proved successful for the military – so successful that they adopted its policies as part of their training, creating simulated battlefields similar to where their troops would be fighting.

# CHAPTER 11: The Red River

A few days passed before I continued with Mr Stuart's interview. The Medical Centre had to prepare for a visit from the Department of Health. Although I had a reprieve from Mr Stuart, I began to find his story fascinating and found myself wanting to continue. As soon as the Department of Health had left the facility ,I went looking for him. When I found him, he greeted me with the familiar sneer but I also noted an inkling of a smile on his face. That was the closest I came to seeing some expression of warmth from him.

"Mr Stuart, good to see you. Are you ready to proceed with your story?"

"Ready like Freddy," he replied.

"Well, ready Freddy, let's go."

"Apparently, the Department of Health gave you a good rating," he said.

"What makes you think so?"

"You are happy and you are smiling," he replied.

"Quite observant of you, Mr Stuart, yes they did. We will remain in business treating patients with mental issues hopefully for a long time."

He smiled and began his story from where he left off.

"Weeks before I began to search for Red Dong, I was given a weapon by a ranger whose tour of duty had ended. The weapon rejuvenated my spirit for battle. It was a sniper's concept weapon, considered the best such military weapon available. The price tag was too high for the military to buy in great bulk but a few were given to the army who made them prizes in their sniper competitions. The ranger and I had competed against each other in target competitions while going through training at Fort Hood. He was the army's sniper champion until I defeated him. But because

I was shipped out to Vietnam, he replaced me in the competition and went on to regain his title. I remember the night he came to my barracks and presented me with his weapon, which he had won in the competition. The act surprised me; he was a white officer and a Special Forces ranger – they do not give away their prize weapons. We had barely spoken and were not buddies.

"Sergeant Stuart," he said, addressing me as I came to attention. "I am giving you this weapon," he continued, handing me his sniper rifle with a scope and sound suppressor.

"Why?" I asked.

"You saved my life twice, Sergeant, and I appreciate those heroic deeds. I would not be going home alive if it wasn't for you. This weapon is a token of my appreciation. It is a special weapon; you can pick off a man as far away as two miles with it. I have never had the opportunity to do that feat. What I am saying is that you are a special warrior. I will have no further need for this weapon but you – you will take lives and save lives with it".

"I accepted the gift and he showed me the weapon and explained all its features. I adored it, I knew this was a superior weapon. I had been using rifles since I was ten years old while hunting, competing in military marksmanship competitions and now killing North Vietnamese and Viet Cong men of war. This was the best weapon I had ever had. It felt as if it was an extension of me even more so than my trusted Enfield. I felt all I had to do was to point and shoot and the bullet would follow my mind to its intended target. I retired my old faithful that night – my Enfield became history."

"You did receive that first prize after all, what a coincidence," I said.

"It was no coincidence. It was meant to be; don't you understand?"

"I don't, but please proceed. Don't let me deter you – some things are best not explained," I said, sensing a miracle, and he continued.

"I remember feeling a tinge of invincibility with my new toy. The day after, one of the soldiers in my unit came busting in the barrack shouting "Incoming, incoming!" We hit the ground as mortars and shells began raining down on our base. A soldier burst through the door shouting, "Sergeant, Sergeant. We have spotted their caller!"

"Where and how far is he?" I asked.

"About a mile and a half.  He is in a tall palm tree on the opposing hill." I had never attempted a target that far before.

"What makes you so sure that it's their spotter?" I demanded.

"He is using binoculars to spy on the base and is using a radio to communicate his findings," he said with no uncertainty.

"The base was located atop of a hill. It was home to more than 20,000 troops. It was a huge compound. We overlooked miles of the surrounding jungle. Our camp was a naked, isolated town in the midst of the jungle. Beyond the base for about half a mile were mine fields. The mines were planted in several concentric circles around the base, interrupted only by the roads leading to and from the base. The area of the mined field had been defoliated leaving it barren except for the unexposed mines. From the protection of the jungle, we were constantly under siege by the enemy but the minefield provided a protective barrier. The enemy bombarded the base with all types of mortars and artillery shells. We would wipe them out and they would return again with new supplies and men. This time, their spotter thought he was safely out of range of our snipers. He sat in the cradle of a tall coconut tree overlooking our base from a safe distance, with a bird's eye view of us. He was giving accurate instructions to their artillery that resulted in more than two direct hits on our barracks and munitions storage.

"This was a job for my new weapon. I heard the familiar whistling sound of the incoming mortars and artillery shells before they exploded on contact. Men were screaming in pain, shouting in anger as their bodies were ripped apart from shrapnel. I tried to put the chaos out of my mind and got my weapon ready. I could see the sun reflecting off the glass of his binoculars.

"He must be giving their artillery unit the coordinates of specific targets on the base," continued the soldier. As I proceeded further away from my barracks to the outer rim of the base, the soldier pointed in the direction of a tall palm tree that towered above us. Again, I saw the reflection of the binoculars. I looked around for a place to make the shot. I remembered the sniper's box in the guard tower and headed there. Soon I was in place to take my shot but suddenly there were three explosions, one after another in quick succession, which rocked the base and obliterated many of the barracks. I heard louder screaming as mortar shells came whistling through the air. I refocused on my objective, adjusting the telescope of my sniper's rifle; I got him in my crosshairs. He was sitting in the cradle of the towering coconut tree doing exactly what the soldier had stated. I focused on him and disconnected from the mayhem around me. I no longer heard the battle, or the screams of the injured men. I concentrated on making this kill. Suddenly it was calm and peaceful as a windless day. I could see my prey as clear as he was standing in front of me. His upper body was visible; the rest of him was concealed by clusters of coconuts. I remember aiming and calmly I squeezed off two rounds. There was minimal kick back from the weapon, which made me wonder if it had the power to propel a bullet effectively. The suppressor had absorbed the sound of the bullets; there were two faint thuds when I had squeezed the trigger.

I looked at the target for what seemed to be an eternity, then suddenly saw what appeared to be the binoculars falling out of the palm tree. Its glass lenses caught the sunrays, reflecting it back to me as a message of my success. I watched as it spiralled down and disappeared in the lower canopy of the jungle. I lifted my weapon again and looked through the scope. I saw the lifeless body of the NVA trooper stuck by his lower torso and legs between two branches of the coconut tree, while his upper body was exposed, dangling from the coconut tree with both arms lifelessly dangling down towards the ground as blood oozed from the exit wound in his head. He was dead, but they continued to rain down mortars and shells on our base.

"As I confirmed his status, I could hear the familiar sound of two F4 Phantoms streaking across the Vietnamese sky to deliver their payload of death and destruction on the enemy. They came thundering from way up out of the sky, dropping bombs and firing missiles on the enemy artillery positions. Huge, deafening explosions followed as the bombs hit their targets, emitting acres of orange colored fireballs mixed with thick black acrid smoke that plumed into the sky, burning our nostrils as we inhaled. The strong odor of napalm was choking while the smell of burning flesh wafted in the air. We cheered as we heard the painful, horrific screams of their dying soldiers and listened for the coming silence of the dead. Soon the artillery fire stopped and quiet reigned. It had been a clear day, but now the horizon was invisible due to the orange and black fireballs that colored the countryside. The mighty thunderous jets disappeared leaving black smoke trailing behind them.

"Weeks had passed since that occurrence and more Viet Cong fell victim to my new weapon. My tour of duty was quickly coming to its end and I continued to plan and prepare to capture Red Dong.

The battle for Hill 875 was raging when we got word that the NVA troops were led by Red Dong and we were suffering great losses. Three of our units were surrounded by NVA troops and were being massacred and, even worse, were being fired on by our air support, an incident of friendly fire. It was a testimony to commander Red Dong's tactics. We went to rescue them, but couldn't go by air as there was no clearing at the top of the hill for helicopters to ferry in troops. We believed the men there had gotten word to make a clearing for the helicopters. But the attacks from the NVA forces were so intense that to expose ourselves was suicide. I remember praying for my unit as they prepared to annihilate the NVA troops. I carried numerous weapons into battle knowing I could reach the point of not having the time to reload. Strapped to my left thigh I carried a loaded automatic colt 45. I had taken that weapon from a dead officer earlier in my tour of duty. On my right leg I carried a Tech nine automatic pistol with a clip of 32 bullets. Over my back I had the Samurai sword. I had an AK47 and my new sniper rifle. I carried two ammunition belts crossing my upper body, which had the ammunition for my sniper rifle and my AK47. I carried a bag on my left hip with two full clips for each of my pistols and my AK47 plus a dozen grenades.

"The Vietnamese battle plan predominantly revolved around the ambushing of our troops. Their ambushes were becoming more ingenious with traps, mines and concealed pits with tipped spears to impale anyone who fell into them. Mines went off, blowing our men to bits as we ran for cover. Suddenly, a group of men immediately in front of me disappeared into the earth, followed by their screams. The ground had given way below their feet as they fell into a pit and were impaled on the spikes tipped in cow dung. I can still hear their screams; it was a painful, horrific way to die. The enemy now tried to encircle us and had troops ready to cut off our path of retreat while they bombarded us from ahead. We had no choice but to hold our ground and outfight them.

"The battle for Hill 875 raged on for days. Eventually a clearing was made atop of the hill and the helicopters ferried in fresh troops and took out the wounded. Reinforced with fresh troops, we went on the offensive. By now, the Air Force was able to drop bombs on the enemy without friendly fire incidents. I knew the North Vietnamese soldiers would start retreating once we got the upper hand. The momentum of the battle had shifted in our favor and they sensed that change. It was time for them to make a hasty retreat. We wondered why they did not overrun us when they had the opportunity, but that chance had slipped away just like they were now slipping away, before we could wipe them out. Into the midnight blackness of the dense jungle they disappeared while we waited, hiding in shallow foxholes clutching our weapons, with bated breath. We waited, but they never came, the battle was over".

# CHAPTER 12: The Hunt

"I waited until daybreak to start on their trail. It was like tracking animals in the wild. Knowing what to look for was key. It would take days for me to be sure I was on the right trail. By the second day I reached what was known as the Naked Forest. It was what the natives called it after we defoliated what was one of the thickest jungles in North Vietnam with Agent Orange. I stopped to observe the standing trees without their leaves, now husks of their once vibrant oxygen-giving selves. As I walked through the dead forest, I saw hundreds of craters created by bombs. Lifeless trunks of trees that were ripped from the ground lay around them. The craters had become mini lakes, emitting a misty smoke with the unmistakable scent of napalm and gunpowder. As my journey continued, I was met with an unholy stench emitting from the rotten flesh of unburied corpses that littered the landscape. Flies buzzed everywhere and scavengers feasted on decomposing bodies. I covered my nose and mouth with a bandana so as not to swallow the viscous putrid odour. I vomited several times at what I saw and smelt. The jungle had become a scavenger's paradise.

"What had we done to this glorious planet? I wondered. What were we doing to this beautiful country? This was the result of the savagery of war, I remember thinking, to placate my guilt I felt as I made my way through the forest. I exited the Naked Forest with tremendous relief. I wasn't sure I was on the right trail until day three, when I found a letter from a General Kwan to Red Dong. Being American it was difficult but I had mingled with the South Vietnamese enough to understand a bit of the language. In the letter, General Kwan expressed his grief and sorrow for Commander Red Dong's losses when we massacred the people of his village. "Commander Dong had lost his parents, as well as his wife and two children. I never gave any human characteristics to the Vietnamese people. I always tried to dehumanize them and that made killing them easier. But here was a letter, written in Vietnamese, addressing the sorrows of the war. They were no different than I. They wanted the best for their children, they wanted to live and grow without any foreign powers dictating to them and slowing their progress. But most of all, they were willing to fight and die to attain this independence just as we, as a colony, fought to gain our independence.

"You seem to empathise with the enemy you were fighting?"

"I saw myself in them," he said and continued. "Red Dong was leading his troops across the border into Laos. I had to close the distance between us quickly. I estimated there were 30 to 35 men accompanying him. It was obvious that after the battle at Hill 875, the retreating NVA forces had splintered into small units and headed in different directions. I could not follow Red Dong into Laos, so I had to strike before they crossed the border. The morning of the fourth day, I came on what seemed to be a battleground. The evidence of small arms fire in close quarter battles was all around me. As I searched around, I found the bodies of eight NVA troops. I went through their pockets and found bits of information, one appeared to be an officer, and in his possession, I found a map that confirmed my suspicions were correct. There, on the map in red, was their path into Laos. I looked around and noticed the numerous trees that were shredded from the top down by gunfire. I remembered that the day before I heard a C130 gun ship off in the distance. Apparently, these men met their fate through its terrifying firepower. Concluding that it was not Red Dong, I took the map and continued on the trail. I was in luck, as apparently one or more of his men were seriously injured and blood trails led away from the killing field. I pressed on and by late afternoon noticed that the blood on the ground was still wet. The wounded had slowed down the men's speed. By nightfall I heard their voices; they were camped not more than 300 yards up ahead of me. I quickly retreated to the edge of the forest, climbing high up into a large tree.

"From there I saw directly into their camp. I got my weapon ready and picked out three singularly isolated individuals. They didn't know what hit them, and nor did the rest of the unit until about half an hour later when they discovered their sentries were dead. By then it was getting dark. I climbed out of the tree and sought refuge 100 yards back in the jungle. I figured Red Dong would get his troops to find and execute me. I heard them scurrying around in the dark on the jungle floor, trying to get the position of where the shots were fired. Remarkably, they did pinpoint the tree from which I had shot down their comrades. From my perch, I distinguished five voices. At daybreak, I saw they had made camp about 50 yards away from the same tree. I had clear view of them. Three were sleeping and two were on guard. I brought my weapon to bear and without a sound the two guards fell. The others never woke from their sleep. I think back now of the cruelty of war. That new weapon had made me a stealthy, invincible force.

"Before long I was back on the tree from where I had shot the three guards. The main camp was now empty. I eyeballed the surrounding area but saw no form of human activity. I waited, knowing that if I was mistaken I would not have the chance to recover. I waited in that tree until midday before I was satisfied there were no more NVA troops hiding at the campsite. Slowly and quietly I approached it. The surrounding grass was more than eight feet tall and as dense as the ocean water. As I approached the encampment, I sensed something was wrong. I got down on my knees and saw that hidden by the grass, leading to the camp were trip wires. This meant there were mines. I looked around without moving and saw how close I had come to stepping on one. I cautiously approached the mouth of the trail leading into the camp, expecting someone to open fire on me. There was no one in the opening but the cleared encampment was surrounded by a buttress of tall grass. I studied the wall of grass and then I saw it – the muzzle of an AK47. Whoever was holding it did not realize that it was partially exposed... or maybe that was what they wanted me to think.

"I squeezed off two quick shoots from my AK47. The sound suppressor absorbed the blast of the bullets but also emitted a distinct thud. I heard a rustle in the grass and squeezed off another two rounds in that direction, which was answered by a fusillade from the trooper's AK47. I was in a firefight and fully exposed. I reached into my bag and grabbed two grenades, pulled the pins and lobbed them at the enemies' position. After the explosions, it was quiet again. I lay in a prone position, listening, waiting for sounds to reveal if there were more of them. That's when I heard movement in the grass beside me. I waited with my AK47 in hand as the NVA trooper came out of hiding to investigate. He was so surprised to see me pointing my AK at him that for one moment he froze in his tracks. I will never forget the look on his face as I opened fire. Another came out from hiding. Instantly he fired away, missing me by inches in his impulsive desperation. I took my time to aim and squeezed off a burst that hit him solidly in the chest, lifting him off the ground and depositing his lifeless body about six feet away. I lay there on the ground looking at the bloody carnage that resulted in the death of these men. I felt no remorse – no sense of guilt at ending their lives. I wondered how many more were in hiding in this field of tall grass, waiting for me to step into that defenceless campsite to open fire on me. I looked at the bodies and saw that the men were armed with AK47 and they had extra clips on them. I put my AK47 on automatic and sprayed the full circumference of the opening with lead. If there happened to be others left waiting to ambush me, I had every intention to wipe them out. When I was satisfied no one else was waiting, I searched the bodies of the enemies for clues of their destination and relieved them of their AK47 loaded clips.  I continued on the trail.

"Again, along the trail I saw speckles of blood. I knew that at least one of their wounded started to bleed again; apparently, movement had reopened the wound. He was likely haemorrhaging; an artery was severed. It seemed as if they were going through great stress to keep him alive and carry his helpless body with them. I concluded he was an officer of great importance. This was not a good sign. Soon they either had to leave him behind – or kill him, because he was now a liability. Could I be so lucky – could this wounded officer be Red Dong, I wondered? I realized they would leave him behind to ambush me. It happened so suddenly I did not have time to react. I was in another large clearing along the pathway. His back was against a tree stump and I did not see him initially, but he saw me. He was so far gone that he could not muster the strength to pull the trigger of his AK47. His clothes were soaked in blood and I noticed he was laboring to breathe. Blood was coming out of his mouth when he attempted to speak. I knew it would not be long before he took his last breath. I disarmed him and gave him water. He drank and looked at me. Satisfied it was not Red Dong, I pull the trigger, ending his long suffering.

"I continued on, knowing that the distance between Red Dong and I had narrowed but without their wounded comrade they would be moving faster. I knew they had heard the last battle as well as the shooting of their wounded comrade. I knew that they would either try to ambush me or try to evade me. My senses were on extra alert when I heard them up ahead. I veered off the pathway into the thick long grass. I travelled a difficult swamp route until I came to the end of the tall grass and the bank of the river. I looked in all directions. To my right I saw a bridge suspended over the river. It was about half a mile away. There was dense vegetative undergrowth to the forest on the other side of the river, which could easily conceal me. I wasn't sure whether Red Dong had already crossed over into Laos. I stood there briefly, thinking of what should be my next move, before I decided to cross the river into Laos. When I reached the other side, I sought refuge in a nearby forest. I peered out at the bridge and saw Red Dong's units now crossing the bridge into Laos. I got out my sniper rifle and took aim. I hit the first three men leading the way over the bridge, which caused the others to retreat, scurrying back to the North Vietnamese side of the bridge. I decided to make my way up toward the bridge on the

Laos side using the coverage of the thick undergrowth. They had not pinpointed where the shots were coming from. They had taken up defensive positions on the North Vietnamese side of the bridge, but a few of them were exposed and, as I picked off those few, others became exposed. In their frantic search to find safe hiding places, they exposed themselves and I continued to pick them off. The sound suppressor was working like a charm. I was firing at will at the enemy but the silencer did not betray my positions as I advanced to the bridge. Red Dong's troops became destabilised and chaotic as they saw their comrades falling and were unable to figure out where the shots were coming from. Most of them lay dead and the rest were anticipating their end as they wildly opened fire in all directions.

"I estimated four were still alive. I continued to work my way up the opposite side of the river concealed by the undergrowth as I headed towards the bridge. Another two became visible. I quickly picked them off, when one came running out shouting something with his hands up over his head. Another member of his unit quickly opened fire on the surrendering trooper, instantly killing him. I fired at him. He fell to the ground, dropping his weapon. By then I had reached the Laos entrance of the bridge. I ran across it, pointing my weapon at this trooper, knowing he was not dead. I saw him reaching for his weapon and fired a shot hitting the weapon, which caused him to back off. I motioned for him to stand. The bullet had slightly grazed his arm. It was only a superficial wound. I searched him and to my delight it was the man I was looking for. It was Commander Red Dong".

# CHAPTER 13: Coming Home

Colonel Carson's spirit had no place for defeat. His will for victory never faltered, his desire to destroy his enemy was constant and his actions left no doubt in the mind of others of his thinking. He was a seriously flawed patriot, like many who fought alongside him.

The Black Forest project had become his personal war. He hoped to leave Vietnam a general. His research on North Vietnamese and Viet Cong's method of fighting had proved beneficial to the army. There was a decrease of more than 30 per cent in the number of fatalities among those men who were trained at the simulated jungle bases.

The military was pleased with the results; the Pentagon heaped praises on Carson and even made recommendations for his promotion to a one star general. However, Carson was now doing duel service for the Air Force and was an active member of the CIA. The Air Force was not pleased with him, although his research benefited the military. His penchant for hanging enemy soldiers was disturbing. If his research hadn't benefitted the Pentagon, he probably would have been dishonourably discharged. Many in the Air Force wanted him gone, but because it was thanks to him that they had gained air supremacy, they swept his disturbing behavior under the rug and only sought to relieve him of his duties. The CIA however, steadfastly supported him and offered him a high-ranking position as a pilot of their SR71 Blackbird, the fastest plane known to man. He accepted their recruitment but refused to pilot, as he was developing a longing for home. He had served three tours of duty in Vietnam and his single seat F4 Phantom fuselage was decorated with the spirits of those he had shot down. As his career now swayed in the balance, he took off on another mission to Vietnam. He was to accompany a squadron of B52s that were on their way to lay waste to Hanoi train yards.

This was a never-ending siege.The Americans bombed and the next day the Vietnamese rebuilt. The mission from its inception was wrought with bad karma. While flying to their target, one of the B52 bombers began having technical difficulties and was instructed to return to the base. It was not a very manoeuvrable plane; bombers are like cargo planes, built to carry a load of bombs, drop them and return to their base. By itself, it was not intimidating to the small, nimble, manoeuvrable, MIG 17. Three of them saw the crippled B52 and like a pack of hungry wolves seeing a defenceless moose, they pounced. The giant bomber had no chance as the savage MIG fighters strafed her fuselage with lead. One of them took delight in blowing one in every one of her four duel packed engines, which blew up the adjacent engine. As she went down in a blaze with her desperate crew facing death, her captain radioed back to her fleet and her base. His last message was "Mayday, Mayday we are going down at the hands of a squadron of MIG17s, please avenge this loss. Let these bastards pay for this." The captain was defiant to the end, knowing he was heading to his demise. The B52 lumbered across the sky, a flying inferno with flames streaming from out of its burning engines, streaking to the ground and exploding into millions of fragments. Its ordnance of approximately 70,000 pounds of bombs shook the countryside as they continued exploding. From miles away, people could feel the continuous explosions and smell its residue.

This was a bad day for the Americans. They went from one catastrophe to another. The rest of the fleet did not manage well, as waiting at their destination were well-equipped and highly skilled North Vietnamese air defence soldiers. They manned deadly surface to air missiles and were willing and ready to give their lives in defence of their country. The North Vietnamese were not known to provide an easy target but this mission was especially difficult for the United States Air Force. Making their way through the clouds, leaving behind a trail of white vapour, the deadly missiles streaked at supersonic speed, locking onto their targets through their radar guidance system and, with great succession, destroyed many of the bombers as they slowly released their payload of bombs on the North Vietnamese resistance. If there was hell on earth, this was it. The Americans were bombing with cluster bombs, incendiary bombs, smart bombs and dumb bombs. The train yard became an exploding inferno with North Vietnamese men bent on protecting their homeland to their last breath. With no flexibility in their will, both sides were determined on destroying the other.

Locked in this mental state, Carson flew his F4 Phantom and fired missiles that made direct hits with a surface to air missile launcher. To do so, he flew at a low altitude but this made him an easy target. Anti-aircraft artillery exploded within yards of his aircraft causing severe damage to his control system that progressively worsened as the battle proceeded. He was forced to retreat and head home. He attempted to glide his big, heavy jet fighter to the base, or as close to it as possible, but the plane was not cooperating. He radioed back to his base, giving them the coordinates where he could be found. He knew that he had to eject from his beloved fighter as the pull of gravity forced it down to earth. Carson gave his last coordinates and ejected. His parachute functioned as he hoped and opened up in the bright Vietnamese sky. He saw in the distance the crash of his plane while simultaneously hearing its explosion. He saw the fiery orange mushroom emitting from the remnants of it, topped by a black oily crown. It appeared as if the jet had released its spirit. The explosion spread violently from its epicentre through the jungle before its force dissipated, but it had successfully informed the enemy of his presence. He knew once he hit the ground, he had to find a place to hide. He had not sustained any injury and, as he looked down at the approaching earth's surface, he recognised the Black Forest off in the distance as the place where his jet fighter crashed. He instantly surmised that his chances of survival had diminished by a large per cent. He knew that many Viet Cong Forces who had amassed earlier around the Black Forest were still in the area.

He drifted down into the jungle canopy, expecting to be fired on, but that did not occur. Once on the ground, he cut himself free of his parachute and began to plan his route back to his base if help never came. He had one flare, which he expected to use to alert the helicopter that would be sent to rescue him. He also had a semi-automatic Colt 45 pistol: an officer's weapon. That's when the thought occurred to him that his luck was running out and he should no longer tempt fate. It was time for him to go home if he were to make it alive out of Vietnam. Every man must know when the momentum shifts from him and – if he does not note and heed these subtle signs – fate will be most unkind. Not even his strong will can change his destiny.

# CHAPTER 14: Purpose of Life

"You actually captured the feared enemy commander, Mr Stuart?"

"Yes, I did, Nurse Gordon."

"That was a great achievement. Please continue, Mr Stuart tell me more."

"Fearing I was about to kill him, he remained in a submissive position on his knees, with his hand behind his head. "Get up," I said, as I motioned with my rifle, making sure they were no others.

"He got to his feet. I could not believe this diminutive man was the feared commander Red Dong. But genius knows of no size and armed with AK47s and given a strategic planning board and purpose for living, this little man had become a giant headache to the US military. I searched him for weapons and found three concealed pistols. Satisfied there were no more, I began my journey back with my 50,000 dollar prize. I concluded that he was no more than five feet three inches, which confirmed that he was indeed the man I had set out to capture.

"Are you going to kill me?" he asked, surprising me with his perfect English.

"Give me a reason and I will be happy to oblige. I will get my 50,000 anyway, dead or alive. That is what is written on the poster," I said with a scowl.

"You are planning to carry my corpse all the way back to your commanders?" he questioned, as I handcuffed his hands behind his back.

"No, motherfucker," I said. "Only your head and hands. That's all they need, so if you want to live through this, you'd better do as I say. And where in the fuck did you learn to speak English?"

"At one of your American universities," he replied. I knew that wealthy Vietnamese sent their children off to universities for their higher education. Most of them went to France.

"What university?" I questioned, a little jealous, being American but never having had that opportunity.

"I got my Bachelor's at Columbia University, and I got my Master's at Berkeley,"he said, with an air of superiority.

"Well – I got my Bachelor's at the American Institute of Hard Knocks and my Master's here in the jungles of Vietnam. I graduated at the top of my class. Do you want to know what I majored in?" I metaphorically asked. "Killing little squinty eyed motherfuckers like you and I am very good at it. You saw what I did with your boys? Now move, or I will take you back in bits and pieces," I said, as envy triggered my feelings of hate for the enemy. I viciously pushed him in the direction leading back to the base. He stumbled along from my constant prodding and pushing.

"So, that's how much I am worth to you Americans. I must have been a thorn in your side and maybe everywhere else," he said, with a clear sense of accomplishment.

"No, buddy, don't blow up yourself now," I said. "You are just a bounty and I am a hunter. I am taking you home to meet Uncle Sam. I will get my 50 grand and you, your life if you are lucky."

"You are a rare type," he said.

"What do you mean by that?" I asked.

"I do not find many of your colour so patriotic. I would expect that from your white counterpart, but from you I expected understanding," he said to me.

"Understanding! Why the fuck should I be understanding to you or your cause?"

"We are both oppressed by the same peoples, don't you realize?"

"Well, 50 grand can make a man forget and overlook a lot of things, including oppression," I said sarcastically, and pushed him harder, causing him to lose his footing.

"What will you do with that money when you return home to America? Buy yourself a home, a car, get married? What will you do with it, GI Joe?" he asked sarcastically, as he got to his feet. "I want to know, because you will become rich through me. Will you think of me when you drive your nice fancy car or when you go to sleep in your big pretty house? Tell me, GI, will you think of me when you give money to the women to make you happy?"

"I told you to shut your frigging mouth, so why are you talking?" I said and hit him harder in the upper back with the butt of my AK47, which sent him reeling to the ground again. "If you don't shut up now, I will blow your fucking brains out and leave your carcass here to rot," I said, as menacingly as I could.

"Here or anywhere, GI, do it. I welcome death for I have nothing to live for. I already know the outcome of this war and that was my only reason for living. Your people have already killed all those I held dear and I want to be with them but I cannot bring myself to do it. Do it for me, GI Joe. Set me free. Allow me to escape this hell."

"I looked in his unflinching eyes and saw that he meant it. '

"We in America have a saying – that one should be careful what they ask for. They may just get it. Now move!" I said with an ugly sneer that brought out the meanness that resided in me. I pushed him again, but this time much harder than before.

"We walked in silence for miles before he said anything again. "I have been wondering, knowing your country's history of hate, oppression, suppression and injustice to people of your color. I am wondering why you take up arms and fight for it. Your people have not been included at the table. So why would you take up arms and fight for your white masters? The same greedy, oppressive white masters who excluded you from the table. Yes, I am talking of the same white masters who enslaved your forefathers for centuries, then created a system of segregation so as to keep your race politically, economically and educationally inferior. They denied your people the right to vote, the right to educate yourself and the right to be treated equally by the law. This confounds me." He stopped in his tracks and slowly turned to face me and said, "Don't you understand that when you fight beside him, you empower him to keep you shackled? I cannot understand your loyalty. They have stripped you of your pride, your dignity, your culture and your identity, yet still you continue to support them. You have become an integral cog in their oppression machinery. You help them enslave others, as they had your people enslaved for centuries. Why? You must look around and see the agony you have created. You will learn and understand the reasons we fight. You will understand the reasons why you must fight and why you must maintain your dignity and create your own identity."

"What are you trying to do?" I asked him. "Trying to understand me or my means of survival, for this is what it's all about, survival. You have chosen your method to do that and I have chosen mine."

"Does life mean that much to you that you will allow yourself to live under those oppressive conditions, without dignity or respect, allowing yourself to be violated by them as they wish? Even now your white comrades make human sacrifices by hanging their black comrades as well as many of my people that were captured and taken as prisoners of war. They hang them while they burn crosses. I never knew that human sacrifice was still in existence, especially in advanced cultures and societies like yours claims to be," he said with contempt.

"That statement stopped me dead in my tracks. "What did you say?" I demanded, not believing what I heard, for he had uttered the only words that could and would cause me to deviate from my objective.

"He turned and looked at me and continued to speak, "Yes your people make human sacrifices in the Black Forest, and I will take you there so you can see of what I speak."

"If you are leading me into a trap, buddy," I said, "you will be the first to die."

"I do not know what will happen between here and there, nor do I know what will happen when we get there, but what I know is that we are going to win this war. We will never surrender; we will not be defeated for what we fight for is our right to exist as we choose and what you fight for is the right to enslave us, to oppress us. In the eyes of your Christian God, which of those are righteous?"

"I am an atheist," I replied, but he was becoming very convincing. The determination he had resonated in his voice. It helped me come to understand their reason and purpose for fighting and I respected it. As a black man in America, I knew what it was like to live without freedom.

"Why do they call it the Black Forest?" I asked him.

"The trees of the Black Forest were grown specifically for the harvesting of a special type of sap from which rubber is produced for tyres. But because of this war, they deviated from its intended purpose and instead it is used for the hanging of our people. They are tens of thousands of those gigantic trees growing in neat rows extending for miles with bodies hanging from them as if they were some type of a human fruit." I was now sure he was speaking of lynching.

"Who planted them?" I asked, trying to lessen the impact of his statement.

"The French did, but the British supplied them with the plants."

"The trees of a rubber plantation are not usually big," I said.

"These were not genetically engineered to keep them small like modern rubber trees. These were planted under the premise of a bigger tree will yield a larger quantity of rubber sap."

"As he led the way I knew I had relinquished my control to him even though I was the one armed and he was the prisoner. I was torn between his information and getting back to the base. There were many NVA and VC units in the area surrounding the Black Forest. Since their victory at Hill 875, they were congregating in the hills and the forest. I had ominous feelings about going there. It took us the better part of the day to reach where I had shot the solitary wounded NVA soldier and when we got back there, his body was still in the same position I had left it. Red Dong wanted to bury his comrade but thought better of it when he met my stare. We continued our journey, leaving the corpse to nature's course. We came to the campsite and again it was as I had left it. So far, no one had come this way. I looked at the destruction caused by the minefields that I had set off earlier. A good portion of the grass field had been burnt. Soon it would be dark; I decided it was better to hide in the tall grasses for the night. I tried to hide our trail off the pathway into the grass, which towered over our heads.

"I cuffed him with another set of cuffs to his ankles, pushed him to the ground and he hit it with a thud. He raised his head, turned his angry face and looked at me.

"You could have told me what you were about to do," he said, glaring at me with hate and anger in his eyes.

"I looked at him and smiled. "You would not have agreed; remember we are enemies. Hours ago, we were shooting at each other and the only reason you are not dead is because you are of some value to me. But I will be paid, whether you are dead or alive. Buddy, you have no rights as far as I am concerned. I am going to treat you as my enemy and my prisoner. You should hope that I kill you – you aren't going to like what they are going to do to you if I get you there alive." I chuckled, knowing the truth of my statement ,and he realized it too by the look that settled on his face. I grabbed the cuff that was around his leg, pulled his legs into a flex up to his butt and connected it using a third cuff to his handcuffs behind his back. He was hog-tied. I looked at him and smiled. He cursed at me. "You nigger motherfucker. I will get you one day, if it's the last thing I do," he said calmly.

"You see," I said. 'I am giving you reasons to want to live. Not so long ago you wanted me to end your miserable pathetic life, now I hear you talking about you wanting to get me.  Dream on, Big Red,' I said.

"You think you are invincible, huh, Yankee?" he said with a sneer. "You are not. Your technology maybe superior to ours, but so were the French and you see what we did to them."

"We are not the French and if you are smart, you would shut up so you could live through this to carry out those threats you're making."

"Why don't you kill me?"

"Do you really want to die?" I asked. "You know – this war will end one day. Your country will need brilliant educated people like you to rebuild it. You could find a new girl, get married and start a new family. If there is life there are possibilities, you know," I said flippantly.

"I rolled up a hard ball of pebbles, dirt and grass in the foot of a sock I carried for this. I knelt with my right knee in the small of his back. I hit him on his shoulder with the butt of my gun and as he screamed I pushed the dirt ball into his mouth and taped it, as he struggled to resist. "That should keep you quiet for tonight," I said, as I rolled him on his side.

"Your night will be an uncomfortable one, but you will live,'"I said, and sat with my back against a tree, clutching my AK47 across my lap ready for action. I don't recall when I drifted off to sleep but it was one of those nights when the slightest sound or total quietness woke me. All my senses were alert; nothing was going to surprise me. Every move he made brought me out of my sleep and every sound was thoroughly analysed with an increasing degree of annoyance each time.

# CHAPTER 15: The Black Forest

"I rose with the first rays of the rising sun; some would say it was still dark but the skies had that early tint of sunlight as dawn took hold of the land. I looked at my prisoner. I observed the rise and fall of his chest, which confirmed he was still alive. As uncomfortable as I had made him, he had still managed to sleep. I went into my bag and brought out the bomb I had in my backpack. I pulled up the back of his shirt, which roused him as I placed the belt around his waist and tightly buckled it. He was in no position to offer any resistance. I undid the cuff that connected his handcuff to his leg shackles. I watched him as he stretched his arms, which I now cuffed in his front at his wrist. I hoped and prayed that the tables never turned against me.

"I said, while I got some rations out, "Here is a stick of beef jerky for you," as I removed the gag. "You are going to quietly wash out your mouth and I will allow you to eat. Now I am telling you – don't get impulsive and try something stupid," I continued, now pointing my pistol at his head. After watching him eat most of the jerky, I went on. "You are a man who likes to think about things. Therefore, you must be wondering what I placed around your waist". I analysed him as he chewed on the last piece of dried beef.

"Yes," he replied between bites.

"It's a bomb," I replied which made him stop chewing.

"I'll show it to you." I lifted his shirt and revealed the bomb belted around his torso. Shock quickly registered on his face and the blood drained from his yellow skin. I lifted my left hand, which held the detonator.

"This is the detonator," I said. "You fuck around, Mr Columbia University, and boom, you are history. Nobody will be able to find a piece of your Berkeley Master's degree ass. You understand me." He was in shock, his mouth gaping, filled with the beef jerky. Then he spat it out. I guess my assault on his senses was too much to withstand and he responded the only way he could at the time.

"I hate you,'"he sneered. "I hate you."

"This is a war," I said, "with all the ugly brutality of it. There is nothing nice about it. Nothing glorious about it. In this game, there is only death and destruction. The idea is total annihilation of your opposition, mentally and physically. If I remember correctly, you, my friend, were doing a masterful job of it before I caught you. You are considered a very bad man, my friend, a very dangerous beast. That is why they have so much money on your damned head. I hold no sympathy for you. Now let's go – do as I say and we may live through this."

"After this war is over, I will find you one day," he said convincingly, "and I will kill you."

"I looked at his ugly angry face. I knew he meant it and I was aware he could do everything he said. "Not if I kill you first, and you are tempting me,"I said. "Now let's go and find those lynched men you were talking about."

"We set out on our journey. Suddenly the booming sound of jet going supersonic could be heard flying in from my rear as if coming in from Laos. I knew they were bombing the Hoe Chi Minh trail, which meandered into Laos and Cambodia near the North and South Vietnam borders. This was a key supply artery for the NVA and VC troops. Supplies coming in from China and Russia to North Vietnam were transported via this main artery, circulating to the NVA troops fighting in South Vietnam. The jet streaked across the sky and released its incendiaries. They were clearing a path in the forest so troops could be brought in. The sounds of the explosions vibrated across the open countryside, fireballs continued exploding with greater frequency and intensity, mushrooming into the sky. Noxious fumes were carried afar by the wind. From miles away we heard the familiar holler of the enemy troops who were being exterminated in these fireballs of death, screaming their last seconds of life away. The closer they were to the centre of the blast, the more completely their bodies would instantly evaporate from the heat and be blown away by the explosions. Nothing or no one was expected to survive within 100 yards in all directions from the epicentre of these blasts. As you travelled away from the epicentre, trees were burnt to a charcoal black, some left standing entrenched into the ground with lifeless roots while the carcasses of others littered the landscape. All life in that area had become extinct through the suffocating effect of these bombs.

"We travelled on, avoiding the areas I knew were occupied by NVA and VC troops. Silently, like ghosts, we closed in on our destination without any event. Then it happened.

"Water," he said. It was more of a demand than a request. I looked at him, knowing our supply was low.

"No," I said, "we do not have enough. We have to ration our intake." It was a hot, steamy day in the thickly forested jungle. Not being directly exposed to the tropical heat had its benefits, but being out of the sun did not provide much relief from it either. We trudged on and I noticed some irritation in his manner. I knew he was ticked by my response to his demand for water. I sensed the irritation in his heavy breathing and by the way he walked.

"You are a commander of squadrons. I am sure you have been exposed to situations where you had to make decisions to limit your troops' intake of water,"I said in an explanatory voice.

"Look here, you condescending nigger Yankee, I do not want to hear shit from you," he said. "I will take you to where you want to go, you can kill me or take me where you intend, I don't care. You will not defeat us. We will fight you to the last man." I felt the anger rise in me as I walked up to him and struck him hard to the face with the butt of my AK47, sending him reeling to the ground. I stooped down with my right knee in his chest and stuck the muzzle of my weapon in his mouth.

"If you dare call me that again, I will send you to Hades without your fucking head," I said, meaning every word. Blood was now flowing from the wound I had opened on his right cheek with the blow from the gun's butt.

"I stood up and listened for any sound. I did not hear anything abnormal. I did not sense anyone else had heard our skirmish. He got back to his feet. I gave him water.

"That is the last you are getting until morning," I said.

"He smiled. "Do you believe that we will live to see the morning? I believe we will be killed either by your people or my people before then."

"That should make you happy," I said to him.

"That is what my people call you," he said now, in softer tones.

"I find that so offensive, so racist, that I will kill you if you utter it again," I said.

"We consider you a warrior to be feared." he said. "You have killed so many of our men in battle, more than any other soldier of your army. That is the reason we respect and hate you. We have made several attempts to kill you and whoever is successful will be greatly rewarded."

" But I am still here and all-comers will be sent on a one-way trip to the lower world," I replied, as I relished my newfound fame.

"I knew it was you who was following us from the time you shot those guards."

"How did you know that?" I asked him.

"Whenever you are sniping, your kill shot consistently enters above the bridge of the nose. I planned to eliminate you by sending troops to search for you and kill you. If they failed. I had an ambush set at the campsite."

"Yes," I said, "and guess where they are now? In hell – the same place I will be sending you if you utter that disparaging remark again."

"But before you captured me, I was able to alert my armies to your presence. They were expecting me in Laos since yesterday. With me not showing, up every soldier in the NVA and VC armies is looking for me. If they believe I am your prisoner, they will not stop searching until we are found," he said with a smile. "Maybe you are the one who should be thinking of that reservation that has been awaiting you in hell."

"You talk too fucking much. I am going to shut your ass up," I said, as I stuffed cloth in his mouth and taped it. We travelled several miles undetected by the enemy, in total silence.

"It was late afternoon when I picked up the faint but unmistakable scent of decomposing flesh, something that had become commonplace in wartorn Vietnam. I stopped in my tracks and, with my nose in the air sniffing the wind, I identified the vicinity from where the odour was coming. I started to follow the scent to its source. Then I heard a moaning sound. He heard it too and stopped in his tracks. We followed the sound until we came on a badly injured Viet Cong fighter. I assessed him and knew he would not make it through the night. I called my captive over and when they saw each other they started to speak. The injured VC was having difficulty breathing and was gasping for air with every word he said.

"Do as I say and nothing more," I ordered Red Dong. "Ask him how many more fighters are there?" He asked the questions as I ordered him. "He is the only survivor of his group. He wants to know how we got here as there are mines all around the Forest. Most of his comrades were killed trying to cross the mine fields."

"Ask him how he got here?"

"He said he was taken prisoner and brought here for questioning. But the bombardment from the NVA destroyed the prison walls setting him and many of his fellow prisoners free. They were hunted down by elite Special Forces, many were recaptured and hung in a ritualistic manner with burning crosses."

"Burning crosses," I repeated. "Ask him if he's sure that's what they did?'"

"He is dead," Red Dong interrupted.

"I looked at the VC fighter and saw that death had settled on his face. I was familiar with that blank stare as I had seen it on many of my dead comrades' faces. He was gone. "Let's go," I said. He was of no use to us and we trudged on following the stench as it got stronger and stronger the closer we got. I wondered what atrocity was about to be revealed. I looked up in the canopies of the trees to see fattened vultures observing us as we got closer. I suddenly stepped out of the thick underbrush of the jungle floor into an area occupied by hundreds of neat rows of huge tall trees. They stretched in straight lines ahead for miles, but what I saw next shocked me to my core. There, from the branches of the trees in the distance, were the remains of hundreds of men hanging. I stood there for several minutes, staring at this unbelievable sight. Many had their hands tied behind their backs. The stench of their swollen decaying bodies in different stages of decomposition was overpowering to my senses and to my emotions. Maggots rained from their rotten flesh, while vultures had their choice of whom they would feed on. There were hundreds of hanging skeletons, some fully dressed, and burnt crosses were everywhere; some were standing while many were on the ground, littering the landscape. I turned and looked at him and I saw the tears in his eyes. I attempted to take the cloth from out of his mouth and he shook his head as if to say no, but I did.

I did not know when I started walking but we walked for miles in that private killing field in total silence aghast at this atrocity. Then we came across several decomposing bodies of black US service men hanging. Why? I asked myself. Why did they leave them like this? Did they not expect this macabre setting to be discovered?

"No, no,"I heard myself saying. "This is not real."

"This is real,' I heard him reply. "This is what your people are doing to us and to their own of your colour."

"Why didn't they bury them?" Then one of the swollen black faces in late decay looked familiar. I took my sniper rifle out, took aim and fired without a sound. The shot snapped the rope sending the edematous body falling. It splattered like a rotten fruit on hitting the ground. I removed the dog tag from the stinking decomposed flesh. It was the remains of Private Rory Jackson. I remembered him because he had approached me when he arrived, asking for survival tips. He told me of his family waiting back home for him. He showed me pictures of his wife and their son who was named after him. I remembered the day I heard that he was missing in action. I prayed over his body.

"Is this what awaits me when you turn me over to your leaders?" Red Dong asked, as we looked at the hundreds of hanging bodies in different stages of decomposition. The vultures were not fighting over the bodies. They were not even rushing to feast. They had become fat and lazy. I did not respond to his question as memories were now flooding my brain.

"I don't want to die like this. There is no dignity to die like this. I am a soldier fighting for what I believe, which is the freedom of my people. We have never threatened you, your people, or your country, yet still you have found your way across the oceans to my country so you could heap on us so much sorrow, death, destruction, hate. For what purpose? To make us slaves to your capitalism, a member of your democratic club. We do not want to join. We want our own identity.  I would like you to kill me now instead of letting me die slowly from the anguish you are deliberately inflicting. Blow me up with this bomb you have attached to my back but don't let me die like that. It is dishonorable and not the way of a soldier," he pleaded.

"I looked at him, feeling a lot of empathy for him, as I was being overwhelmed by the memories of seeing my father and uncles lynched. It was all coming back. The door to the room in which these memories had dwelt was now open. I had kept them locked in the recess of my mind, now the memories and emotions were free and roaming. I looked at the many faces made grotesque by the tight noose around their necks and the swelling of their decomposing bodies. Their heads were tilted to one side where the cervical break had occurred. I found a reason to live that day; I found a purpose for my existence on this planet, something to dedicate my life to that day. I looked at my prisoner who had tears rolling down his cheeks. I watched him as he looked at the hundreds of hanging corpses of his countrymen, hanging from a Klansman's noose. I could not do it. I could not deliver him to them after seeing this.

"I walked over and removed the bomb. I said to him. "Your country needs you. I hope you help it rebuild itself. I am giving you your life." I unlocked his cuffs, removed the bomb and set him free.

"Why do you do this?" he asked.

"I now understand the reason why you fight," I said.

"My purpose is just and honorable," he said. "Why do you fight?"

"I am still searching for the reason," I said. "But I am a soldier, a robot. I kill because I am told to, that is my reason for being here, I follow orders. Now go – before I change my mind."

"No, you are no robot. You are a man, a brave, courageous and wise man. You are willing to sacrifice your life for your country, but you are also capable of discerning its ills and against all odds are willing to correct them. Your battle will not end here in my country but will continue in yours." I watched him as he walked away and disappeared among the burnt crosses that littered the landscape and sprung from the ground like an aberration. I took one final look at the endless number of grotesque bloated decaying bodies hanging from the trees, their stench overwhelming my senses.

"After all you went through, the risk you took to find him – you set him free," I said. "I can't believe you gave up the reward, the money – why?"

"There are some things, Nurse Gordon, that are of a greater human value than money. What he was fighting for was within that righteous realm."

"He got to you."

"No. It was what he was fighting for, the reasons – after I saw what was there in the Black Forest – that got to me. I began to wonder if that fate in some way or form awaited me at home.

"I started out walking for miles before the forest ended. It opened into an endless green valley, with shrubs and grass that reached as high as my knees in places. Before I moved, I thoroughly scanned the terrain. I checked my compass and was satisfied I was heading in the right direction. I continued walking, ever alert, realizing that this terrain did not offer much cover. I knew that an open plain like this favored the person who first saw the adversary, allowing him to get off the first shot. The sun was beating down on me. It was as if I was walking through a furnace. I took a sip of my water, looked around and continued. That was when I heard the unmistakable sound of Huey helicopters. I also heard the distinct sound of their M60, chattering away. I hoped it was sending many of the enemies to their demise. I looked and saw them in the distance not more than a mile away. The lead helicopter gunner was shooting at the ground. I began a slow run in that direction trying to keep as low a profile as possible. The helicopter was receiving small arms fire and then in an instant, it was blown from the sky. It exploded in a huge fireball. The remaining helicopters opened fire at the targets on the ground. They were trying to move into position to rescue someone. Between me and the helicopter, I distinguished about 20 NVA troops dressed in camouflage gear with their backs to me. They were armed with small arms, including RPGs, and were firing their AK47s at the helicopter. I was within 100 yards of their rear and started picking them off one by one, always taking down the one closest to me. Before long, I had taken out about ten of them with headshots.

"The sound suppressor was working like a charm. I hit one and the impact of the bullet caused him to lurch forward into the back of another. I instantly aimed and fired at that one, on seeing that he had turned to hold up his dead comrade and was now realizing what was happening. But before he could sound an alarm to warn his comrades, he was dead. The bullet went through his skull, lifting him off the ground. This caught the attention of the others, who now turned to see what was happening behind them.

"That second of respite was all the distraction the Huey needed to open devastating fire on them, almost wiping out the rest of their unit. The survivors ran off and as they did, I aimed and got two more before they disappeared. One of the Hueys descended and someone came running out of the bushes. Suddenly he froze in his tracks, I saw and he saw another NVA trooper taking deadly aim at him with his AK47. But before he could fire, I did, and the NVA trooper fell. The down pilot turned and saw me for the first time. I ran to the down craft to check for survivors. There were none. We retrieved the bodies and put them aboard the Huey and took off.

"The down pilot was a Colonel. I looked at him and there was something familiar about him. Yet I could not place him. His tag said he was Colonel Christopher Carson. I looked around to see him looking at me. He never took his eyes off me, which made me uncomfortable. Finally, he said. "Thank you, Sergeant, I owe you my life."

"Think nothing of it," I said, with a certain amount of bravado.

"Sergeant, where did you get that rifle?"

"A friend gave it to me, Colonel, when he had completed his tour of duty," I replied.

"It's a beautiful weapon."

"Yes, it has sent many men to meet their maker."

"May I see it?" He asked with outstretched arms as if to receive it.

"No, Colonel," I said. "No one touches any of my weapons." He looked at me for a minute, then withdrew his outstretched arms. "It's not an army issued weapon, is it?"

"No, Colonel. It was a prize from a divisional marksmanship contest."

"Your friend won it in a marksmanship contest and gave it to you – such a beautiful weapon?"

"You should be happy, Colonel. It saved your butt."

"What are you doing out here by yourself, Sergeant?" he inquired.

"I was looking for a man, Colonel."

"Who is the man you were looking for soldier?"

"Commander Red Dong,"I said, which piqued his interest.

"I know of Commander Dong. He has a bounty on his head. Why do you seek this man?"

"For the bounty, Colonel," I said.

"By chance, you don't have his head in your backpack?" He asked, which brought a chuckle from the crew of the Huey helicopter.

"I did not get him, Colonel."

"What is your name, soldier?"

"I am Sergeant Stuart," I said.

"The Sergeant Stuart?" he said.

"I don't know about the, but I am Sergeant Stuart," I repeated.

"I have heard of your many exploits, Sergeant. You are a courageous man. I am pleased to make your acquaintance and am sorry to hear you did not get your man."

"There was something familiar about this Colonel's face, but I could not place him. I knew him from somewhere. He was an Air Force pilot, more than likely a pilot of the new F4 Phantom.

"What are you doing out here, Colonel?" I asked.

"I was shot down," he replied.

"Air Force F4 pilot," I said.

"Yes," he replied.

"How is that?" I asked.

"My guidance system flaps and rudders got toasted while bombing the North Vietnamese rail yards. I had to ditch my plane."

"Lucky to be alive, Colonel," I said. "But that F4 is a great weapon system, a great plane."

"He looked at me and smiled. "It is now – but when it came out it was a coffin with some missiles attached."

"Why do you say that, Colonel?"

"The belief was that the era of dog fighting was over. The old jets were armed with air-to-air missiles to shoot down enemy planes from a distance. It worked sometimes, but most times the enemy never complied. They devised tactics to stay out of the range of our missiles, making them ineffective. When we used them all up chasing them all over the sky, they turned on our defenceless F4s with their cannons and blew us out of the skies, sending our pilots down in flames."

"I looked and listened, knowing I knew him from somewhere, sometime before.

"I hope the Pentagon learns from their mistakes and appropriately arms those jets so your pilots can realistically fight the enemy at all quarters, with confidence in your weapons and strategies. Too many have died fighting this war with theoretical ideas instead of the realistic proven weapons of war." I said, having an urge, a need, to shift the direction of the conversation. "A bit of all America has been transported to this country and has found itself on the battlefield. I have witnessed the good, but mostly the bad and the ugly side of America here in Vietnam and I now understand why they fight, even in defeat," I said.

"What have you seen, soldier?" asked the Colonel.

"I looked at him, knowing in my heart that although he was on my side, he was not a friend. Our difference in color divided us like day and night. Although we were at war, representing the same nation against a common enemy, he was a greater threat to my wellbeing than the North Vietnamese or Viet Cong troopers, but I had to know where I knew him from as his face seemed so familiar. Then suddenly, like a catharsis, it came back to me. He was the boy on the horse who wanted to lynch me with my father and uncles. It was him. There was no doubt about it. But where was that ugly scar that crowned his face? I wondered.

"I have walked through the valley of death," I said, "and I feared no evil. I have seen the work of the nightriders here in Vietnam and wondered why and how. I certainly don't believe it resulted from strategic planning, but from the hate we carry within us to this country."

"He looked at me, not responding, studying me and my words. His silence spoke volumes, for his silence to me showed that he was aware of what occupied the Black Forest.

"Finally, he broke his silence. "There are things we know of that are best kept silent while they are being investigated," he said, looking me in the eye.

"How can I bring just men to face justice when those who are responsible for justice are corrupt and unjust?" I stated, "knowing the man who I am bringing to face justice is the one who is trying to change an unjust society to be a just one. We should be reaching out to him instead of trying to hunt him down and assassinate them. We do not have to be the new age Rome."

"You found your man and you let him go, didn't you soldier?"

"I found myself, Colonel," I said as the Huey landed at the base.

"You are a soldier, representing the interest of the United States. That man you set free was one of our deadliest enemies. You had the right to kill him or bring him to justice but you had no right to set him free. That is treason, soldier," said the Colonel.

"I am a civilian, Colonel not a soldier. I am no longer owned by the military. I can make my own decisions about the things I do."

"How many more men must die at the hands of that butcher you have set free before he is brought to justice?" he demanded.

"How many more black soldiers like me as well as women and children must be lynched by the Klan before our nation puts an end to it? When America starts to consider my interest, then I will consider America's interest," I replied in disgust.

"You have not heard the end of this, soldier," he said as he walked off.

"What happened to the scar on your face, Colonel Carson? I see losing that did not change you from being a hateful, lynching, Klansman.' That statement brought him to an abrupt stop. I noticed the change in his demeanor. Slowly, he turned and looked me in the eyes. Death now occupied his countenance. "Who are you, Sergeant?"

"I am your past, I am your present and I will be your future. I know who you are and I know what you do, Colonel. I have experienced the effects of your work and I have seen its imprint here in Vietnam." I walked off without saying another word and I felt in that moment that he suddenly recognized me as the young boy his father had spared from the hangman's noose about a decade ago.

"I went to the airport on base and caught the next transport flight back home to the US. For me, Vietnam was no longer a place to be. For me, the war was finally over, I had served my country and finally came to see the light."

"You walked in with a patriotic bang and you left with your eyes open. It's as if you discovered as a black man putting your life on the line for your country did not matter –they still saw you as less. Mr Stuart, for all your bravery and the number of enemy soldiers who met their demise at your hands as you grimed your way through that war, I want to know how come you never received any medals of honor, distinctions for bravery or courage, for something. Make me a believer. Make me believe this is not a figment of your imagination, or one of your moments of grandiosity?" I said.

In his slow calm manner of speaking, he said. "I was never injured during the war and I did not make this up. Wait here until I return" – and he got up out of his chair. In about ten minutes he returned with a bag, which he proceeded to open and took out about ten medals with pictures and newspaper clippings of generals handing him medals of honor. All but two were from the US military. One of the others was from the Australian Government – it was their highest military medal of courage and the other was from the French government who awarded him with their highest medal of honor. He identified and explained each and the reasons why he received them. Now I had seen the proof, I was convinced of his story.

# CHAPTER 16: Homecoming Queen

The following day, I sought to avoid Mr Stuart to concentrate on the problems of other clients. There was a new female who was diagnosed as sexually preoccupied in the unit. She was actively seeking satisfaction, the doctors said. Lisa Garcia was a slim, pretty, young Hispanic female, which made my job that much more difficult for her presence was causing incidents. Since her arrival, she was caught having sex twice and was involved in three fights with other females over men. Although she was on one to one observation, she still found a way to have sex with her lovers. Her roommates complained about her attempting to sneak male clients into their room late at night. Many of the clients were HIV positive. At the time, she wasn't, and our aim was to prevent that from happening. She found ways of evading her constant observation to satisfy her sexual preoccupation. My job required me to prevent her from having sex. Most psychiatric patients when acutely ill, even those over the age of 21, are not considered capable of using good judgement or making viable decision for themselves. Therefore, they are under the protection of the state and if she became infected while under the protection of the state, the state would be considered at fault and held accountable.

I was sitting at a desk in the nursing station when a young male client approached me and struck up conversation. He was known to be a ladies' man. He was a very charismatic individual. He was about six feet three inches tall, a light-skinned black male. He was diagnosed as a borderline schizophrenic and was equally manipulative. As he spoke with me, I noticed the sexually preoccupied patient, Lisa, walking in the direction of her room with the tech behind her. I observed as he turned to acknowledge her. Instantly I told him to stay away from her. He smiled. At that instant I got a call from my supervisor requesting information on specific patients from their charts. In answering, I temporarily lost track of the male client while speaking to my supervisor. I quickly scanned the clients in the sitting room. He was nowhere to be seen. I looked for the promiscuous female. She was nowhere in sight but the tech who was assigned to her was speaking to another client in the day room. Right away I knew what was happening. I told my supervisor I would call him back with the information later and hung up the phone. I asked the tech for the patient.

"She is in the bathroom," replied the tech.

"With whom?" I asked as I scrambled to retrieve the keys for all the doors on the unit. I ran to the room to see her roommate standing there.

"Who is in there with her?" I asked in no uncertain terms.

"Ian," she responded as I fumbled with the huge key chain containing dozens of keys. As I stood by the door, I could hear their sensuous moaning. Then, as I placed the key in the hole, I heard her saying. "Hurry up and make me come, they are trying to open the door." The tech, a West Indian woman, was now visibly upset and began shouting "Lisa, open the door, now!" I continued trying the different keys. I could hear her gratifying cooing as she urged him on. "Oh God, Ian you are so sweet, do it to me, Ian, do it to me, baby, oooh," she kept repeating. It continued and with each repetition, she vocalised in a higher note and slightly louder, but still soft enough to remain sensuous. "Do it to me, Ian," she said, coaxing him on. "Do it to me baby," she said from behind the closed doors. "Oh God, fuck me, Ian, fuck me," she said in a cadence that had me turned on too as I fumbled with the key. At that point I wondered what I would or should say when I got the door open while they were still having sex. He was now heard on the other side giving her instructions.

"Let me do it from behind," I heard him say.

"Oh, my God, that's my favourite position," she said in approval. Soon after I heard her vocalising in ecstasy, saying "Yes, yes, Ian, yes, yes, Ian, do it to me, baby, it feels so good." She was now breathing very heavily, repeating "Oh God, oh God it feels so good," louder and louder. Soon the yeses were replaced by his name, Ian, leading to a heavy panting and in a moment she was screaming again, "Fuck me, Ian, fuck me, fuck oh God it's good, it's good. Don't stop, Ian, don't stop. Ian, they will have to pull us apart if they open this door," followed by, "Ian, don't stop. It feels so good, it feels good, Ian, aaaah, fuck me, Ian fuck me." I could hear the steady increase in the intensity of his strokes, working to reach a climax.

Suddenly, there were gratifying screams from behind the door followed by her shouting, "Yes, yes, Ian, yes do it to me, baby, yes, yes." I turned and looked at the tech, rolled my eyes and shook my head. Her gratifying high pitch chatter and scream reached a crescendo and then she let it all out as she achieved her climax, "Oh Ian, Ian, that was good, so good we must do it again." They were talking as they cleaned up and then it went quiet. Before I could find the key, the door opened and they both exited the bathroom happily smiling, without a care in the world. She was already on one to one observation and I placed him also on one to one observation until he could be removed from the unit. This was going to be a major incident. I could feel its stressful presence weighing me down. This one would not be easily dismissed. This incident would run its course and possibly heads would roll.

After meeting with the psychiatrist and doctor, as well as department heads, I met with the tech who was assigned to watch the patient. Like me, she was visibly stressed, knowing that she was at fault, but I was the nurse in charge.

"Ms LaFleur," I asked, "do you know the details and reason for the policy of constant observation or one to one observation?"

"Yes," she replied timidly.

"What is the purpose of one to one observation?"

"To provide physical protection and emotional support to the self-destructive patient," she replied.

"Were you the person assigned to a one to one with Ms Lisa Garcia during the hours of two pm to four pm?"

"Yes," she replied.

"Why is Ms Lisa Garcia on one to one observation?" I asked.

"She is sexually preoccupied," replied Ms LaFleur.

"And that makes her a danger to herself and others especially if she has STDs or she has sex with someone who has, isn't that so, Ms LaFleur?" I knew that although she had committed the infraction, I would be the one who would be held accountable.

"Yes," she replied in agreement.

"Isn't the main requirement of a person assigned to do one to one is to remain approximately two arms lengths keeping the patient in your sight at all times?"

"Mr Gordon, she said had to use the bathroom and I was helping another patient."

"While she was in the bathroom having sex, Ms LaFleur, the same thing you were there to prevent," I said with my voice elevated in anger. "What time did this incident occur?"

"Approximately three pm," she replied.

"During that time, you were scheduled to be observing Ms Garcia and no one else," I said as she reluctantly shook her head in confirmation of my statement. "Ms LaFleur, do you agree that one to one observation means that the staff who is assigned to do the one to one observation is not allowed to assist another patient if it will take them away from their assigned task." She looked at me very hard, sensing that she was now cornered. I saw the change in her mannerisms, becoming defensive and angry.

"I wasn't observing another. I was helping another patient."

"Ms LaFleur, you neglected your assignment. Helping someone else was not your assignment."

"It was not wilfully done; I was only waiting for her to get out of the bathroom. I did not know he was in there."

"You did not check, nor did you stay with her. Ms LaFleur that was part of their plan to manipulate us. They created a diversion to keep you occupied while they snuck away to the bathroom to commence their rendezvous. You have got to recognize that. The patients we work with are mentally ill but they are not stupid. That's the gist of it Ms LaFleur. Due to that error in judgment, we are now in big trouble. What you should have done is check the bathroom to make sure it was empty before she went in, and wait outside the door so that no-one else enters."

That day I started a new system to easily identify the keys. The following day at morning rounds, the incident was officially reported and I was called to my supervisor's office to explain. I presented the facts as they were. I too was written up because there was a breakdown in my unit awareness. In my mind, I rehashed the moment when he began speaking to me with the intention to manipulate me. I remembered how he turned to look at her as she walked by when she was entering her room. I remembered what I said to him. I knew if I had taken a more assertive position it would not have occurred. I should have confronted the problem then. My instinct was correct but I had left it up to the tech to do her job. This made me as culpable as she was.

My assignment required me to speak with the clients that I had charts on, among them was Ms Yoa Matoma. I wanted to see what was taking place in her mind. We spoke about her homeland of Japan and her family. The conversation progressed to her assimilating in the American culture. She was now beginning to realize that her short stay here did not adequately prepare her. She had fallen in love and married a man of western culture without understanding the culture or people before she did this. I found her a virtuous individual, still seeing things and operating from her cultural background.

"What you have experienced is an occurrence most American women have become versed in sometime in their life. To be cheated on by your spouse is abusive and deplorable, but it's not unusual. Take time to speak with them and you can learn from their resilience and their determination to overcome and move on to make their lives better."

"This is not about American women. This is about me. I have disgraced myself and my family. I will never be able to face them again."

"What will it take for you to understand that what you did was just a part of living and growing? The things you both did were mistakes you will overcome in time. It's not the end of the world."

"I will not overcome this" she responded.

"The only way you will not overcome this is if you do not allow yourself to. You did nothing wrong – do not beat yourself up over this."

"My disgrace is greater than life. I do not expect you to understand."

"You are in America now and this is your first American problem. So you must use American means to resolve this problem. The ultimate disgrace in America is succumbing to your adversity and thus taking your life."

"What are the American solutions to my problem?"

"The willingness to live and overcome. You must attain the willingness to thrive while knowing and accepting that adversities are a constant of life. You will one day gain the knowledge that the richness one attains from living comes from resolving the problems one is faced with in life and the wisdom gained from these solutions are what fuels your growth. Death is not a triumphant means over adversities. It is the finality in the journey of life. Therefore, life will present you problems along the journey which you must resolve. Ending life is not and will not be a solution to any of your problems."

"I do not understand," she said in a subdued tone.

"Do not allow the perceived disgrace of the incident to dictate your solutions. Defer to that bright light, that beacon I see shining through your eyes and face. It does not want to be extinguished; it desires to live. It's a time to live and grow. Your objective is to get your green card. Allow your husband to do that for you in a business manner, and when that is accomplished you can divorce him or pursue a relationship if you both so desire, but either way it's time to live and continue with your life. Do not make your journey on earth a short and unenlightened one by running away from your problem. For its purpose is not to kill you, but to enlighten you." I wondered if I had made contact, wondered if I had convinced her to live. Did I give her any concrete material to use as a solution?

As the days passed, I observed her as she plunged deeper into her depression. Eventually she stopped speaking to her carers, now convinced that death was her only solution. I attempted talking with her but the entrance to her mind was closed like a door. I watched her as she walked aimlessly in the dayroom. Her eyes lifeless, her vigor had flickered out like the flames of a lamp. Her highly intelligent wit had been replaced by a blank stare. Where had she gone? I wondered. Where was that energetic, engaging, acutely ill individual that initially walked in here? Where was she hiding in that impressive but now troubled mind? What was I failing to understand and what block was preventing me from reaching her? Initially I had not seen her as a mentally ill person but an individual who had made some error in judgment. But her insanity was now dominant and it was dragging her deeper into depression. As she had stopped speaking with the staff she remained on constant observation for suicidal ideation.

I could not avoid Mr Stuart any longer and his familiarity had become a welcome predictable change in the day.

"Mr Gordon." I heard his voice calling my name like an old friend. I turned to meet his smile. "Are you avoiding me today?"

"Mr Stuart, welcome to the table. I have time for you now," I said.

"Do I continue my life story?" he asked.

"With every violent moment of it," I replied.

"I didn't think you were being judgmental," he said.

"I would not have you change a moment in your life story to appease me and that is not being judgmental," I said.

"My life has been a violent one," he said, "and it continues to be such."

I looked at him; an older man who never presented a violent incident to the unit was now telling me he was still violent.

"How is that?"

He looked in my eyes and calmly said. "I will tell you everything in time."

"Mr Stuart," I said, "did you kill anyone since you were discharged from the military?"

"Yes," he replied without a trace of doubt in his voice, "I was a bounty hunter for years. I hunted down some of the most dangerous criminals who were wanted by the law, dead or alive. Many were taken in alive to face justice. Others were not as fortunate."

"Death follows you doesn't it, Mr Stuart?"

"It doesn't follow me, I am an agent of death," he said in no uncertain terms. "I do his work for him. You see that Japanese girl you have been trying to save. You will get news of her demise in the coming future. In fact, she is already dead; she is waiting for the opportunity to finalise it. She will not do her death act here because she respects you, but she will do it."

Stunned by his statement, I looked in his face, peering deep into those cold black eyes and I saw the truth of what his grandiose mind had deduced.

"How do you know that?"

"My instincts, Nurse Gordon. I trust them. They are telling me she will be killing herself and you already sense it."

"What makes you think I already sense it?"

"You have good senses and a great instinct. Trust them and allow them to be a part of your guidance system. You know when you make judgment calls based solely on rationality, that is when things go wrong. When you are instinctively in touch with your spirit in addition to your good attitude, you can do no wrong."

I looked at him in wonderment sensing the truth in what he said. "Mr Stuart, will you continue your biography?" That was all he was waiting for to continue his tale. It was my assignment to listen.

"After I was discharged from the military, I went to find the family of the lynched service man I had discovered back in the Black Forest. I had been given an address for his family in Bedford

Stuyvesant Brooklyn, New York. I remember that hot summer's day when I arrived in Brooklyn. It was my first time in New York. The streets were littered with garbage. The heat and humidity were unbearable and the stench of ripened garbage wafted in the sweltering heat. I could not believe this was part of the famous New York City I heard so much about. Yet still the streets were teeming with kids playing stickball, disregarding the dog faecal littered sidewalks. Others were cooling themselves off by soaking in wide-open hydrants. The ice-cold water was coming out at an unimaginable force, beating against the side of passing automobiles, but the youngsters did not seem to mind. It was all a game to them, growing up on the sinful streets of New York City. In years to come, not having any positive means to channel their energies, many would fall victim to these streets. The water ran along the streets like turbulent rivers and spilled onto the sidewalks before it found its way to the opening of many littered-covered sewer openings, where it descended to find its way to its destination. As I walked along the streets, I never saw a place with so many small parks with basketball courts, handball courts and junkies sitting on the benches getting high. The neighborhood seemed hopelessly lost. I wondered if this was the repercussion of fighting this ungodly war in Asia and if so why were the black neighborhoods the ones that had to suffer. Many brothers from these neighborhoods were fighting in Vietnam hoping that, on their return, their country would reach out to them. If that was to start, it would have been then. It never happened and it will never happen."

I listened to his monologue and in agreement I said. "Every man is in-charge of his life, to create what he sees fit for himself. Poverty will not be kind to those who are not prepared to take control and shape the path to their destinies. Those who become the victims of poverty will fall behind and become the pawns of the bureaucrats."

Stunned by what I had said, he looked at me with some disbelief before he responded, "Mr Gordon, you are wise but your heart is cold. You have no compassion for your unfortunate brothers."

"We all have been given similar opportunities. That's what education is about. Those that you call unfortunate are the ones who did not take advantage of the opportunities offered. They made a choice and this is where their choice has taken them. I am concerned about their plight but I am more concerned about me and my family's achievements."

It was as if we came to an understanding and he continued his story. "Finally, I arrived at the family's address of my fallen comrade. It was a private home. I rang the doorbell and a plump, greying elder woman opened the door. I instantly recognised the resemblance; it was his mother, I never thought she would be there. I introduced myself and asked for his wife."

"Are you here about my son?" she asked.

"Meaning no disrespect, ma'am, I would like to speak to the wife of private Rory Jackson."

"Pauline, Pauline," she shouted, "come now, someone is here from the army to see you −" all the time looking at me with a scowl as if she already knew what I was about to say.

"He is dead, isn't he?" demanded the old lady, at the same time the young woman she had shouted for entered the foyer. "Hello, I am Sergeant Stuart,"I said, with an outstretched arm. "This is an unofficial visit. I am not representing the army."

"He is my son, so whatever you have to say to her, you will say to me. I brought him into this world. Now say what you have to say and leave."

"Give the man a chance to speak," said the young woman.

"I suddenly realized I had not prepared a statement. I reached into my pocket, pulling out the dog tags. I presented them to both women.

"The old lady instantly broke down and started to bawl saying, "My son, my son, my only child is dead, you killed him, you killed him.". The young woman wrapped her arms around the old lady to comfort her and assisted her to a chair. I tried to help, but she did not want me to touch her. I stood there not knowing what to do, but I felt I could not leave them like this. I looked at the face of the young woman, who had tears rolling down her cheeks.

"How did he die?" she asked.

"I could not bring myself to tell her the gruesome story of how I found his body hanging from a tree by a rope, lynched. That truth was too heart-breaking. To know that the ones you had entrusted your child and husband's life with had done such a despicable act would be intolerable. So I heard myself saying, "I found the remnants of a body that was blown up and with it was this tag. I knew your son and your husband. Although we were not of the same platoon, we had spoken several times. He once told me of his wife and family, including a young son. I felt it was my duty to bring this home to you all.'

"What did he look like?" asked the wife wiping tears from her face with a towel.

"There was nothing recognisable about him; he had stepped on a mine which blew him up," I said, using data compiled by multiple observations of that happening during battle.

"So, you are not sure it was him?" asked the old lady, clinging to a ray of hope.

"I did not see when it happened, but through other eyewitnesses, I am sure it was him," I said.

"They are lying, they are lying, my son is not dead," said the old lady, in denial.

"He is not dead," she said, now sobbing uncontrollably.

"I am sorry," I said. "I wish it was your son that was here now instead of me, but I cannot undo what has happened. Your son was a brave man, a courageous soldier." I brought myself to attention, saluted the family and took my leave.

"I walked along the streets of Brooklyn with the intention of going back to my hotel room and drowning myself in liquor. I was shaken, despondent at what had just happened. I found myself muttering as I walked along the streets, internally exploring the brutality this country's majority had practiced against its minority population and taken across the oceans to perpetuate on others. As a soldier, I was one of its key agents, taking its violent hate wherever it chose. I gloried in killing and I had killed hundreds of the enemy's men, women and children. Suddenly I saw some of their faces. I understood the reason for their fighting. That's when I felt someone tugging on my sleeve and heard a woman in a raised voice saying, "soldier boy, soldier boy." I snapped out of my daydream and looked at the woman. The first thing that struck me was her good looks. She was gorgeous, tall and slim with dark flawless skin and long legs, dressed in a white blowsy cotton dress and matching white sandals.

"What's the matter soldier boy?" she said, "I have been trying to get your attention for two blocks now."

"Do I know you?" I asked.

"No, you don't, but I saw you going by old Mrs Jackson's house and I wondered if it was about Rory."

"Who are you?" I asked her.

"My name is Jacqueline Blast. I have known Rory since junior high school."

"You are the other woman, aren't you, Jacqueline?" She did not respond. "Well, baby, you better start looking for another man." I walked off, but she followed.

"How did he die?" she asked.

"I already went over that with his family and they are the only one I have any obligations to tell," I said. "If you want to hear about his death, go speak with them."

"You know I can't. You already said it. I was the other woman and they hate me."

"I wonder why?" I muttered to myself.

"Please," she said, "I have waited so long to hear something and it seemed like he disappeared shortly after he went to Vietnam. I got one letter from him. He said he met a great soldier he would emulate, a man who was never injured in battle. He said this man would show him the path home."

"Who was this great warrior he spoke of?" I asked.

"A soldier by the name of Sergeant Stuart," she said in response.

"Ma'am," I said with a faint smile that disappeared as I started to speak. "Rory is never coming home again. He is dead. All the memories of him, the good and bad, the drama and laughter you shared, cherish them for that will keep him alive in your mind.' I started up the steps to the elevated train station when she let out a wail, which spun me around and next thing I knew I was holding her in my arms comforting her.

"I remember saying, "I envy Rory so much. In his short stay in this world, he impacted so many. I wish his life was spared so his loved ones could greet him with joy on his return instead of me bringing them the sad news of his demise."

"Why are you envious?" she asked, wiping the tears from her pretty face.

"Nobody came to meet me when I returned. Nobody cared if I lived or died. I am the last person he should have picked to emulate."

"She had stopped crying. I don't know how long we sat on the steps of that subway platform but I remember her saying. "You sound so lonely, so alone. Where is your family, soldier boy?"

"I have none,"I replied. "I am alone in this world."

"Where are your parents?" she asked.

"My parents are dead," I replied coldly.

"I am so sorry to hear that," she said. "How did they die?"

"I don't want to relive that," I said. "That grief has not died, it's fresh and it burns in me as if it occurred yesterday although it was more than a decade ago."

"She looked at me for a few minutes then replied, "When you are ready to let go, you will."

"I have to go now," I said.

"Why?" she asked. "Where are you going?"

"To my hotel room," I replied.

"To do what?" she asked.

"I turned and looked at her. "For a stranger, you sure ask a lot of questions?"

"I don't feel like being alone," she said.

"I am sure you must have many friends who you could be with at this moment," I said.

"I do, but I want to be with you," she said.

"Me?" I said in disbelief. "Why, are you my homecoming queen?"

"And more," she replied. "Don't you want me?"

"I looked at her now very seriously. "I wanted you from the very moment my eyes settled on you."

"I felt likewise about you, when I saw you walking to the Jacksons' residence," she said. "You looked so handsome in your uniform; I was taken by you."

"We met only a short time, yet I feel like I have known you all my life. You are bringing a certain joy to me that I have never experienced before."

"It's called love, baby," she said. "That's one of the many things your queen will present to this relationship." I stood there looking at her. I was taken aback by her use of the word relationship. I hadn't had a relationship with a woman before, much less a loving one.

"Don't be afraid," she said. "This is the beginning of something special." Inside I felt like screaming out in joy. I could not believe what I was hearing. "You are my girl. Is that what you are saying?"

"I am your woman, but I have one request."

"What is that?" I asked.

"That you treat me right, with love and respect. I require you to treat me with the appreciation of the love I will give to you."

"I will," I said, without hesitation.

"Many men have tried to get me. Many have wanted to hear me utter those words in their ears but I never felt it flowing from my heart until now."

"I gently took her in my arms and our lips met. We kissed. It was electrifying. I felt so aroused, so alive. I did not want the kiss to end and when it did, I saw that pleasing joyous smile on her face. "Wow," she said, "Soldier boy. You are a great kisser." I laughed and said, "No one ever told me that before."

"You are lying," she said, feigning disbelief.

"I am not lying about this now. That I want you," I said, with the seriousness of my thought all over my face as I looked in her eyes.

"If I was to give myself to you now, would you respect me tomorrow, or would you think of me as easy?" She asked as we now walked holding hands.

"I will always respect you," I said hoping she would change her mind but knowing she was not about to. This was going to be a chase.

"Only one man ever had me before," she said, "and it took him years before I gave my virginity to him."

"That was Rory?" I said.

"She turned her head, looked at me and nodded in agreement. "Who was the lucky lady that took yours?" she asked me. The question stopped me in my tracks. She turned and looked me in the eyes. I was thinking of a lie but she already saw through me. "I can't believe it," she said, bursting out in a laugh. "You have never done it before, I can't believe it. You are a virgin," she said again. "You mean you went off and fought a war and never had a woman before you did? Don't worry, baby. I will change that," she said after getting her fill of laughing. "I am going to allow you to love me and to make love to me, but you will still have to wait, because I am not some easy girl and I don't want to be treated like one. Remember I am your homecoming queen," she said with a smile.

"The day went by so quickly, soon it was midnight and I was kissing her goodnight. I was in love and there was no doubt about it. I had never had such a beautiful woman wanting to be with me. She had captured my heart with her sweet uncompromising personality and my soul was already longing for her presence although she had just closed the door to her home.

"As I turned to walk away, the door reopened. "Don't be discouraged," she said "when we make that physical connection, I will make every moment a memorable one." She smiled an infectious smile that had me burning up in anticipation.

"That's what you all say," I said ,now acting with displeasure.

"Look at me," she said. "Do you believe for one moment that you will not be satisfied by this?"

"You are a pleasing sight to my eyes, and my mind will never free itself of your image".

"Pray that tomorrow comes soon, my love, so that your eyes again will dwell on me as we grace each other's presence."

"Tomorrow cannot come soon enough. However, I will wait an eternity if it takes that long to be in your inner core."

"You are addressing two separate issues, my love. Tomorrow we meet to continue building our relationship. When it's time for us to make love, you will feel it like I will."

"I am feeling it now," I said.

"That is not love you are feeling," she said. "That is lust you are feeling from being in my presence, which is normal for most men," she added with an impish pout.

"Aren't you feeling it?" I asked.

"Yes," she replied, "but that is not the way I want to start our relationship."

"I walked over to the door and kissed her a final time and my wanting increased a thousand fold. As we separated, she said, 'Goodnight, my Romeo.'"

"As I walked away, looking back at her peeping out from behind the unlocked door, I said, "Goodnight, my Juliet." I had found the woman I wanted to spend the rest of my life with."

# CHAPTER 17: Reclamation of the Dark Side

Carson's adjustment to a peaceful world was slow. He needed time to cleanse himself of the effects of war and the thoughts of killing. He needed time to adjust to the serenity of peace and to think of people as friends, not enemies trying to kill him. He needed time to accept that he was no longer in Vietnam. His recovery was slow, and as night fell and sleep overcame him, his dreams took him back to the war-torn jungles of Vietnam. In those dreams, he did as he pleased to his enemies. He delighted in slaughtering them. He enjoyed torturing them and most of all he received great pleasure in watching them hang by their necks. His dreams always carried him to the Black Forest. There, he did those things with impunity. His dreams were so vivid that on awaking he had difficulty adjusting to being back home.

As word got around of his return, his friends began trekking by to see him. At first he delighted in telling them his war stories. But as the days turned into weeks and then months, he wearied of reliving Vietnam and began letting go. Many of his friends had also recently returned from 'Nam and were having problems adjusting to the peace of rural America. One warm summer's day, five of them sat in the backyard of his father's estate drinking beers by the poolside. In the gathering was Rick Cassidy, Charles Caldwell, Michael Carmichael, James Dewitt, and Carson. Six months earlier, they had all been respected, purposeful, high ranking military officers. Now they struggled to find their purpose in society.

Rick Cassidy and Charles Caldwell were graduates of the Naval Academy. They served their time in the navy on the carrier Enterprise. For three years they were stationed out at sea off the coast of Vietnam. From there they flew bombing missions deep into the interior of Vietnam. They were both Top Gun trained pilots and, like Carson, had an impressive history.

Michael Carmichael was a graduate of West Point. He was considered to be the next George S Patton. But those great blitzkrieg tactics at West Point did not fare well in the jungles of Vietnam. He didn't adjust well to the hit and run tactics of the Viet Cong's guerrilla forces. He tried an assortment of strategies to counter them, but all proved ineffective against an enemy that was as elusive as the wind. He convinced the American military to convert tracked troop carriers into machine gun carriers, which led the troops out into battle. They became the mainstay of each platoon, providing the firepower of four machine guns. Because they were halftrack vehicles, they were able to go almost anywhere, but not in the thick wooded area of the jungle. As time went on, these vehicles became armed with surface-to-surface missiles. This innovation brought him back into the good graces of the army officer corps. He received numerous accolades and was promoted to captain.

James Dewitt was a graduate of MIT and, while there he joined their Army ROTC training. After graduation, he joined the army as a first lieutenant. He spent a year in Vietnam and later continued training to become a green beret officer. On leaving the army, he joined the CIA from where he had recently retired.

Here they were, former military men sitting in a backyard trying to focus on what they saw as a bright future. They were part of America's dream.

It was Michael who posed the question. "Now that we are finished with our military careers, what are we going to do next?"

Rick, who was always sure of his destiny, replied first. "I'll start working at my father's company. Someday it will be mine and I must know it inside out so I can take it where I want it to go."

"I will be his right-hand man, as always," said Charles Caldwell. They had been friends since nursery school and were seldom without each other. They had both joined the naval academy together and were stationed on the same carrier. As a pilot, Charles was Rick's wingman.

"I hope you both don't fall in love with the same chick," said Chris.

"If they did, you know Charles would differ from Rick," said James. "He can't think for himself and wouldn't know what to say or do if Rick doesn't tell him." This brought a round of spontaneous laughter as they knew that the relationship between the two was built around honor, respect and their competitive spirits.

"What about you Chris? We all want to know what you plan on doing with yourself?"

"He is going to run his father's company like you are planning to do," said James, "except he will not run his father's company into the ground by buying expensive sports cars and supporting fast bitches like you will, you corrupt son of a bitch."

"James," replied Rick. "Have you ever considered filtering some of your thoughts before opening that mouth of yours and letting your waste out?"

"I call as I see it, man," said James with a deadpan expression. "What's the matter? Nobody interested in what I'm doing with the rest of my life?"

"Not really," replied Rick. "You're not really part of this group like we are. We have known each other since kindergarten. Our families lived in these towns for centuries, generation after generation. We plan on keeping it that way. Maybe in three more generations, if your family is still around, we will consider them as a member of the community."

James got to his feet, put up his middle finger and left.

"What are your plans, Chris?" asked Charles.

"Politics, man. I'm going to run for Congress to represent this district. Dad is the senior state senator and I intend to follow in his footsteps. One day I will be president, or die trying."

"Why don't you create your own path instead of following your father's?" asked Charles.

"My father's footsteps are those of a distinguished and honorable man. He did nothing to be ashamed of. He is a senator as well as an accomplished businessman. Those are footsteps any man would be proud to follow."

At the same time, another young man arrived. He was warmly received but his harried disposition betrayed the trouble that he carried.

"Rob, what's got your feathers ruffled?" demanded Rick.

"Those damn niggers in town, especially those returning from 'Nam. They're trying to change everything in the community. Demanding jobs, better pay, and talking about voting a nigger into Congress. Soon they will be demanding to run the country!"

"Not if I can help it!" said a startled Carson. "That congressional seat is mine and no nigger is going to get it while I'm alive. This is God's country, a white man's country, and it will remain that way."

"Well, you go tell 'em and kick their asses in the process 'cos that's what they did to me and a few of the boys over there at Lex's tavern."

"A bunch of niggers beat you boys up and got away with it?" queried Carson. "I long for the old days when we rode with hoods, guns, ropes and flames. We kept them in place then. How do we do that now?"

"They're talking about running one of their own for the congressional seat because they have the number to win this district and get some niggers in power."

"They are the majority now in this community and may be able to pull it off."

"That's my seat," replied Carson, "and it will take me to the White House. No nigger is getting in the way of my dreams."

"What can we do?" asked Rick. "They have the majority population in the community."

"We can use the same old methods to stop them. They worked before – why wouldn't they work now?" asked Carson.

"Times have changed," said Rick, "and even the old methods would need new approaches. We could do it like a well-organised military strike. Using stealth and secrecy," said Michael.

"I want them hanging from the nooses of ropes," said an angered Carson.

"So be it," said Rick as Charles nodded in agreement.

"Do you have any names?" asked Michael.

Rob gave five names to the group with their addresses and other information. Carson took leadership of the group as he was the most familiar with Klan activities. It gave him great satisfaction. The body of James Dewitt was found on a farm of a reclusive Vietnam Vet by the name of John Lincoln. He was a black man who had returned from Vietnam after serving two terms in the rice paddies. He had killed many men there but now he was racked with destabilizing nightmares from post-traumatic stress disorder. Once in town he lost awareness and his subconscious took control, back to the battlefields. You could hear him shouting, screaming, making inappropriate noises and acting as if he was in the middle of a battle killing enemies. The town's people quickly ran out of his way in fear, seeking cover as they watched the crazy man perform his violent antics. Eventually he was subdued by the police, handcuffed and taken to jail. He was seen by a psychiatrist who diagnosed him with PTSD and after therapy he was released. Now his life was about to dramatically change for the worse, as Carson plotted to make him the fall guy in his plan to destroy the town's black community.

Dewitt had been reported missing by his family for several days and as the community came together in search of him, they found his battered, decomposing body on Lincoln's farm. Word got to Lincoln that the body was found on his farm and as police vehicles with blaring sirens sped to his house, he armed himself and made a run for the mountains overlooking his property. To the police this was a sure sign of guilt. They went into the mountains in search for him and in a terrific gun battle, fatally shot him after he killed many of their officers. His body was brought back to town and he was pronounced guilty of killing James Dewitt. The event triggered anti-black sentiments in the town as Carson had wanted. Organised strategically by Carson, a series of fights broke out in which white town folks were beaten up by black mobs. He used this to his advantage and started a law and order campaign, saying he would bring order back to the community if elected to Congress. The white town folks bought into it while the blacks organised around their leader. He was one of the five men on Carson's list.

Henry Morton was a graduate of Howard University with a degree in community affairs. He was among the top of his graduating class. While working within his community, he discovered the need to be aware of politicians and their influence, so went back to school and studied political science. The community became aware of the many things he was doing to improve their standard of living and asked him to represent them in Congress. Unlike Carson, his work knew no racial boundaries and benefited all within the community.

Henry Morton had taken prescribed medications to the home of the Eversons, a white family in the community with three teen daughters. Not knowing they were collaborating with Carson's political machine, he unwittingly sought their support. When the sickly grand matriarch needed medications, he offered to get them for her from the pharmacy and delivered them to the house. The next day one of their teen daughters made the most damning accusation a white woman could make against a black man in the South. She accused him of rape. Before he could deny it, the white community was up in arms. His picture was on the front page of their newspaper with a headline that read; "Negro community activist raped white woman." That night, after his white attorney left his home, the white knights donned their white robes and cone shaped headgear. It was late at night when they arrived, surrounded his house and burnt it to the ground. There were no survivors. The entire Morton family was erased. Carson went on to represent the district in congress.

A few days afterwards, while celebrating his victory as a new congressional representative with some of his close friends, his most inner circle, one of them asked. "Chris, I know you are planning to eventually run for the presidency. What will you do if you were to run and win?"

"First, I would give you an important cabinet position and second, I would enact the King Alfred Plan."

"What's the King Alfred Plan?"

"You never heard of the King Alfred Plan?"

"No," they all replied in unison, "what is it?"

"The King Alfred Plan was put together by the FBI under J Hoover and the CIA to exterminate the black race if they are involved in uncontrolled civil disruption nationally or if there is a race war. It can only be ordered into effect by the President."

"Are you kidding, how did you come to know of such a plan?"

"Remember I work for the CIA and I was privy to a lot of classified information. There are many like us who want niggers out of our country and are willing to support our hidden agenda."

"How would they do it?"

"How did Hitler exterminate millions of European Jews? Trust me – there is a plan."

"Chris for President," chirped one of the members of his inner circle after a brief pause.

"Chris for President," they all shouted in unison as they raised their champagne glasses in endorsement of his hidden agenda.

# CHAPTER 18: For Your Love,  I Became a Man

"After I met Jacqueline, the hours in a day were not sufficient to be in her company, and at nights when we were not together I found myself thinking of her. She brought direction and stability to my life. Each day when we met after work we spoke of being together but she made me aware of what together meant. It was her or the bottle and she won. I have not drunk any liquor since. The therapeutic effect of love quickly carried my mind from the post-traumatic effects of Vietnam to the sweet seductiveness of its embrace. Each day we met my love for Jacqueline grew and increased the distance from my past. I cherished the love she gave; it healed my soul and nurtured my spirit; I discovered what I had longed for and needed. I appreciated the happiness she brought into my life as I was ready to receive it. I honored the moments we were together for I valued them and would not do anything to violate our unspoken sacred pact. I knew she was my woman and I was her man.

"It was a cold winter's night in the first year of our courtship. We lay on the bed together; she was still fully clothed after arriving home from work. We laughed and talked of the events that occurred in our lives that day, but most of all I longed for her. As we began kissing, she gently pushed me away.

"No," she said, "no more. I cannot continue like this. Each night you leave me in torment. It's as if you pick me up and drop me off the edge of a cliff. I will not allow it anymore."

"Then let me make love to you," I replied.

"Do you truly love me?"

"With my all heart yes, I do, from my soul I do and through my spirit I do."

"If you love me so much then what are waiting for? There is no such thing as the right time, honey – you cannot build me a castle and then take me there. The object of love and relationship is that we build it together, we struggle together and accomplish together. We become a unit as one."

"Jacqueline, I want to make you my wife."

"Then make me your wife but understand this. You will not get there until you have placed a ring here," she said, finally pointing to her ring finger.

"You gave yourself to Rory Jackson, didn't you, and he was married to someone else."

"That relationship was different. I wanted to give him something special, something he never had before, and I gave him myself. He was going off to war, to fight. He never returned. He died serving his country. It is the ultimate sacrifice a man can make. I gave the ultimate gift a woman can give. I have no regrets for what I did."

"Did you love him?" I asked her.

"Yes, I did," she replied.

"Why didn't you marry him?" I asked her.

"The question is why didn't he marry me?"

"Do you know the answer to that?" I queried.

"Yes," she replied

"What is it?" I asked.

"I was too black," she replied.

"What?" I uttered.

"Yes, the colour of my skin was a problem with his family. They thought I was too dark. They never considered the content of my character," she said looking deeply into my eyes as if searching for a sign.

"Tomorrow I will make you my wife," I said to her.

"Making me promises again."

"No," I replied. "Tomorrow you will not go to work. Call your girlfriend Sheena and I will call Cayan. Tomorrow we will meet, go to city hall and you will become Mrs. Stuart". I plucked the encased diamond rings out of my pocket and revealed them to her. She screamed in delight as she held them, stared at it and hugged them to her bosom. It was a dream that came true. I looked at the happiness from this one act I had perpetuated and now I fully understood the true meaning of love.

"When did you buy these?'"she asked.

"Yesterday,"I replied. "Do you remember?  These were the ones you said you liked the most when we went shopping," I said, as she placed the engagement ring on her ring finger. It was a perfect fit.

"Of course, I remember," she said in delight. "But it was so expensive."

"That's why it took me so long," I said. "Try on the wedding band."

"No, no," she replied with an engaging smile. "You put it on my finger."

"I took the box and removed the ring. I felt it as I gripped it between my fingertips and knelt to the floor on my left knee. I took her left hand in my left hand and gently placed the ring on her ring finger. It also was a perfect fit. We stayed in that position for minutes admiring the reflection from the diamonds and she hugged me as I said to her, "I love you, Jacqueline Blast, and tomorrow I will make you my wife. I will cherish you," I said as I kissed her longingly on her face. "I will honor you." I said as our lips gently met and her hands hugged me behind my head. "I will provide for you and make you a proud mother of our children," I said as my lips brushed along the length of her neck. It aroused her and I felt a tremor going through her body. The next day I did as I said I would and Jacqueline Blast became Mrs Stuart.

"We could not afford to go away to any fancy hotel or resort. So, we went home. That night I became a man and soon after Jackie became pregnant with our first child. It soon became apparent that where we lived was not large enough for a growing family. I worked in a supermarket while Jackie worked in the nearby post office. With our combined income, we lived quite well. But that too was about to change if I did not do something about it.

"On one of my days off from work I went to meet Jackie after her work day was over. While waiting, I noticed several pictures of men wanted by the law posted on a bulletin board. They had all committed serious crimes and were now fugitives with a price on their heads. The posters said they were extremely violent men and were wanted dead or alive. One of them drew my attention. It said he was a Vietnam vet, who had killed his neighbors while hallucinating on drugs. When everything was over he realized what he had done and went on the run. There was a reward of 10,000 dollars for his capture. I remembered how I had tracked Red Dong in Vietnam and I knew I could do this. The money was an additional incentive, as it would take more than a year for me to make 10,000 dollars at the supermarket. I ripped the poster off the wall, folded it and placed it in my shirt pocket above my heart as the woman of my heart arrived. She had apparently seen me putting the paper in my pocket.

"What is that?" she asked, her warm smile still enveloping her face, yet fading. It was not time to tell her my new objective because I had not thought it through yet. Before I answered I hugged and kissed her.

"You never ask me what I did in Vietnam," I replied as we walked, holding each others' hands.

"What did you do in Vietnam?" she asked.

"Basically, I hunted men down and killed them. I was very good at it," I replied. She let go of my hand and stopped walking. "That is what war is about and I have a bag full of medals home which confirms my abilities."

"Is that something to be proud of?"

"My country which trained me to be a warrior strongly believes so," I retorted.

"I am your wife and I believe that poster of that man you took off the wall will take you to the Americanization of Vietnam. You will bring it home and continue that war here on American soil. So, let it go. Let that man go. Let someone else hunt him down and bring him to justice. Let the police do their job." I looked at her and agreed, but there was a driving force within my soul telling me this is what I had to do. It was to be my destiny. We walked on in silence with my quietness betraying the disingenuousness of my agreement. She knew and felt it.

"How would you go about capturing that man?" she asked.

"I don't know yet," I replied. "I would need to get lots of information on him."

"Information like what?" she asked.

"Like who is he? Is he a member of a gang? Does he have a routine? Where does he live?"

"He is a dangerous career criminal. Since he returned from Vietnam, he's been robbing people at gunpoint in the community and it's strongly believed that was not his first killing. That was his first killing of a white man and woman. They were a Jewish couple who owned a store on Broadway. It's believed that he went in the store, stuck them up and demanded their money. He taped them up and after he got their money, shot them in the head. He was seen by many leaving the place.'

"Why?" I heard myself asking.

"He has a drug habit he has to support. It drives him to do unreasonable things," she said.

"How do you know so much about him?" I asked her.

"He is my brother," she replied. It was then I noticed the tears in her eyes. "We have the same father but our mothers are different. He never lived with us. In fact, he grew up in foster homes," she said, now sobbing. "The drugs have got a hold of him, and he has no self-control anymore. He feeds his addiction – that's the reason he does bad things. I was told that one day he visited his mom and demanded money. When she told him she had none, he almost beat her to death. He is no longer human. If that is what you decide to do, this is where he lives – and like you, he has a bag full of medals for killing enemy soldiers in Vietnam.'

"I was stunned by this information, as she handed me a piece of paper with his address and I wondered then what I should do next. I took the paper and placed it in my pocket. With that, I had made a life changing decision. There were times I regretted making that decision, for if I had not done so, we would still be together, my sweet Jacqueline and I. No need to say – I went on and captured her brother and the money became an incentive to continue along that path. It became a way of life until it led me to my true purpose in life."

"Which was or is?"

"In time, all your questions will be answered, Mr Gordon. Be patient and listen," he replied with a warm reassuring smile.

# CHAPTER 19: Ways of the Street

He was a tall, big individual with a nasty disposition. He had arrived on the unit a few days before and his presence was generating an uneasy affect of anxiety and fear among the clients and staff. He did not say anything threatening, nor did he do anything violent. But through his intimidating presence personified by his youth, height, muscular build and blackness, he generated an undercurrent of fear. He was so big and so strong that the staff feared one day he would become agitated and lose it. I saw him as being much more cerebral than they were giving him credit for. There were rumours of him being acutely ill in the Psych Emergency room, where it took six staff and five security officers to subdue him. They gave him a cocktail of Ativan 2mg, Haldol 5milligram and Benadryl 50 milligrams IM. Instead of calming him, his agitation went to a higher level. He was restrained on the stretcher, tied down by all extremities. He was so tall that his legs extended several inches beyond the foot of the stretcher. Then a staff member found him standing with the stretcher attached to his back. She approached him and he swung the stretcher, knocking her off her feet. She screamed, bringing other staff to her aid only to be met by the behemoth. He had all intentions of hurting the staff. After he was finally subdued, it was documented that three staff and two security guards were injured. Now he prowled our unit, with a very deep scowl to his youthful face, telling a few of his peers of his days as a drug dealer on the mean streets of Harlem and what he did to those who owed him money.

I found him to be an eloquent, intelligent, young man, searching to find his identity. With conviction, he had bought into what his community had endorsed as their leading role model. Although he had used drugs, he had decided that he was not going to be a junkie. He had dropped out of school some time in his sophomore year, which now limited his growth potential, but he was determined to make it as a gangster. He said he drove a Cadillac, which was a sign of prestige for him. He said all the boys around his way either admired or envied him but he knew they all hated him and some day, he said, he knew one would be brave enough to end his reign and start their own. "That is the nature of the game. There are no survivors. It chews you up and then devours you. All the young girls try to run some silly game on you but you drug them up and soon they are willing to do anything for the high," he said laughing.

"You have no qualms with that?" I asked.

"Qualms!" he exclaimed. "Man, I am providing a service. If I don't do it, someone else will," he said, with a half-smile concealing the sneer that projected the disdain he had for me.

"But doesn't it bother you that so many lives and families are destroyed by this scourge that you are producing and selling?"

"Sure, it bothers me. I am not totally insensitive," he said, "but you know what, it's only the weak that are being affected by this product. They would have been done in by something else if drugs weren't available."

"There are a lot of weak people in our communities then," I said, "and you and your type take pride in robbing them of every bit of their dignity before you dance atop their graves."

"Doc," he said, "this is survival of the fittest, the smartest, and the strongest. You, I believe are among the smartest. You would not pollute your body and soul, nor endanger your spirit with the shit I sell, would you? But there are many hopelessly lost souls who yearn to find Nirvana and their first true high gives them that feeling. The thing is – once they have experienced it, they will never experience it again. Nor will they ever let go. But they don't know that, so they keep on trying because to them the feeling was so sweet and so mellow they are hooked from that first time and they go on trying to achieve that experience again. I know what it's doing to them, but I will never stop them because while they are killing themselves, they are making me rich."

"Don't you feel any attachment to your community?"

"Why?" he asked.

"You are a part of a community. Instead of destroying it, you should be working to uplift it," I said.

"I want to uplift myself. Everyone is responsible for themselves. I want to be rich and I won't stop trying until the day I die," he said with the sneer again and an unmistakable look of determination.

"That's okay, but you have to find a means to achieve that without bringing despair to your community. I have never met a happy soul that uses or sells drugs."

"You don't get happiness from using drugs," he said interrupting me. "You get a euphoric sensation which can be confused with happiness; those who are smart analyse the feeling and understand that. They know the difference and what it can lead to. Then there are those who seem to pursue the sensation hoping to live it repeatedly, never letting go, and so it consumes them. They are labelled as having an addictive personality. The truth is— they have felt something they will never again feel in their lifetime and maybe even in death. Do you notice how depressed they are when they are coming of their high?" he asked, with a smile on his face.

"You have a great understanding of people's needs and wants and what motivates them to purchase this vile product you sell," I said.

"That's my job, Doc, and for me to survive I must know my clients' needs and I must meet them or they will go to someone else."

Those words I thought could be coming from any fortune 500 CEO. I looked at this young man in his early twenties and thought: here goes another brilliant mind to waste. "Have you ever been to jail?" I calmly asked.

"Never been," he replied with conviction, "and not planning on getting caught either," he said confidently.

"Well – plan on it," I said laconically.

"Why?" he asked. "Are you planning on turning me in, Doc?"

"No, but your choice of occupation will take you there for a very long time. Sooner or later that will happen, or even worse a more horrific demise by the hands of your peers. That is the nature of your field. The worst thing about it is someone else will be there to take your place and continue destroying the community for additional generations to obtain mad money in their unquenchable pursuit for the almighty dollar."

"You said it, Doc. You understand the game. This is all about the almighty dollar and nothing else. I provide a service."

Interrupting, I angrily declared, "An illegal one for which you must eventually pay the penalty."

"I have nothing else to say, Doc."

"When one set out and breaks the laws, they are usually apprehended, judged by their peers and a sentence is handed down if convicted. Some are lucky – they are not caught immediately. Like you they continue to poison the community, leaving it blighted until they are apprehended. Based on your longevity perpetuating this crime, your sentence will be tenfold. I guarantee you will be caught someday and end up spending most of your life in prison, regretting every glorified moment you excelled at being an illicit drug merchant. Then, just then, you may have the time to reflect on all the weak souls you rob of finding their inner strength and their place within the community, including yourself as you are one of those weak souls you so despise. You will have time to find your inner strengths and discover your true calling. However, it will be too late for you to pursue your purpose for living. In this transient moment of reprieve, here and now maybe, just maybe, if you ask for forgiveness, amend your ways and give your life to the Lord you will find your way before you are caught, before it's too late, so that you can go on to do what you truly were meant to be – a great leader, which is your true calling. It's your gift. Do not waste it being a drug dealer. Pursue your education and make that your goal."

He looked at me intensely, got out of the chair, opened the door and walked out into the day room. I hoped I would not lose him because I wanted him to change his ways and look in the direction of education to achieve his goals.

But I too had a reprieve in the form of a vacation.

*****

On returning from my vacation I was greeted by tearful staff bearing sad news. Ms Yoa Matoma had been discharged. The day after, she left her dorm room at New York University, travelled down to the Bowery, entered a building, and instead of taking the elevator walked up six flights of stairs, got onto the roof and jumped. They said her death was instantaneous at contact with the ground. I felt anguish for such an early death. I felt grief and loss that such a bright life shone no more. I was informed that her remains were to be transported to her homeland for burial.

As the day passed, I reflected on the many conversations I had with her. I felt a sickness in the pit of my stomach as I heard some of the staff crying over the news. She was so young with such a bright and promising future. She had it cut short by her perceptions and beliefs.

"Why are some of the nurses crying?" queried a familiar voice. I looked up to see Mr. Stuart towering above me.

"I am not at liberty to discuss that, Mr Stuart, but it's good to see you again," I said with a smile.

"It's good to have you back again, Nurse Gordon; you seem as if you enjoyed your vacation, only to return to the open arms of the grieving."

"Yes, I did, and I am wishing I was still there," I said without volunteering any other information.

"Where did you go?" he hesitantly asked.

"The Caribbean," I responded, still not wanting to give much information regarding my life.

"I have been told the countries there are most beautiful, like paradise."

I smiled on hearing this description. "One of the privileges of life is to be able to visit and interact in a friendly manner with the people of other countries," I said as he looked at me, apparently in deep thought, searching in his mind for an appropriate response.

"I don't know about that," he said. "My only encounter overseas was in the military and I saw the people of that country through the lens of my sniper's rifle. Anyway, Doc, I am told I will be discharged in two days," he informed me. I looked at him, knowing that he was ready to face the outside again.

"You are looking forward to that, I presume," I said, not giving him my undivided attention as I checked the charts of the patients I was assigned to work with for the day. As usual, he was among them.

"I wanted to finish telling you my story before I am discharged," he declared.

"Is it that important to you that I hear your life story?"

"I want you to know and understand me. I want you to know that this man had a purpose for his existence."

"Tell me the purpose."

"I could do that, but to give you only the purpose would make your judgment of it out of context. The text is my life and the deeds I indulged myself in are the events. I have sacrificed myself to make this country a better nation for all its peoples."

"How is that?" I said now perked up by his strong statement.

"Listen to my story and be the judge," he said.

"Continue with your story, Mr Stuart," I said, feeling some annoyance about having to hear him harp on about his battlefield prowess.

# CHAPTER 20: Thinking of a Family

"Love motivates you. I was motivated to be successful. I wanted to give my love Jacqueline everything in the world. I did not want her wanting for anything.  One day I met her at her job and went looking on the bulletin board again for pictures for more men wanted by the law. They all had huge bounties on their heads, which was the carrot being dangled to whoever had the balls to go out and attempt to capture them. The next day I found myself at the nearest police station, being instructed about being a bounty hunter. My first case was to apprehend a well-known east Harlem pimp known as Johnnie Lightfoot. He was the instrument of more than two women's brutal demise. Although wanted by the law, he was seen driving his white Cadillac Eldorado around town. He was arrested several times but was always found not guilty and released back into the community. It was believed he tampered with jurors by intimidation or paying them off. It was also believed he did the same with the witnesses and those he could not influence, he killed. The violent deaths of three prostitutes in a hotel room were linked to him but there were no witnesses.

When questioned by the police he denied any involvement and had a confirmed alibi. He was in jail when the murders took place, doing a short time for assaulting a woman. Now he was directly linked to the killing of two corrupt police officers. Jonathan Jefferson was his birth name: the name Lightfoot came about while playing football in high school and stuck throughout his years as a professional football player including a six-year stint in the NFL. He was a tall man, not particularly big, but very fast and strong. He played the position of safety for a major NFL team and inspired so much fear by intercepting passes that most quarterbacks threw to the opposite side of the field whenever he played. His career was cut short when he became involved in a motor vehicle accident that left three dead. Although not at fault, he was sued by the survivors and lost his fortune. After years of rehabilitation, he regained his strength and agility but not at the level to compete again in the NFL.

"One of his sordid friends enticed him into a life of crime and leisure, living off the work of women, and he grew to like it. Soon he had about a dozen women working for him and he protected them and their territory with the same zeal he used on the territory he considered his domain in the NFL. He was a vicious hitter then, and a fatal one as a pimp. It just so happened that his territory overlapped with that of two corrupt cops. As his business expanded from the streets into bars with nude dancers and brothels, the officers noted their revenue diminishing. They were about to clash. The officers gave Johnnie Lightfoot an ultimatum: either he worked for them or they would let him disappear.

"The two police officers were partners and had a history of providing protection and information for a sizable fee to major drug dealers, pimps and prostitutes who worked in their district. Any of their clients who did not come across with their fee were put out of business. In their greed, the police officers sought to continue their illegal operations beyond the boundaries of their precinct. They plundered the booty of their criminal partners and threatened them with jail time if they reported what was taking place. As time went on, most of the criminal masterminds operated their empires to gratify the grandiose dreams of the two corrupt white police officers. It was not long after that the criminals began to plot to get rid of the officers. The officers got wind of it and in a merciless coup they killed each of the crime bosses and replaced them with people they considered loyal. Some of the men were not qualified and new young bloods sprang from the streets and surpassed them.

"Johnnie Lightfoot organised a meeting of his underworld partners. Unanimously they decided to eliminate the corrupt officers. The corrupt officers became victims of a bloody, vicious death. Johnnie Lightfoot paid off a group of Jamaican gangsters to do his dirty work and they hacked the officers to death using machetes. One of them was later caught for another crime and gave up Johnnie Lightfoot for a series of murders, including the police officers, in exchange for a lighter sentence. For years the New York Police Department (NYPD) knew those officers were corrupt. They did nothing about it; they looked the other way as the officers made sure they had no rival on the streets of Harlem. The NYPD saw it as a way of controlling the street crimes. Now, after their brutal deaths, they honored the officers as if they were heroes.

"Johnnie Lightfoot was wanted dead or alive for murder with a 20,000 dollar bounty on his head. I organised a team of seven men, all former military men, all Vietnam vets. We took time to tail him as he went about his business. He had an expanding business that included drugs, gambling and prostitution, and he was attempting to come clean by buying into franchised fast food restaurants. He always had three bodyguards. All of them were proficient assassins, men who would kill without a second thought. Each had recently been discharged from the army after serving a tour of duty in Vietnam. I know the face of men who are killers. Their eyes take on a certain look. It is a look I became familiar with while fighting in the jungles of Vietnam. If you survived the jungle patrols and ambushes, you would eventually grow into that look. It was a look that said your senses were functioning at such high levels that even the ground below your feet was subconsciously checked for mines with each step without looking at it. It was a look that came about after surviving and seeing many others succumb to the ambushes, traps and mine fields that sprinkled the jungles of 'Nam. Men like those did not just depend on their vision to know of the enemy's presence. They could feel, hear and smell the enemy on the wind as it blew. These men's minds never wavered beyond the objective of their present situation while out on patrol. I remember a platoon leader, stopping his men and telling them to take cover because he smelt the enemy. A few new recruits snickered. He sent a couple of them out on point and they walked into the ambush without realizing it.

"He proved his point and that afternoon the surviving new recruits learned the need to trust their senses as they observed the remnants of their fallen comrades' bodies being sent home in body bags. They never snickered again. They had experienced the grim reality of war.

"We created a plan to surprise Lightfoot's well-organized gang. Every individual on the team knew his role and when the day came, we stuck to it. It turned into a shootout – three of Lightfoot's gunmen were killed and he was injured. We collected close to 50,000 dollars, since two of Lightfoot's men also had bounties on their heads. We each made more money that day than we had made all year working from nine to five. At that juncture, we had no doubt what we were going to do for a living from then on.

"The months went by quickly and we continued bringing in dangerous criminals. They were men who had committed serious crimes and were fugitives, eluding the law and its enforcers. We took on a case of a young man known in Queens as Jimmie Fabulous. He was also a former vet and a F4 Phantom pilot in Vietnam. After his discharge, he sought but could not get employment with any of the airlines, even thought he was a fighter ace in the skies over Vietnam. He drifted around until one day someone gave him a large sum of money to fly a plane from somewhere in Florida to a remote field in the jungles of Jamaica. There his plane was filled with bags containing ganja, as the Jamaicans call it. In a few hours, he was back in Florida. Fabulous was a great pilot in Vietnam – he shot down more than five enemy planes in dogfights. This new game gave him an adrenaline rush similar to what he was accustomed to in 'Nam. The thrill of playing cat and mouse with the DEA, CIA and other secret services that are protecting our coast from being infiltrated with drugs gave him a rush he was never able to duplicate. He had found himself, even though he was playing on the other side of the law.

"For more than two years, Fabulous made regular trips to the Caribbean and Mexico, bringing tons of marijuana to the US. Then the public was introduced to cocaine. The demand was unbelievable. Fabulous began flying to Colombia; he was a middleman, buying cocaine from the cartels selling to the street gangs who eventually sold it to the public. He became one of the links between Colombia and the United States. Flying low and at nights, he became known as the cocaine express. His people were making so much money, they lit cigars with hundred dollar bills. Guided by their greed and their lust for money, the gangs demanded more from Fabulous. Fabulous was forced to make three trips weekly to Colombia in his attempt to meet their demands. He became concerned with the DEA and other government agencies now declaring a war against drugs. But before he could do anything about his concerns, a war erupted among the gang.

Many of the main leaders were killed and the only major player left standing when the smoke cleared was Fabulous himself. He reorganized the gangs around him and became their main supplier. For years he did this, before he was finally exposed. His gang broke up after the DEA and other drug agencies hunted them down. Those that survived were incarcerated for life. A few talked. Fabulous went into hiding but he was eventually caught. In a daring plot, a member of a Colombian cartel broke him out while he was being transported to Sing-Sing with a life sentence. He made the FBI's ten most wanted list with a bounty of a million dollars on his head. That's when he became a major interest of mine. Fabulous fled to Colombia where he became a major transporter and drug runner for the Madeline Cartel. For more than two years he baffled the major drug enforcement agencies as he brought in tonnes of cocaine. As his brinkmanship increased, so did the bounty on his head, which had now reached two million dollars. For a time, it seemed that every shipment of cocaine that entered the country was said to be brought in by the new Fabulous gang now working directly with Colombia and Mexico. Then I did a raid on a gang down in Miami that changed our luck for the better. The man we were seeking went by the name of Ricardo Crespo, another elusive drug czar. He was not captured, but some of his henchmen were. As we searched their office, we found documents of the times and places Fabulous would be making his drop offs. I made copies and put the papers back where we found them. We followed the schedule and locations of the various drop offs, but they had changed their plans and rescheduled them.

"It was a hot sticky night when we made our way deep into the bushes of Alabama, filled with anticipation and trepidation, knowing this was one of Jimmie Fabulous's last scheduled drop offs, as per the schedule we had found. I had my group of bounty hunters with me: John, Steve, Robert, Roy, James and Cayan. His men were a dangerous group but were also a well-functioning unit. We made sure we arrived a day ahead of the Fabulous gang. We slowly trudged our way through the forest in the darkness to the place where the expected drop off was to take place. By early morning we found the clearing where he would be landing. While we waited, John prepared for battle by planting mines. We searched for positions that we knew gave us the advantage and took turns resting, but the bugs made it an unpleasant experience. We were well armed and took time discussing our plan to capture Jimmy Fabulous himself, but we knew this was not going to be easy. Most of the members of the Fabulous crew were well versed in combat. As daylight drew near to its end, a queasy sensation took hold of my stomach that evolved into a tight knot. I knew the coming battle would take its toll among us. As my men took up their positions, I bade them farewell. Steve was manning one of the M60s machine guns; John was armed with a reusable hand-held missile and grenade launchers. His objective was to blow up or disable the plane and other major vehicles the Fabulous gang was using. Robert was armed with his Thompson submachine gun. These men were the members of the kill zone. Cayan and I were the snipers at opposite ends of the field. Our job was to cut off the escape routes by picking off the members of the gang if they fled in our direction. On the opposite side of the kill zone, Roy and James were in hiding with another M60 and an AK47.

Our ambush was set. By 9pm it was pitch black. Not one star lit up the Alabamian night, nor did any nocturnal beast give away their presence. I knew as they observed us that they too were caught up in the anticipation of what would occur next. Suddenly the wait was over and I heard the oncoming rumble of vehicles as they made their way to the landing zone over the uneven dirt road. Their lights penetrated the dark night. The sounds of their engines invaded the quiet of the rural forest. They took up position around the airfield to guide the plane to a safe landing. I counted 21 men. There were three trucks and a car. Soon we heard a low- flying plane. The trucks began flashing their lights as a signal to the plane as it circled above. The lights stayed steady as the plane went into position to make a landing. After it landed, the pilot got out while the trucks drove in and the gang began to unload the cargo. Everything was like clockwork. The first rocket propelled grenade (RPG) struck the plane and it blew up with a tremendous boom. It lit up the forest, startling the wild life, which reacted with an alarming outcry and flight to safety as the machines guns started. The gang was caught by surprise. I didn't know how many had died in the initial explosion but I could hear the screaming of the injured. It instantly brought back memories of 'Nam. The second RPG hit the truck that was being loaded; it exploded and went up in flames. The night was momentarily consumed with the sound of gunfire. I took my time and began to pick off members of the Fabulous gang; one by one they went down. They were caught in a fierce crossfire. I heard the unmistakable sound of the M60s as they blasted holes into the bodies of the Fabulous gang who were armed with mostly M16s. They tried to make a run for it in one of the trucks, which brought about another huge explosion as it set off one of the mines John had planted. Before long it was over and the Fabulous gang was out of operation. We collected close to three million dollars in bounty for bringing these men to justice. Jimmy Fabulous was caught and incarcerated.

We divided up the bounty among ourselves. Never in my life did I imagine that I'd so much money. I went to Georgia and purchased a big brick house outside Atlanta. I paid cash for it. I came back to New York and took Jacqueline to her new home. I continued to do my bounty work. With my earnings, I bought a Cadillac for Jacqueline and a Jeep Wagoner for myself."

# CHAPTER 21: Flight from New York

"They were lots of gangs and great gang violence in the Bronx in the 1970s. These gangs ruled with an iron fist and any who dared to venture on their turf was at risk of losing their life. One Saturday morning the front page of the New York Daily News showed a black man hanging by the neck from a light pole with his hands bound behind him. It was a brutal sight and brought back memories of my father's and my uncles' demise and those I had discovered in the Black Forest of Vietnam. Someone was sending a message. They could have simply shot him but they lynched him instead. The NYPD was afraid to go into the neighborhood and investigate but a gang defector who said he was there when it occurred gave valuable information. He was granted immunity in exchange for being a key witness of the Spanish gang, as it was known: its rise to power, it actions and those it had eliminated. He told them of the gang's brutal history, led by the butcher Hector Alverez and the elusive brain, Ricardo Crespo. Most of all, he told them of the gang's various burial sites.

"Recently a group of white Columbia University students went missing after they went looking to buy drugs in the Bronx. They got lost and ended up in gang territory. They were robbed, killed and buried there. The informant gave the NYPD all the information they needed to find and retrieve their bodies.

"The following day the NYPD with a force of close to 500 men invaded the area and dug up the remains of over 20 people. Included were the remains of the four Columbia University students. Alvarez's and Crespo's names were now the two names on the FBI and NYPD most wanted listed with over 250,000 dollars attached to each of their heads. They were considered armed and dangerous. The wanted poster said they could be captured dead or alive.

"The news travelled fast and bounty hunters from all over the country began preparing. A team of five, all Vietnam vets, led by a former highly decorated army major, were the first to venture into the gang's territory. They thought they were prepared for anything but they soon discovered they were up against a disciplined, well-organized force, trained like the military. The overwhelming force quickly captured and took them as prisoners. The gang extracted information from them about their families and dispatched several assassins' teams. These teams were assigned to wipe out the families of the men and they did so with great efficiency. Because the families were in different states, the FBI became involved. The team of bounty hunters was killed and buried at a new site in the South Bronx. As word got around about what the gang had done, most of the other teams of bounty hunters who were planning on going in backed off, exactly as the gang wanted.

"I organised a team of seven members, with me as their captain. The majority had intense military training by being members of the green berets and other special forces. All but one was a veteran of the Vietnam War. The only member that was not a vet was James. He was a peace officer, a Federal Marshal. He was useful as he had access to files of the men wanted by the law. Most of these were born killers and they had honed their skills to a higher level while fighting in Vietnam. This was one of the unspoken requirements of the job. I needed men who were dangerous, as the job was dangerous. I wanted men who had faced death and survived either by their wits, skills, courage or a combination of some or all those attributes.

"The gang was wreaking havoc in New York. The Governor of the state of New York and the mayor of New York City increased the bounty on Alverez and Crespo's heads to one million dollars each. They ordered the NYPD to show a greater presence in this crime-infested neighborhood. Pairs of police were seen cruising the neighborhood patrolling, attempting to attain some control and reverse the growing crime epidemic. Even though the South Bronx was burning, people came from far to purchase their drugs there.

"I had followed with keen interest all that was going on in the Bronx. Like certain areas of Brooklyn, the population of the South Bronx was greatly addicted to heroin. Like a dark cloud, it had blighted the area. It had changed the focus of the populace that dwelled there from achieving the American dream to that of robbing and killing their neighbors for money to satisfy their addiction. Their downward spiral in human morality and behavior could mainly be attributed to their addiction that came about through the shepherding of Alverez and Crespo.

"Listen up," I said, addressing the members of the team, "we are gathered here today to make some life changing decisions. I have been pondering, wondering how to bring to justice the chiefs of the Spanish gang. The way has been finally revealed to me. There is a change that is sweeping the drug culture of this nation. The addicts are moving away from heroin to accepting cocaine as their number one drug of choice. Somewhere during this transition, we must strike. This is our window of opportunity. The first step of preparation is to move your families out of New York. Their whereabouts must become confidential information. Do not share that information with anyone you are working with.'

"Why are we doing this?" asked Cayan.

"To prevent a reoccurrence of what happened to that bounty team happening to us and our families if we are captured. You know what happened to them," I replied.

"We know what happened to them, but that will never happen to us as we never underestimate our quarry," said Mack.

"They outnumber us almost 300:1. If we were to go in like some of the other groups have, what will prevent us from ending up like them?" There was a moment of silence as they mulled this thought over in their minds. Cayan broke the silence with a question.

"Why do this when you have the answer to capturing the chiefs of the gang?"

"You make this sound like a God thing," said Robert.

"I am a believer, a man of faith. I strongly believe our success so far has been because of his anointing," I replied.

"You really do not have a plan?" questioned John.

"Yes I do. This is the first step in the plan, and we meet here again in one week at the same time to discuss the other steps," I replied.

"The plan is to hide our families from the Spanish gang. I thought we were gathering here to go and capture them," said Mack.

"In one week, we will speak of their capture."

"We will have lost time and maybe whatever element of surprise we may have."

"There are no elements of surprise, with this gang especially if we have to go to them. Mack, they are prepared and waiting for anyone who wants to take them down, especially on their turf. We will not attempt to go head to head with them. We must plan and prepare to take them on our terms. There is a reason why over five million dollars are on their heads, and it is not because they are choirboys. Before we proceed, we will have to take all precautions to protect what is dearest to us and that's our families. We have seen how they retaliated. Our wives and children must not become victims of our work. If they know of anyone related to us, that person will be endangered. I am sure they will not stop until they have gotten us all. Therefore, we must prevent any retaliation from happening. If any of us are captured, we must take our own life rather than fall into their hands. It is a fact that they will kill you after they have interrogated you and gotten all the information they need to strike back at anyone affiliated with you."

"We finally adjourned and went our ways to do what was best for our families. I had been thinking of this move for months since the gang had hanged the black man from the light pole. That week, Jacqueline went back to Georgia, after visiting her family in New York. We did not return to our home as I thought the gang could find that information. We looked around and rented a house in a rural area outside of Atlanta; it was to be our safe house. Jacqueline had already packed our belongings and was ready to move when I arrived home.

"You believe this upheaval of our family from New York and Atlanta to the Georgia woods will keep us safe from your gang?"

"That's the idea," I replied. "After they are captured, you will be able to set up your beauty parlor and get your business going again."

"Or I may go back and work for the post office like I did before we met," she concluded. "But what about you – how safe will you be. I heard about the Spanish gang on the news and I have read about them in the papers. What they did to those men's families was inhumane. I don't want you going after them," she said, as we drove along the Expressway heading to Georgia.

"I explained I loved her and she meant everything but it was my purpose to rid the world of people like this. This job had chosen me. She went along with it because she loved me.

"The week went by and I returned a day earlier to prepare for the meeting with the team. The doorbell rang. I was expecting someone that would reveal information that would make the capture of the Spanish gang an easy task. I approached the door with my semi-automatic Colt 45 in my hand. I peeped out the peephole and saw the stranger.

"Who are you?" I asked.

"I am a friend," said the stranger.

"I don't know you – what do you want?" I asked.

"We need to talk," he replied.

"Talk about what?" I asked.

"The gang," he replied. It was the person whom I was expecting. I opened the door and beckoned him in.

"Show me some ID," I demanded. His ID indicated that he was Mossad, Israeli secret police.

"What do you want with me?"

"I am going to do you a favor. In exchange, you will do me one."

"And if I refuse?"

"We all have the right to our choices. You can refuse," he said laconically.

"What can you do for me?"

"We can give you Alverez and Crespo," he replied.

"How is that?" I asked.

'We will get to the details later," he said, with the assurance of someone who meant what he said.

"What do you want me to do?"

"Two Jewish boys were killed in the South recently in your Civil Rights War. One of them was one of our people, so we need you to investigate," he replied.

"Who killed them?"

"I am sure it was the Klan," he replied.

"Why can't you do your own investigation?"

"We do not have the personnel to do that."

"Why don't you go to the FBI?"

"We are not supposed to be here," he replied.

"Why me?"

He paused for a moment before he answered.

"In a sense this Civil Rights war your people are fighting is our war also. We are looking at areas in the United States to settle in large numbers and develop our communities and our businesses. But our people are hated by the Southerners as much as yours are, although for various reasons. That is why we are supportive of your war against hate. We march with your leaders in their battles, in their struggle to make this experiment a righteous one. We are willing to die to change this system to make it inclusive of all. Your people are willing to die to have their rights as Americans and, when they win, all Americans win, including my people. So far, they have won the battles in the American cities and have gotten a bill to guarantee their rights to vote but a battle is still being waged in some rural areas of the South. The Klan still marches and is stronger than ever. They have not been defeated and will not be defeated until they are dead", he said.

"What has that demagogy got to do with Alvarez and Crespo?"

'You will see. You are about to have a life changing experience. I just hope you can cope. It will not always be satisfying. You will experience both sides of the coin," he said.

"Why should I do that to myself?" I asked.

"Mr. Stuart," he replied, "you can be a man and live a life that men will forever respect, or you can be like Tom, Dick or Harry. No one will ever know of or care about your existence."

"What's the problem with a man who chooses to be inconspicuous?" I asked.

"You did not become one of the best in your field by being inconspicuous. You did it by creating and executing your plans with a belief that you are right and you will succeed. You wanted to make a difference, and so you did. You have apprehended some of the most vicious and dangerous criminals who have walked the face of the earth. I want you and your team to train with us for a short time and we will hand you Alvarez and Crespo. It is a part of the plan."

"Are you saying we will not have to work in their capture?"

"No," he replied. "Alvarez and Crespo are buying cocaine from Colombia. We are their connections. In a few days, we are to meet for a major buy. That is when you will intervene."

"That is going to be violent. They will be at their highest alert," I replied.

"There is never an easy way to capture a gang who has made it to the top of the chain without some violence. But in this case, it will be easy, especially when you begin to train with us. We have a bunker with one way in plus an escape route. We will use that escape route once we have them all inside. They will be locked in; we will rig the place with teargas and explosives. Once they are inside, you will remotely set off the explosives and tear gas. As they lay there injured, we will stop air from entering the room and in a few minutes, they all will be dead."

"Why the tear gases – why don't you go directly to stopping the air flow?" I inquired.

"A group such as this gang should be given the opportunity to see and experience the terror they inflict on others before they die. We call it retribution", he replied.

In a meeting the next day, I informed my team of our new allegiance. Some questioned it, while others accepted it. But what they objected to was what we had to do in return.

"We have given up our independence – our right to choose," Cayan said when he heard. Two weeks after that, we captured the Spanish gang chief, Alvarez, and other important members of his gang, just as the Mossad agent had planned. However, one major gang member was not present – the elusive Ricardo Crespo. We made over three million dollars in bounty. We dreaded the thought but it was our time to reciprocate".

# CHAPTER 22: The Making of Senator Carson

Four tumultuous years had passed and Carson had served two successful terms as a congressman. He had penned and voted for bills that had enriched his state and eventually the district he represented in Congress. As a junior congressman, he was well thought of in both houses. His father's stellar performance as a senator representing his state for five terms had paved the way for him. The familiar name of Carson allowed many doors to open to the junior congressman that would not have been available to most unknown freshman congressmen. Many in both houses knew of his father's views on race relations and many shared those views. When young Carson arrived in Congress, he was well received and found his way to the racist old boy network. He became part of the status quo.

It was about a year into his second term when he got word that the senior senator representing his state would not be seeking another term due to his poor health. Carson immediately decided that it was going to be his seat and he started preparing to run as a candidate to represent his state in the senate. He gathered his people and created a plan based on what he and his consultants figured would get him elected. His first idea was built around getting higher paying jobs into his state and making higher education more affordable. He had extreme thoughts and ideas, not to mention things he wanted to keep in the closet. But the people who came to hear him speak demanded he speak out his extreme views so they knew he would represent their thinking. His conservative Republican opponent was expressing his right-wing ideology and, the more he did, the larger the crowds turned out at his rallies. It became clear to Carson that in order for him to win, he had to express his views and not appear as what he wasn't.

His consultants guided him to change his platform to that of intolerance for anyone who was not white. With all the racist ugliness he could muster, he sanctioned crimes against blacks and total discrimination.

One of his advisors pulled him aside after a shockingly vitriolic speech of racist intolerance and hatred.

"Mr Carson, I would advise you not to be so open with your views. You are intentionally alienating the black votes and they are not as impoverished nor as weak as you may believe. The seat you held as a congressman will be won by a black Democratic candidate. Three other seats held by white candidates, two Republican and a Democrat, are going to be won by black candidates. They are currently ahead in the polls and their district has a majority black population with a majority black number of registered voters. If you are to appropriately represent your state in some way, you must show you are willing to work with these people."

"Mr Bujurand, I will have no need to be working with them niggers. They, on the other hand, will have a need to be working with me, and they will always find my door closed to them."

"I fail to see how that will benefit the people of Alabama. What kind of supreme representation will that be Mr Carson? You are allowing your racist emotions to be your guide and not your intelligence. I cannot fathom the hate you have for those people simply because of the color of their skin. They are no different than you and I. The reason for their impoverished state is because they have been denied access to the path of prosperity, education and justice. We white Americans cannot continue to live that way; we must treat all Americans equally. If we don't, the rest of the world will pass us by while we expend our energies in trying to repress the growth of people who are different from us."

"Mr Bujurand, it appears that you are not seeing the surge of people coming to our rallies since I began verbalising intolerance as my central theme."

"I have noticed the difference, Mr Carson, but I believe you need to widen your base."

"No. What I need to do is to have more people with that type of thinking as my supporters. I want more white supremacist flocking to my rallies. Therefore I need to increase advertisement directed at them. They will provide me that victory I want. If you are not here to support my cause, then leave. If you choose to remain a member of my consulting team, then advise me how to let my words reach more people who will support me in the primaries and the election."

"I cannot advise you when you have chosen to have that as your theme. You see – I am not pure white. My extended family has black folks in it also. I cannot speak of hating them, and then at the next family reunion, look them in the eye. I am not a hypocrite, Mr Carson. Here is my resignation. Remember this: America is changing, the world is changing and somewhere along the line, if we do not learn to be tolerant of others, others will learn not to be tolerant of us."

"We are Americans and the world has more need to be tolerant of us than we of them. They all are trying to come to America. They're all seeking to become residents and citizens of our country."

"That too will change, Mr Carson – maybe not in our life time, but that too will change." He prepared to exit Carson's office for the last time.

"We have enemies, Mr Bujurand, and no one knows how to destroy the enemies more so than we do – and that we start learning and practicing at home. That is the American way and we are Americans –we make no bones about it," said Carson with a smile on his face.

"As your political career grows, I have reasons to be afraid. Your progression does not bode well for Americans who are different to you. It does not bode well with people around the world who are different to us. It does not bode well with most Americans, as your views will cause much turbulence and strife. Your policies will have men thinking and feeling they are better than their brothers. Mr Carson, your ambitions scare me. I believe you and your supreme men will follow the path of another who believed and practiced white supremacy. We know him as Hitler."

In the days that followed, the crowds increased in numbers at Carson's rallies as he spoke at the different community centres, attracting thousands who hung on every racist word he uttered. His supporters came dressed in their Klan outfits and the media initially did not challenge him or them. Even though they noticed the growing numbers of Klan members and other white supremacist groups coming to his rallies, they failed to challenge him and scrutinize his message. The major media networks passively made people aware of it, but their analysis was minimal and ineffective. For them, this was only a senatorial race in one of the poorest rural states of the union. The media's lack of coverage allowed Carson and his opponents the ability to reach back in time, bring thoughts from a pre-civil war era and express them as what he would implement as policy as a state senator. Without the media there to scrutinize and publicize his words, the candidates pandered to their racist supporters. The media's superficial coverage failed to discover the violence and hate that was taking place behind the scenes deep in rural Alabama.

# CHAPTER 23: Acceptance of my Purpose

"The Mossad agent stood by a VCR and pressed its play button. "I want you to see something, and when you are finished you will wonder if this is your America. These are not actors; these are recent happenings in the South. It troubles me to see this occurring in this country, but it is the plight of your people's continuous persecution. I am showing you this, hoping you will do something about it."

"What was being shown on the VCR?" I questioned Mr Stuart.

"I watched as the VCR played out this gruesome story of a rural family found hanging by their necks. The family consisted of husband and wife and their three sons ranging in age of 14 to 18 years of age. There was a burnt cross nearby."

"Life has a way of pulling you back into what you were really meant to do, doesn't it Mr. Stuart? I remember your noble reason for setting Red Dong free, but the money from bounty hunting had you sidetracked from your stated purpose in life."

"No, Nurse Gordon. It was preparing me."

"Go on with your story, Mr Stuart," I said.

"The Mossad agent continued: "No one has been questioned by the law. No one has been brought in by the local sheriffs as suspects to this evil crime. The state has turned a blind eye and the FBI is not investigating. The Klan is known to have a large contingent in the county yet none of its members were considered as suspects. The family was buried but no one in law enforcement is seeking answers or trying to resolve this heinous crime. About two months afterwards, a body was found hanging by the neck from in another county. This young black man was reported as a missing person for about five days before his body was found. Again a cross was found at the site. Turns out the black communities which had suffered for centuries at the hands of the Klan are now living in fear, wondering if the Civil Rights battles they had fought, that eventually took Martin's life, were worth it.  It appears that things remain the same and possibly have gotten worse with these Klan hangings. For two years, there has not been any recurrence in Alabama. However, in Texas and Georgia there were a total of seven such hangings, which finally brought forth the involvement of the FBI. Recently the hangings of three Jews in rural Alabama has shocked the Jewish community. One was the son of a wealthy Jewish family who immediately posted a 100,000 dollar reward for information leading to the capture of their son's killer. That's why we got involved. We protect Jews everywhere in the world – even here in America. We were able to gather information and discover the atrocities going on in the South – however, we were not able to find any of the individuals who carried out the hangings of the Jewish boys or the black families,' said the Mossad agent. 'We need your assistance. I want you to meet John Greenberg, whose son was hanged, and has posted a reward of 100,000 dollars. I would like you to take this case. I will provide you with whatever you need to help you resolve it.'

"We are not a detective agency," replied Cayan. "We are bounty hunters. We bring in men who have been convicted by the law for crimes they have committed."

'I know no one has been convicted of any crimes. But heinous crimes have been committed, crimes against humanity, crimes against your people, merely because of the color of their skins. No one has been convicted. No one will be convicted because even the DOJ is complicit, but you know and I know crimes have been committed," answered the Mossad agent.

"I knew he was right, for even to that day no one was brought up on charges for the brutal hanging of my father and his brothers. I met the family of the deceased Jewish boy who had offered the reward. They questioned me, wanting to know more about me and my work as a bounty hunter. I informed them of my intentions, but they wanted the proper authorities, meaning the police, to be the ones to resolve the case. The Mossad agent informed them that was unlikely and that members of law enforcement were also members of the Klan. They grew to accept me as their next best bet and said they would pay the reward if my investigation led to justice. Me and my men were paid a stipend. I gathered my group together and we made plans to resolve the hanging of the Jewish boy. It was sad that it took the death of Jews for some action to be taken. Blacks were being lynched all over the country and no one batted an eye. Not having the money or influence, only blacks cared whether we as a race lived or died. My unit came together and vowed to protect each other. The media, which had dehumanized us as a race of criminals, saw no need to cover our story, so nothing was said of the hangings of our people on the news. I concluded we were treated as disposable; America saw no value to us here and in the world. That was when I saw our need to create value, to create wealth so that we could have the power to be noticed. We needed to reach the point where we were seen and heard without uttering a word, where our needs were met without us having to state them. We had to become so valued that the world would fail to exist without us. We would not travel the road to extinction nor forever dwell in poverty. I accepted the case as I valued myself and my people as we journeyed to the point of being indispensable.

"Seven of us set out in two Jeep Wagoneers the next day for Alabama, to investigate the site of the Jewish boys' hangings. About seven hours after leaving Atlanta, we arrived at the nearest town on the map to the site. It was a main street town with a little nondescript motel on the outskirts. We got rooms there and decided that this was going to be the headquarters of our operations. The clerk and manager was an older black man with tufts of grey hair where a beard should have been. He had suspenders holding up his pants as his big pot belly distended above the waist. It was a hot sweltering day and he had a wide oscillating fan blowing the stifling air around. It did not take much to get him talking about the hangings. He even drew us a map of the location of each of the hangings of the Jewish boys and gave us directions to get there. He warned us not to be caught anywhere near the town after dark.

"Why?" I asked.

"That's the reason those boys were killed. They were in the wrong place at the wrong time," he retorted.

"Who do you believed killed those boys?" I asked.

"Only one set of people kills like that," he said with anger contorting his fat greasy face. "The Klan," he finally said. I felt his anger and his pain. I felt his hopelessness and despair all in that one answer.

"What makes you think that they did it?"

"Mister," he said, "them there people want the South back the way it was. They don't want us making any progress and this is their way of controlling us, with fear. They hanged a prosperous black family recently, burnt down their mansion too. Those people were business owners all over the South, and the law never responded. By hanging that wealthy family, the Klan sent us a message. They told us no matter how large we get, they are still in charge down here."

"Do you honestly believe that?"' I asked. "Or was it that they feared they were losing their supremacy, knowing if the masses saw a wealthy self-made black man, other blacks would be influenced to become like him?"

"Mister, I have lived here in the South all my life. I had hopes and dreams when I walked with Martin. I prayed for better days, but when they killed him, my dreams permanently stopped in their tracks and my motivation ceased. I had intentions of owning a slew of these motels all over the country. When he died, I already owned this and this has been the only one I owned since."

"You should not have allowed your dreams to die with Martin, my friend. You have made him die in vain. Remember he said he would lead us to the promise land, but he would not make it there with us. If you gave up, brother, that has nothing to do with Martin – it's your lack of confidence and courage. Prosperity does not come easy. It takes a lot of work, a lot of sacrifice and good money management. All the marching and protesting Martin did was in vain – you failed him and you dishonored him by giving up. You should have made your dream of prosperity a reality for you and your family. In so doing, you would have fulfilled your purpose and honored Martin."

"He looked at me with astonishment and said: "Mister, you are right – but how can I do that with those people lynching and terrorizing us daily?'

"You must stand up to the cause of your fear. Don't allow it to defeat you and leave you in a state of mental paralysis. You must search for your answers and weigh the possibilities of their outcomes and then act on them," I said. "To overcome fear, you must not fear death. You cannot fear pain. You must understand and accept that your death is also a possibility in the equation of achieving your goal. If you want something, you must be willing to die or kill in the fight to achieve it." I looked in his unflinching eyes, knowing that he understood all I had said. "Organize groups of like-minded men who have similar visions and dreams as a means of support. Network so that you are not alone. Then you must act on your dreams and your visions and make them real. If anyone gets in your way, go after them, hunt them down and destroy them, put fear in their hearts so they will never have any desire to challenge you again. Activate the power within you instead of living in the grips of your fear," I finally said.

'That's un-Martin-like," he said meekly.

"Martin is dead. He took us to the promised land. Now we are there. We must fight for it. Martin was our Moses and after Moses led the Jews out of Egypt, they had to fight for what God promised them. We have been freed from our physical but not our mental bondage. It is time we acknowledge that and free ourselves of those chains, cast them aside and stop living in fear. Organize, network and make your plans. Act on them and reap your success. It's time we take responsibility for ourselves. It's time we make our mark on this land and create our legacy. Allow your fear to be your guide and it will provide you wisdom. You must act on your dreams or they will remain dreams," I concluded.

"What you are saying is blasphemous, Mister. They would destroy us if they saw us doing that."

"It's for us to prevent that from occurring. Do you like living without dignity, without respect, and being called a nigger by every little red neck that passes by? That is not living. You will die an angry bitter man because you never allowed your mind to meet its challenges; you never allowed your spirit to act on it visions. You never allowed yourself to be embroiled in the tasks of acting on your dreams and making it, and your visions, a reality. That is what living is about – and thanking the almighty for your successes and learning from your failures. In so doing you will accept the purpose of your life. The reason you were put on this planet is not to live in fear but to thrive and strive in prosperity."

"But there are so many of them," he said.

"Are you a righteous man, a Christian man? Pray to God to show you the path and he will lead you to your answers. You are never alone when you proclaim yourself to be a child of God. Go and organize and network, unite with others who share your vision of prosperity, chart your course and begin your journey to success and prosperity. Live your dream!" I said and I gave him a tip for his information and told him to remain mum as to our presence in town.

# CHAPTER 24: Mission in the Heart of Dixie

"**W**illiam, Mack, Robert and I set out to find the locations he had documented as the sites of the lynching. We knew we would eventually draw unwanted attention in the heart of Dixie, and the consequences could be fatally brutal. We were well armed and ready for the unexpected and that was the key to survival in this business. But here in the land of Dixie, black men's lives meant nothing. We were less than human and we had fewer rights than animals. Even our contribution to America, such as the recognition and acceptance of the people's civil rights, which were significant to the growth of the country's Democratic ideals, meant nothing. What it did was to bring us under greater scrutiny and public ridicule by the main hatemongers of the country – the Klan and the media.

"All the hangings were off the same highway. We found the dirt road that the motel manager had told us about and we followed it for miles into a densely forested area far from the town. We drove for more than an hour deep into the forest. William, a new member to our crew, a former green beret and now a Federal Marshall, was driving. Slowly he traversed the gravelly dirt road, trying but not always succeeding to avoid the huge water filled cavities in the way. We heard the babbling sound of a river off in the distance, just as the motel manager had stated.

"Smell that clean fresh air," said William.

"Smell the scent of death – it's mixed in with that fresh air you are smelling," said Mack.

"It's carried on the wind," said Robert, teasing.

"No, motherfucker," said an unwitting Mack. "You can smell it – like it's just sitting here." Mack never went on any of these expeditions without his trusted Tommy gun. "Well. I have a sure fire way of resolving any of these good old boys' problems and its name is Tommy," he continued.

"Shut the fuck up, you damned idiot. Let any of these crackers know that you have a gun and they will hunt you down like rabid dogs and kill your motherfucking ass," said William.

"Then they will hang your dead body from a tree and disembowel your dead ass," I added, which gained a boisterous round of laughter from the group. It was not funny to me because I had seen them do that to my father and uncles.

"We headed to the river. We were surprised by the many boot imprints we found on its muddy banks. We identified about 50 distinct sets of boots, shoes and sneakers imprinted. Those good old boys were not even concerned with being caught. There were also imprints from a variety of fast boats at the shoreline. We decided to follow the shoe imprints from the riverbank that led into the nearby forests.

"That is how they got here," said Mack. "They must have kidnapped the boys, brought them here by boat, took them into the forest and hanged them."

"Where?"

"What?" said Mack.

"Where did they hang them?" I asked.

"I don't know," Mack replied, with some indignation in his tone.

"Let's follow the footprints into the forest," I said, leading the way "and see what is revealed." We retrieved our weapons from the Jeep, locked it up and proceeded to follow the trail into the woods. It was not long after that we found the tree that displayed signs of rope marks around a sturdy lower branch. In another short distance, a burnt cross lay on the ground. We noted the evidence of many men being there at that site. They had left clues that corroborated their presence and their actions.

"Now that we have found how they got here and what they did, we must find out where they came from and who they are," I said.

"They came from up the river," volunteered William.

"What lead you to that conclusion?"

"By the angles of the boat imprints as well as the shoe imprints on the river bank."

"Therefore we can start looking for a town up river where they left from?"

"We could do that," I replied. "Maybe we could drive up river from here to see what we find".

Slowly William navigated the big jeep along the grassy banks of the river.

"This is one bumpy ride," commented Robert. "When I get home, I am going to need to rest my ass from the assault it's going through."

"Don't you know this is the future in motor vehicles?" said William. "Boys, you must learn to appreciate what Detroit is coming up with for our driving pleasure!"

"Driving pleasure?" quipped Robert. "Shhidd, if I want driving pleasure you would find me in a Cadillac Deville. This is giving me a sore ass and I don't find that pleasurable."

"Can a Cadillac take you to places like this?" asked William, deftly manoeuvring the vehicle around a huge hole in the ground that was filled with water. Without waiting for a response, he continued. "That's what I am talking about. There will come a time when these four-wheel drive vehicles will litter the landscape and no environmental obstacles will hamper them like it does cars."

"You better watch where you are going before you have an accident and have our remains littering this landscape," said Mack, chipping into the conversation.

"Do you smell that?" I said, scenting a faint odor of smoke.

"Shit, man, you always smelling some shit," said Mack. "What is it you smell now?"

"You don't smell it?" I asked, now sure of the scent.

"No, we don't smell it," said Robert.

"What do you smell?'"demanded William.

"Smoke," I said.

"There must be a fire going on nearby,'" said Robert.

"Somebody's cooking," said Mack.

"Where is the odour coming from?" William asked.

"Good question," I replied.

"Stop the vehicle," instructed Robert. Exiting the jeep, he walked towards the river and began pulling on blades of grass and tossing them in the air.

"What the fuck is he doing?" asked Mack.

"He is trying to find the direction of the wind," I explained.

"Direction of the wind!" exclaimed Mack, with an incredulous look on his face. "There isn't any wind blowing."

"Yes," I replied, "that is why he is plucking blades of grass and tossing them in the air. They are then caught by the wind current and blown before settling back to the ground, and the same is occurring with the smoke. But the smoke particles are lighter than the grass, so it is easily carried by the wind for greater distances."

"Teach that boy, teach that boy", said William. "When he is finished learning, he will be graduating cum laude from the school of hard knocks" - which brought a smile to my face.

"It's coming from up the river," said Robert, as he got back into the vehicle. "I can smell it now."

"We can all smell it, genius," said Mack. Soon we saw the smoke overhead and followed it to its source. We came to a large frame house in a clearing of more than two acres. There were thick tall hedges and many trees separating the yard from the riverbank. If one was going by on the river, you could miss the house if you were not aware of its presence. We stayed in the woods, hoping to see someone. A big older black man came out and sat on the porch. We could not make out what he was saying, but he was speaking to someone. Suddenly three young boys came running out of the house, laughing and throwing a football. They were followed by a woman, a young girl and two grown men. The boys took to throwing the football to each other on the large grass lawn. The girl and the elder folks took to sitting on the porch talking, totally unaware that we were observing their every move. Seeing that they were black folks like us, I decided to approach them as a possible source of information. We retreated to the Jeep and entered their property by an unpaved dirt road we discovered leading directly to the front of the house. We did not want them to know we were spying on them. As we entered their property, the boys ceased throwing the football and took to watching us. The elder folks stood up to acknowledge our presence, but there was only one of the elder males now present. I took it that the other two had disappeared into the house where they would by now have targeted us with their hunting rifles.

"Howdy, mister – ma'am," I said from the front passenger's' seat, trying to sound as friendly and nonthreatening as possible.

"Howdy, stranger," said the elder man, "what bring you folks around these parts? You lost or something?"

"No, mister, we are searching for answers."

"Answers?" he asked.

"Come in the house, you boys," said the woman, frantically hurrying to retrieve her sons from what she sensed as possible danger.

"Aren't any answers around these parts to what you are looking for mister."

"I haven't told you what I am looking for yet, friend."

"Aren't no answers around here, mister," he said again, sticking both his thumbs behind the thoracic area of his dirty suspenders and gripping them with his index fingers.

"Listen to me, friend," I said. "We are lawmen looking for the men who lynched those three Jewish boys down there in the forest by the river. From what we have seen, their boats must have come by here. We have seen where they came ashore and dragged their victims into the forest to be hanged but we do not seem to know where they came from."

"Sorry, I can't help you mister," said the man. I imagined he was afraid and did not want to become involved.

"Don't be afraid," I said. "We are not going to tell anyone about the information you give us". I was trying to put his mind at ease.

"Hey," said William, sensing that my tactics were getting nowhere. "What makes you think that you won't be next? You know that down in Alabama, they killed off a family just like yours, husband, wife and three boys. They are passing by here in their boats going down the river to do their hangings of black folks like you and you don't see anything while living out here. You know they are coming for you. Sooner or later they are going to get you."

"It's a matter of time," I said. "They know you have seen them and you know who they are. Believe me, they are going to come after you. Come on," I said to William, "let's go – we are wasting our time here." As he turned over the vehicle's engine to depart, the woman came running out of the house shouting, "No, no! Don't leave! Don't leave?"

"Shut up and get back in the house, Sara," shouted the man.

"No," she said defiantly. "We must tell them what we know."

"It will cost us our lives," he said.

"It already has. I cannot live like this. We cannot live like this while they are killing us off and we hide our heads in the sand and do nothing. It will not stop until we are all dead. No one is caring while we are being killed off."

"I care," I said, interrupting their drama. "That is why I am here."

"You all aren't anything but a bunch of niggers! You can't stop them," he said.

"Talk to us, Sara," I said.

"They are men from the town, important men not from just this town but several of the towns off the river. Some of them are lawmen, judges, doctors and lawyers. They are key members of the community and they are the ones who make the decisions. They have foot workers who do the actual work of finding the victims."

"How do you know that?" I asked.

"I used to work in the town and one night, instead of coming home, I decided to stay in town. There was a meeting and the streets were filled with Klansmen. They stood at a podium in the centre of town at the square and made speeches saying that now Martin was dead they must take back the rights that were given to the niggers."

"Where were you staying when you overheard this vile crap?"

"I was staying with a white family who I worked for. The family hid me," she said, "and when they came to recruit them into joining the Klan, I heard everything they said. They said that America was for the white man and Africa was for the black man and if we did not go, they would hang us all by the neck until we were all dead. They did not know that I was there listening and the people I worked for did not make them aware. The next day, they hid me in the trunk of their car and drove me all the way out here."

"Sara! Did you recognise any of them?"

"Yes, it was a hot night and most of them did not have on their hood and mask," she said. "I recognised the sheriff, the judge and many other people – even our town doctor," she said, without a flicker of doubt.

"Damn the town doctor too," said Mack. "Please, Lord, don't let me ever get sick."

"We need to find a Klan member that is involved in all these lynchings. We have to capture such an individual for questioning," I said to the group.

"That would be old man Carson or his son, Christopher,"she said. "He lives in a mansion outside of town called the Little Log Cabin. It's off the highway. It's a big plantation house where Senator Carson lives. He is one of the most important Klan members around here. From what I have heard, since his son Christopher returned from Vietnam he has been the leader of the Klan revival and the person behind all these hangings."

"Colonel Christopher Carson?"

"You know him?" she asked.

"I am acquainted with him and his work," I said.

"He's not a nice man," she said. "We believe he is behind these hangings but we have no proof. Ian Carson is our senator. He is a very powerful and influential person. We are afraid of him."

"It was strange how fate had brought us back together. We were on a collision course and only one of us would survive. If he died, it would be the end of an era in American history. If I died, that history would continue. It was getting dark; we had to make it back from where we came. "Thank you, Sara, for your time and wisdom. Someone must stand up against bigotry and hate and you did tonight."

"You cannot leave now," she said. "To get to Carson's place, you must drive through town and they will see you. You will end up like all the others. That's how they got caught – by driving through the centre of town, right into the arms of angry and hateful Klansmen. In the morning, you can drive back down the river to the road and come back around to old man Carson's place."

"You are offering us a place to stay, Sara?"

"Yes," she replied, "and you should take it if you want to live".

"What will your husband say?"

"If he was alive, he would agree with me. This is my place and what I say goes," she said in an assertive tone.

"How can I ever thank you?"

"By taking those hateful bastards to jail," she replied.

Night came quickly in rural Alabama and the sky lit up with a million stars. I sat on the porch in the dark with the family and my men shooting the breeze before going off to sleep on a big couch in their living room. Being in a strange environment, I fell off into a light sleep just like I used to in 'Nam. Although I was asleep, I was so alert I could hear a pin drop a mile away. It was about 2 am when I heard someone quietly approaching. I gripped my Colt 45 semi-automatic below my pillow in my right hand.

"Wake up, mister, wake up," whispered one of the boys. "Come follow me."

"Where are we going?"

"They are going to have another hanging." I quickly jumped out of bed and woke the others.They led us to the clump of trees and bushes at the edge of the property facing the river. We saw about five boats coming down the river with approximately 30 armed men. The boat engines were turned off so as not to give away their arrival. Instantly, I knew what was happening. "They are coming here. Get the guns; we are the ones they are coming for tonight," I said, as we hastily retreated back to the house and took up defensive positions with our guns. I told the members not to fire until I told them. I watched them as they came out from the protection of the trees, and quietly made their way across the huge lawn in the moonlit night, not aware we had seen them. Each was armed to the teeth and when they reached about half way across the lawn, one of them lit a torch and ran toward the house. That was when we opened fire. He was the first to be hit and the torch fell out of his hand onto him and began burning his freshly minted corpse. I knew I got him with a headshot. We opened fire on the others and they fell by our first volley. Although they were surprised by our initial volley, the survivors quickly recovered and hurriedly retreated to the cover of the woods. They went about surrounding the house from the cover of the woods. Hunting was a way of life in these parts. Most boys by the time they were 16 were expert marksman, a skill they learned from their fathers. This battle had  become a battle of attrition. It was becoming clear that it was our skill against theirs. I had my sniper rifle with me. I still never left home without it, and tonight it was going to do its work. From behind the trees, I could see the flashes of rifle fire. I responded with my fire,  directing it about two inches above and two inches to my right of their muzzle flash. As usual, there was no return fire. As time went by,  I noticed we had sustained a large quantity of casualties. Most of Sara's family had been wounded or killed. The

Klan had managed to surround the house and set it afire. It grew into an inferno and we were trapped inside – with them waiting to pick us off on exiting. They began throwing tear gas and grenades into the house.

I saw Sara coming down the steps with the limp lifeless body of her daughter clutched to her chest, but before she reached the last step she momentarily froze in her tracks. I saw the blood squirting out the back of her head. Her body fell in a limp heap as she released the dead body of her daughter. A bullet had found its mark. I looked around the burning room and the only person who showed signs of life apart from me was Mack, and he was severely injured. Suddenly the door was blown off its hinges by a grenade, which killed Mack. The fire bellowed out of the back door and windows, stoked by new supplies of oxygen. I looked around and saw that they were all dead – my men, Sara and her family. I thought it would be suicidal to go out the door, but it would not be long before the smoke or flames would claim me if I stayed there in the burning building. I looked over and saw Mack still leaning with his back against a wall with a bullet entry wound above his nose. I knew his death was instantaneous. His beloved Tommy gun was at his feet. I reached over, took hold of it and put in a new clip. I placed my sniper rifle over my shoulders and it hung from my back. The frame building was now a total inferno. I crawled out quietly onto the porch on my belly clutching Mack's Tommy gun. As I made it outside I started to hear their voices. "Nobody could survive this fire," I heard one of the men saying.

"I want everyone who lives in this house accounted for," said another. "I want all those niggers dead. There will be no witnesses. Get all the men together and check for their bodies after the fire", said the speaker. One of the henchmen let out a loud whistle and the surviving assassins came running.

"We are all here," he said. "We are all that survived out of 30," said another.

"You want us to wait until the fire stops and get a score of their dead?' questioned another. They had gathered on the lawn in a group of about 14, discussing the possibility of finding any bodies alive in the inferno that was once a home to a beautiful family. They had their backs to the burning building. It was their final and fatal mistake.

"We have sustained heavy losses. I have counted 16 dead among us. This should not have been. We were supposed to come, kill them and leave. There were supposed to be no casualties," said one of the Klansmen. I gripped Mack's Tommy gun and came up firing. Taken by surprise, I easily killed six in the initial blast. Before they recovered, I came around with a second fatal blast. They all had fallen. I sprayed their bodies with more lead to make sure that no one survived. The heat from the building was tremendous. I wanted to go back in and get Mack but the top floor of the building was now collapsing down into the main floor. The temperature was above 2,000 degrees and I began remembering the villages we had torched in 'Nam. I grabbed my rifle and Mack's Tommy gun, ran to the Jeep and drove off into the bushes from where I came as the angry flames devoured the building. As I drove away, I heard the building collapsing as the fire caused it to crumble, entombing all those who had given their lives so I could survive the carnage."

# CHAPTER 25: Searching in a Quagmire

"I returned to the little motel and told the others about what had happened. We prayed for a few minutes together for our departed friends, William, Mack and Robert. Only I, John, Cayan and Steve were left. After this we headed out, two in each Jeep, to find Carson's place. On arrival, Cayan and the rest of the men were impressed by his well-manicured estate with tall oak trees lining both sides of a long drive that led to a huge white-painted plantation house. The vast estate had a beautiful lawn that was sprinkled with a variety of trees, shrubs and gardens with flowerbeds. I immediately thought we could use these for cover in our advance on the main house. Surrounding the estate was a tall spiked fence. The main house had two floors and was a sprawling building with smaller attachments. It had six tall round marble columns at the front of the building, equidistant from each other, and a veranda on each floor. It reminded me of the plantation houses one would see in movies of the South, such as Gone with The Wind. On three sides of the estate, thick forest and bushy undergrowth stretched up to the fence. This provided a good hiding place for us as we spied on Carson. Over a century ago these were cotton fields, a main staple of the Carson plantation and means to its prosperity. From the cover of the bushes, we waited and planned. We watched and saw an older man dressed in a robe exit the main house at the back and sit in a chair under an umbrella by the pool. He picked up a phone and began speaking. We were about 300 yards from him. Old man Carson was without doubt a rich, powerful man and more than likely had many influential friends. This was not going to be any ordinary hate monger criminal.

"This does not look like any log cabin I know of," I said, a little bewildered, wondering if this was the right place. "Sara said he lived in a little log cabin and I am sure this is the direction she gave to Carson's residence."

"I wonder why she told you that," said Steve.

"Maybe if she had told you the truth, you would have been intimidated by it," said Cayan.

"John, who was looking through the binoculars, said, "I know why." Handing me the binoculars, he said, "Look at what is written above the main gate."

"I focused the binoculars on the crown above the main gate and there, written in wrought iron, in bold letters, was 'THE LITTLE LOG CABIN'. I don't know if this was a show of humility, but it made me 90 per cent sure I was at the right place. Just then a man ran out shouting, "Mr Carson, they said there was a massacre at Sara Wilson's place! Everyone is dead, including the men we sent!"

"What?" he screeched, springing to his feet. "How is that possible?"

"We just lost the element of surprise," whispered Cayan.

'Not totally, they may not know anything about us yet,' I replied.

"They certainly will be on their guard from now on", whispered John, "making it harder to get to Carson."

"That's for sure," said Cayan, addressing me as he inquired, "What will be our next move?"

"We have to be like ghosts, unidentifiable and stealthy in everything we do. We cannot bring any attention to ourselves, we cannot afford to have them see us, or we will have lost the war. They know we're here but they don't know who we are or how many we are. We're vastly outnumbered. One little slip up and we will blow our cover – that's what they're waiting for and if that occurs, we have lost the only thing we have going for us. We can only attack at night. It is imperative we get a confession from Carson taped and on video".

"How are we going to get him?" inquired John.

"We are going to get him tonight when he is asleep," I said. "We will start preparing now."

"The house will be like a fortress. There will be guards all around protecting him from any intruders," said Steve.

"Our objective is to get Carson and find out what he knows about the lynching of the Jewish boys. The question is – how do we get to Carson? How are we going to get to Carson?" repeated Steve.

"First, we have to get into that house without blowing our cover," said John.

"No, the first thing is to get across the lawn without being seen. If we're seen, they'll open fire. Then we will have lost all element of surprise. We will use the landscape to our advantage," said Cayan.

"How is that?" I asked.

"I looked at the oak tree he was looking at and saw that its branches would be supportive. But I knew that if we took that route, we would be leaving ourselves open and defenceless to the guards. "Yes, one of us will do that," I said. "We will use that tree to get to the top porch. After getting there, we will then suspend a rope and the rest will use the rope to get to the top porch. Who will do the honors?" I asked, seeking a volunteer.

Immediately Cayan responded. "I will do it – it was my idea. I did things like that in the military."

"You were special forces?" asked Steve.

"Special forces and I also fought with the Green Berets,'"replied Cayan proudly.

"Home boy – you could take out this place all by your lonesome," said Steve.

"If that was the plan," he replied.

"What are we going to do when we find Carson in the house?"

"We are going to abduct him by knocking him out with a quick-acting drug and bring him back here with us where we will question him."

"What makes you think he will be cooperative?" questioned Cayan.

"The drug I've got will take away his will to resist."

"Will it harm him?"

"He'll be dead by the time we are finished interrogating him."

"Are you joking? That is a US senator! We cannot kill him," responded Steve.

"Why not? He has been killing black folks long before I was born," I replied.

"I'll do it," said Cayan. "When do we start?"

"At midnight," I replied.

"What is the name of this drug and what do you know about it?" asked Cayan.

"We used it in the field in Vietnam whenever we were interrogating Viet Congs or North Vietnamese prisoners of war."

"War is hell, isn't it?" said John. "We kill our fellow man and consider it humane."

"We all looked at him, knowing he was the only one among us who was in the military that did not make it to 'Nam. He was drafted and served, but it was during the time the nation was at its highest peak of turmoil regarding our occupation of Vietnam. Millions were protesting all over the country demanding withdrawal, chanting, "Bring the boys home."

"You a pacifist?" asked Cayan.

"Why?" asked John.

"I don't want a man who is assigned to cover my ass hesitating to cap the enemy's ass when he shows his ugly face. You hear me? I want you to lay down some serious fire if any of those assholes shows their face. I want you to blow their heads off and think nothing of it. I guarantee you this –  if the positions were reversed, they would think nothing of blowing you to kingdom come. Survival is not built on hesitation but on the one who can get off the quickest and most accurate shots."

"Amen to that," I said with a smile.

"We were all expert marksmen, but I knew I was the best shot among them followed by Cayan and Steve. Because John had no war experience, it was difficult to tell how good a shot he would be under fire. The men had not lost faith in him but I sensed a drop-off in their confidence for him as he hadn't killed before nor had experienced enemy fire. John was a big, tall man, approximately six feet six inches of pure muscle. He said when he was young people called him Hercules because he was so strong. Well, tonight he would have to prove it, I thought, because he would be the one assigned to carry Carson. Steve had drifted off to sleep in the jeep and the others look weary.

"Sleep, brothers" I said. "Sleep, for tonight we will face death. Don't worry – we will either make young handsome corpses or live to be old men with grandchildren, who will gather around and listen to the tales of our great exploits."

# CHAPTER 26: A Bitter Fruit

"Now that you had found your nemesis, what did you do, Mr Stuart? Kill him?"

"No, Nurse Gordon. Listen and don't interject until there is a need for you to do that, please," he replied, and continued.

"I was awakened by John at approximately 6pm. He had been replaced by Steve for guard duty. We had rested in the Jeeps and were prepared for what was to take place. He gave me his report, which I found disturbing. He informed me that there was a flurry of unusual activity occurring at Carson's estate. There were still two hours of daylight to go. I made my way to where Steve was in hiding in the thick underbrush observing the house.

"What's happening over there?" I asked, taking up position beside him on the ground, making sure they did not see or hear us.

"Something is going on. They have been pretty busy. I believe they have discovered the ruins you told us about," said Steve.

"What gives you that idea?" I asked him.

"First they doubled the guards on the property. They have sent out search teams. There are two men driving around the perimeter of the property in a jeep checking with the others who are on foot. Their guards work in pairs. I counted five pairs so far and they are holding a brother in captivity. It seems like he was badly burnt."

"What did you say?'"

"They brought in a brother earlier who appeared to have sustained third degree burns on his back and arms. Looked like he's in severe pain and they've been interrogating him since his arrival. I heard him screaming in pain. I wonder if he is still alive, I haven't heard anything from him in the last hour."

"It has to be someone from last bight's fire."

"Why is that?"

"If he was not from there, he would be of little importance to them and they would have killed him already. They are trying to get information from him about us. If he's as severely injured as you say, he won't be able to resist, and if he knows anything about us he would have already told them. When did they start reinforcement?"

"Not too long ago," replied Steve, "and they brought him in approximately at 4pm."

"More than two hours ago," I replied. "Why wasn't I informed? This event has changed all our plans,"I said, seething.

"Why?" asked Steve.

"From what you have said, I sense he has told them all he knows. If they know of us, they will be waiting for us. They have doubled the guards. They know of us. We have to think of a different plan."

'I have an idea. If they should leave with the brother, why don't we tail them?'

?Why should we do that? It will only give away our presence."

"They already know we are involved; they just don't know where we are."

"We can't get careless and give away our position."

"When they have gotten all the information they want and have no further need of him, they are going to lynch him. I doubt they are going to do that on Carson's property. They are going to find an appropriate spot to do it and that would be somewhere in the woods. If they are going to the woods, they must pass by us, so we could follow them."

"And then what?"

"When we are sure of what they are doing, we will call you and you will join us."

"Continue," I said ,wanting to know where he was taking this thought.

"I have a movie camera with me," Steve said. "When I was with the CIA, I used it in the field, especially in Vietnam. We flew in Huey gunships over enemy territory taking pictures. On development, if we found enemy troops massing in large numbers preparing to attack, we would call in the real deal, a C130 gunship, and that would come and massacre the enemy on the ground. That camera is so advanced that from as high as 10,000 feet in the air at midnight we could get pictures of the enemy as clear as if they were in a photo shoot. Instead of fighting them, we could get pictures of them lynching the brother and send it to the FBI and the media. Let America see what is going on here in her backyard here in the deep South."

"I thought it was less risky than my original plan. But what if we were spotted while tailing them? There was still risk. We were no longer operating from a position of surprise. They knew of us and were ready and waiting for us to show our heads so they could blow them off.

"Get the camera," I said to Steve. "We will start our film production from here. Tell Cayan to go and keep an eye on the main road so we have no surprises when we have to move out."

"He returned with the camera, surprisingly a not too bulky device. He immediately went about shooting images of the property, the estate house and the men patrolling it. He filmed everything we saw that was relevant. While he filmed, I had time to think through the new plan. Who would do the tailing? It had to be Cayan and John, while Steve and I made the film of their main force. I went back to the camp and woke John and told them of the change in plans. They got the weapons they needed, which included a sniper rifle, an AK47 with four clips, a grenade launcher with a dozen grenades and one of the two M60 machines guns with three belts. They took one of the two radios, and I reminded him of our signal before breaking silence. We had to respond with a code before they started with any message. We then proceeded over to where Cayan was hiding while he observed what was taking place on the road.

"Anything to report?" I asked.

"It's been quiet out here," he replied.

"I informed him of the new plan, its objective and the importance of their roles in it. Cayan listened attentively and accepted his new role just as if he were in the military. He summarised everything, making sure he understood the plan. Both he and John had all intentions of attaining their objectives. They were well trained and knew how to use the weapons I had selected for them. Our intentions were to meet up in the woods. If anything went wrong, they had specific orders to resist being captured, and if they survived we would meet at a safe house in Brooklyn, New York. They were to wait in their vehicle in the woods until the main caravan went by. We would signal to them that the vehicles were leaving Carson's place and, after they had bypassed, they would follow at a distance without attracting any attention. When we were ready, I said my goodbye to Cayan and John and headed back to the camp. I packed everything away in the remaining Jeep Wagoneer. I made sure our weapons were ready for us, including the Thompson submachine gun for me, an M16 assault rifle with a grenade launcher, my sniper rifle, a Colt 45 side arms and the other M60 machine gun. I always thought of the M60s as the equalisers. What we lacked in numbers, we made up for with the M60s' firepower. The rest of the weapons in our arsenal were in the back of the vehicle. I went back to where Steve was hiding, observing the house. Three armed men were entering a vehicle.

"Those are their boys," said Steve, "their point men."Steve filmed as I observed Christopher Carson giving instructions to the one who oversaw the group. It was the first time I'd seen him since that incidental meeting back in Vietnam and this confirmed my belief that he was at the root of the hangings. Soon they left in a Chevy Blazer.

"What are we going to do about the brother?" Steve asked.

"What do you mean?" I asked.

"Are we going to rescue him?"

"Are you serious? That's not in the plan."

"We're just going to sit by and let him die! We are going to let them lynch him like that!" said a now-emotional Steve.

"If we attempted to rescue him, it would be suicidal. He would certainly die and we would not achieve our objective. Steve, like it or not he is a pawn, a man to be sacrificed for the greater good. It's for us to make sure what he is about to give is not lost and not given in vain."

"Steve turned and looked at me, then went back to filming the departing Chevy Blazer.

"Is that nigger still alive?" I heard Carson bellow at the top of his voice.

"Just barely," replied one of his underlings.

"Give him water and tell the doctor to give him something for the pain. Make sure he is still alive so we can hang him tonight".

"Yes, Mr Carson," replied another of the underlings as he scurried away to relay the message to the doctor. Carson turned and addressed another group of Klan members.

"You get in touch with the others and tell them to bring the other one and meet here in half hour. Let's go, time is wasting. Tonight, we lynch two niggers. Tomorrow, when I am president of the United States, we will activate the King Alfred Plan and get rid of all the niggers here in America. But be on the lookout – there is a bounty hunter on our tail, trying to get information on the three Jewish boys. He's a dangerous man, a natural killer. He is a nigger and if you come across him do not hesitate to shoot – for he won't."

"Did you hear that? They know we are here. What are we going to do?" Steve asked in horror.

"Stick to your plan," I answered him.

"They have more than one of us. They are planning to lynch more than one of us," interjected Steve, shocked at Carson's statement.

"The plan does not change," I said in a reinforcing tone. "We must stick to the plan and gather all the incriminating evidence so the law will put them away."

"Are you crazy? This is the South. No white man has ever gone to jail for killing a black man here."

"Our objective is to change that and hold the Department of Justice accountable for its actions. When we are finished here, the intent is to have them respect the lives of all American citizens no matter their colour or creed. The Declaration of Independence said all men are created equal, and that law must be upheld at all instances by all."

"You're crazy," Steve retorted. "It was meant as a guideline for democracy. But as far as blacks are concerned, it was never meant to apply to us."

"We may never see it happen in our life time, but we are on a journey to make all men equal in the eyes of the law and justice a reality for all."

"Did you hear what Carson said? When he becomes president, he will activate the King Alfred Plan and get rid of all of us."

"I heard him,  and if I am alive he will never become president. What the hell is this King Alfred Plan any way?'

'I've never heard of it, but it sounds like a plan to get rid of the black population."

"That sounds like a thing Carson would do. I remember the first time our path crossed, when he and his Klan group lynched my father and uncles. He said back then that all of us niggers will die and – he meant it."

"Shortly, other Klan members began arriving, dressed in their full Klan regalia. Many got out of their vehicles and gathered in groups on the lawn of Carson's huge estate. It was great for filming as most did not have the flap of their cone-shaped hat covering their face. We filmed them as they talked and socialised with each other before they got to the matter at hand. Soon a van arrived and a young black man was pulled out by a leash, which was tied to a black leather collar around his neck. He had a bag over his head with holes in it so he could breathe and see. He was handcuffed behind his back and shackled at his ankles. He wore no shirt and his back was scarred with marks he had received from whippings.

"Get the other one from the basement and let's begin," shouted a jubilant Carson. "We are going to have a lynching tonight like the good old days. I want the niggers to discover the bodies and become agitated, angry, creating civil unrest nationally and seeking vengeance. Then, when I enter office, I have justification to implement the King Alfred Plan."

"The other black man was dragged from a room attached to the garage. Like the newcomer, he too had his hands cuffed and was shackled at the ankles. However, unlike the other man, he had no covering over his head. I felt my heart skip a beat as I saw his face. I recognised him as one of Sara's brothers. I was speechless for a moment. Steve noticed the look on my face.

"You know him, huh?" Steve said, confirming the look on my face.

"Barely. More like an acquaintance," I replied.

"Who is he?"

"I told you about Sara. It's her brother, James."

"We are now sacrificing her brother to make a point," said Steve as he scrutinised me, making me uncomfortable by arousing feelings of guilt.

"She would have wanted it so," I said, to suppress all feelings of guilt and honestly sensing how Sara would have acted in this moment.

"How do you know what she would have wanted? You only knew her for a few hours before she was dead."

"I knew her for hours and in that time she projected to me what she stood for in her lifetime. I can safely say without a doubt in my heart – I am making the right decision."

"What about him?" Steve inquired.

"His character was not as well defined. He never gave any indication that he really stood for something during our conversation. He walked in fear of what the white man could do to him if he stepped out of line. Like most black men here in the South, it is a means of survival. But on adopting that submissive attitude, they lose touch with their true sense of self, their self-worth and their inner strength. If that is so, he has told them everything he knows about you. I hope you or the rest of the crew did not divulge much of yourselves that night. No black man is beyond the reach of the Klan. That's why we cannot attempt to rescue them,– that's the reason we would not succeed," I said as I looked at him. I remembered how much we had stated of ourselves last night to have them feel comfortable in accepting us in their home, knowing we meant them no harm. I had spoken of the most important thing to me, my family. I only hoped they were safe as I prepared to take on this hazardous task. I knew any moment could be my last. I didn't remember having any such thoughts as I rip-roared across Vietnam, killing, maiming and destroying. Within the last 24 hours, three of my closet friends had died and we were about to make their sacrifice worth it. I had shed no tears and I had no feeling of loss. Death was a way of life for me. It happened around me as I was its main conduit, its main perpetrator. 'Nam had taught me how to be a stone.

"Get them in the truck," one of Carson's underlings shouted. My attention was abruptly drawn back to the happenings on Carson's estate. The high-ranking Klan members were gravitating toward their vehicles while the lesser members loaded the vehicles with necessities for their sacrifice. Soon, the funeral procession began to move. Slowly the lead vehicle made its way down the driveway, while the others took up position behind it. They gained momentum as they headed out onto the street. I wondered what these poor innocent men were feeling at this moment, knowing that their end was drawing near. We caught everything on film, even the two men who were being led to their deaths. It was a full moon now and its reflection lit up the countryside. We returned to our vehicle and made it to the edge of the forest, looking onto the road but still invisible to passing vehicles. I disembarked and cautiously made my way to the side of the road. I looked in either direction and saw the tail lights of the last vehicle now disappearing in the distance. We followed, and by the light of the full moon were able to see them from a distance. They turned off the main road onto a dirt road, the same one I had used when I was in flight from Sara's home. Cayan contacted us and gave us directions to where he and John were hiding while from a distance, they watched. They did not dare risk being spotted. They directed us to where they were. I remembered the spot as I had been there when we investigated the other hangings earlier. We pulled off the road and hid our vehicle in the bushes on the other side of the road so no one could see it in passing. It took us a little time, but we found Cayan and John.

"What has happened so far?" I inquired, fearing that we had missed the most incriminating moment. Steve was already filming.

"You've not missed anything so far. They've been preparing for the cross burning. They just erected it and are about to light it," Cayan whispered. I looked to where the Klansmen had converged around a huge cross, towering above them, wrapped in thick cloth and bound by a rope that snaked its way around the huge planks to the top. Even from where we were, we could smell the kerosene with which they had saturated the cloth. One of the Klansmen walked over to the cross with a torch held in his right hand, said some words and lit it. The cross burst into flames. It was so vibrant that it appeared to take on a life of its own.

"Look there," said Cayan, pointing towards a tree. I was shocked when I saw two nooses hanging from a thick sturdy branch of a tall, big, oak tree. A pick-up truck was parked below. I saw both men being lead to the truck. Sara's brother James offered no resistance. I thought to myself that he saw this as an opportunity to escape the pain and suffering he had experienced. The other young man was combative and not about to slip away quietly into the dark.

"Take off this fucking hood from over my head – allow me to see!" he kept yelling as he struggled against them. The Klansmen took to beating him with their whips. He fell to his knees and as they converged on him, now punching and kicking him, Carson shouted,

"Stop, stop, let's grant him his last wish. We will take off the hood." I watched as he removed the hood from the young man's head. I did not recognise him. He got to his feet and they all took a step back. He was a tall, well-built man. I could see the fire in his eyes and the strength of his spirit in his character. He was not going to be broken and he would carry that to his grave.

"You think you are killing me?" he said as he looked them in the eyes. "No, you're not. You are killing a piece of what is right and decent about this nation, this country we all occupy. I committed no crime and I offended no one. You treat me as if I am the problem and hanging me would be the solution. But let the truth be told – you are the problem. Sheriff. You are this town's chief law enforcement officer, yet you have sanctioned this unlawful act with your presence. You will one day regret this, when you must answer to a higher office. You, senator, prove that hate knows no limits to the minds it occupies and the soul it stirs. Doctor, you stopped this man's pain and preserved his life not so he would live but so that he could live to be lynched. The rest of you brandish your hate for the rest of humanity by your association with the Klan and what it stands for. I will have no mercy for you and I cannot find it in my heart to forgive you. One day, even hell will refuse your spirits and you will never again be a problem to humanity." He turned and stepped on to the back of the truck. A tall Klansman placed and tightened the noose around their necks. After getting off the truck, he banged on its roof signalling to the driver of his readiness. The driver looked at Carson who nodded his approval and he stomped on the accelerator. The truck lurched forward and two audible cracking sounds were heard as their cervical spines broke from the weight of their bodies against the resisting rope from which they were now suspended. Their violent kicks and twitches slowly came to an end. Their necks were broken and their heads tilted awkwardly to the side. For them, life in hell had ended and I was sure they had gone onto a better place. It was all caught on tape.

"Suddenly a gust of wind flared up the vibrant flames of the cross and it tumbled over, setting ablaze the two Klansmen who were standing near it. They shrieked in fright and pain as the flames quickly consumed their outer garments and met their skin. They shouted, "Help me, help me!" and threw themselves to the ground, rolling around to put out the flames. Others grabbed blankets from their trucks and sought to smother the flames, but their robes caught alight and soon they too were engulfed in flames. The others gasped in disbelief, rooted to where they stood. No one had water; no one knew what to do but watch in shock and disbelief. One ran over with a fire extinguisher he had in his vehicle. He put out the flames. Six men had received third degree burns over most of their bodies.

"Did you see what happened?" said John. "It is a sign."

"Why don't we open up on them now?" asked Cayan.

"No," I replied. "We are here to gather information to send these men to prison."

"This opportunity will never present itself again. They are confused, disorganised and shaken by that event. If we hit them now, we stand a chance of completely wiping them out," said Cayan.

"That will be murder, and then we will be hunted by the law."

"This decision will come back to haunt you," said Cayan. "This is an opportunity from God himself, telling us to strike them down. Those hateful bastards have been killing our people for centuries. It's time we took the fight to them."

"No," I said. "If God really wanted that, he would have struck them down himself. Remember we are here to gather information to bring these people and their practices down by presenting it to the media, the FBI, the DOJ and all other responsible government agencies."

"Fuck the media! And Carson – he is the government! They have all been complicit in our oppression. We must handle our own business and stop waiting for others to do that for us. This is the perfect ambush. They will never know what hit them."

"Let's remain quiet until they leave," said John. "Otherwise they may open on us instead."

"We watched as the doctor assessed the burn victims. Then they gathered themselves and left. When we were satisfied that they were all gone, we came out from hiding, took close up pictures of the hanging men and then we fled. We sombrely got back to our vehicles and headed for New York. It was a long drive, Steve and I in one vehicle and Cayan and John in the other. We never said a word along the way. Three men who we had called brothers and friends had died in battle and we watched as the Klan lynched two others. I had been there more than once before, but for the others it was their first time seeing this. To see those men hanged because of the colour of their skins brought forth emotions that made me want to kill or die doing so, but I refrained by not giving into my impulses. We knew then that this racial hate had no boundaries and the genocide of our race was in Carson's plans if he got elected president.

# CHAPTER 27: Back to Reality

"**S**topping only to refuel and refresh ourselves we travelled all night and the better part of the next day to arrive in Bedford Stuyvesant, Brooklyn. I remember it was a hot, sticky summer's day. With heavy hearts and troubled minds, we observed the many black children sitting on stoops, playing on the sidewalks and in the streets, far and safe from the dangers of the South. Yet still, I thought, dangers were waiting to claim their lives in these mean streets.

"Mothers could be heard shouting from the windows of their apartment buildings attempting to gain the attention of their wayward sons, who were captivated by the fun of the moment. Some of them were on their way to being lost and conquered by the distractions of the streets, never to find their true calling in life. The sweet sounds of Motown wailed over the streets, making the scene seem deceptively serene as young boys formed alliances and were initiated by gangs in the wrong ways of the street. It was good to be alive, even if it was in the ghetto. I felt an easing of my stress as we sought dwellings in a cheap fleabag motel. I was among my people again.

"Can you make copies of that tape?" I asked Steve.

"Yeah," he replied, "and what are we going to do with them?"

"We are going to mail them out to the FBI, the news media and the Department of Justice. I will keep a few copies and I will give one to our client when we meet with him," I replied.

Cayan laughed. I turned in anger to look at him. "You have a better idea?"

"Do you think they are going to show that on television?" he replied.

"They showed the war, didn't they?"

"That is their war, against a foreign enemy. This is our war, against them. Do you think they will show that on their television?'" he asked again.

I felt my leadership was being challenged. "We will see," I replied.

"No, we won't," he replied. "You will see. I already know."

"We should give it to effective black leaders and let them deal with it. Let them take it to the news media. Then it will be shown," said Cayan.

"Do you know of an effective black leader? I know of none. Since Martin was murdered, all the others have been on the run, hunted down by the law like common criminals, bullied into submission and discouragement. Their followers are now strung out on heroine. There are no black leaders, brothers. It's just you and I. The choices we make and the chances we take will determine our future."

"I cannot do that, brother. I have made the choice and taken the chances but my results must also be affirmative or it is all a waste of my time, and this has been a waste of my time."  With that, Cayan gathered his things and he and John walked out the door. I would never see them alive again. We sat there in silence. I wondered whether the difference in our ideology mattered that much to him that it created a divide we would not overcome. I uttered to Steve, "Make the copies now." I distributed them as I originally thought, sending a copy with an anonymous letter to the FBI. I also sent copies to the major news media and the Department of Justice. That evening I also met with my client, Mr Eisenberg and Mr Greenberg.

We met in a restaurant in Williamsburg, and after our initial greeting, he took me into a back room and watched the film.

"Is that all you have?" he asked.

"That's it," I replied.

"I need more than that," he said.

"What more do you need?"

"We need documents," he said, "and him admitting that he lynched those Jewish boys."

"He already admitted that. If you need more evidence, you will have to get it yourself," I responded. "If you don't believe what you are seeing is enough to put away this individual, then no matter what I have, it will never be enough."

"Don't you see – the people that are being hanged in this picture are black? They have been doing that in the South for centuries. It's the way of life there. If he was caught hanging Jews, we would have no choice but to act on it. Furthermore, you know who is in your little picture show?" he said. Not waiting for me to respond he continued, "That is Senator Christopher Carson, one of the most powerful senators in the senate."

"Are you scared of him?"

"I am," he said, looking me in the eye. "He came up through the CIA. He is a dangerous man and if you had any sense, you too would be very afraid of him. You can have your tapes back," he said, handing the tape to me.

"I have my own," I replied. "No matter the color of a human skin, when wrong is done, all those in the human community should stand up and make their voice be heard. When I took on this assignment, that was my belief and I am more rooted in that belief now. Yes, the color of the people being hanged in this picture is black, but to me it makes no difference if they were red, white or other. They were lynched and that is not right. They need to have justice done on their behalf. Your concern cannot be only for your people. If so, no one will be concerned when it's your people being lynched. Three of my men were killed during this assignment. The first time I ever lost men in battle – but I am sure you are not concerned because they were not Jews. I must compensate their families. They died in the process of getting information to help make your case. We provided you a service and we expect to be compensated, 100,000 dollars – that is the bill for our services."

"100,000 dollars", he repeated. "I don't have that type of money".

"How did you expect to pay off a reward of 100,000 dollars if you had no money? Under false pretences, three men died trying to gain information to help you break open your case and when we did, this is what you are saying? They died to present you a suspect, the same man that is seen committing the same crime that took your people's lives and now that you have that information, you say it's not enough? You claim to be dissatisfied and broke? Mr Eisenberg, you are a man without honor, lacking moral fortitude. You are indeed despicable scum," I said as I stood, took up the films and walked out. He was still sitting there as I left the building. I was only sorry I could not wipe his brain clean of the film I showed him.

"For one week, I stayed in New York waiting to see something related to what I had presented to the newspapers, radio stations and television stations. The media was not showing it. I saw nothing on the evening news regarding the lynching of the two men. One day as I sat there studying Carson's face on a poster on the wall of my room, the phone rang. The constant ringing was pulling me away. I was torn between answering and staring at Carson's pictures, wondering about putting a bullet between his eyes. After several rings, I picked it up.

"Mr Stuart?" I heard a voice asking.

"Who is this?" I asked.

"It's Eisenberg. Are you at that motel on Myrtle Ave?" he asked, sounding alarmed.

"Why do you want to know, Eisenberg?"

"I want to give you your money so you and your boys can get out of town as soon as possible."

"Why?" I demanded, interrupting him.

"Your tapes were turned over to Senator Carson and now there are some dangerous people looking for you. Come and get your money."

"No," I said. "I will tell you where to take it, and make sure no one is following you."

"These are CIA people," said Eisenberg. "You don't know when they are following you."

"What does the CIA want with me?" I demanded.

"What is the matter with you – don't you read the papers?

The communists who took over South Vietnam are charging us with war crimes and you were mentioned as a witness to the hanging of thousands of North Vietnamese and Viet Cong prisoners of war, including women and children. The Chinese and Russian Embassy are putting thousands of pictures on display of lynched Vietnamese and even some of our own black troops. They said a Major Red Dong of the North Vietnam military is leading this campaign. He claims you set him free on seeing these thousands of bodies hanging from trees by ropes in the Black Forest in Vietnam."

"I could relate to their suffering, I said.

"You did set him free, it is true," Eisenberg stated.

"You can't imagine. There were thousands of bodies, hanging by the neck, suspended from branches of large trees. They were on display for the North Vietnamese to see. It was supposed to have a psychological effect, but it only incited them to fight harder. We can thank our friend Carson for this, because he was the leader of it all."

"I know,' said Eisenberg. "That is why both the US government and the CIA want you dead. If it gets out that you set him free because you could relate to their sufferings, those are grounds for treason. You will be tried and if found guilty. You will hang. But you know they do not want it to go that far. If it does, it will be a major embarrassment for this nation. They will try to cover it up, and that means no loose ends. You are the primary loose end, the only person that can say this heinous act occurred. You cannot be trusted because your ideology prompted you to set one of their high-ranking officers free. That one act of setting him free allowed him to come back to haunt us. You should have kept your perspective about you and remember who and what you were, an American soldier. If you get on the stand, you will confirm their story of the dirty little secret of all those lynchings. You are better off dead than alive and that's what the CIA intends to do. I will give you your money, but don't let it be known that I was the one that tipped you off," he said. "Something else – the CIA got hold of your films from all the news media, the FBI and the DOJ.  They turned them over to Carson. I did mention before that he is a powerful man."

"Yes, you did," I said, "but how did you find out about the tapes?"

"I am Israeli secret service. I have my contacts too," said Eisenberg.

"I am impressed," I said sarcastically.

"At no time should a man betray his country," he said, looking at me with contempt in his eyes when he handed me a bag filled with money.

"I have one more question for you. Have you ever heard of the King Alfred Plan?" I asked.

"Where did you hear about that?"

"I overheard Carson saying that when he becomes president, he will enact the King Alfred Plan."

"You and your people are in great danger. It was conceived by J Edgar Hoover of the FBI with aid from the CIA. It's a plan to exterminate your race."

"I was shocked at his words but I believed him, I knew it was not beyond Carson to do that. I took the money and walked away. I divided the money among the team giving Cayan's cut to John, as they kept in touch. I headed home to Atlanta, where my wife and children were waiting my return. This, I hoped, was the end of a chapter in my life. Little did I know it was just the beginning. I had left Vietnam in September of 1970, America had pulled out in 1973 and now in August of 1977, I was being pulled back in a conflict I had left behind seven years ago. It was threatening to do something that the Viet Cong's or the North Vietnamese could not do and that was to make me a casualty of war. I was about to be dragged under by a moral act I did in Vietnam and because of it, the CIA was now on my tail and my country wanted me dead."

# CHAPTER 28: Death of an American Family

"Mr Stuart, you speak lovingly of your wife and children. Did they die, and if so, how?"

He stared me in the eyes for a long time before he started speaking. "I was informed by one of the men who was involved in her murder about how they did it. They said they relished killing my family, and so I brutally killed them for that."

"What did they tell you?"

"He said they went to my home hoping to find me there but that was not the case. They found my children who were startled by their presence and screamed. This is how I have imagined it must have happened from what I've been told. Jacqueline must have jumped out of our bed at the sudden terrifying screams of the children and the loud commanding voices in our home. There were strangers invading our house and I was not there to protect my family from them. They said Jacqueline burst into the room, armed with a pistol in her hand, and saw them, two fully dressed in Klan regalia. They said she pointed her weapon at the one who stood by himself. The other two were holding my son and daughter in their arms with guns against their heads.

"They said they threatened her but she stood up to them, trying to protect my childre and demanding what they wanted from her with a pistol in her hand. The thought is awful for me to comprehend. They explained to her my reputation as an uninhibited killer in Vietnam, and that I had killed 200 of theirs. She apparently didn't believe it and told them to get out. But they had another member of the Klan with them who she hadn't seen. He was the one who shot her. They boasted that she didn't see it coming; he shot her from behind. What a coward. My poor children had to witness this. They lynched them as they burned my house down. My whole family gone in one night." He trailed off, looking wearily into the distance. I felt a sudden pang of sorrow for him in that moment.

"That's how they killed your family?" I asked quietly.

"Yes, Nurse Gordon, that's how they were murdered."

"I am so sorry, Mr Stuart, to hear of the loss of your family at the hand of those terrorists. No one should die like that. No one should experience such hate just because of the color of their skin. I cannot fathom it and I cannot see any reason behind it. We were the ones who were enslaved, we are the ones who have reasons to be bitter, angry and hateful, but somehow they are the ones who are openly expressing those symptoms after we were emancipated." He looked at me blankly and quietly nodded in agreement.

"Nurse Gordon," said Mr Stuart "Even before I discovered my family had been murdered, I drove through the night thinking how easily my universe had imploded. I had the Klan on my tail as well as the FBI and the CIA hunting me down and I was considered an enemy of the state. My enemies were clearly defined. As I drove, I remember a sense of danger grew. I was determined to remain calm and not let my emotions drive me into a higher state of anxiety. I sped through the night along I95, headed for my home, a place I had not been in months. I wondered what awaited me and what was happening to my family, hoping that I would arrive in time to get them out of harm's way. I remember wondering where we could go to be free of the Klan and the CIA. I thought of Africa or Angola, but Angola was amid a civil war with millions dying. Nigeria also was going through governmental changes with its military. I remember the sense of doom growing with each passing second.

"As day broke, I concluded something had dramatically taken place in my world because of my Klan hunting. The last four hours of the drive were awful. Because of the weapons I had in my vehicle I couldn't drive fast and attract attention. Finally, I made it to my exit. I was paranoid, thinking there would be someone there waiting for my arrival, but there was no one. My need to remain inconspicuous took control of me. To surprise my prey was a distinct advantage, rather than to have him alerted to my arrival. As a sniper in Vietnam, I had developed those skills for my life depended on my ability to be stealthy under all conditions. Slowly and silently I drove the back streets of my neighborhood, eventually making it to my block. I stopped and canvassed the periphery and saw no guards. There was no one visibly watching, awaiting my return. My house was at the opposite end of the block.

"The sense of foreboding intensified as I approached my house. As I advanced from the far end of the block. my heart skipped a beat at the sight that greeted me. In the middle of the lawn stood a large charred cross. The neighbor's hedge and a huge tree blocked my immediate view of my house. I sped up. The only thing remained standing of my house were the brick walls. The beams from the roof had collapsed and what remained of the ceiling was now on the charred floor. They had bombed and burned my house down. Where was my family? Were they alive? I had to know, I had to find out. That was when the resounding words that Cayan uttered back in the Alabama woods came ringing in my ears. "The Klan had the ability to reach out and touch you no matter where you are in this country," he had said. I should have consented when he sought my permission to kill all the Klan members in their moment of disarray after the hanging of Sara's brother. Now that decision came back to haunt me. This was Carson's doing – I knew it. As my vision settled on the charred cross boldly standing in the middle of the lawn, imposing the hate it symbolised over the charred remains of my house, I screamed in anguish. At its base was a box. I walked over to investigate it. It was not booby trapped as I expected. I slowly opened it and I jumped to my feet, ran, screaming when I saw the contents. After the initial shock, I gathered myself together and slowly returned to the open box. I could not touch it but I recognised the faces, the dried bloody heads of Cayan, Steve and John were all in the box.

I could not bring myself to touch their heads and I could not bring myself to walk away. "Forgive me," I said, as I closed the lid to the box and picked it up and carried it under my arm.

"My emotional dam burst open as I walked around what remained of the structure of the building which was home to my Jacqueline, my homecoming queen and our two children. This was the castle I had built for her and the two children she had given me. Michael Stuart, my loving son, and Cynthia Stuart, my beloved daughter –where were they now? What hell had the Klan heaped on them? There were no signs of their bodies, no indication that they had become victims of the fire but I sensed they were dead. Just then I noticed a figure standing across the street from my house. It was the old man. I had seen him wandering these streets ever since I had moved here. He was well into his seventh decade of existence. I always greeted him in passing; he was approximately six feet tall, slim of body but with the stooping posture of an aged individual. His full head of hair was as grey as the ashes that covered the ground of my burnt-out building and his skin as black as the charred remains of the fallen beams. However, his face often bore a pleasant smile with white teeth and a sunny disposition. He stood there watching me from across the street from behind his thick-rimmed glasses. I sensed he knew something about this. I approached him.

"Do you know who did this old man?" I inquired.

"Son," he replied, "look around you. The signs reveal who the culprits are. They want you to know who they are – that is why the cross is there. They are not hiding. They were deliberate in their task. In fact, they were waiting for you. They grew tired of waiting and left before you arrived."

"Did you see them do this, old man?"

"With my two eyes. Like many, I watched from a distance as they burnt your house down."

"Why didn't you call the police?"

"Many of us did, several times in fact. But they never came, neither they nor the fire department showed up."

"That's because they were busy burning down my house. What happened to my family –where did they go?"

"The old man stared into my face for what seem to be an eternity without answering.

"What happened to my family?" I repeated. "Tell me if you know". He said, "Come with me, son," and I followed as he led the way into the bushes. I followed close behind, listening to his monologue. "I thought white America was on its way to adopting a more tolerant disposition in dealing with all other ethnic groups – a maturity, you know. I was wrong. Their hate is still as strong or stronger today than ever. It's just not as clearly displayed as before. I marched with Martin and was amazed with his teachings. That great prophet, a vessel of the almighty –they murdered him. His words which were meant to enlighten all of mankind fell on deaf white ears. We are all God's children, but their heart is full of detestation and intolerance for others, so they find it easy to do God-awful things like this to us."

"They are not God's children. Their souls are possessed by evil and they must be stopped."

"The old man stopped in his tracks and looked up at the muscular branches of a broad based oak tree whose sturdy trunk reached to the skies. "This is where I found your family, hanging from this tree. Your wife who was shot in the back and later lynched with your son and your daughter. With the help of others, I cut them down and buried them in those graves over there," he said, pointing to three unmarked graves.

"No!" I screamed. 'No!" The news hit me with the force of a bomb. I fell atop of the graves of my beloved in grief and cried. The impact of this loss was even greater than that of my father and uncles. I did not realize that the sun had set and darkness had settled over the land. I had been there at the burial site of my traumatically deceased family for hours, talking to them, praying for them, grieving for them. I felt as if my heart had been savagely ripped out of my chest as I went from talking to crying. Now I knew what it was like to be on the receiving end of this deed, which I had seen so many times in Vietnam. We had burned entire villages and killed so many helpless women and children and rationalized their deaths as casualties,' of war. Now here I was in my own country, a recipient of the same treatment from my fellow Americans. There was no doubt in my mind what I would do next: an eye for an eye, a tooth for a tooth. This act was the declaration of war and I swore I would take this war to Carson and destroy every man, woman and child that stood in my way to revenge the murder of my family. I planned to put fear in the hearts of all men that wore the Klan robe and wanted them to know I was coming and I would be merciless in taking their lives.

"Forgive me, my beloved Jacqueline, for not being there to defend you and the children against such tyranny. Without a doubt, I am the cause of this action. In my work, I have revealed this evil monster that has preyed on poor black people across the South and in Vietnam. I first met him as a child when he took the lives of my father and uncles. He took his hate with him across the seas to traumatize the people we fought there. Now he is back home doing the same thing to poor black folks here in the South. He knows he has been exposed and is now bent on keeping me quiet but it won't be so. Mark my words – I will avenge your death, I will avenge our children's death and Christopher Carson and all his minions will feel my wrath. This is now a war and I will not be at peace until I have avenged your deaths. I will look forward to joining you in heaven where I know you await me. You will always be alive in my heart. Let Michael and Cynthia know my love for them will be eternal. They will live in my heart forever. Your murder will be the fuel to my action and through my actions I will heap an abundance of brutality on the Klan Band all its kind. I will show no mercy as I kill, maim and destroy the members of that organization and what it stands for. I love America and the goodness for which it stands. That is why I became a soldier and was willing to die in her service. However, this evil dark side I cannot allow to continue to exist."

*****

"You declared war against the Klan?" I asked in disbelief.

"Yes, Nurse Gordon," he replied. "You are from the Caribbean. You would not understand."

"I am a black man, so I have experienced the pain you feel. I have walked your path. But my journey has not been as toxic as yours. Your battles and victories have made my journey more palatable, just as I will make my children's lives easier and less toxic than mine. I therefore understand that any man faced with injustice will feel the need to stand and fight for what is right. But declaring war against the Klan is like declaring war against the United States."

"Exactly," he said in agreement, "the US dearly holds to that racist ideology of the Klan and calls on it whenever needed. However, it will not publicly acknowledge its racist ideals nor disavow the Klan. There was nothing forthcoming that would satisfy my need for justice and so I became judge, jury and executioner. Vengeance would be mine."

"Did you ever question yourself regarding the righteousness of your act?"

"No, never did I question myself. The Klansmen never question themselves about their deeds."

"The Klan is made up of white men who are the majority in this nation. They will never convict one of their own when the victim is not white like themselves."

"Does that make it right for them to hunt us down like we are animals? Does it make it right for them to hang our people by the neck because they feel like it? No, Nurse Gordon – it's not right, it cannot be justified and because our justice system was not doing anything about it, I took justice in my hands and I punished those who had perpetuated those heinous crimes against us."

"Most white men are not Klan members."

"Most of them innately harbor the ideology of the Klan. They are closeted Klan members. Millions of men and women of other races have perished and met their demise at the hands of white men who felt they have the right to end the lives of others simply because they are different. Like animals becoming extinct, races of people have become extinct because of their brutality and greed. I am angry. Through me, billions of tormented souls cry out in anger, going as far back in time to when Columbus set foot in this hemisphere, bringing his European ideals with him. The American history bears witness with its manifested destiny. From Africa to the Americas and the Caribbean this legacy of hate, slavery, genocide and imperialism has left billions of angry souls seeking justice but only getting laws to repress, suppress, and depress their spirits and still, more laws to frustrate their lives. Don't believe that their deaths have put an end to my demand for justice. My peoples' spirits are still angry from the treatment they received at the hands of those conquering imperialist forces. I fight this war on behalf of all those souls, to right the wrongs and injustices that have been showered on them and us since the discovery of this New World. Many have forgotten or chose to forget the torment and torture their forefathers had to endure, believing that it is a better world today, never taking time to research the history of the racial conflicts. They choose to be assimilated into the system, a system that does not really want them but cannot outwardly refuse them. I am a man. I want to be treated like a man and nothing less than a man."

"How come you are still alive? You started this war in 1975 and it's now 2006. More than 30 years have passed. What have you accomplished in those 30 years?" I asked him. "Have you been hiding from reality in asylums like this one?"

"Off and on, yes – they have been my sanctuary from those who hunt me. It's my haven, the only place I can be at peace and the last place the law would think of looking for me."

"What do you mean by that?" I asked.

"I am tired," he said. "I need some rest." He stood up from his chair and walked to the door. He stopped with one hand on the doorknob and turned his head half way. Without looking at me he said: "One day soon you will have all the answers – all the information you need from me to enact your role. Eventually you will know why I fight. Read about the King Alfred Plan and get to understand it. It will be enacted in some part or in full during your life time." He exited my office. Strange character, I thought to myself. Many times, I did not consider him mentally unstable. What he yearned for was what every man sought throughout their lives: love, respect, integrity and dignity. If his story was true, that was what he was fighting for. I asked myself then if this King Alfred Plan he kept referring to was true.

# CHAPTER 29: Striking Back

The unit was quiet; it had been without any incidents for days. Mr Stuart had remained in his room for most of that time, coming out only for his meals and medications. At first I did not disturb him because I imagined he was still in pain from reliving his family's deaths. I checked his chart to find he was compliant with his medications and had denied having any hallucinations during this time. However, he was not socialising with the other clients and staff, and this bothered me. After our last meeting, I sensed he was slipping into a depressive state of mind. I went to his room to see what was happening with him. As I walked into the sunlit room, which he shared with three other male patients, I noted the curtains were drawn back from the window that made up the eastern wall of the building. Mr Stuart was lying on his back in his bed reading a book.  I looked around the room and saw that another patient was asleep in a bed, covered from head to toe. I heard him breathing and knew he was alright. He was a newly admitted patient. I called his name twice and waited for his response. He removed the cover from his face and angrily looked at me.

"What do you want?" He demanded of me in a gruff tone.

"I wanted to see that you are okay," I said.

"I am okay," he said as he pulled the cover back over his head. "When do they serve breakfast in this joint?"

"They are serving lunch right now. If you make it to the lunch room in a few minutes you will get a meal. You must respond to the bells whenever you hear them ring. They ring at every mealtime and every meeting time. Please respond to them, as once a meal is served there won't be any until the next meal. We do not keep food on the unit." Quickly he got out of his bed and headed for the lunchroom. "Mr Stuart, aren't you hungry?"

"Yes, but my hunger is neither for food nor drink, but for words and wisdom that will quench and fill my brain like food would do my guts. Did you look up the King Alfred Plan?"

"No," I sheepishly replied. I had forgotten about this King Alfred Plan he had mentioned and I quickly sought to change the subject. "I don't believe you will be filled by what you are reading."

"Then get me something that will, for I yearn to read something that will grab and keep my attention. You know, with all the restrictions they have on us crazy people, I am not able to go and come as I please and there is no bookstore or library in this place so I can choose what I want to read."

"What is it that you want?"

"I want some books to read."

"I will get you books," I said, "but I want you to finish your story!"

"Why?" he demanded, "so you can tell your friends about crazy old me?"

"Legally I cannot discuss my clients with anyone who is not involved in their care, and I am sure you don't believe I would do such a thing," I replied.

"But you still do, Nurse Gordon, you still do," he repeated.

"That would be improper, illegal and I would lose my license if I was found doing that. I have worked much too hard to achieve it. I would never do anything that stupid to jeopardise my livelihood and why would you say that?"

"Your livelihood," he sneered as if I had said something offensive, now sitting on the side of his bed with both legs firmly planted on the floor. "Your livelihood. Is that all you care about?"

"It's one of my major concerns – the preservation of my major accomplishments. To achieve that required a lot of studying to become knowledgeable and attain my degrees, sacrificing having fun with my friends for studying, planning, working to reach where I am today. In learning I came to understand the responsibilities it takes to be a Registered Nurse. My education was costly in money and consumed a lot of my time as I dedicated myself to gain that knowledge and experience. It took great effort. Without a doubt, the rules of my practice are important to me and I make sure I adhere to them. They are among the guidelines that I have used to alert me that something troubling is going on within my patient's brain. I need to assess to find out what is troubling you, causing you to withdraw and isolate yourself from others."

"I am telling you my life story and sometimes your comments show that you are being insensitive and judgmental. All I want you to do is listen. I already know what the outcome will be and you cannot change it. I have accepted it and am mentally prepared for it, for the day I walk out those doors I will turn myself over to the authorities, but before that time comes I want to tell my story. Once I am in the hands of the authorities, they will let me appear as a serial killer, a murderer, a common criminal or even a terrorist. But I see myself as martyr who will bring about change using violence to achieve my goals."

I looked at him as I processed what I heard and mulled over in my head which of his statements I would first address. "Violence within itself does not change things; it usually exacerbates situations, making them worse. That's why Martin chose non-violence in bringing about civil rights changes, for he knew what violence would lead to. The Southern whites chose violence, and the media then exposed the vile hate they harbored through their use of violence and the world came to see and know what was happening in America. Public opinion drastically changed and sided against the whites because of the violence they demonstrated against innocent black people seeking human rights as citizens of this nation. Do you remember the newsreels on television of the police attacking the non-violent protesters with their dogs, beating them down with their batons and blasting them with tear gas as they ran in fear of losing their lives? It was an ugly sight to behold but it swayed the public's opinion in favour of the non-violent protesters and they won the war, but most of all they won their rights.

"Mr Stuart, within the scope of my job I must formulate nursing diagnoses based on the information I am receiving so I can correctly care for the patient I am working with. If that makes me judgmental in your eyes, then so be it. I will not turn off my senses while I am listening to you or others. I sleep only at nights, not while I am here, and your story does not allow for any naptime. I have not encountered any boring moments in your life that would render me to sleep yet. I look forward to hearing your story. So far in your story you have not mentioned anything you have done that is considered a crime of murder, so get on with it and finish up your story."

"You want me to continue?" He asked with a smile on his face, as if relieved of a burden.

"Yes sir, I find your life story compelling and, so far, righteous."

He furrowed his brows and looked intensely at me. I felt as if he was peering into my soul for hidden meaning to my choice of words, but I was genuinely wrapped up in his life story.
"Yeah," he mumbled not finding any disingenuousness in my heart. "The following day I dug up my wife's and children's graves to make sure that it was them buried there in the ground. I had to be sure it was them. By then some of the fire and hostility had dissipated from me and rationality began taking its place. I re-interred them after I was certain, and prayed over their graves. Again, night caught me in the woods and I started hallucinating. I saw my father and uncles hanging from the tree, like when I last saw them, when they were lynched by the Klan back when I was a boy. They started talking to me.

"This was not meant to be son; your family was not meant to be sacrificed. But that is the way of your enemy. He has no regard for our people's lives. You must put an end to this," my father's voice said. "You must venture into their midst to accomplish your purpose in life. All this training to kill and all the experience you have had in killing is for a reason. It was not by chance you became proficient at this. You were chosen, favoured by the almighty to bring an end to a dark history of the US and prevent it from taking on the racist ventures of Christopher Carson if he becomes president. If you accomplish this my son, this nation will survive and continue to grow, spiritually accepting its people as one. If you fail, your enemy will take this hate he has for our people and use it as the rationale to wipe us all from the face of the earth. The pain you are feeling for your lost loved ones will be motivational in you accepting this mission."

"Father, I am in pain. Allow me to grieve the loss of my loved ones", I remarked to the apparition standing in front of me, looking like my father.

"Your heart has already accepted your mission, son, for it yearns for vengeance," he said, "but not your mind. Your mind must accept what your heart is telling it and then it should go about planning to do what your heart has told it. Have no fear – in doing this you will discover the true meaning of life. Have no fear of death and of accepting it when it's your time. Son, you must have faith in the almighty. You will need him to accomplish this mission."

"Suddenly there was an unearthly sound. I looked at the ghostly figure of my uncle Joe. He was morphing into another ghostly figure with the most hideous face I ever saw.

"You are all ghosts," I said. "You are all dead. How can I be speaking with you? How can you be speaking with me? Am I going crazy? This is not real!" Just then, the ogre of a figure began morphing again. This time the spirit of my sweet Jacqueline stood before me.

"Listen to what they say, my love," she said. "Only you can stop Carson. He will not reveal what truly lies in his heart and mind to the American people. He is very crafty; he knows what to say to his audience to win them over to his thinking. He will not reveal to the American people what dwells within his heart. If he did, they would not elect him to the White House. You must prevent that."

"How can I do that?"

"You will kill him. Be aware – there are forces out there whose mission is to prevent you from achieving your goal. The children and I died hideous deaths; we are calling on you to not let that occurrence be in vain. You are here to hear our message and avenge our passing. We are angry spirits although we are in a better place. We cannot be at peace until you put an end to the existence of Christopher Columbus Carson. I love you, my husband, and I wait for the day when you join us in this better place then we will all be in peace."

"I love you, my wife," I said to her spirit.

"I love you, my husband, and the spirits of our children miss you." And they were all gone."

Mr Stuart sat there with a forlorn look on his face. For minutes, silence reigned, only to be broken by my question.

"Mr Stuart, was it you who assassinated Christopher Carson?"

"It's more than 30 years since that night and I have left a trail of death and destruction behind that will amaze this world when they come to find out." That brought me up in my chair. I knew he was serious and what he was about to reveal could not be discounted.

"Mr Stuart, was it you who assassinated Presidential candidate Christopher Carson?" I repeated, wanting to have him confirm his previous statement, but he ignored me and continued with his story.

"At first, I did not know where to start, but I had learned how to make bombs and explosives while I was in Vietnam. The old man had told me of a Klan meeting hall deep in the Alabama bushes. He provided me a map with its location and other Klan meeting places. I questioned him on how he had attained all this knowledge of the Klan.

"Although we lived in fear, we never always turned the other cheek. We had our skirmishes with the Klan and  a few of its members met their demise at our hands. But we never openly confronted them. Unknown to them, we scouted them, got to know who they were and where they met, lived, entertained and worshipped," said the old man.

"Mr Stuart, you are not answering my question. Did you kill presidential candidate Christopher Carson?"

"All your questions will be answered Nurse Gordon. Listen to my life story".

*****

"We did our best to avoid them," the old man continued. "We humbled ourselves and we cowered. As black people, we bowed to show humility and we acted stupid when we had to so as to survive. We made them feel we were not a threat to them. We tolerated their hate, prejudice and everything else to survive. But knowing that things could change we prepared for war. We stored our ammo, our people worked in their homes as housekeepers and they furnished us with information about them. Those old people who work as servants and maids were among our greatest spies. Throughout all the states where our people lived, we gathered information, hoping the day would never come, but preparing for it so that we would be ready to fight to prevent our annihilation."

"When did this start?" I asked the old man.

"After World War 2, many of our black veterans were returning to the South after fighting Hitler and defeating Nazism. They could no longer tolerate Jim Crow. They wanted to take up arms and fight, but cooler heads prevailed and so we planned and prepared for their ultimate onslaught on our people. That never came, but we were prepared if it came. Eventually other minds and thinking prevailed. Now we fight to be included and to be integrated into this system. In so doing, we have lost most of the things we created while we were excluded from it.' I looked in the old man's eyes and saw the pain and fear he and others who came out of slavery had endured. It all made my mission clearer."

# CHAPTER 30: The Meeting Hall

"The old man furnished me with additional maps of the meeting places of various white supremacist groups throughout the South and across the nation. He also provided me with the things necessary to make bombs. One of the Klan's meeting halls was not very far from Carson's place. With that as my objective, I planned and prepared for my first encounter. In a few days, I set out to avenge the deaths of my loved ones. I was embarking on my road of no return. I travelled mostly by night. Hidden below the rear car seat were my guns, bombs, grenades and launchers. I also had five missiles and a reusable hand-held launcher: this was for a special mission. It was late at night when I pulled off the road and drove into bushes near the Alabama town that was known as the major Klan stronghold in America. If there was any fear that America would eventually become like Nazi Germany under the Confederacy, this was the place that would be the soul of that driving force. I knew if I was spotted I would not make it out of there alive. I hid my vehicle deep in the woods. With my weapons on my back I trudged through the thick dark wilderness. It did not take long before the morning sun began to light up the vast forest. Even in the dark I had managed to follow the old man's directions and there in front of me, as the thick bush thinned out into a meadow, was the building he had described. The building was locked up and showed no signs of life.

It was early morning and the sun was already providing enough heat to force me to remove my backpack. Satisfied there was no one there, I decided to move in for a closer look. There was a big steel-covered drum against the wall close to a window of the building. I moved it below the window and climbed up. The first floor had a bar and there were several tables with chairs around them in the main room. This was not just a meeting hall but also a place to socialise. There was a dance floor. I looked closely at the window, checking for alarms. There was none and to my surprise, the window was unlocked. I looked in the hall before I entered. I gripped my Colt 45 automatic as I trespassed. I was feeling at peace, comfortable with myself and my plans. I did not know that an adrenaline surge could be so comforting. Its instantaneous boost of energy brought me to higher levels of awareness. I made my way through the building looking for places I could place the bombs where they would be devastating but would not be seen by the Klan members. I placed all of them out of sight under the floor and ceiling throughout the building. On exiting, I returned the drum to its original spot. I sought out a tree deep within the clustered forest that was tall enough so that I could see any approaching vehicles and what was taking place at the cabin, but far enough that I would not be seen. The tree was a distance from the dirt road that led into the meadow and to the hall. There I mulled over my plan. I figured Carson would be at this Klan meeting. If not, I would get him at his mansion.

"I had a few hours of REM sleep. I dreamed that I was so alert I heard the sound of the growing grass in the meadow. I had not forgotten this feeling. It was always there, waiting to be called on. It was as if I was back in Vietnam, crawling through Viet Cong's tunnels with gun in hand, doing a search and destroy on their underground camps. All my senses were alive. I was ready for war.

"Slowly the day went by; I checked the devices, rethought my plans looking to make improvements, and reached the point of readiness. It was late afternoon when the first vehicle crashed in on the sounds of nature as it made its way up to the building. It was a jeep like mine except of a different colour. Four men dressed in battle fatigues got out of the vehicle and made their way to the main entrance of the building. Within half an hour, another two vehicles arrived and another four men entered the building. I observed them preparing for the night. I prayed that none of them would stumble onto the bombs and reveal the violent destruction that awaited them. As time went by, more of them arrived. Soon the meadow was filled with cars and groups of men dressed in white robes and matching cone hats standing around chatting, not having a clue what massive destruction I had waiting for them in the hall. As dusk fell, they began to head indoors. I had stopped counting at 200, but my prey was not among them. The meeting was called to order, and they began to read the minutes from their previous meeting.

"As they became increasingly involved in their meeting, I started to battle with myself, knowing that Carson was not there. I questioned myself if setting off the bombs and killing these Klansmen would not send Carson into hiding where I would not be able to find him. Then I remembered the last time I did that — and its consequences. I knew some of these men were involved in the murder of my family. I pushed the buttons that detonated the explosives. All 12 exploded simultaneously, their shattering blast ripping apart the building in a crescendo as the intense pressure tore into the unsuspecting Klansmen's bodies, ripping apart their flesh and blasting their bones into tiny fragments. Their deaths were quick and unexpected. They were dead before they could scream. Bits and pieces of human bodies and tissue were blown all over the cars in the beautiful green meadow as smoke and fire took hold of what was left of the building. As I stood up to take my leave, the head of a man fell to the ground in front of me. An incredulous look of surprise was still on his face and he was still trying to speak, which horrified me. I thought how fitting an end this was for them, knowing many of my people had met a similar death at their hands."

I could not believe what I had heard. "Mr Stuart," I said slowly. "You have just admitted to killing more than 200 men in cold blood. This is a terrible crime. I have to report this crime to the police. Confidentiality cannot save you."

"I am not seeking any protection, Nurse Gordon," he said. "I welcome you reporting this and everything else I have to tell you. I am ready to face the law, for I know I have accomplished my purpose for living. I am ready to die and that is what the state will do to me. However, I am asking you to allow me to complete my story."

"There is more?" I asked.

"There is much more needing to be told," he replied.

I did not know what to believe, or whether this man was delusional or creative. I myself had migrated to the US in June 1988. I came with a goal to be an engineer, but I met Sharon. We fell in love and she became my wife. She was pregnant early after graduating high school. But we both struggled and became Registered Nurses. We lived comfortably in a predominantly West Indian neighborhood. Although we had seen and experienced prejudice and hate sometimes when we ventured into neighborhoods that were occupied by whites, we were never exposed to the degree of hate Mr Stuart encountered in his lifetime. We had professors in college who we sensed were prejudiced but had learned how to ignore them outside of the classroom and we worked to achieve the grades we wanted while we were in their classes. Would I have acted like he did if I was exposed to that degree of hate? I don't believe so. I began to ask myself if this was all true. I had read and heard of the violent racial history of the US from the time of slavery to the time of the Civil Rights movement. I read of the intolerable conditions my ancestors had to  endure. What blacks had to tolerate here in the United States was severely inhumane.

Things had changed. I was no longer an audience to Mr Stuart. I was being pulled into being a participant in his dramatic tale. As I listened, it became clear that I had major decision to make. I had to act on his revelation, because he was disclosing personal, classified information about his life. I was now realising that he was counting on me to inform the law of his deeds. I was beginning to understand my role in this tale.

"How will you portray me in my life story, Doc?" I heard him asking.

"I am a Registered Nurse," I replied. A faint smile came over his face.

"Will I be presented as a heartless monster when you write my life story? That's not how I want to be recalled. The reason why I am telling you all of this, the good the bad and the ugly, is so you can present me for what I believed, what I perceived and what I will die for. Tell me you won't present me as an inhumane, heartless, murdering psycho?"

"What are you, Mr Stuart? I want to know the good the bad and the ugly about you. If what you have just disclosed is true, aren't you a heartless, murdering psycho?" Our eyes met in a heated stare-down. "I need to believe what you have been telling me, Mr Stuart, and if you have not furnished proof, your life story will not be written by me in any place but your psychiatric chart. Your claims after Vietnam are preposterous. They are the insights of a man lost in thoughts of delusions of grandeur, a mere figment of your imagination."

Silence prevailed for minutes thereafter. He stood up, went to the main desk and requested his suitcase. After it was given to him, he opened it and took out a New York Times article with a headline dated August 14 1978. It read, "Are the coloreds striking back? 220 Klan men blown to bits by explosives in rural Alabama Town hall." I was shocked as I read the New York Times report of a Klan meeting that ended in their horrific demise. I remembered when he showed me pictures and newspaper clippings of him receiving different medals of honor during the Vietnam War. He had explained to me many of those medals he had received during that war, presented by high-ranking military officers. I had accepted the fact that this was not a tall tale from a crazy man's imagination.

"Let me see the contents of your suitcase!" I demanded.

"You will be given it all in time, Nurse Gordon," he replied. "I ask that you only listen to my story and write it when I am gone from this world. It may make you a wealthy man by becoming a best seller," he said, with a smile on his face.

"You killed more than 200 men and you expect me to sit here and continue listening to your tale of brutality? You smile about it and think I want to profit from their demise. You are a heartless, psychopathic monster. I have my obligations and even laws of patient confidentiality will not prevent me from turning you over to the law," I said.

"I want you to do that," he said coldly, without any hint of remorse. "But I want you to hear everything I have to say before you do that. At the end I will present you with all the proofs, my medals from 'Nam, all the newspaper clippings, all my documents of how I planned and went about doing what I did. Most of all, the weapons I used to achieve my goals. Yes, I am a heartless monster. I started to become one from the day they made me watch as they lynched my father and uncles. My journey to Vietnam made me numb to the feelings of others and finally whatever heart I had left was lost when they lynched my wife and children."

I closed the door to the room so no one would interrupt us. I sat in a chair and bade him to continue his murderous tale.

"This is not a tale of murder," he said. "It is a tale of redemption."

"It does not matter how you rationalise your story, what I see and hear are constant killings by your hands."

"I cannot get you to understand, and it's important that you do. You have not shared my experiences nor borne my pain. I was mistaken – you are a black man but you have not felt the pain of the black masses here in America. You bask in the light of the American dream, a falsehood it sells to the masses to get you focus on an illusion while so many of us are attacked by unjust law and their enforcers. You have attained an education, a profession, a family, a home – yes, you have gotten everything that a man would want in this experiment we call the United States of America. I am asking you, Nurse Gordon –  where were you when the Federal government had to provide troops to protect black kids on their way to integrated schools in the South? Where were you when blacks were fighting to have the right to vote? Where were you when Martin was assassinated?"

"I never thought of the white man as an obstacle in my path to achieving my goal, Mr Stuart. I never saw him as such. The only thing I saw that could prevent me from reaching my goal was me and my thinking. I never allowed it to become an obstacle. What you need to do is inform young men that education and not crime is the path to success. You need to inform youths to take control of their destiny not through marching but through education by becoming the attorneys, the judges, the legislators, the district attorneys... the people who make the decisions relating to the law. And then they will have justice. Now get on with your story, Mr Stuart."

"Do you think the drug laws and the war on drugs were meant to stop and prevent the trafficking of drugs? If so, they are a terrible failure. Do you believe the three-strikes-you-are-out laws are meant to stop people from committing crimes? No – they are not. They are just a continuation of the Jim Crow laws that have been part of the history of this nation. If those laws were meant to do as they said, more whites would be in jail – they are the majority drug users and dealers in this country. But if you follow the media and those who are warring on drugs, you would believe we are the only ones doing it. Their true objective is to prevent the advancement of black folks.

"Possibly there are a million young black men in jail with life sentences for minor nonviolent infractions. You think that is not a plan?" he asked. "You have to belong to something more than just the American dream, Nurse Gordon, for that is a fallacy sold to the masses to keep them focused while the brutal reality grinds you to a pulp. You are one of our success stories. Wake up and see the cause and effects. Be aware of them, for they will eventually affect you and your offspring."

"My commitment is to my family," I replied.

"Get out of your comfort zone, Nurse Gordon. Don't just live your dream but help some little black boy or girl live theirs."

I felt some embarrassment to have this psycho instructing me on the need to participate in the growth of my race. But his thoughts were noble.

"I instruct many young people at my community centre in making career choices, making life choices. I listen to them and offer counselling and give guidance if I can. However, that is enough about me; I would like you to continue with your story, Mr Stuart."

"I headed for my vehicle making sure I left no evidence behind. I had expected lots of police vehicles to be swarming the area by then, but to my surprise, none came. I thought the explosion was heard all over the county. Then the answer came to me as I heard an explosion from a distance away. There was an ongoing strip mining nearby with the sounds of constant explosions. The population thought the bombs I had set off were from the miners. I waited until about midnight and headed out of hiding. I had my RPG next to me as I drove to my next destination. It took me less than an hour, but I was finally there on the street in front of Carson's estate. I loaded the rocket launcher and fired five times from the cover of the dark. Five times I had a direct hit followed by an explosion. The house went up in flames as I made my way to the vehicle and slowly drove away. I heard the screams of the bodyguards who were caught in the house; they were being incinerated by the furious, overwhelming flames. There would be no firemen or policemen to rescue them for they were all dead, victims of their own indiscretions as members of the Klan.

"You blew up a US senator's home?" I asked in disbelief.

"My intentions were to kill him, but he was not there at the time. I later learned that his father was killed in that incident."

"How come you were not caught?" I asked, still in disbelief.

"I don't know and I never tried to figure it out. I was always careful never to leave any evidence behind. Maybe, as the apparitions had said, they would protect me. Maybe they veiled the eyes of those who were looking so they would never see me."

"I don't get, it," I said. "You are telling me that you blew up buildings killing hundreds or possibly thousands of people and the police never thought of you as their primary suspect. Carson must have known it was you. Why didn't he turn you over to the police?"

"Maybe because I had the goods on him. I still have copies of the tapes of him hanging those two men in the woods in Alabama. It will be among the things I will give to you before I go. I was never picked up and questioned by the police or treated as a suspect," replied Mr Stuart.

"After committing this violent act, I remained inactive for the next years. I went into hiding; I returned the vehicle and weapons to a place the old man had told me. There I was furnished with a new identification and I was taken across the border into Canada and to Alaska where I worked on the Trans Alaskan pipeline."

# CHAPTER 31: A Cover Up Brewing

Christopher Carson was in the Senate when he heard news that his home, the place where generations of Carsons had resided for hundreds of years, had been fire-bombed and burned to the ground. Additional news of the bombing of the Klan's town hall was forthcoming. Over a hundred years ago, that building had been built by his great grandfather on their land. It had been a central meeting hall for members of the Klan since its inception. The building had been visited by some of the most influential politicians who were members of the Klan when it was righteous to be a Klan member. As he stood staring at the remnants of his family estate, he was approached by FBI agent Donald Carwell, who was assigned to the case.

"Do you have any idea who could have committed this crime Mr Carson?"

"Only one man has the audacity to do this – and that's Mr Stuart," he replied.

"Why would this Mr Stuart have a reason to use such deadly force against you and your family?"

"I don't know," replied Carson.

"Mr Carson, this is like a war zone. For someone to blow up your home, you must have done something to piss them off."

"Whatever was done gives them no right to kill all those men and my father, a prominent US citizen, a former member of the senate, a man who dedicated himself to serving this nation."

"You mention the person named Mr Stuart as being your suspect and responsible for this crime. Would you describe Stuart?"

"He is black. He is a nigger."

"That is helping us some," said the racist, corrupt FBI agent.

"Officer, I will take care of this, I don't need your help. I will find him and I will bring him to justice."

"Mr Carson, I know your background, I know you are CIA but it is my job and duty to resolve this crime. Where do you think he is at this moment?"

"I do not know. More than likely in one of our great urban ghettos blending into the community."

"Senator – tell me more about this man, Stuart."

"He was among the most decorated men that fought in the Vietnam War. He is a dangerous killer and if he does not want to be found, you will never find him. You must do something to draw him out."

"Have you tried that?"

Carson looked at the FBI agent and continued his narrative, "This man Stuart is a traitor to this nation. He actively supported our enemies at the end of his tour of duty in Vietnam, leading to the death of thousands of American soldiers and the withdrawal of our troops from Vietnam. To answer your question – yes, I have tried. And this is how he retaliated."

"What did you do?"

"I am CIA."

"What did you do?"

"I killed his family."

The FBI agent could only stare at Carson for the moment on hearing this information. "You have made this a personal war between you and Mr Stuart. Don't make it spill over into the communities, otherwise we will be involved. We cannot provide you any logistics of his whereabouts and if we find him we will apprehend him. However, if you should find him before we do, make sure he does not survive or you will be going down with him."

"You don't seem to understand the nature of the being we are dealing with."

"We understand your being, Senator. We have a long history of you, your father and generations of Carson men here in America. We know of your involvement in the Klan and of the lynching of thousands of African Americans by you and your family members.

We know what you have done in this country and abroad. But you have privileges – something he does not have. If he is found, he must not remain alive to present his story. Like you, he does have an impeccable record of serving his country and he will be heard if he can present his story to the DOJ. If you fail to do that, you will have many FIRST degree murder charges brought up against you, Senator Carson. We have tapes of you lynching black folks in Alabama."

"Why are you not offering me more protection from him? You saw what he did to those men!"

"You don't need protection, Mr Carson. You have your bodyguards and CIA working for you."

"You must excuse me – the longer we speak, the greater distance he puts between the crime scene and himself. I have an interest in finding this man. Allow me to do that."

"Senator Carson, if Mr Stuart remains alive to confirm what happened in Vietnam, you and this nation will be tarnished forever."

"Are you threatening me, officer?"

"War crimes were committed in Vietnam, Senator, and they seem to point to you and your CIA secret society."

"I hear you loud and clear," replied Senator Carson. He turned and addressed his nearby underlings. "We must find Stuart and kill him. I cannot have my record tarnished by what some nigger saw in Vietnam."

"We have no idea where he disappeared to, Senator Carson."

"Find him."

# CHAPTER 32: Toy Soldiers

"Did you kill anyone while you worked in Alaska or resided in Canada, Mr Stuart?"

"No, Nurse Gordon I did not. While there I used my time to plan my next attacks on returning to the mainland. After completing my obligations to the pipeline consortium, I crossed over back into Canada and stayed there for an additional five years. I hunted and lived off the land as I had learned to in my youth and in the military. While there I occasionally sought information regarding Carson's thriving political and economic progress.  He had relocated to Texas after I destroyed his mansion, and became the governor of that state. His ambitions had driven him to now declare himself a Republican presidential candidate. This prompted my desire to return home. After many days of pondering, with a heavy heart and a troubled mind I gave into my desire. I had been away for approximately eight years and had grown to like this new life. However, I knew I had unfinished business back in the US.

"As I travelled along the magnificent byways and highways of my native country, I was informed of the racist militia groups, skin heads they called themselves, that had sprung up and flourished all over the country in the time of my absence. I sensed that like franchises, they were affiliated with the Sons of the Klan. All across America, white supremacists spouted their ideology as they trained with weapons of mass destruction, hoping that one day they would use them against the black population.

"The Federal government did nothing about it. We had fought and shed our blood in every war this country was involved in to uphold its philosophy. We helped in the settling of this nation, but one would not know that from her history books.

"I drove around the country formulating my plans, in no rush to get from point A to B. I noticed the people as they were one and the same, the only difference was their setting. The older ones looked at me with contempt and the children with curiosity. None were willing to know and accept me as a human being. I could see it on their faces and in their eyes. It burnt through my armor and pierced my heart. Racism had affected us all; it had stunted their growth and development. Their superior attitude, their arrogance and privileged life prevented them from understanding the effects their prejudice had on their lives as well as the lives of others.

"It takes courage to venture beyond our comfort zone to know someone that is truly not like us, and accept his difference and his right to existence. That is the secret to understanding that we are all our brothers' keepers. It's their culture to kill anything that is not familiar to them. You see it in their movies, in their books...it is so easy for them to kill.

"My thoughts on racial discrimination consumed me over the weeks following my return to mainland US. Then it started again. The voices, they were returning, but they were not talking to me, they were talking to each other in my head. It was as if I was eavesdropping on a group of people having a conversation. I tried not to give it my attention, fearing that if I did, it would drag me further into this illness that was now quickly consuming me, the insanity that was taking over my mind and guiding my thinking. I feared that if I was acquiescent to its presence, we would become one. Little did I know that leaving it unchecked had allowed it the time needed to become one with me. Hearing it was proof of my fall from grace into its abyss. I found myself driving around the country listening to the hate mongers as they heaped their hate on us for no apparent reason. There are those who wanted us to go back to Africa where we belong, and others whose vile thoughts made me cringe and I kept asking myself – why?

"More than eight years earlier, I had set off an explosion that had taken the lives of many Klansmen. I gave no thought to that act then. What had time away from from mainland USA done for me? I was introduced to a culture that was not driven by racial ideology as it was here in the US, and it had affected me. I had assimilated that within me, but now I was home again in the great US. One night through my aimless wandering, I found myself sitting in a bar in a hot, sleepy, little Texas town. I sat at the counter drinking a cold beer with an old white man serving up tall tales of his Korean War exploits.  It took sometime but I eventually found myself laughing at some of the things he said.  I was truly beginning to let down my guard when in walked a group of five young men seeking and wanting trouble.

"As they walked in the bar, I noticed the way they were looking at me.

"Al, give us each a pitcher," demanded the loudest member of the group to the bartender as they headed to a table. "Look boys, a nigger," said one of his friends as he set his sight on me.

"Al, who is the nigger?" demanded the first man. "Haven't you told him niggers are not welcomed here?"

"Look here, boys,' explained the barkeep, "I want no trouble here."

"I was always armed. Strapped to my lower legs just above the ankles I had my pair of Glock nine millimetres. I had my British commando knife strapped to my thigh and I could reach it through my right pocket in a split second.

"What are you doing here, nigger?" demanded one of the young thugs.

"The same thing you are doing here, boys – drinking a cold beer."

"What did you call me?' he said, getting out of his chair and coming closer.

"Disrespect is a bitch isn't it...boy?" I answered without getting to my feet. At the same time, I noticed that one of them had gotten up and headed out the door. He has gone to get their weapons, I thought, as the loud mouth proceeded toward me.

"Are you ready to die?" I asked him.

"Are you?" he demanded of me.

"Yes, I am. I've been waiting for someone to do me in for a long time," I said, without any uncertainty or hesitation in my voice.

"We will grant you your wish," he replied, smiling. "I never met a man so willing to meet his maker before, but nigger, I will grant you your wish as soon as my friend returns."

"You never answered my question,"I responded. "Are you ready to die?"

"He turned and looked me in the face, now less angry and more thoughtful, but before he could answer, his friend returned with baseball bats. He tossed one to the instigator and to the others who were now up and taking positions around me. At the same time, the barkeeper came up with a double barrel shotgun from below the counter.

"You are not going to kill anyone in my establishment. Sit down, all of you!" he barked with his gun pointed at them. Caught by surprise, they slowly retreated to their seats. "Mister, you get the hell out of my place."

"I gathered myself, finished my beer, walked towards the exit door and before I left, I turned and addressed them. "I am ready to die," I said. "If you are ready to kill me, follow me. I will be heading north." I got in my vehicle and did exactly as I told them. The urge to kill was taking over my thoughts. It was as if I had no control. The impulse was consuming me and I hoped the five of them would soon follow. However, I knew five would not satisfy my appetite. I needed to feast; it had been more than eight years since I last killed a man.

"I drove a few miles out of town and saw an area on the side of the road where I could park. I got out of my vehicle and made my preparations. I knew they would follow and it was not long after that I saw the lights of their vehicle approaching. They arrived and alighted from their vehicle.

"Are you all military men?" I asked.

"Texas militia," replied one.

"Toy soldiers," I retorted.

"Toy soldiers!'" repeated one of them. "Well, this toy soldier is about to kill your ass," he said as they took up positions around me with their baseball bats.

"It's clubbing time!" shouted one in glee, as he lifted the bat above his head with all intent of bringing it down on mine, but before he could complete his motion, I drew and started firing my glocks. In a second, all five of them lay on the ground with serious bullet wounds. Now injured, they were no longer willing to fight. I got my duct tape and restrained them, and dragged them into the woods. I bound all five of them together with each of their backs against each other.

"I asked you before if you were ready to die."

"No!" shouted one, "set us free!" This evoked a chuckle from me.

"Freedom is now based on conditions, partner," I retorted.

"You isn't a fucking partner of mine, nigger,"countered their leader. I walked over to him, separated him from the group, his hands still bound behind his back. I escorted him to stand by a tree trunk and continued speaking. "I want you to be aware that your deaths are imminent, but if you cooperate, you may live. To show you how serious I am, I'm willing to do this." I quickly pulled one of my Glocks and fired one shot. It penetrated the head of their leader directly between the eyes. He was dead before he crumbled to the ground. The remaining men were now petrified.

"God, he shot Rich in the head just like that," I heard one of them say in disbelief. Another one said, "He killed Rich." I raised the pistol and fired in the air to cease their chattering, and continued speaking to restore order. "You do not have to suffer the same fate as your friend. All you have to do is answer my questions and you will live," I uttered, knowing in my mind they were all dead. I walked over and stood directly in front of one of them.

"What's your name, boy?" I demanded.

"Joey," he replied timidly.

"Joey," I repeated. "You are a member of one of these hate group militias, aren't you?" I pried, hunting for information that would lead me to one of their groups.

"Don't answer any questions Joey," shouted one of his comrades.

"Boys, wherever you go – there are rules. Here I will make them up as we go and you are aware that I will enforce them as I see fit. The first rule is that no one speaks until I have given them permission. Young man, I did not address you. You have broken that rule. Consider this as your final warning," I asserted and went back to questioning Joey.

"Joey, before we were interrupted, I asked you a question. Now give me an answer."

"I belong to the Texas fourth militia, a member of the Sons of the Klan," replied a fearful Joey.

"Don't answer anything that nigger asks you, Joey!" shouted the rule breaker again.

"Bobby, I want to live," replied a petrified Joey.

"I walked over to him and calmly said, "Bobby, you apparently have no respect for me and my rules."

"Without that gun, you wouldn't be so brave would you nigger?"

"Bobby, close to a thousand men have thought that and they have all met the same fate. It's time you joined them, Bobby.' I said, as I placed the gun to his forehead, contacting his skull. His eyes suddenly opened wide with surprise. I pulled the trigger again shattering the quiet of the early morning. Bone particles, blood and brain matter went splattering from the impact of the bullet's penetration.

"They all had their eyes closed tightly now. "Boys," I said "you are soldiers; you must know how to look death in the eyes without flinching. Open your eyes. I am death and I am here to claim what's mine."

"What's that?" one bravely asked.

"Your spirit and souls," I responded.

"What will you do with them?" he inquired.

"Send them to hell where they belong," I replied.

"You are going to kill us all, aren't you?" he sheepishly stated.

"Not if you cooperate," I lied. He instinctively sensed my lie and confronted me.

"If you are going to kill us, have the decency to be honest with us."

"I am the devil," I replied. "Honesty is not one off my strengths."

"Guys, we are dead," the braver one stated.

"Clever indeed," I responded. However, Joey was governed by fear and did not comprehend the revelation of his braver partner.

"Joey," I inquired, "do you want to live?"

"Yes, yes, I want to live". He affirmed his cowardice as I placed tape over the mouths of the other two members.

"Then answer my questions truthfully and honestly – for if you don't, Joey, have no doubt, I will kill you, like I killed your friends."

"What do you want to know?" demanded Joey, ready to spill his guts to save his miserable pathetic life.

"Why did you join this militia?"

"So I could have friends," he replied.

"Don't lie to me, Joey," I calmly rebuked.

"I am not lying," he said, crying.

"Isn't this militia a hate group of white supremacists who profess to hate blacks?" I interrogated.

"Yes," he replied in a low tone, so that I had to strain to hear him.

"I can't hear you, Joey, son of the Klan – talk louder," I demanded.

"Yes, yes, yes!" he screamed back at me.

"How many niggers have you all killed, beaten up, harassed and just put the fear of the devil in? Answer me truthfully, Joey – remember you want to live and, if you do answer, you will live."

"Many," he replied, now shaking.

"How many do you mean by 'many', Joey? 5, 10, 20? Give me a number, Joey."

"50 that I know of – maybe more from before I joined," he revealed.

"More than 50," I reiterated. "You are lying to me again, aren't you, Joey?"

"No, I am not! They weren't all niggers; some were 'spic, wet back laborers up from Mexico. In fact, most of them were."

'How do you know that?' I continued interrogating.

"It's part of our initiation as Sons of the Klan. After they finish training us, they bring in a group of niggers, spics and wet backs. Usually five of them, lightly arm them, then they are released in the wilderness. They have us hunt them down and kill them. We work as a team."

"This was your team?" I asked, smiling.

"Yes," he replied.

"Interesting, truly interesting. Where is your camp located, Joey?"

"About 50 miles south of here, in the Diego forest," he replied.

"Unexplored country. How come you're so far away from your base?" I asked.

"We were out hunting to find some niggers or spics for the next group initiation."

"And you ran into me. Isn't that a bitch?" I replied. "Who is hunting who now, Joey? The tables have turned on you and your boys here. How do you like being on the other side, Joey?"

"He sullenly stared at me. "I will allow you to be reticent for that one, Joey. You can keep your thought to yourself," I said with a sneer. "How many of you are in the camp?"

"He did not answer. "I will not repeat myself Joey."

"Close to 300," he replied.

"What type of weapons are they using?"

"Mostly small arms, AR15, M16, AK47 – anything we can get our hands on. What you planning on doing, nigger?" Joey quizzed. "Attacking the camp would be suicidal."

"You think so, Joey?"

"There are 300 well-armed, nigger-hating, bad men there. You don't stand a chance."

"Who am I, Joey?"

"A fucking dead nigger," he replied, smiling.

"No, Joey, remember I told you who I was when we first met".

"The devil," he said sheepishly. "Who the fuck calls themselves the devil?"

"I am who I am, Joey, and I am here to collect lost souls. You have described a place where there is an abundance of them. That is my destination."

"They are going to kill you."

"You don't get it, Joey. When you have lived with death for long as I have, you grow to accept him and respect him. You know he is not the finality but the means to the next order of life, the unknown. For a man that professes to have killed others, you sure as hell are afraid of dying, Joey. My day will come too and I will be accepting of it. I will not fear it."

"I have never killed anyone, mister," he confessed.

"I didn't think so, Joey, but surely you have made a lot of black people lives miserable, through harassment, beatings, and participating in lynching. Haven't you, Joey?"

"Yes, I have," he replied in a remorseful tone.

"What did those poor defenceless people do to you that provoked such hate and animosity that you saw a need to build militias to wipe them out?"

"They exist and that is enough of a reason," he said, now with a sneer on his face.

"That's right, Joey. Reveal to me all the ugliness of your soul, say those nasty things that you believe or been taught, don't be concerned about how I feel, Joey because that's who you are – a white supremacist." I taped his mouth. I had gotten all the information I needed. I walked over to the cool-headed leader.

"I like you. You are very clever, very smart. Maybe one day you would evolve into being wise – you have that gift. Pity you won't make it there." I pulled my weapon and fired once. He was dead. I turned and looked at Joey. He was struggling to say something I did not want to hear. I walked over to the other one whose name I never got. I removed the tape from his mouth.

"What's your name?" I inquired.

"Fuck you, nigger," he said, and spat on me. I wiped it off, looked at him, smiled, took aim, fired and he too was dead.

"I walked over to Joey, who was still struggling to speak. I removed the tape from his mouth.

"You said if I told you what you wanted know you would let me live," he said, with tears in his eyes.

"I also told you who I am, Joey. You didn't listen."

"You lied to me?"

"Yes, Joey, I lied. That's what I do. I am the devil, remember."

"I want to live, I want to live, I want to live!" he cried.

"Joey," I said "if you are willing to kill for your belief, you must be willing to die for it too. And you, my friend, have been killing for your belief. That's the reason why we are here. You followed me to kill me. Tell me, Joey, when you were beating, maiming and killing those niggers did they beg for their lives, Joey? Did they beg for their lives? Ah, Joey, answer me, Joey, did they beg for their lives before you killed them?" I screamed at him.

"Yes, yes!" he shouted back at me as he hollered and his voice trailed off as he cried. "Yes, they begged, they begged."

"Did that stop you from killing them, Joey – did it?"

"No," he replied, still sobbing, now sensing that his fate was sealed. "They were only niggers!" He sobbed even more.

"No, Joey, they are human beings like you and me, people with dreams and aspirations. They wanted to live just like you want to live." I paused for a moment and looked at him. He seemed so pathetic, but I knew I had to do it. "It is time to die, Joey. Now die with dignity." I placed the muzzle of the Glock against his forehead slowly, giving him time to think. He stopped sobbing, our eyes met and I pulled the trigger. It shattered his skull and splattered his brain matter. I searched their dead bodies for the keys of their vehicle and for additional information. This was my undeclared war. I walked back to the desolate road to where their vehicle was parked and drove it off the road into the bushes where it would not be seen by passing motorists. I searched it and found a map of the campsite and its location. I got in my vehicle followed the map to the militia camp.

"I drove avoiding the main roads, using the seldom travelled back roads. The narrow road twisted and turned before it forked into what seem to be a slightly wider and more used path. Soon I was driving on an open road with a large lake to my right. It was almost a mile across the lake and on the other side I saw several barracks and other military type buildings. I pulled over to the side, got out my binoculars and looked. It was a campsite with a sign nailed to a post, which towered above the other buildings, as he had described in the interrogation. It read, 'White Power.'

"I studied the camp and drove to a place where I could not be easily seen. For days without detection, I studied the comings and goings of the campsite. I spied while they conducted one of their initiation rites. I witnessed them as they brought in about seven men, mostly black youths. Not long after their arrival there was a flurry in the camp as they made preparation for the initiation. This was followed by lots of yelling and shooting. The shooting continued sporadically for hours. Finally, there was jubilation and a lot of whooping it up. I interpreted that as the new members successfully completing their initiation. They were now fully-fledged skinheads.

"The only way into the camp was via the road or directly across the lake, which offered no cover or protection. I knew they would be prepared to defend the road but anyone assaulting from the lake would be a sitting duck. Yet, I chose to go via the lake. I chose my weapons, my four pistols and a hand-held version of the Gatling gun with six belts of ammunition, and a Russian made grenade launcher that was built like a revolver. It carried eight grenades when fully loaded, an automatic AK47 with six extra magazines. I also took my sword, which was sharpened on both sides. I had explored the lake as far away as possible from the campsite and found a kayak in good condition with a paddle. I was down wind from the camp.

"I had plans to launch my attack by paddling up the lake, hugging the shore line all the way to the campsite. It was after midnight when I arrived at my destination. The campsite was in darkness except for minor lights here and there. There was no doubt this was a deserted old military base. The white supremacists had moved in and occupied the deserted fort. After all the chasing, hunting, shooting and killing earlier in the day, they were overcome by fatigue and most of them had turned in for the night. As I made my way into the camp, I saw the gasoline pump. I opened fire on it with my grenade launcher; it erupted into a fireball followed by a huge explosion that almost knocked me off my feet and another fireball twice as large as the first which abruptly brought them from their sleep. To my right was the building in which they stored the arms. I fired three rounds from the grenade launcher. It was like a bomb going off. Suddenly there was a greater blast from below the ground of the gasoline station. Its force launched me back into the water from where I came. I gathered myself and waded back to the shore with my finger now gripping the trigger of the lethal hand-held Gatling gun. By now several members of the militia were running around trying to stop the resulting inferno caused by the many explosions, from their ammunition and the gas storage. They were not aware of my presence and as I made it back onto the shore I opened fired with the Gatling gun. The constant spinning of its barrel sounded like music to my ears. It spewed out hot lead, which ripped and chopped, blasted and tore apart the bodies of the toy soldiers.

"They were fleeing in fear and screaming in confusion as hot lead ripped into them. I was slaughtering them and had no remorse. In their confusion, they were trying to escape by running into the woods. I fired a series of four grenades that landed in their midst and the ensuing explosions tore apart their flesh and their death screams were amplified by their fear.

"I walked throughout the camp blowing up vehicles, setting buildings afire and killing every man I saw and others I did not see. They were all victims to my lethal wrath. Many kept running into the woods and I pursued them to the edge where I continue to fire, reload and fire my grenade launcher again and again. Then I cut loose again with my Gatling gun. Whoever survived the onslaught would not be coming out to fight again.

"As I made my way back to the lake, I found about three severely wounded men. I tied them together. I did what I saw a platoon leader did in 'Nam. I taped three sticks of dynamite together, placed it in the space that was created by their backs. I lit the extend wick and walked away as it burned down to the sticks. The explosion was deafening. I returned to see what was left of them. It was not much. That was when I realized I had crossed the line. That one act of depravity in my mind made me a murderer. I was no longer human. What had I evolved into? I had rationalized it to myself by saying it was a war. As I got in the kayak to row away, I took a last look at the hell I had created. The towering infernos were consuming the buildings and the continuous explosions gave credence to my rationale. The campus was littered with dead bodies waiting for the day someone would come by to find, identify and lay them to rest. To me, my job was done here. Since then, I returned into hiding, though I did occasionally hunt and kill pockets of Klan members all over the country. They were not safe from my onslaught but there was one killing I prided myself on for I knew I had become a master assassin then. However, it is of such enormity I will tell that story another day."

With that said he got up from his chair and left the room.

"Mr Stuart, Mr Stuart," I said as he left the room, with many questions in my mind wanting to be answered. He did not respond and kept walking.

# CHAPTER 33: The Vetting of a Presidential Candidate

Christopher Carson was serving the second year of his second term as Governor of Texas when he began preparations for his presidential campaign. He was now a seasoned politician and had come to terms with his ambitions and knew how to win over the voting public. He proved that by relocating to Texas where he defeated a popular incumbent governor. He had two years to run, two years of kissing babies' cheeks, shaking millions of hands and saying the politically correct things that would get him into the White House. But it was obvious to those who interviewed him that he was hiding his views on many issues as he chose his words too carefully so as not to appear offensive to voters. Immigration was becoming a major issue in the US. Large pockets of illegal aliens were flooding through the southern borders and the racist South did not like it and sought ways of dealing with the problem.

Carson was being interviewed by a young journalist and was approached about the issue. "Governor Carson, if you were president, how would you deal with Mexico and the large numbers of its people illegally crossing the borders into our nation?"

He thought for a moment and said. "We must meet with Mexico, maybe help them create jobs so the people of that country will not have the need to come here illegally seeking jobs."

"Does that mean that you would be sending jobs to Mexico to keep the Mexicans in their country, Governor Carson?"

"No," he replied. "We can help Mexico develop its economy and become a great trade partner by directing their government in ways of economic development. Over the years that will help provide substantial employment for its people. We also can partner with Mexico in helping develop its education system to make a larger middle class base. We could direct them into valuing its entrepreneurial population by making it easier for its people to go into business by providing direct government assistance and instructions in their business ventures so as to nurture their growth and development."

"Governor Carson, you see education and employment opportunities as the answer to stopping the ongoing flood of Mexicans into our country?"

"Yes, I do. I believe that most Mexicans are here to work, not to milk our system like some other minorities do. I strongly believe that if we were to begin on that premise we would eventually find the solutions to our problems."

"Governor, recently you were in Arizona. Arizona has more people crossing its borders than any other states that share a border with Mexico. You said you supported whatever the good people of Arizona did to resolve that problem. You also said that this is a white man's country and you are afraid of the constant influx of Mexicans into our country which would lead to whites eventually becoming the minority in this nation."

"Yes, I did say that and I do believe that is a valid concern among the white population. We did not create this nation to hand it over to others. New laws are needed to adapt to the changes that are occurring. We would be foolish to surrender this nation to people who do not have the same commitment to its culture and its future as we who created it. Our great founding fathers fought and died in the formation of this nation. They carved this nation out of the wilderness that existed here. For generations, we have worked to make this the most prosperous nation on this planet. This is the result of our stewardship, our vested interest. The rest of the world wants to come here but unfortunately, we can no longer accommodate them. It is for them to stay in their countries and make commitments to develop their countries as we did ours."

"On the Statue of Liberty, it says send me your poor, and so on. What do we say now?"

"We say the inn is full here; there are no more vacant rooms. So keep your poor hungry mass, that's what we say. We can no longer accommodate them."

"The greatest asset a country has is its population, its people. It is the greatest resource to any nation. That's the fuel to its growth, they provide the vision, the creativity, they have the imagination and they provide the workforce. We once used slavery as our work force and then Asians came to help us build the railroads. Before and after World War 1, we had a large influx of Europeans who all contributed in the making of this nation. Now we have people coming from Latin American countries doing jobs that most Americans are not willing to do. So in that sense, are we not inadvertently making a place for them? And is it because they are non-whites that you are supporting Arizona and other radicals in creating these new selective immigration laws?"

"No, we must protect our nation from the invasion of others. We have many enemies out there and most would like to attack us from within. It's to our benefit to adapt a policy of selection over that of an open door. Most nations that are considered a threat to us are non-white in population. We are at peace with most white populated nations and are willing to grant residency to people from those nations because they are unlikely to bear ill will against us."

"Governor Carson, you are favoured in the polls to be the Conservative Republican candidate. Would you tell us some of your plans if you became president?"

"The polls can be misleading, but if I was to become president I will not be raising taxes. There will be tax exemptions granted to large corporations to stimulate the economy and to keep jobs here in the US instead of sending them off to someplace in Asia. I will do what's best for all Americans. I will see to this nation becoming prosperous again. I will see to the formation of great paying jobs and the redevelopment of a strong manufacturing base."

"Can we do that, Governor Carson, without a large and varied work force?"

"Yes, we can and yes, we will. We did before and we will do it again," he replied to the delight of his conservative supporters. Carson went on to win the first five primaries, distancing himself from the other candidates in the delegate count. He was the early frontrunner and this prompted the media to begin an in-depth investigation of him. The New York Times and the Boston Globe began a full story on his military background, starting from the time he entered the Air Force Academy. They wanted to reveal the times candidates used bad judgment and how it affected others, so the public would know what kind of president they would be. The media saw it as their duty to educate the public to who these men were, especially the frontrunners.

The media went through his records as a student at the US Air Force Academy and they stumbled onto the report of him framing black Air Force students. The New York Times discovered that the Air Force Academy had covered up their findings to avoid damaging Carson's father, who at the time was a powerful senator. He did things that benefited the Academy, even though it was not in his state. The Times found the first unethical misjudgement by Christopher Carson. He continued his campaign as if nothing happened, even when the principal of the Academy, who was now retired, committed suicide when the story broke. He could no longer live with the shame he brought on the institution. The Boston Globe interviewed Governor Carson to find out more about this story, after it had questioned other participants who were involved. One of the students whose reputation was ruined reported he was not accepted at any other university after they were wrongly accused of cheating on their exams. And even though the Academy requested for him to return and complete his education, they did little to remedy the situation after they discovered that it was Carson's group who had manipulated the incident.

"Governor Carson it is documented here that you were involved in staging, implicating and destroying the future of black

Air Force Academy students by creating a false involvement of them cheating on their Academy exams?"

"I did not imply I exposed their cheating ways. I exposed their unethical response to the Academy's rigorous demands to make us men of honor. I will not apologise for what I did as I have very little expectation of men who gain through Affirmative Action."

"It has been proven that your group placed test papers in the lockers of these students, then alerted the Academy to these tests being there. Are you denying your involvement in this?"

"Why would I do such a heinous deed? And how would I have been able to get my hands on such tests?"

"That is the question we are all asking. The Academy did not explain how you did this in their report."

"The Air Force Academy is one of the most highly respected institutions of higher learning. Its teaching and practices of ethics are irreproachable. The fact that I was not expelled and graduated while those students were dishonored explains everything. I will not dwell any further on an issue that took place over three decades ago."

But The Globe was determined to expose the man who was seeking the highest public office before it was too late. Its reporters continued to dig through his history. In the meantime, his supporters grew and he won more delegates and more primaries. He quickly approached the required number of delegates needed to represent his party. The closest other Republican candidate had approximately 500 fewer delegates than Governor Carson.

*****

"Governor it appears that you have a history of confrontation with the minority population of this nation, in particular the black population, as well as involving yourself in keeping Mexicans from crossing the border."

"I have never supported racial injustice and I will not do so anytime in the future. However, I expect the same standards from the minority population as from the majority. I will not be giving the minority population a free pass because of history. We have gone beyond slavery and Jim Crow, so I expect them to keep up with us. We are all Americans and Americans have always been able to find a way. The best way to succeed, no matter their origin, is to get a job."

"Governor Carson, are you planning to do away with all the Affirmative Action perks that blacks were granted?" a reporter asked.

"Under my leadership there will be no more Affirmative Action. Blacks must succeed based on their merit. The market place is a varied one, with numerous people of all backgrounds participating. It is time the minority population starts participating in it to achieve some form of prosperity instead of waiting for government handouts. I am not a racist and no American, be they Native Americans, blacks or Hispanics, will have any reason to fear me or my policies," he said with a stone face. "I want all of America to prosper under my leadership."

It sounded good, but the media did not buy it. It was then that the New York Times received an invitation from the Vietnam War museum. They did not reply immediately, choosing to follow the nation's presidential race. Again, they received an invite to a museum in China regarding crimes of the Vietnam War. 'This is a final invite', it stated. 'Your pursuit to find the truth should take you everywhere your subject has walked. If truth is what you seek, come and we will show you the truth.' This time a red flag went up.

The New York Times investigative reporter arrived in Peking. He was met by the curator of the museum, Mr Xi, who spoke fluent English. He was an alumnus of Oxford University, a former Rhodes scholar.

"Mr Xi, how nice it is to meet you," said the reporter and his staff to the Chinese official who bowed in response. Getting immediately to the point, he asked. "What truth do you have for me?"

"I will reveal horrendous deeds by men who claim to be honored men. How it affects your nation's presidential race depends on your reporting. You should not seek to influence the public's thinking; just allow the pictures to speak for themselves. Let the American people see and discuss it among themselves."

"What is it that you want to show me?" questioned the American.

"The Vietnam war was not only a war of different ideologies, but of racial conflict. We will show you pictures to support this claim. The man who is running for president of your nation was key to this deviation. He was highly decorated, but it is time the world got to know him as the Vietnamese people did. We have invited many major newspaper reporters to the opening of this exhibit and they will report to their papers what is revealed here today."

The museum was a large modern building. "There are 30,000 pictures on display here which all are part of the Vietnam War exhibit. You will see pictures of the many battles that were fought but I want you to focus on those pictures exhibited under the title the Black Forest Atrocities."

"What is the Black Forest?" asked the American journalist.

"The Black Forest was a rubber plantation of approximately 20 square miles. There was a rubber factory there as well as a residential area for its French workers. It had a landing strip for planes and a two-way highway leading in and out of the plant. It produced Black Forest rubber which was used predominantly in the manufacturing of tyres."

"Why did atrocities occur there?"  The journalist was now developing an interest in the story.

"During the war, the Black Forest was surrounded by a mine field, isolating it from the surrounding jungle occupied by the American CIA. They kept a lot of prisoners of war there. They used it to conduct experimental war games and ritualistic hangings on its campus."

"What?" the journalist said in shock.

"The pictures will tell their story," replied Mr Xi.

On seeing the pictures of the victims of the Black Forest, the journalist could not walk away from it. The barbarism of it made him sick. He turned to see that journalists from other nations were looking at him with contempt and he knew that was the way they were now seeing his country. He turned and looked at the American soldiers, some dressed in Klan regalia. They were hanging prisoners of war. He looked at their pictures and shame consumed him.

"Do you see anyone of notoriety in these pictures?" asked Mr Xi.

Maybe it was the initial embarrassment, but he had walked past a picture in which there were many soldiers in Klan whites but without their cone hats covering their faces.

"Look at this picture. Does this man look like your Republican presidential candidate, Governor Carson?" The journalist was amazed at the likeness. The resemblance was startling. He placed a call to his office to check on the military background of the Republican frontrunner. A picture of him in his uniform was made available to the media to use as verification. The military confirmed his service with the CIA in the area that was known as the Black Forest. After a week of intensive study, research and verification, the story broke.

The New York Times was the first to run the story with a headline of:

"Republican nominee, former war hero disgraced his country in the Black Forest of Vietnam."

The New York Daily News countered with:

"Republican presidential candidate disgraced his country by dressing as Klansman while lynching POWs during the Vietnam War."

The story drove home the point with pictures of Carson dressed in Klan regalia with his face exposed, while he presided over the hangings of prisoners of war. The Pentagon scrambled to verify the story. The Republican hierarchy was in denial as they rallied around their nominee. They met behind closed doors to assess the damage done to their party and the candidate's chances of getting them to the White House. The nation, meanwhile, became fixated on the story as public interest rapidly grew. Many Americans were appalled by the acts depicted and were even more repulsed by the fact they were dressed in Klan garbs. The Pentagon tried to save face by immediately sending its personnel to China and requesting copies of all Black Forest pictures. They then requested the Federal Government to arrest all military personnel who were involved in the Black Forest Incident. However, the Republican president pressured the legislative branch to disregard these as war crimes.

For days the media tried to interview Carson. He had released a press report to assist in putting out the fire, but it did not help. The other presidential candidates seized the opportunity by demanding that the men who were involved should stand trial as criminals of war.

Carson called a closed-door meeting with his top advisors. "Gentlemen we are here today to find an answer that will overcome our present situation and allow us to stay the course to the White House."

"Governor Carson, did you do those despicable act as described by the media?" questioned a well-known Republican senator.

"Did you see the pictures, Senator?"

"Yes, I have," he tersely replied.

"Pictures do not lie, Senator. I will not lie to you and say I did not do those deeds. But one thing I will say, is through those acts, several thousands of American soldiers were saved."

"I cannot and will not be supporting you from here on, Governor Carson. I will withdraw my delegation support to your candidacy. I will not try to persuade my colleagues to do the same but I believe they will."

"We will see, Senator. I will not release any of my delegates and I have more than the required amount to win the Republican nomination."

"That too will change, Governor Carson. As the American people get to see and hear of the things you did in Vietnam, they will quickly withdraw their support. They will rightfully abandon you for what you did was not in the true spirit of what Americans are known for, nor do we want to be known for such vile acts."

"Vile acts, Senator! Our history is full of vile acts. We built this nation based on vile acts. We practiced genocide against the Indians. We enslaved the negroes and when we set them free we terrorized them with Jim Crow laws and the Klan."

"Governor Carson, we have grown beyond that. Those behaviors are no longer acceptable. In my book, any man that practices those behaviors is unacceptable as a candidate for the presidency."

"I will let the people decide. I will not shrink and hide. I am a candidate and I intend to win. The fight has just begun."

"Governor Carson," shouted another senator representing a southern state. "I am supporting you and the delegates of my state will continue to support you."

"All of you who will support me in my time of need and during these moments of crisis, I thank you. For those who have absconded, the truth has yet to be told."

"Governor Carson, I strongly urge you to treat the media with respect for they will use this incident to destroy you," said one of his advisors.

"What do you suggest I do?" asked Carson.

"I suggest an interview in which you tell your side of the story, then based on the result you launch a revival of your candidacy by barnstorming through the South and quickly through the North and the rest of the nation. You cannot wait for primaries to go and speak with the American people. You must do it now and you better have a good explanation for why you did what you did. If you don't, Governor, you will not be elected the Republican nominee."

Days passed by and he continued his campaign. During an interview with the Washington Post, he was bluntly asked by the interviewer, "Governor Carson are you a member of the Ku Klux Klan?"

"No, I am not, never was and never will be," was his reply.

"Governor Carson, in these pictures you are dressed in Klan regalia, hanging Vietnamese prisoners of war. What do you have to say about that?"

"Have you ever fought in a war?" he asked the Post interviewer.

"No," she replied.

"I did," he said, "as a fighter pilot and as a CIA Green Beret. We lived with the constant fear that any moment could be our last. It was kill or be killed and that is something you don't want to experience. I got good at killing and that came about because I decided to take an offensive approach to the war and not wait for the enemy to dictate the terms of the war to me. War is brutal and unforgiving, there are few moments of civility and these are usually far and few between. I have here pictures of American soldiers who were captured, tortured and killed in an obscene manner." He took several pictures of American soldiers who were tied to trees and their heart was cut out of their chests, some others had their heads blown off by grenades that were tied around their necks.

"You have to understand the nature of war. It's the ultimate practice of hate and evil, with few restrictions. If I breached any of those restrictions, I ask for your forgiveness. While in service for my country in a time of war I felt a need to terrorize the enemy as much as he was terrorizing us. We lost that war, and tens of thousands of our boys died there in South East Asia. Many died a gruesome death at the hands of our enemies. Every minute we lived we knew it could be our last. It was no time to shrink and hide, it was a time to die or a time to kill and I chose to kill. I fought to attain victory for my country and that required putting fear in the heart of an enemy who had no fear of our superior technology and killing power. Unlike us, they had no fear of dying for what they believed in nor did they have any delusion about what it took to attain victory. That was the difference between us. We won the battles but they won the war. This battle they will not win, this war they will not win. I will continue to run for the presidency. No foreign country will dictate the qualifications required of an American to hold such an office. My interest is for the growth and prosperity of my people and my country. I will not bow to the wishes of a nation in which we were once locked in a bitter conflict that took the lives of tens of thousands of our men."

Carson made many speeches in which he stood firmly and unapologetic about his actions in the Vietnam War. The American people at first had their doubts but as time went on, he swayed them to his side and they came in droves to hear him speak and to support him in the polls. In the following weeks, he won two major primaries, which assured him of the nomination at the Republican Convention. The media now coddled him with kid gloves by making statements that he was the leader America needed and longed for. They failed to uncover his post-Vietnam horrendous deeds in the South.

Then one-day Carson got news of the mass killings at a former military base. Close to 300 men were found dead, all members of a militia led by a member of his Secret Society.

"That nigger is back," he said. "He's back from wherever he had disappeared to. Find him and kill him," he ordered his security chief.

*****

With the Republican convention days away, Carson looked out from behind the curtains and scanned the crowd of more than 50,000 people seated on the lawn of the Brooklyn park. He felt secure in his decision to continue his campaign; he was here to capture the north. As he strode onto the stage and approached the dais he was greeted by a standing ovation and thunderous applause that resounded throughout the crowd. There was no doubt in his mind that he was about to be the next president as thousands more people came streaming into the various entrances of the park to see and hear him speak. As the crowd swelled to more than 70,000, he imagined the tremendous power he would attain with them voting him into the White House. They quietened down as he started to speak. He spoke of his intentions to have a maximum cap of 10 per cent on the interest rates of credit cards. The crowds cheered even louder. Suddenly, in mid-sentence, he crumbled and fell to the ground. In unison, a gasp escaped the lips of those in visual range and then silence as people tried to figure out what happened. Those nearest saw the blood pooling onto the floor of the stage beneath his head. They screamed in disbelief, the crowd panicked and stampeded as the would-be president took his last breath as his security team raced to his side.

# CHAPTER 34: Mr Stuart Exposed

Again, I was having difficulty accepting and believing Mr Stuart. His stories of excessive violence and hate disturbed me and I found myself wondering if most of this was true. Mr Stuart, however, did not seem disingenuous. I found him to be quite straightforward. But I had to know what was fact and what was fiction. I could not rely on the words of a man that could be diagnosed with delusions of grandeur. His rambles on race relations were indicative of a troubled man. I was not qualified to rationalize his actions nor analyse what was occurring in his head and attribute it to a mental disorder or dysfunction. That was the role of his psychiatrist. No, I would not venture down that path, but what I would do was verify the occurrence of those events in the stories he told. I had written down most of what he had told me.

I called the army department of personnel. Like all government institutions, they refused to give me any information over the phone. They instructed me on how to proceed to attain the information I sought. I toiled with their legal documents, following every bit of instruction before I finally achieved my goal.

I confirmed Mr Stuart had a distinguished military career. He was decorated with medals of honor while on tour of duty in Vietnam. My respect for Mr Stuart grew immensely at that moment. But I realized that meant he had the training to do all the things he said he had done. I set out to find what was fact or fiction regarding his alleged mass murders committed in Alabama before fleeing to Canada and those he said he committed in Texas after he returned from Canada.

After failing to find any information on the Internet regarding these crimes, I contacted both the Alabama and the Texas state Department of Justice. I specified the crimes using limited amounts of the information Mr Stuart supplied in his story. I did not expect any positive results, but when each state confirmed these mass murders, I began to question my next move. Was Mr Stuart's story something I should treat as confidential, or should I turn him into the law? How would my institution react if I proceeded to the justice department knowing that I would be disregarding Mr Stuart's right to confidentiality? He had disclosed his life story to me hoping that I would write his biography, but here I was trying to decide if I should turn him over to the law. One day, while I was still procrastinating, I was called to the main desk to be greeted by two Federal agents. My inquiry in these cases had sparked their interest and they wanted to know why I was inquiring and where I had got my information. It was now summer of 2006, almost 30 years since the first crime was committed according to Mr Stuart, in the summer of 1978 and also summer of 1987.

I decided to go to my chain of command with what I had discovered. However, at the same time the states involved demanded any documentation I had on the cases. They wanted to know what I knew, if I was involved, or if I knew who was involved in the cases. They threatened to subpoena the institution's charts of all patients and demanded to meet with me. They implied that the information, which I supplied them in my research indicated that I knew too much about the cases. To them it meant I was either involved or I knew who was.  I was their closest lead to the cases and neither state was going to let go until I divulged what I knew.

Ms Walcott was the director of nursing and the person I would immediately report to in such an event. She was a wise individual but grounded in the old-school methods of thinking and problem solving. I presented her with Mr Stuart's chart, which I had documented a lot of the information he had revealed to me. I quickly went over this with her. She immediately concluded that he was a danger to all, although he had never taken any actions or verbalized any thoughts of harming himself or others while on the unit.  She read the part of the chart that dealt with the mass murder in Alabama and Texas.

"This man has some wild imagination," she concluded.

"Ms Walcott, it's not imagination, these crimes did happen. I have validated their occurrence with both states' departments of justice. They have corroborated everything there. They are now in contact with the FBI which has visited us seeking to find out what I know."

"How did they come to know of Mr Stuart's files?"

"I called them to confirm his story."

"Why?" she angrily asked.

"Because that is what Mr Stuart wanted me to do. He wants closure. He believes he has accomplished the purpose for his existence. My unit manager, Dr Charles, has been informed of what Mr Stuart has been telling me. I also have documented whatever he has disclosed."

"What instructions has Dr Charles given you about this patient?"

"To make sure I document everything he told me," I replied.

"Have you done that without adding any of your feelings or thoughts in his chart?"

"Yes," I replied, knowing with certainty that this chart was now to become the major part of any court case against Mr Stuart.

"Why did you call the justice department knowing that everything the client reveals to you is confidential information?"

"Firstly, I wanted to know if any of this was true. Secondly, I knew what he said was confidential, but if what he said was true and it is, I could not cover it up by using his rights of confidential information. He has claimed to have killed more than 500 men in two states. And he does not want me to cover it up. He wants the world to know what he has done and he is willing to go to the electric chair for his crimes."

"You have discussed this with him?" Asked Ms Walcott.

"Yes, I have. That is why I know how he feels," I said.

"Mr Gordon, we are moving down a slippery slope here. You have gone beyond your boundaries by investigating this patient without first addressing it with your team or the hospital police. You have supplied those states information about a patient, which has prompted them to start investigating an incompetent patient and the institution. He has informed you that he has a history of auditory, visual and tactile hallucinations. Furthermore, it is not your responsibility to inform the justice department of his crimes. Your obligation is to your team and to your patient. What you have done is an egregious act that will lead to your termination."

"Ms Walcott, the patient also has rights and if he requests to be turned over to the law, that is his right. He did commit those crimes and he knew what he was doing then, just as he knows what he wants now."

"Mr Gordon, show me some document that Mr Stuart wrote giving you permission to do this. You are a nurse, Mr Gordon, not the patient's psychiatrist. That was not your call. Closure," she responded in disbelief. "Mr Gordon, this is a mental health institution. There are channels to go through to do this and you have breached them all."

"Don't you believe those who died at his hands need to have justice enacted on their behalf?" I questioned.

"That man is not fit to stand trial. He hears voices' telling him to kill. That is why he is here. You wrote that in his chart. What judge will see it fit for him to stand trial? They will demand to have access to his chart to make decisions before they sentence him to spend the rest of his life in a long-term care facility, never to be free again."

"Then, why am I being threatened with my job termination?" I asked her.

"What you did was without the consent of your superiors. You have taken information from a patient chart and given it to others who are not part of this patient's care team."

"What I did was confirm the brutal killings of several hundred men by a patient to whom I was assigned to care for. He willingly provided me this information, requesting me to write a book about it and present it to the law. I decided to confirm his information. I now know this is not the ramblings of a delusional grandiose psychotic old man but the actual deeds of a trained killer who is using our institution to hide."

"And those he killed...isn't it in his chart that they too were killing others?"

"They were not my patients," I half-heartedly replied knowing that we were ideological adversaries and that Ms Walcott was going to make sure I lost my job. "Ms Walcott, I did what I thought was best for Mr Stuart and the institution. I do not believe the institution wants to harbor a mass murderer knowing his crimes. That would make us complicit."

"What the institution wants to do is not for you to decide. That is left to others whose job it is to decide such matters and you did not allow them to take part in that decision."

"No matter, I did what I thought was in the best interest of the institution."

"Your job is to care for patients. You are educated to do that. We have other people here who are educated in seeing about what is best for the institution."

"The man is an admitted mass murderer. He killed hundreds of men. Do you expect me to turn a blind eye after my investigation corroborated that information as factual?"

"Mr Stuart has been coming to this institution for over two decades. He has been a model patient. If what he says is true, it is still confidential information and should be treated as such. If he wants to reveal that information to the law, it's up to him to make contact with the law enforcement of those states and turn himself in. It's not our job to do that."

"You knew about it? He told you and you did nothing."

"You were assigned to care for a patient, a person who cannot care for himself now. You are not there to add additional stressors to the patient life by calling the FBI on him. You are here to care and to protect that individual. You are here to see that no harm comes to him and see that his rights are not violated. You were assigned to be his advocate. But you have decided to be the advocate of the Klan, a group of people who have terrorized, killed and destroyed the lives of many thousands over the last centuries while the law turned a blind eye. It's all there in the chart – you wrote it. Mr Stuart took a stand even in his insane state. He stood for what was right. I will support Mr Stuart. What he did was one giant act of righting human wrongs. Yes, I knew. He told me and other nurses his story and, to us, Mr Stuart is a hero. He fought when white men terrorized and killed us at will. He did not tolerate that. In my eyes, what Mr Stuart did was heroic."

"What's next?" I asked knowing that I had set into motion something bigger than I could imagine.

"What's next?" She replied with an unmistakable vehemence in the tone of her voice. "What's next is that I will meet with the director of nursing, as well as with your team leader, Dr Charles. Make no mistake about this. It's going to the top and heads will roll. The ball is no longer in our court. You have given it to the states of Alabama and Texas. You said they are in contact with the federal government, so I presume the FBI will be involved."

"We have nothing to be afraid of," I responded. "We did nothing wrong."

"You have initiated an investigation into a mental health patient without consulting your superiors or getting a written consent from that patient. How do you expect us to support you? You still do not seem to understand what you have done. You are not to contact this patient; if there were a bed available on another unit I would transfer him immediately. Mr Gordon, make sure that Mr Stuart is placed on one to one observation, for after he has heard what you have done you may be his next victim. I will see to your transfer from this unit as soon as possible."

I was left to ponder my egregious deed as Ms Walcott left my office.

# CHAPTER 35: The Assassination

Days had passed and meetings had addressed the recent events, but I sat at my desk still hearing Ms Walcott's words ringing in my ears.

I saw Mr Stuart sitting in the day room. I took to observing him from a distance. His face was peacefully calm almost to the point of serenity. There was some measurable peace in his life and it showed in his countenance. I beckoned him to my office, letting the tech who was assigned to constantly observe him know that he would be with me for a time and, when I was finished, he would need to continue his assignment. It was already determined from that he would be transferred to a long-term care facility, but that would be done after his meetings with both states Department of Justice and the FBI. I asked him to sit as he entered the office.

"Mr Stuart," I said, uncertain of how to proceed but knowing where I wanted to go with this conversation. I expected him to be angry. I had known him long enough and I expected him to understand. "Mr Stuart," I repeated, "there will be changes in your care."

"Am I going to prison?" he poignantly asked.

"No. Because of your mental health history you will be transferred to a long-term facility. However, I must tell you that I investigated your past and found that you have been truthful."

"Is that unusual?"

"Mr Stuart, I have never experienced anyone with a history like yours and I hope I never will again. That is the reason you will be going to a long-term care facility," I concluded.

"Mr Gordon, I always wondered what was missing from your life. Your spirit lacks passion. Your life is too limited and bland. You are living for all the right reasons but it appears you do not extend yourself beyond that. You need to explore your mind. You need to entrench yourself into your beliefs and make them an integral part of your life. They will bring passion, zeal and a purpose to your life. They will give you reason for living and a reason for dying. I don't believe there is something out here that you would die for. Therefore, I don't believe you have started living. I will be locked away for the rest of my life but I know I lived for a cause, I served a purpose trying to right the wrongs of my country and change the beliefs of its people."

"Mr Stuart, is that how you go about righting the wrongs of your country, by killing those with whose credo you disagree? I do not look forward to having a difference of opinion with you, Mr Stuart. I may not live to see the next day."

"You are being sarcastic Mr Gordon. The reason those men died was for their practice of racial supremacy, racial hate. For this country to evolve and move forward we must recognise what is holding us back. Prejudice and hate is the sickness that is preventing us from evolving socially. Those words from the Declaration of Independence that say all men are created equal. Those words were not accidentally placed in the Declaration. The men who wrote those powerful words were conduits to God. That thought was perfection, but the men who wrote them, they were far from perfect. They were slave owners believing in the inequality of men. It was not a thought of theirs but a thought and an act of God for those words to survive and appear in the Declaration of Independence. Now it is for us as a nation to let this noble thought prevail. I have done my part by killing those who would see to the suppression and denial of such a dignified human right."

"Are you saying that your goal was to kill racism?"

"Yes, but I could not kill thoughts of racial hatred without killing the men who harbored them. Those men relished the violence pervading their thoughts. Their thought was embodied in their physical beings whose spirit and soul stood firmly in their belief of racial hatred and racial supremacy – and they acted on it. Until that thought has become extinct, those words, 'All men are created equal,' remains a hollow echo of what it was really meant to be."

I looked in his eyes and finally understood him. I knew what he meant. The vision he held was shared by Martin Luther King and many others. It was a dream of what this nation was meant to be. I wondered now if it would ever reach that place. Or would its sickness prevent it from evolving to that lofty position? The following day, on my way to work, I read a newspaper headline about the acquittal of four police officers who had shot and killed an unarmed black man in the Bronx, New York. They had fired more than 50 shots at him. This was a recurring incident in our society and now I wondered why. It dawned on me that we were being given the opportunity to move forward, but we could not move forward until the men who were trusted with the duties of law enforcement were held accountable for their unjust acts. For us to evolve as people, those officers had to be found guilty for what they did. Until then, this scenario was destined to repeat itself until the right thing was done. None of our white judges dared cross the line to do what was right, so injustice for black people prevailed as the law. I knew that the end of racism had to start in the chambers of justice. It had to start with men who are trusted with the position to be held to a higher standard so that the blackness of their robe could not be equated with the blackness of their hearts and minds. I looked at myself and people of my color and wondered what our place was in this nation. I concluded we are its conscience, its uncorrupted soul, righting its wrongs from its long history of racial injustice. We are its surviving victims who fought and won the battle for civil rights.

"Mr Stuart, did you kill anymore?" I found myself asking. It was followed by a long period of silence as Mr Stuart stared at me. I instantly thought of apologizing, but before the words could escape my lips, he waved them off with a subtle gesture of his hand.

"I know you mean no harm, nurse. You are just doing your job. Do you really want to know the answer to that question?"

"Yes," I said just above a whisper.

"Yes, I have."

"How many more have you killed?"

"Many, but one very important one comes to mind," he replied with certainty to the tone of his voice.

"Tell me about it," I demanded.

A smile came on his face. "It was Carson," he said.

"Are you talking about the senator, the governor, the man who was a presidential candidate? You killed him?"

"The same, but when he was assassinated, he was no longer the senator of Alabama. Carson had moved from Alabama to Texas and become governor of that state. It was during the year of 1988 while he was campaigning for the presidency.  At first many did not believe he would make it. But as time went on the country began to embrace his ideas. I knew where he was about to take us. Carson would be our Hitler and we blacks would take the place of the Jews in his holocaust. During his campaign, he blamed us for all that was wrong with this nation. We were the cause of all the crimes, we were the reason why white males were losing jobs, and we were the boogy man waiting in the dark to rape white women. We were the reason for the abuse of the welfare system, we were the reasons for all what was wrong in the country and he said he would get tough on crime in the rest of the nation just like he did in Texas. He had instituted a prison building program in Texas which now warehoused more black men than any other state in the nation and many companies benefitted from their slave labour. He attempted to make the death penalty as one of the means of punishment for non-violent crimes such as drug trafficking. It was defeated in the state congress. He was successful with the 'three strikes you are out' law. I remembered those days; a simple thing as walking the street was unhealthy for a black man. He could be gunned down by a racist cop who thought he saw something he considered as a dangerous weapon, but would not take the time to be sure. White women inadvertently branded us as thieves and muggers by clenching their pocket books extra tight as they walked by any of us.

Many would cross the street rather than take the chance to walk near us. The media took pleasure in making sure that every black criminal was made the centre of the evening news. They and the police department always put on a show at our expense."

"Was it you who killed him?"

Without answering me, he continued, "I took notice as his message took hold and the nation began to embrace him. I remembered him as a boy sitting on his horse the night he and his Klan members lynched my father and uncles. This is who we were embracing to lead us for the next four to eight years. No one accepted his affiliation with the Klan and if they did they did not care, but I knew and I cared. I was there in Vietnam when he and his crew lynched thousands of Vietnamese as well as many black soldiers, men who were considered missing in action. I saw the result of that with my two eyes. I could not allow him to become president. I set out to stop him the only way I knew. For the final time, did you take time to read about the King Alfred Plan?"

"Which meant you had to kill him?" I said with some certainty knowing his history.

"Did you read what I asked you to read?"

"No," I replied. "I still have not read anything about this King Alfred Plan."

He scowled at me and I could see the disappointment in his face. I made a mental note to read the King Alfred plan.

"What is it all about anyway?"

"It is a plan to systemically round up African Americans all over this nation and place them in concentration camps and proceed to exterminate them in nuclear powered ovens, similar to what Hitler did with the Jews during WW2."

"What?"

"Take time to read and understand the world you live in. You are living on borrowed time. The plan describes in depth how this nation would exterminate the population of black nations to get the resources of those countries in times of war. Our lives are of no value to these people, no matter where we are. If they want something we have, they will take it by force and wipe us out in the process. Go on the Internet and read about the King Alfred Plan."

"Do you believe it's authentic?"

"Yes, it is. It was created by J Edgar Hoover."

"What has this to do with Carson?"

"He is the first person I ever heard mention it. Carson is CIA and I heard him saying that if he became president, he planned on enacting the King Alfred Plan."

"How do you know that it is still considered policy? Many presidents have been in office since then and none of them enacted it."

"Many presidents have enacted parts of it, but never in totality. That is where Carson differs. Carson was the frontrunner of the Republican Party's presidential candidates. He was the person with the most delegates, pledges as well as the most popular votes. Knowing what I knew I could not allow him to become president. He was protected by the secret services everywhere he went and they knew how to spot a potential assassin in a crowd. I had to make myself inconspicuous and could not appear at too many of his rallies or they would spot me. I had to appear at the site weeks ahead of the rally to find that certain place where the kill shot could originate. I could not chase him all over the country. I knew I would only have one opportunity. For more than six months, I had travelled ahead of his security team searching for that ideal spot – and I found it."

I still could not believe what I was hearing. This was beyond anything I could imagine, was Mr Stuart about to tell me how he killed Governor Carson?

"He was scheduled to have a rally in Brooklyn's Prospect Park in New York on the lawn. There was a band shelter in the park where he would make his speech. I began looking for a place I could make my kill shot and entered one of the few high-rise apartment buildings on the north-east side of the park. The building was more than 30 floors tall and towered over the densely forested hills of the park. From where I was to the band shelter was more than a mile. I had made shots of longer distance in 'Nam but that was several years prior. In my spare time I practiced my shooting each week while I was in Canada. As I prepared, I found a place to hide my weapon after making my kill shot.

"I prepared to make that kill shot and to disappear in the Brooklyn crowds after. For my escape, I thought of entering the hospital. I thought I would go to Kings County Hospital, which was also known for its mental health services in the G building. There I would make complaints of being suicidal, actively hallucinating and hearing voices. And I was hearing the voices. Sometimes they battled in my head, trying to become my dominant commander and it was disturbing. Yet here I was following the commands like a puppet on a string. I walked to the area in the park where he would be speaking. It was a beautiful park with huge lakes and playgrounds. On the west side was Park Slope, one of Brooklyn's nice neighborhoods with blocks of million-dollar brownstone homes. On the north-east of the park was some of Brooklyn most well-known cultural centres including the Brooklyn Museum, Brooklyn's Botanical Garden, and the main branch of the Brooklyn Public Library. It was the neighborhood of the Caribbean people. Many of them from the islands of Jamaica, Trinidad and Tobago, Barbados, Grenada and other islands of the Caribbean. They are proud people with strong links to their country of origin steeped in tradition and culture; they are hardworking and a prosperous set of people which balanced well with the wealthy whites on the west side.

"Finally, the day came for his Prospect park rally. I stuck to the steps of my plan. I had placed my weapon in its hiding place in the building two days prior. I could not believe the heightened security. The NYPD were out in force, walking the streets, riding bicycles and scooters in the park and driving their squad cars.

Their snipers were atop every high rise and their helicopters flew overhead. Even the building I was to take my kill shot from was occupied by police officers. But I knew of a way in and a way out. I came up through the sewers and took my shot from the 28 floor, which was two flights below the security location. That day, hours before I was to make my kill shot I went to Kings County Hospital and signed in at their emergency room. It would take hours for me to be seen. I wonder why they call it an emergency room knowing the services are so slow in coming. I waited for hours before I was registered. Once that was completed I was told to wait to see the triage nurse to whom I made my complaint. I knew it would be hours before I was seen by an emergency doctor, who would refer me for a psychiatric consult. I was left in the waiting room. Now supplied with my alibi I set out to complete my goal. I walked along a deserted block with vacant New York State University office buildings on one side and its affiliated parking lot on the opposite side of the street. I entered the subway station and onto the platform. No one saw when I slipped off into the tunnels where I followed the tracks to my destination. Several times I had to hide from oncoming trains but it was a fact that many homeless had descended to the underground where they dwelt in the catacombs. Finally, I was at my destination. I entered the building through the sewer in the basement and made my way up to the 28th floor. I entered a deserted storage room, opened the window and, through my optical gun lenses, had a perfect bird's eye view of the west side of Prospect Park and the band shelter. On the stage sitting beside the guest speaker was the mayor of New York City. I wanted to shoot him too. The current speaker was the State Governor who was introducing the Republican frontrunner. I did not have long to wait before Carson was at the dias. A few minutes into his speech and I was ready. My sound suppressor was attached to the end of my killing tool. I took aim and the rest is history.

"You assassinated Governor Carson?" I found myself asking Mr Stuart.

"It had to be done, son, it had to be done," he replied.

I could not believe what I was hearing. This man was confessing to the assassination of a presidential candidate.

"I have to inform my team of this immediately," I uttered still in shock. "Would you excuse me for a few minutes?"

"I understand," he said as he arose from the chair and left the room.

*****

"Watch him carefully. Don't ever leave his side," I said to the tech who was assigned to observe him. I picked up the phone and called my team leader Dr Charles.

"Dr Charles," I began. "Mr Stuart informed me that he was the person who killed Governor Christopher Carson of Texas in Prospect Park."

"Governor Carson, the presidential candidate that was assassinated back in 1988?"

"The same," I concurred.

"Is his story credible?"

"Yes," I replied. "He told me of how he stalked his prey during his campaign and finally found the ideal spot from where he took his kill shot."

"Where is the weapon?"

"I did not ask him," I said in response.

"If he can produce the weapon, then his story will be credible."

"I believe him," I replied.

"I do too," said Dr Charles, "but until there is proof, all we have is the rambling of a delusional old man. Now get that proof and call me back."

I called Mr Stuart back into my office. He was still being cooperative. I wondered why he was so willing to give himself up.

"Mr Stuart this has been your secret; you have lived with this information for years. Why are you now divulging it? Do you believe that your being in a mental health facility will prohibit the authorities from getting to you?"

"On the contrary, I want them to do to me what I have done to those men. I want them to extinguish my life."

"Why?" I inquired.

"I do not want to live anymore. I have fulfilled my purpose in life and am now being haunted by the voices I hear. They torment me. They are the voices of the 1,023 men, women and children I have killed by soldiering."

"What?" I asked, wondering if he was becoming suicidal.

"Yes," he retorted. "I live with the voices of all those I have killed and they torment me every day of my life."

"What do they say to you?"

"They are angry I took away their right to live. They say I took away their right to human happiness. They say I denied them the right to grow and evolve. Everyday they tell me how much they hate me; everyday they curse and torment me. I can hear them, but they can't hear me."

"Where is the gun you used to kill Governor Christopher Carson?" I asked.

"I left it in the sewers," he replied.

"Do you remember where in the sewers you left it?" I asked.

"Yes, I took time to place it in a special spot for safe keeping, in case I had to use it again."

"Would you direct us to it?"

He went about doing that and the hospital police with the aid of the NYPD followed his directions and retrieved the weapon. His fingerprints were still on it and it was still in working order. The weapon was turned over to the FBI who conclusively reported that was the weapon used to kill Governor Christopher Carson. Immediately, the state of Texas sought extradition of Mr Stuart. However, the state of New York did not comply with the requisition knowing that Mr Stuart was not mentally fit to go on trial. They also knew the intention of the state of Texas was to give Mr Stuart a trial no matter his mental condition and hang him as quickly as they could.

The state of Texas was holding three men in their penitentiary who had committed murders in New York state, including the killing of two police officers. The authorities of each state went about making a deal in which a swap was made. In the end New York got the three desperados they wanted from the state of Texas and in return they gave up Mr Stuart to the state of Texas.

The day Mr Stuart was extradited was my last day working at the facility. True to her word Ms Walcott saw to my termination. The state of Texas had subpoenaed me to testify for the prosecution against Mr Stuart. I was very disturbed about this and could not bring myself to do it. Before Mr Stuart was extradited, we had spoken and decided to remain in touch, even though I was being forced to be his Judas.

# CHAPTER 36: The Grand Juror

After Mr Stuart's extradition to the state of Texas, a date was set for his Grand Jury inquisition. He was assigned a court-appointed attorney who had too many cases and too little time to prepare to address the issues of Mr Stuart's case. The reason he was chosen to represent Mr Stuart was because the Texas justice department saw him as being incompetent, which was a quality they wanted. He had a history of tardiness in representing his clients. The state wanted a quick conviction of Mr Stuart and they were seeking the death penalty if he was found guilty of his crimes. But first because of his mental history, he had to be seen by a court appointed psychiatrist who would determine if Mr Stuart was mentally competent to stand trial. It had to appear that they went through all the right channels without any compromise of his rights because he was one of the country's most decorated war heroes.

In the meantime, the media ran stories about the man who killed thousands of Klan members, dehumanising and demonising him as a black, ruthless, cold-blooded killer. They began stirring the emotions of the uneducated masses. Over the years, the hate and prejudice that had simmered below the surface within the white community rose to the top, boiling with anger and hate. Like the Klan of old, they sought vengeance for every Klan brother who died by Mr Stuart's hands and wanted to turn back time to an era when blacks had no rights. There was a backlash of violent crimes against the black population in Texas and throughout the nation. Influenced by the media, gangs of armed angry white men, many of them members of white militia groups, rampaged throughout the South and Midwest violently attacking black men, women and children. They struck on university campuses where young black men and women were the minority.

Many of the black ghettos of the nation went up in flames as the white gangs began engaging in what could be considered open warfare. In the suburbs and rural areas, old white men who were once Klan members remembered their old alliances. They got hold of their rifles and began hunting down their black neighbors. The country quickly fell into chaos. Law enforcement were not vigilant in their duties and the world watched as black families fled as refugees from the 'land of the free' and sought safety in Canada, Mexico, and Central and South America. Many fled to Africa as they saw the events escalating into a race war. Other black men and women who claimed their rights to be citizens of the US took up arms to fight against their white oppressors. Congress quickly revoked the rights of an out of control media who were fanning the flames of ethnic cleansing. The Federal government called in the military and were eventually able to quell the storm but more than 100,000 black people had been killed by the white militia gangs.

The day of the inquisition arrived. The site of the meeting was a small room in a highly secured long-term facility. There was a small rectangular table with four strong and firm spindle legs, one at each corner. The table was placed in the middle of the room; it was the centrepiece of the stark and gloomy room. Around it was three chairs. The first to arrive at the table was Mr Roberts, the court appointed imbecile of an attorney representing Mr Stuart. He was given a copy of Mr Stuart's files a few days prior to this meeting. He had received two more boxes that day containing Mr Stuart's charts from various hospitals that had treated him. It never troubled him that he did not win many of his cases because the cases never stopped coming. There were too few lawyers and too many poor black and Hispanic criminals who could not afford a high price attorney to get them out of their legal problems. Guilty or innocent, they were given representation that did not prevent innocents from going to jail or to the electric chair, as Texas has capital punishment. Mr Roberts took up his position.

Next came in the assistant district attorney, who was there to instruct and present the state case to the Grand Jury so they would vote to indict or dismiss Mr Stuart's case. The Jury was made up of 23 white men and women. They were all members or former members of the Klan. The district attorney, Mr Rhodes, was an attorney by trade but had degrees as well as a practice as a psychiatrist. He was a man of many interests, attaining millions through his private practice. After leaving his private practice he sought a medium through which he could achieve high office in his state and maybe the nation. He developed a 20-year plan, at the end of which he envisioned himself as president of the US. His first step was to become an assistant district attorney. The successful handling of this case would be the vehicle to challenge the Republican incumbent senator at the next election. He was a tall man standing six feet four inches and weighed about 220 pounds. He was muscular and fancied himself a good athlete. His hair was jet black except for the irregular sprinkling of grey at his temples, which was slowly diminishing his youthful appearance.

This visible transformation he accepted as a way of life and an indicator of the early transition into his midlife, although Mr Rhodes had no intention of readily giving into it. His arrival was followed by a procession of armed lawmen taking up position in the room and hallways as Mr Stuart was lead in, cuffed by an iron bar that restrained his bilateral upper extremities at the wrist with a thick chain that was connected to his bilateral lower extremities at the ankles. The chains restricted his range of motion and he could not walk fast. With each baby step he made, the clanging of metals against metal announced his coming like an alarm alerting everyone to his presence. A total of 10 armed sheriff deputies took up position on the floor from inside the room to the hallways outside of the suite. The block on which this Supreme Court building was located was closed off to the public by state troopers. Mr Stuart was considered a very dangerous man, a person to be extremely afraid of. But there were many who wanted him dead including the militia groups. It was rumoured some would try to break him out of prison to kill him.

The Grand Jury was called to order and the assistant district attorney read off the names of more than 250 people Mr Stuart was charged with killing in the state of Texas.

After instructing the Grand Jury of what was required of them and reading the charges that were to be presented against Mr Stuart, the inquisition started. Mr Stuart was sworn in and took a seat on the witness stand.

Mr Rhodes addressed the court.

"Ladies and gentlemen of the Grand Jury, we are gathered here today to decide if Mr Stuart is mentally competent to stand trial in the state of Texas for the murder of Governor Christopher Carson, and 250 other individuals who were members of the Brotherhood of the Anglos militia. Do you or your attorneys have any questions?"

"How are you going to do that?" asked Mr Stuart.

"By ascertaining the thoughts that were in your mind during the times you committed such violent acts," replied Mr Rhodes. "Mr Stuart, will you state your date of birth?"

"April 17, 1948," he replied stoically.

"Here in your chart it is written that you witnessed your father and three uncles being hung by men wearing white robes and cone shaped hats, is that true?"

"Yes," replied Mr Stuart.

"Do you remember the date of this incident?"

"July 20, 1958. It was that night the Klan lynched my father and uncles."

"As it was at night, how were you able to identify whether it was Klan's men or your own people dressed in those robes acting like they were Klan's men?"

"I saw them; many of them lost their head piece in the battle to subdue us. I saw their faces. No black man would ever put on a Klan robe."

"Did you recognise any of them?"

"Yes," replied Mr Stuart, "I recognised Christopher Carson. He was a boy of about 16 years then."

"Is that the same person as Governor Christopher Carson?"

"Yes," answered Mr Stuart, "he was just a boy then."

"What made you so sure that it was Christopher Carson and not some other boy?" inquired the inquisitor.

"He spoke to me."

"What did he say?"

"That if it was not for my age I would certainly be hanging from that limb like my father. He continued by saying that one day my time will come, he would see to that."

"What did you think he meant by that?"

"That eventually he would lynch me like he did my father."

"You did not tell me why you were so sure it was Governor Carson?"

"I know him, I saw him then and I saw what he did in Vietnam. There are pictures of him hanging NVA and VC troops. He admitted it. He wanted me dead."

"Was old man Carson there that night?"

"Yes, he was the leader of the pack. They were about to lynch all of us but he said not the boy, let him live. We do not lynch nigger children. Eventually his day will come. I cried and begged them not to as they lynched my father and uncles. It was after that Christopher Carson addressed me, revealing his intentions."

"How did you feel seeing your father and uncles getting lynched by the Klan and you being unable to stop this incident?"

"I lost my righteous spirit that night and my soul set out on a journey into darkness as I swore to avenge their deaths and accept the consequences. Until this very day, I cannot separate myself from that incident and thus I am now ready for my lynching. That is the consequences of my actions and that's the reason we are here to prepare me for the consequences."

"Was it that incident that drove you to kill?" Probed, Mr Rhodes looked at Mr Stuart's court appointed attorney knowing that he would not object to his questioning. 'The lynching of your family members, is that the reason for your premeditated killings?'

"Yes and also the lynching of my wife and children. Those incidents drove me to kill every Klansman I could."

"Therefore, you planned all of these mass killings you did in Texas and Alabama and the rest of the country?"

"Yes I did, driven by vengeance I plotted, planned and I carried them out."

"What are the other reasons why you kill?"

"I kill because I have seen many of my people lynched, abused, intimidated, and harassed by you whites daily for no earthly reason, without any protection, regulation or response from law enforcement, or the department of justice."

"Mr Stuart, here in your chart it says it was after that traumatic event of the death of your father and uncles you began hearing voices?"

"Yes," replied Mr Stuart.

"Are you hearing voices now?" asked Mr Rhodes.

"Only yours," answered Mr Stuart.

"I take that as a no. When was the last time you heard voices or had any sensation of hallucinations? That is seeing, feeling, or hearing things from people, animals or things that are not there?"

"I can't remember," responded Mr Stuart.

"Were you hearing voices before you walked in the room?" grilled Mr Rhodes.

"No," replied Mr Stuart.

"Did you hear voices yesterday?"

"No."

"The day before?"

"No."

"Any time this week?"

"No."

"Last week?"

"No."

"This month?"

"No."

"Last month?"

"No."

"This year?"

"No."

"Last year?"

"No."

"Mr Stuart, it's fair to say that you have been free of your hallucinations for some time now, measurable in years. Is that correct?"

"Yes," replied Mr Stuart.

"Mr Stuart when was the first time you began hearing voices?"

"After the lynching of my father and uncles," he replied.

"Whose voices did you hear?"

"My father and my uncles."

"The same people you said were hanged by the Klan."

"Yes, sir."

"Did they give you any instruction or tell you what to do and, if so, what were the instructions?"

"They told me to have my auntie's husband teach me to hunt and how to use a gun."

"Did you follow the instructions of the voices you were hearing?"

"Yes, I did."

"Even though those people were dead?"

"I had nothing to be afraid of. It was the voices of the people who loved me."

"You never thought it strange that dead people were talking to you or that you were being given instructions from the grave?"

"No, not until my wife Jacqueline made an issue of it."

"Your wife Jacqueline brought this abnormal behavior to your attention?"

"Yes."

"When was this, Mr Stuart?"

"In the summer of 1974. I was hallucinating and she was aware of it and she told me that it was not normal. She said I was sick and she took me to see a doctor who referred me to a psychiatrist."

"Mr Stuart, when you were hearing voices, what did they tell you to do?"

"It depends on whose voice I was hearing."

"How many voices did you hear?"

"At first it was my father and uncles. As years went by and killing became a way of life, I soon began to hear the voices of those whose lives I took. I obeyed only the commands from my father and uncles."

"What did they tell you to do?" Mr Rhodes demanded.

"They guided me through life by telling me to go to school and get an education and to hunt and get to be proficient with weapons. They instructed me to join the military. They guided me through Vietnam and, when I returned, they guided me to my victims."

"Did the voices tell you to kill?" asked Mr Rhodes.

"They told me who to kill," answered Mr Stuart.

"Did you always obey the voices?"

"I tried to resist them but I eventually ended up doing as they wished."

"Did the voices ever tell you to kill someone and you did not kill them?"

"I was too weak. I could not resist."

"Why?"

"Because when I did, other voices were then set free and they wanted me to kill many others. Can you imagine hearing more than 2,000 voices in your head screaming instructions at you to kill others?"

"No, I can't. Insanity has not been one of my life experiences."

"You are a fortunate man," replied Mr Stuart.

"When was the last time the voices told you to kill and you did it?"

"It was Governor Christopher Carson. But after that I had committed myself to the mental health institution at Kings County Hospital in Brooklyn, New York."

"What happened there?" Inquired Mr Rhodes.

"I began taking medications. After a time, the voices disappeared. I was set free but soon ran out of medication and the voices began to return. I have been in and out of mental institutions since 1988, going from a short term to long term care facilities only to be set free and to start that cycle all over again so as not to hear the voices."

'You told your life story to Nurse Gordon of the facility in which you were a patient. Why did you do that, Mr Stuart?"

"I am seeking forgiveness and I am ready to accept the consequences of my actions."

"Seeking forgiveness from whom – God?"

"He has already forgiven me. However, I am seeking forgiveness from the spirits of those I killed while in service of this nation. I have robbed them of their right to grow and to love and be loved. Through war and an insatiable hate, I have done this, not realizing what I was doing was wrong."

"You hear the voices of our enemies who you killed while fighting in Vietnam?"

"I hear those the loudest, for I later came to realize they were fighting the same tyranny I was fighting here in America."

"Why is being forgiven so important to you Mr Stuart?" asked his court appointed attorney, Mr Roberts.

"I am 58 years old. My death is imminent. I must cleanse my soul and spirit before I meet my maker."

"You are aware that if the state finds you competent to stand trial, they will be seeking the death penalty."

"Maybe that is how I will be forgiven by those I killed who were not Klansmen," said Mr Stuart.

"Have you ever thought of killing yourself?" asked Mr Rhodes.

"No," replied Mr Stuart.

"Mr Stuart, you are not as insane as I thought you were. Were you ever considered or diagnosed by the military as being insane while you served in Vietnam?"

"I have tried in vain to escape, to forget Vietnam. But like a nightmare, it's always there. No I never told anyone that I heard voices or that hearing voices made killing easier."

"Why didn't you, Mr Stuart?"

"I thought I was normal. I thought it was normal to hear the voices of my deceased family members. I thought it was normal hearing the voices of dead people telling you what to do."

"You were one of the most honored and decorated soldiers of that war?"

"That's what I am told, but what honor is there in killing innocents?"

"How many men did you kill in Vietnam, Mr Stuart?"

"Why do you ask me that question? Don't you understand I am trying to forget that stage of my life?"

"How did it feel, Mr Stuart, when you were killing all these men? Tell me how it felt." Mr Rhodes was now probing Mr Stuart's psyche.

"If you are good at something and you are aware of the feeling it gives when you are locked in it, then you know how it feels. What are you good at, Mr Rhodes?"

"Questions leading to a person's state of mind when they committed their horrendous deeds, Mr Stuart. I am as good with those as you are at killing."

"What feeling does it give you when you are at your best?" asked Mr Stuart.

"An electrifying joy that is comparable to man's most base of pleasures," he replied.

"Then you have answered your question, Mr Rhodes."

"Are you equating my feelings to yours when you were killing in Vietnam?"

"When one is good at something, the reason is because one enjoys it – it brings pleasure. I was trained to be a soldier. I was trained to kill. I was placed in a war zone where it was kill or be killed. I discovered from the instant I arrived that I was good at it and as time went by, my peers grew to respect me because I was so good at it. It brought joy to my heart as I slew the enemy. I went out in the battlefield seeking the enemy so I could slay him, day after day and when I did not kill, I felt disappointed."

"Were you reckless while soldering in Vietnam?"

"Some say I was. I knew I was invincible."

"Why?"

"My father, my uncles they were there with me all the way and they spoke to me giving me guidance every minute of the day."

"You heard their voices?'

"Yes, when others had lost their way and fell victim to the enemy they were there to calm me, guide me, soothe me and save me. The enemy began to recognise that I owned the battlefield and would destroy them. They began to call me the living ghost. They feared me so they put a bounty on my head. Needless to say, none lived to collect it."

"Gloating, Mr Stuart. Tell me how did you feel about killing your fellow Americans?"

"How did my fellow Americans feel about killing my kind for generations, physically, and also mentally through legislation? There is no difference between slavery, lynching and Jim Crow laws. They were all meant to do the same, kill a man physically, mentally and spiritually. How does it feel to kill your fellow American, Mr Rhodes? That is your purpose here, now, to clear me so that the state has the right to perform the final act."

"How did it feel when you blew up that building in Alabama and killed all those men, Mr Stuart?" Mr Rhodes was now feeling that he was losing some of his control.

"You would never know, Mr Rhodes. I could spend the rest of my life telling you, but you being a white man, you will never understand. The only feeling you could have for me is resentment, but maybe your forefathers who fought with Washington to gain this nation's independence would understand, for our roles are similar. Now we have taken on the role of England and you are its General Cornwallis, so you cannot understand. To know first you would have to be my color, have walked in my shoes and have lived as my people from the time of slavery until now. You had to be treated as less than a man to know. Then maybe you would understand the purpose of my war."

"You are a terrorist, Mr Stuart. An enemy of the state, you knew what you were doing. You planned your terrorist activities against the Klan. You executed them in masses and you want to use insanity as your defence. No, Mr Stuart – not here in Texas. As deplorable as the Klan is, Mr Stuart, there is no excuse for your murderous actions." Mr Rhodes was now losing his objectivity in his pursuit of justice.

"I see the Klan as representing everything that is hideous in this nation. It must be stopped. I have chosen to remove them from the environment like a surgeon removing a cancerous tumour, preventing it from harming surrounding tissues. The hypocrisy of the law baffles me. It is said that justice is blind; it sees no color. But justice is a thing practiced by men who see color – and an all-white jury has a history of convicting people of my color. Is this justice or a sanctioned lynching? When the Klan murdered my father and uncles – where was justice? When the Klan murdered my wife and children – where was justice? When the Klan marched across the South lynching black men, women and children as they pleased – where was justice hiding? Now I have retaliated against such terror and those who terrorized us, and you are here talking about justice."

"They are not the ones on trial here today. You are. Those are people we are talking about, Mr Stuart. They are Americans like you and me."

"Americans, maybe. Like you, certainly. But not like me. It is their ideology I fear the most and they have spent generations perfecting it. The art of racial supremacy has woven itself into the policies of this country, both domestic and foreign, and grown to become a part of this arrogant nation's way of thinking, acting and doing things. It has become so embedded that we can no longer differentiate it from our normal thinking. Once those whom we practice it on have come to see it, it changes its appearance and continues. It's time we stop, grow beyond that and evolve to achieve that lofty dream of treating all men as equals. That is the purpose of my war – equality in America. The Declaration says all men are created equal; it does not differentiate. When they were lynching us, where were you to prosecute them, Mr Rhodes? When they were burning down our houses and shooting us down ,where was your department of justice? How many thousands of my people must die before there is justice? We too are Americans regardless of the color of our skin. Sustaining the dominance of the white race is the present goal of white America. In so doing, you find it difficult to treat others as equals. You have lost sight of the Declaration of Independence and have embraced the Constitutional amendment that gives you the right to bear arms. It allows you to stock up on guns and wait for the day when it is legal and okay to kill us. The Declaration of Independence is a sacred document; it has a greater meaning than you think."

"You speak so eloquently of this nation not being able to evolve. What about you, Mr Stuart? Have you evolved?"

"The beauty of life, Mr Rhodes, is to know and accomplish your purpose in it. I was not put here to evolve. I was put here to extinguish some of those who stood in the way preventing my people's progress. Those people, the gatekeepers of a time past, continue to influence the minds of the young, to maintain their hateful way of life. They must be removed so we can evolve. That was my mission and I accomplished some of it to a degree. Now by the law I must suffer the consequences of my actions."

"Why did you kill Governor Carson?"

"To prevent him from leading this nation down a path like which Hitler led Germany. This tape will explain my reason," he said, attempting to hand Mr Rhodes a copy of the tape he had made in the forest decades ago. Unknown to the DA, he had again sent copies of the tapes to various media outlets.

"Speaking off the record, Mr Stuart, I find you very repulsive, hateful of this nation and its white population. I think you are quite sane to stand trial and if you are indicted by the Grand Jury I will request to prosecute your case. I will make sure you are found guilty, I will send your murderous ass to the electric chair and I will be there on the day of your execution to watch you burn."

"I have fought and killed for this nation in war. That gives me the right to look at the flaws of this nation I love. It gives me the right to set this nation on the right path by the means I know best. This nation has been taken hostage by a radical hateful group and I want to liberate it from its grip and make it what it was meant to be. I visualise the people of this nation coexisting with all others on this planet without trying to dictate or suppress other nations' journeys as we all seek to find our place in the human society. I have lived with violence and I presume I will die by violence, but this nation and its people who I dearly love will evolve, seeking to achieve those lofty words of its Declaration of Independence that all men are created equal. Through the violence I have perpetuated on the Klan and those who share their ideology, I hope I have created a path to equality. Personally, Mr Rhodes, I find you no different from those I have attempted to eliminate. You share the same base thinking."

"Mr Stuart, your history of insanity will not save you from the electric chair. In the meantime, you will be locked in isolation in a long-term facility until the day of your execution."

"I will not be alone. I will have my voices to be my company and I am ready to die. I will kill no more."

Mr Rhodes instructed the Grand Jury to vote Mr Stuart guilty on all counts to indict him allowing him to be tried by a trial jury. The Grand Jury reviewed the transcript of the inquisition and did as they were instructed.

# CHAPTER 37: Thy Spirit Will Meet

"I testified in the trial of Mr Stuart and he was found guilty on 251 counts of first degree premeditated murder. He was convicted and sentenced to the electric chair. When I went to see him, he was accepting of his fate and his spirit remained unbroken. Convinced of his righteousness, his spirit remained strong and steadfast in his relationship with God.

"Mr Stuart," I said. "I hope you will find it in your heart to forgive me for the role I played in your incarceration and your sentence."

"Nurse Gordon, you did as I hoped you would. I have forgiven you long ago," he said. We kept in contact until the day of his execution. Leading up to this, it was said that he could be seen with his bible as he sought forgiveness for the wrongs he had done. He thanked God for directing him and using him as an instrument, a tool to assist in the eradication of hate from this world. Convinced of his impending demise, he sought peace in the remainder of his life and forgiveness from God, which was his ultimate objective. He accepted the peace within him as the accomplishment of this desire. The darkness of his cell calmed his raging heart and he rebelled no more. He knew that heaven awaited him because he had accepted and acted on his purpose in life. This world of man-made rules, which sought to suffocate his soul, was preparing to perform its ultimate penalty through the act of separation leading to the death of his body. I know he did not betray his country, not for a moment. He loved his country; he fought and was ready to make the ultimate sacrifice for his nation and welcomed the thought of the end, as he knew it.

As he languished in solitary confinement on death row in a maximum-security Texas penitentiary, a prison guard walking by his cell stopped and peered in. Mr Stuart was lying on the cot in his cell. The prison guard said. "You will be happy to hear a black man is president of the United States."

"Don't play with me, boy," said the crotchety Mr Stuart. "I don't like people making fun of me."

"This is true," said the guard as he turned the lights on in Mr Stuart's cell, temporarily blinding him, and gave him a newspaper so he could read the headlines.

"How long do you think he will live for?" He inquired as he read the paper.

"I hope he will live to serve his two terms," said the white guard. "I voted for him. I felt something special about him I have not felt in any other candidate. He is a good man and he is concerned about the people of this nation."

"May I borrow your paper?" Mr Stuart asked the guard as he looked at Barack Obama's picture on the front page with a caption that read; 'Our 44th President of the United States of America'.

"You can have it. I will be back in 15 minutes to turn off the light," said the guard as he watched Mr Stuart retreat to his cot. As the guard walked away he heard Mr Stuart calling his name.

"Hey Harry, let the warden know I am ready to exit this stage. I have done my duty. Harry, let them know I have rid the garden of some of its weeds so the flowers would grow to bloom and they have just done that. I am ready to die like my father and uncles did." Mr Stuart was granted his request to die while the world was fighting to spare his life. He met his demise as his father and uncles did by a hangman's noose in the dusty courtyard of a Texas penitentiary with many of his peers looking on from their cell window. He died a happy man as he knew a black man had become president. He was elected by most of the people of the nation, which meant blacks, white, Hispanics and all others had voted for him. It was historic and it showed his vision of the Declaration that all men were created equal was taking root to becoming a reality.